FOURTEEN

Fourteen

by
Colette Black

Cover design by Steven Novak. Copyright © 2015 by Colette Black
Editing by Jen Hendricks

Published in the United States by
Drapukamo Publishing
PO Box 21
Higley, AZ 85236

FOURTEEN

Colette Black

Also by Colette Black

To my Mom
for her spectacular
vocabulary.
Thanks Mom.

1

Fourteen pulled himself from the concubines' river as mist billowed around the waterfall behind him, suffusing the air with the smell of fresh rain. He shook his pale strawberry-blond hair like a pleased dog, the damp strands reaching his shoulders.

He didn't wait to dry this time. He only had a few minutes before his science course with Master Den. In the shade of a broad-leafed bunton tree, he coerced his dark trousers up over his wet underwear and pulled on a wide-necked shirt that blended with the profusion of greenery surrounding him. The fabric clung to the skin between his broadening shoulders, but Fourteen was used to that. The humidity in Beht province made everyone's clothes stick, wet or not. At least the sun was high overhead, so it wouldn't take too long for the late summer heat to dry the outermost layers.

He stretched against the tight fabric of the shirt, gratified by the way it pulled against his arms. At nearly seventeen years old, he hoped for another digit or two above his three arms' height and that his narrow frame might bulk up a bit. Maybe that would finally give him an edge over his older, taller, brothers.

He stepped to the river's edge, giving a final wave to the women's misty silhouettes standing behind hedges on the other side, where he'd hidden only a few minutes ago.

One of the dolphins, having left the calm water farther down the river to frolic with him and the concubines, barked at him, flapping a white flipper as if joining their good-byes. With some twirling acrobatics above the waterline it disappeared behind the wall that split the unnatural river in half. Originally the river followed the valley's slopes, meandering its way toward the sea; but his father, the emperor, in his supreme wisdom had channeled the waterway to make a wide semi-circle around the palace grounds. Somehow, he'd built an immense wall through the river's center, dividing it into calm waters on the palace side, and a turbulent moat on the other—the Numbers' side.

Jumping the metal-linked fence that kept young ones from the dangers of the moat, Fourteen caught a muffled voice sounding from the loudspeakers inside the Numbers Compound; probably a change in schedule for the younger kids' classes. Fourteen trotted through the line of trees he wasn't supposed to have passed, weaving through bushes to the approved pathway. A narrow stream, dividing itself from the river near the falls, tripped across stones and branches between him and the Numbers' wall, an echo to the barrier inside the river, the Numbers Compound squeezed between the two fortifications.

Occasionally, Fourteen heard the rattle of autocars on the other side, in Han City. He imagined roadways full of them, rumbling by one another, taking beautiful women to musicals, acrobatic displays, and daring sports competitions; the kind Numbers only saw on rare occasions like the Festival of Unification or an Imperial Betrothal Celebration.

To see the world outside, to be free from the daily grind as a Number... nothing filled Fourteen's thoughts and dreams more than that, not even the emperor's concubines.

He passed the military barracks kept on the west side of the compound, the glaring-white buildings as immaculate as the soldiers' shiny black shoes and green-and-white pressed uniforms. Beyond the buildings, Fourteen jogged beside the training grounds, ignoring the familiar sound of gunshot, the slide and clip of the bolt-action weapons, and the thump of bullets hitting soft wood. Here, soldiers practiced their skills, hoping to raise tier and be placed in the emperor's palace. Unfortunately for the Numbers, the guards' tests included keeping them trapped inside the compound.

"Hey, troublemaker!" Fen waved to him from the side of the arena, the black fourth-tier tattoo on his forearm momentarily sparkling red in the sunlight. He jogged up to Fourteen. "You keep sneaking past that waterfall, none of us are ever going to make it to palace guard."

"Sorry, Fen. But some things are worth a little sacrifice."

"So you get all the pleasure and we get all the sacrifice?"

"As the next emperor, I think that's how it's supposed to work."

"Potential emperor. You're not there yet." Fen peeled away, heading back for his turn on the firing range. "Get yourself ready. I'll catch you next time, green shirt or no."

Fourteen laughed. "Sure. You'll catch me for the first time ever, next time."

If only Fen were as easygoing about the wall as the river. To date, the man had caught Fourteen eight times. No one else had even come close. Fen probably couldn't get his deserved promotion for the very fact that they didn't dare let him leave.

Passing a long table with a multitude of fist-sized translucent white and pale pastel lightstones charging in the sunlight, Fourteen ducked through the foliage near the little stream as it wound toward the laundry houses. Racing past the learning hall, he trusted to speed more than stealth. If Master Den saw him, he'd pull Fourteen in early for his science lesson and there'd be no lunch, especially if the man decided it was a good day for weapons training.

Out of sight from the back windows, Fourteen snuck past the communal eating area and into the kitchen's side-door. The smell of fresh-baked bread made his stomach growl. In the city, people probably ate whenever they liked, probably had better food, too.

Snatching a long-roll half the size of his arm, Fourteen grabbed a chunk of ham from the table. He scurried through the back door as Frieda stepped away from her cutting board, shaking a finger, her fifth-tier tattoo wiggling, showing her as the lowest tier allowed inside the Numbers Compound, fit only for the most menial tasks.

"Hey, I seen that you youngster. You shoulda be here for lunch like all them good Numbers."

Fourteen waved the bread above his head as he disappeared. "Love you, Frieda!"

With the bread halfway to his lips he stopped. Behind the red-brick building as it formed an L to accommodate the kitchen's bulking stoves inside, Twelve had his back to Fourteen.

Like all of the emperor's children, Twelve and Fourteen appeared identical in most ways, near-replicas of their father. Twelve was the only Number who didn't have to resort to different haircuts or flamboyant clothing styles to differentiate himself from his brothers. Yet, he always wore hyefus wrapped around his torso and snapped along the side instead of the common pullover shirts, as if he thought himself the emperor's assassin or one of the guards. Today's was bright yellow, but the pompous freak didn't need it to be noticed, not with his black frizz sticking out from his head in every direction like a dog gone through a drying machine. Despite the garbage bins blocking part of his view, Fourteen immediately recognized his year-older adversary. He also recognized Twelve's prey.

2

"What do you think you're doing?" Fourteen took another step closer. Twelve positioned himself to more fully obscure the girl he'd trapped in the corner. The blue of Aednat's skirt, the green line along the bottom marking her as Fourteen's servant, disappeared, as did the edges of her dark, auburn-tinted hair. "This is a private conversation. Go be a whang elsewhere."

"I thought I made it clear last time, freak. You're not to have any private conversations with my servant. She's off limits, especially to you."

Twelve's gaze narrowed as he took in Fourteen's wet pants and half-dry hair.

"You get your fill in the concubines' garden. You don't need an exclusive servant that nobody can touch but you."

"Don't be stupid. Nobody touches the emperor's concubines. Not even a Number."

Aednat rushed at the space between the wall and Twelve, her arms full of damp laundry, but Twelve thrust an open hand against her chest.

She stumbled, crying out as her back hit the wall. The clothes fell into the muck surrounding the bins, revealing her fifth-tier tattoo.

"Please," she begged.

"You'll stay there," said Twelve, "until I'm done with you."

Fourteen dropped his food in the dirt, taking the first swing. "You daffing..."

Twelve leaned back, letting Fourteen's forward motion, combined with a solid shove, send him into the trash containers. As they collided with a resounding clang, Fourteen put out a hand to keep from tumbling inside. It came back covered in a putrid slime of rotten fruit and pork fat.

Twelve laughed.

With a flick of his wrist, Fourteen's muck splattered across Twelve's silk hyefu, his eye, and into his brother's open mouth. Twelve spat, gaze murderous.

Taking a step back, Fourteen drew Twelve away from the wall. Aednat only hesitated a second, but with a person like Twelve, a second was too long. He grabbed her arm as she tried to run. She screamed as he flung her back. Landing in the laundry, her head struck one of the bins and blood blossomed from the shallow wound.

Taking advantage of the brief distraction, Fourteen kicked Twelve in the stomach, doubling him over.

Aednat's scream turned frantic. She stared at her blood-covered hand, her face pale as un-dyed silk.

Now Twelve took advantage of Fourteen's distraction. His knuckles drove into Fourteen's cheek. Pain exploded across his jaw. With an open-handed thrust, Twelve knocked him to the ground then straddled him. His fists pummeled Fourteen, driving his face back and forth into the dirt. Fourteen tried to push him off, but accomplished nothing. Then with an "oomph" Twelve's weight disappeared.

Forcing his bruised eyes to open, Fourteen saw the emperor, hands clenched into fists, ready to beat Twelve into limbo.

"Thank the Vasheri," Fourteen said.

The man standing above him turned to look at Aednat, giving Fourteen a clearer view of his face. Fourteen realized, not for the first time, that this wasn't the emperor, but a nineteen-year-old version of him—high cheekbones, strong, narrow jawline, one green eye, one blue, but with his white hair crop-cut. Eleven.

"Good thing I happened along, aye?" Eleven said.

Fourteen frowned. "Good thing you didn't miss your appointment. With *my* servant."

Twelve scooted away, his nose bleeding and one of his eyes swelling to match Fourteen's. "This is none of your business, Eleven."

Clenching his fists, Eleven stalked toward Twelve. "I'll make this clear to you for the last time, dog...she is off limits and so is my servant. There are plenty of other girls here willing to give you a roll. Stay away from the rest."

Twelve scrambled to his feet, shuffling toward the river. "You'll regret this. Someday, I'll—."

Eleven picked up a stone, chucking it at Twelve's head. "Get out of here, dog."

Giving them a rude gesture as he ducked, Twelve ran toward the Numbers' apartments.

Aednat still hadn't risen from the dirt. Kneeling beside her, Eleven pulled off his red silk shirt, obviously worn in anticipation of their meeting, revealing a matured version of the same broad-shouldered, slim-waisted physique he shared with Fourteen. Holding it to her shallow wound he asked, "Are you okay?"

She nodded. "The blood. I need to get—" She wiped her hand on her skirt, but then brought it to her face and stared. "Oh," she groaned. Heaving into the foul mess at her feet, vomit splattered half of Fourteen's laundry. Between the garbage and this, he didn't want to ever wear those clothes again, no matter how well-cleaned.

Eleven pulled Aednat's long hair back, smoothing it out of the way.

"You can take care of what Twelve started," Fourteen warned. "You can beat me to limbo, but I'm telling you the same thing I told him, she's off limits."

Eleven's look could have frozen water. "She'll decide who she wants to be with, and if you're treating her like that dog treats his own servant, I'll make it so you can't piss while standing ever again."

Fourteen couldn't say he hadn't seen it coming. It was obvious by the way Aednat blushed around Eleven, how they talked to one another as if nobody else existed, and the way she swung her hips and drew attention to her well-developed breasts whenever Eleven might be watching. She should be showing off for Fourteen, not one of his brothers. They'd been together longer than any other Number-servant pair in the compound, since they were both ten, and she belonged to him.

Aednat's green eyes flashed. "I may be a servant, but I'm not an old watch to be bartered in some outer-city pawn shop. Don't talk about me as if I don't have a say."

Fourteen could forbid it, but that would only push her farther away. He wanted her to come to him by her own choice. "She's right. She can make her own decisions. If that means you, for now, then I guess I'll have to live with it."

Eleven helped Aednat to her feet, clasping Fourteen's forearm in a comrade's handshake. "You're a good brother."

"What in limbo happened here?"

Fourteen spun around, more than familiar with the authoritative voice. He and Eleven bowed in unison.

"Master Chid Den." Fourteen formally acknowledged his teacher and mentor, remembering to use the family name first as the master was a native

Zhandanese and not from one of the empire's other countries.

Wearing a blue old-style hyefu, a green strip at the sleeves marking him as a Numbers' Master, silken ties were knotted along Master Den's left side instead of the more modern snaps. The material crossed so that the neckline was much higher than normal, especially for someone Master Den's age, less than thirty years. The only person under the age of twenty who voluntarily wore a hyefu was Twelve. Den was also the only master without a tier-tattoo, like the Numbers.

Master Den returned the bow with a terse nod of his head. "Beht Fourteen, Beht Eleven. The two of you?"

"No, Master," said Eleven. "Twelve started a fight with Fourteen. I helped when it became unfair."

Master Den scowled at Fourteen. "You needed assistance?"

Fourteen nodded, averting his eyes and clenching his jaw. Even Ten, older than him by two and a half years, would think twice about confronting Twelve. Eleven might have had some trouble if he hadn't taken their freak brother by surprise.

"The emperor is arriving through the gates," Master Den said. "You boys have about five, maybe ten minutes, to get yourselves cleaned up and present yourselves at the assembly grounds."

Master Den took in Eleven's soiled shirt, his voice softening in the way it only did for Aednat. "She has no stomach for blood. Once she's cleaned up, she'll be fine."

"I'll take her to her quarters," Eleven said.

"No. She'll only receive more reprimands. Take her to the washrooms and explain that she was detained by one of the Numbers. Don't mention any harassment or they'll lecture her on keeping her masters happy. Get yourself cleaned up and in a proper hyefu while you're there."

Aednat gathered the laundry, the green hem of her skirt swishing along the bottom of her shapely calves. The slits in her jeyfu-shirt slid up and down over her hips. On most Zhandanese women the square pattern, tight at the neck and loose everywhere else, completely hid their figure, but Aednat's fuller breasts stretched the fabric, filling the top out so the rest draped down like a tent, hinting at the voluminous treasures that lay within.

"Leave it," Fourteen said. "Even if you wash it, I don't want to wear those again. You can go into town and buy me more between your chores tomorrow."

Shoulders slumped, Aednat mumbled something Fourteen couldn't quite catch, but she dropped the soiled shirts and trousers in a bin. Eleven guided her down the sloping trail from the kitchen, toward the narrow river where the women did the washing.

Master Den crossed his arms. "In order to buy new clothing she'll have to admit she sullied yours."

"She shouldn't have arranged to meet Eleven without telling me."

"What was she supposed to say? 'I have feelings for one of your brothers?' She may be your servant, but she's still a teenage girl. Gabrick, she will be severely punished because of this. Don't you care?"

Fourteen's hand clenched. "Don't call me that. I've told you before."

"It's the name your mother wanted you to have."

"Maybe it's true and you did live in the palace as a child, but even if you knew my mother, it doesn't matter now. I'm the emperor's son. My name is Fourteen." He released his fist, wiping his grimy hand across his trousers. His nose curled at the smell. After another second, he cupped his hands round his mouth and yelled down the hill at Aednat. "I was growing out of them anyway. That's the reason I need new ones." He turned back to Master Den. "I've got to get cleaned up."

To Fourteen's disappointment, the man continued to walk at his side. "He's going to announce the trial today."

"How do you know?" asked Fourteen.

"How often does the emperor come to spend time with his children?"

"Not much, but that doesn't mean—"

A chattering squirrel interrupted him as it clambered across their path and into a stand of bamboo.

"I know him," Master Den said. "You're nearly seventeen and he's grown impatient."

"You think he'll want me? Eleven has a much better chance. He's bigger, stronger, and he's identical to our father. The emperor likes his successor to carry on his divine looks and identity."

"He's not divine,' Master Den growled. "He breeds his children to get the changes he has a whim for. You're almost exactly what he'd hoped, and you're his fourteenth child."

"Why would he want the Number closest to the cursed thirteen?"

Master Den's eyes grew dark. "The number thirteen is only cursed because he decreed it. He murdered your thirteenth brother for the sin of being born. And he murdered the baby's mother for bringing him life. You want to emulate such a man?"

Fourteen refused to listen to any more of the master's blasphemy. "The emperor is supreme ruler over all, he is Lingdow, our source of enlightenment and our guide to Paradise at the world's heart. All of Dixho is subject unto him. So yes, I want to follow him. And if he wills, he will teach me and enlighten me, so I can follow in his footsteps."

"Perfect." Master Den spat into the dirt as they turned a corner. He remained silent as another Number passed, but Fourteen hadn't shut him up. "That man is a blistering tyrant. Twelve hundred years ago, Dixho was the name for Beht province, now you think it describes our whole world."

Fourteen stopped, glaring nearly eye to eye with the smaller man. "You can't know that. You may be a genius, but you're what, maybe twenty-five years old?"

Master Den sighed. "Twenty-seven. But there are records in the palace. Records no one is allowed to see."

"But you found them and read all of Dixho history at the age of twelve? I don't believe you."

Fourteen stalked to his apartment door. Master Den grabbed his arm, spinning him around with a strength that reminded Fourteen this smaller man could outfight him without sweating his hyefu.

"What?" Fourteen said.

"Listen to me, boy. Whether you win or lose the emperor's challenge, you will die. Your only chance is to run. I can help you."

Fourteen pulled his arm free. "How dare you? You tell me the emperor is crazy and evil. Suggest I run from my destiny. I could have you killed for treason."

Master Den folded his arms over his chest, piercing Fourteen with the intensity of his gaze. "Would you? You obviously believe everything they've been teaching you, despite all my efforts. Will you do your duty? Have me hung?"

Fourteen took a deep breath. How did he answer such a question? According to everything he'd learned in temple, he should report the man. But since Master Den had shown up at the compound seven years ago, he'd taken a sincere interest in Fourteen. He often seemed angry for no reason, but at least he saw Fourteen as a person, not just another Number. And he'd given Fourteen a name, even if he couldn't claim it.

"No. I won't say anything." Fourteen turned away. "But you can't speak of this again. If it's time for the trials, then I'll compete to win. I'll leave this compound as the next emperor, or the next dignitary in his service, but I'll leave with my head held high."

Fourteen unlocked his door. Stepping into his apartment, he heard Master Den whisper. "And like all the others, you'll never be heard from again."

3

Mariessa woke to the familiar touch of a knife hilt. She caressed the smooth ivory as she slid the blade from beneath her mat, wishing again that Sando would allow her to sleep in another hut or even out in the forest. But he claimed that as his step-daughter, she must stay in their home. He claimed she was other things, too. She clenched the knife tighter.

Pulling the sleep-cloth from her face, she scanned the small hut. The morning sun peeked over the verdant hills, its light shimmering through the window—a square opening in the hut's bamboo slats, covered by a blue slip of course-woven fabric.

Sando had already rolled his flax-woven mat and tucked it into the corner. Nothing would convince him to rise with the morning light, nothing that didn't gain him either prestige or money. What was the crazy caribou up to this time?

Pulling a bestit from a small box in the corner, Mariessa discarded the one she'd worn the day before. Most Panginans slept nude, nothing but a thin cloth over their bodies to discourage insects. Despite the heat, Mariessa slept wearing the day's bestit. Any barrier between her and Sando was a good thing. Tying the brown-patterned wrap at her shoulder, it modestly covered to her knees. She secured a knife at her thigh in a warrior's sheath, but unknown to Sando, she had another wrapped around her hips with two more knives, both well-balanced and sharp.

Men's voices carried from the far edge of the bangay, where the hunters' huts formed the community's perimeter.

"Of course. Welcome!" Sando boomed.

The rest of their conversation blended into a cadence of indecipherable rising and falling tones like warning drums from the lookout trees.

Mariessa strapped on her leather sandals, a necessity, especially as the late-summer rains had begun. She rushed out the open door, the sash already secured back to let in the morning breeze. Tripping down the tall ladder to the spongy soil below, she took in the unusual bustle of the village women.

She came round the edge of Sando's hut, its stilts higher than the others as befitted his undeserved station as the community leader. Termien passed, carrying an armload of tinder for the morning cook-fires.

Mariessa grabbed the girl's arm, nearly spilling her bundle. "What is happening?"

The younger woman tried to duck away, refusing to meet Mariessa's eyes.

Mariessa yanked the girl closer. This time the bundle fell and scattered. "Whatever Sando has done, there's no more hiding it from me. Is he trying to sell me to another tribe again?"

Termien met her gaze with wild eyes. "It's not a tribe this time, Essa."

"Tell me, Ter."

Sando approached the bangay center, followed by two men, the taller wearing a coat that almost covered the belt holster at the waist of his dark slacks, the other in a long-sleeve hyefu with purple and pink bands on the sleeve, a design she'd only seen once before, when living in Keran. The outfits belonged in cooler weather farther south or on the Zhanda continent to the north.

Ter shook her head, eyes frightened but filled with pity. "They're from the capital."

Mariessa released Ter, eyes going wide. "From Keran?"

Ter swallowed. "No, not our country's capital. *The* capital. For all of Dixho. Han City."

The blood drained from Mariessa's face. That's where she'd seen the design, from the imperial house. "How—"

Ter shook her head again. Her eyes darted behind Mariessa, tears welling in sympathy. The sticks nearly tripped her as she ran, joining the other women around a large rock on which Sando and the men waited.

Looking behind her, Mariessa realized what had sent her friend scrambling to her mother's side like a frightened tree lepur.

The men of the village, according to custom for a gathering, had circled the bangay. Their paldas, wrapped at the hip and extending to mid-thigh, swung as they closed around her. The circle tightened like a noose round a wart pig's neck. Soon, they would force Mariessa to join the others.

Mariessa faced Dangan who was closest, her eyes darting to the forest behind, pleading as his wide frame closed the distance between them one step at a time.

Though there was indecision in his eyes, he shook his head. He hadn't believed her before, and he didn't trust her now. He would remain obedient to his piuno, Sando, their trusted leader who kept them safe and prosperous. No matter the cost, Dangan stayed loyal to his tribe, even if the price included her.

Turning to the bangay center, Mariessa lifted her chin and joined the others. True, Sando had brought a better trap, but she'd escaped before. She'd get away this time too, and she wouldn't come back. She took one last glance at Dangan. This time, she had no reason to return.

Sando's booming voice carried over the small crowd in halting Imperium. Even a child born to a low tier like Mariessa, had enough schooling to understand and speak the Imperial language. "These most worthy men have come from the paradise capital of Han City. Meester Peder kil Straun and Meester Xo Paen are agents representing ICRO, the Imperial Concubine Recruitment Office. We are honored by their presence." Sando bowed to them as he'd already done three times during their approach to the community rock. "Mariessa, come forward."

The women parted, keeping their chins high as a token of their superiority and Mariessa's supposed fallen state.

Taking her time, eyes forward, she approached the massive flat rock. She inclined her head but refused to bow, addressing them in her best city accent. "Mister Straun, Mister Xo." She gave Sando a sly grin, happy to embarrass him with her superior pronunciation, remembered from a time before she'd arrived in this backward jungle village.

"Call me Peder," said the larger man. The other remained silent.

Sando grabbed Mariessa's arm, extending it as he pulled her close, making the seventh-tier tattoo even more obvious to these second-tiers. One set of stubby fingers pressed through the wrap into the flesh at her ribs. If not surrounded by witnesses, she'd have pulled a knife on him.

"You see," he said. "She has skin the color of warm honey, and the black in her eye is up and down like a cat's from her Uradi father. Very unique."

Towering over Sando, pale hair and pale skin a direct opposite from the native Panginans, Peder turned her arm back and forth. "It is pleasing."

"And she has acquired marrying age," said Sando, "Fifteen years this last winter."

"She is short," said Xo.

"Yes." Sando's breathing came faster, his eyes darting from Xo to Peder. "But her father was taller than most Uradi. She has much of her father. You can see the difference from the other Panginans in our village by her coloring, the way her hair curls, her round eyes that only just turn up at the very edges like a proper Keroka. On the whole island of Kerokos, you would not find another like her."

Peder studied her, his accent holding a slight twang compared to Xo. "You are right. Perhaps she will make good breeding stock."

When Sando didn't immediately correct the man's assumption, Dangan's head cocked to one side, questioning his piuno for the first time. Everyone knew the emperor didn't take used girls for mothers.

Sando caught the looks of doubt from his followers. "As I told you, she is no longer a virgin."

"She may still have value as a concubine." said Peder, and Mariessa finally caught his Uradian accent like her father's though the only physical traits in common were their height, strong jaw, and vertical pupils like her own. "A most prestigious honor."

Mariessa sniffed in disgust. She'd heard about the emperor's women, brutalized to the point of insanity, many of them resorting to suicide.

Xo sneered. "She has small breasts."

"Proportion matters more than size," said Peder.

Before Mariessa realized his intent, he gripped the side of her wrap in his muscled hand, and yanked.

Mariessa stumbled into him, crying out.

He wrenched it again.

Her knot held tight, but the fabric didn't. It ripped from collarbone to waist, then fell to the cool rock at their feet.

The crowd gasped. From somewhere near the back, Dangan muttered a complaint.

Mariessa didn't bother to request their aid. It wouldn't come. Without thought as she'd practiced a thousand times, the hip-knives flew into her hands, the tips at each of the strangers' necks.

"No, Mariessa," pleaded Sando. "It would be the ruin of our entire bangay."

"You have no right," she spit in Peder's face.

He chuckled, eying her revealed body despite the knife aimed to kill. Quicker than thought, Peder grabbed hold of both her wrists, twisting one while pressing the other forward. One blade clanged across the rock, falling to the dirt. The other plunged into Xo's neck.

Blood spurted over the white hilt, over her fingers. Mariessa released it, horrified. It fell like an echo, spinning to the rock's edge behind its brother. Wide-eyed, Xo followed the knives, tumbling face-down in the dirt, his legs at an odd angle atop the rock.

"We will take her," Peder said with a businessman's grin, wiping blood from his hand on a handkerchief then tossing it on Xo's body. "The emperor will enjoy of her spirit even more than her figure."

It took Sando a moment to recover. He swallowed hard then forced a grin. "Good!" He almost clapped Peder on the back, but must have thought better of it, returning his wide palm to his side. "We'll have a celebration tonight, in your honor."

"In the emperor's honor," Peder corrected, his tone threatening.

"Um, yes, yes. That's what I meant, of course."

Xo's blood pooled below the rock, running into damp crevices and foot-sized depressions. "What would you like me to do with the man Mariessa murdered? If we bury him in the next few hours, Shangsan should take four or five days. That's the soonest we could dig for his heartstone."

He was lying. This time of year, with the soil so soft, the body would be decomposed and the stone ready to dig up in no more than three full days.

Peder's vague smile chilled Mariessa more than his cold-blooded murder. "Prepare and bury him. After Shangsan, you may keep his stone for your village. I doubt it'll be anything more creative than a lightstone, but that will be for your judging." Peder trained his lustful gaze on her. "Just make sure the girl is ready to leave first thing in the morning. I don't like to be kept waiting."

Sando called two of the men forward. "Put her in the hut and stand guard. She can pee in the corner if needed, but she's not to leave. I don't want her slipping away like last time."

Fists to abdomen, they bowed. "Yes, piuno."

Mariessa struggled as they dragged her away, but it did no good. They took her thigh-knife, and threw her through the open door, tying the cloth flap round the thick posts with tight knots. She waited a few minutes then found her hidden knife, sequestered between the corner bamboo stilts and the woven wall. She slipped it into her thigh holster, wrapped on a new bestit, and waited.

When the moon rose, blue and bright in the night sky, she would have her chance. Nobody, not even Dangan, would hold her back this time.

4

In a clean hyefu, Fourteen ran onto the open field by the compound gates. The stiff fabric itched where the lower panel snapped at his side and the shirt barely reached the top of his trousers, but he didn't dare show up at an assembly in common dress. His shoes, shining as black and mirror bright as the guards', pressed patterns in the thick grass. It would look trampled for a couple of days, but return to normal as Numbers were normally kept from nearing the compound's only exit.

The emperor's frown followed Fourteen's hasty arrival, watching from the raised guard tower at the end of the compound's short entrance road. His black, cabriolet-style autocar, called a Shtedler by Master Den, rested on the brick-paved road inside the gates, guards at each end of the running boards and another at the sleek bonnet-hood, the emperor's chauffeur waiting in the front seat.

More guards in black and gray uniforms and carrying the new self-loading rifles, flanked the emperor, stood by the tower's ladder, and circled the area in key positions on the green's periphery. Standing in the back corner of the platform, the coordinator for the Emperor's Citizen Safety Organization, the CSO, stood in a black hyefu and slacks which matched his second-tier tattoo. The man, Bow Quing, represented the emperor's eyes and ears around the world; Master Den claimed the man's main role was that of chief assassin and personal bodyguard. Bow Quing watched the proceedings without expression. The compound guards, stripped of firearms in the emperor's presence, stood off to one side carrying only sabers.

Studying the emperor's stance as well as the bulges in his opulent robe, Fourteen wondered why the man even needed guards. He had a pistol in plain sight at his waist and a knife in his boot. By the way he shifted his arm across his chest, he probably had at least another pistol strapped beneath the wrap of his green robe, at his chest, and maybe a knife or two. A round bulge near the waistline suggested a grenade of some sort. By the way he shifted his weight, he had something strapped to his thigh and another knife or small gun hidden inside the other boot.

Fourteen glanced at Master Den who appraised his study and raised an eyebrow. Hiding a smile, Fourteen spread out eight fingers, keeping them low and out of sight. Master Den jutted his chin to one side, no one but Fourteen would equate it with a shake of his head. He spread both hands, pulled them back, then put out two fingers.

Twelve? Fourteen watched the emperor a few more seconds, realizing his father also had weapons strapped to his forearms. After closer study, Fourteen suspected he might have a small knife tucked into his whitish-blond braid, tied at the base of his neck. But for all of Dixho, he couldn't figure out where the emperor could have stashed anything else, or what kind of weapon would fit in another space on his body.

"If we're all assembled?" the emperor drawled, staring at Fourteen.

Fourteen blushed but stood his ground. He'd learned early on, his father might get angry if he faced him, but the punishment became ten times worse if he cowed.

"In accordance with tradition," the emperor boomed in a loud voice, "it is time to choose my successor. As Emperor Han II said centuries ago, 'A progressive government is not to be ruled by old men.' So, it is time for the most worthy of my children to take my place as emperor of the world. I have chosen four candidates from among my Numbers. They will enter competition to determine who is most sound in body, mind, and spirit. The winner is not guaranteed as the next emperor, but it plays a major factor in my decision. Now, our competitors will be... Nine, Eleven, Twelve, and Fourteen. The competitions will commence in one week. May the warrior most worthy have the Vasheri's blessing."

Led by the emperor's guards, the lawn erupted in applause.

From the corner of his eye, Fourteen watched Master Den sneer derisively, clapping his hands so they didn't meet. The man had better watch himself, or he'd get his head stuck in a noose without Fourteen's help.

As their father made his way to the ladder, Eleven sidled next to Fourteen. "You know I've never cared about becoming emperor."

"I know," Fourteen said, glad for the reminder of one less brother to worry about.

Eleven lowered his voice a bit more. "To be fair, I thought I should tell you,

I'm going to do my best to win this competition."

Caught off guard, Fourteen stared at the only brother he'd ever liked or felt any kinship with. "Why?"

"Aednat. If you win, you'll take her to the palace with you, probably as your servant. Or worse, your concubine. I can't allow that."

"And if you win," said Fourteen, "she'll be in the same situation."

Eleven shook his head. "No, I'll marry her."

"An empress? There's never been one. The law doesn't even allow it."

"Then I'll change the laws."

Fourteen half-chuckled. "You say that, but once you go through ascension, you'll become Lingdow. Your responsibilities to the empire outweigh personal desires."

"I'll find a way."

"You're assuming you'll win. I'm not going to hand it to you, Eleven. I've dreamed of becoming emperor for as long as I can remember. With that kind of power and freedom, I can go anywhere. No walls. No rules. I'll see the entire world." *And Aednat will want to come with me.*

"The same goes for you as goes for me, brother. The emperor hasn't left his palace more than a few times in the last twenty years, some say longer."

"I'm not like him," Fourteen insisted. "I'll bring more bodyguards if necessary, but my people will know me, the real me, not just posters and laws."

Eleven smiled, but the expression didn't reach the worried lines of his brow. "Good luck to us both then, aye?"

Fourteen extended a hand. "May the warrior most capable—"

Grabbing his forearm, Eleven glanced over at Twelve. "—get pummeled to dust, left to drift in the lost spaces of limbo."

Fourteen followed his gaze. "I can agree with that."

Through a break in the small crowd of Numbers, masters, and servants, Fourteen watched the emperor summon Master Den into the privacy of his autocar. His father rarely acknowledged the instructors, let alone had conversations with them. The door to the back seat shut as the chauffeur scrambled out, white-faced. Two guards led the trembling man away from the vehicle, forming a solid perimeter about seven lengths' radius around the autocar.

What had the loud-mouthed Master Den gotten himself into now?

Fourteen watched, curious, but he needed to focus on what mattered most. In one week, the emperor's competition would determine the rest of his life.

5

Emperor Beht Han rubbed his hands together, an old nervous habit he'd never bothered to break, and stared at the younger man.

Master Chid Den—Han hated the family name Den had taken rather than retain the name of his parent. Den remained absolutely cool. Not a nervous tic, not a shift in the seat, not even a bead of sweat at his temple. Han could have him executed with a flick of his finger, but Den didn't seem to care.

Den smiled, no wrinkles creasing his mouth or movement in his eyes. "Curious. Why not Ten? He's big enough, his appearance fits your requirements, and he's the smartest of them all. Ah," Den answered his own question without pause. "Too smart. He's figuring out your secret, isn't he?"

Han went motionless. He could swear that he didn't change expression, but somehow Den read some flick of the eye, some minute movement of a single muscle. He gave up keeping anything back. "He's being killed as we speak. Bad dinner fungi."

Den nodded, seemingly unconcerned, though Han knew he'd taken a liking to some of the boys, including Ten, and especially to one in particular, the least likely of them all.

"You seem to spend more time with Fourteen than the others," said Han. "Is that because your girl is his servant?"

This time Den did react, the muscles in his chin tightening. "I had an obligation to Aednat's mother as I'm sure your spies have already informed you. I wanted her where I could keep a close eye."

"Somehow you've convinced the boy to limit their relationship. I commend you for that."

"He has a natural sense of right and wrong. There's been no need for convincing because he would never do anything to hurt Aednat."

"You like him," Han said.

"Sometimes. Sometimes I hate him. Because of him, Kerise is dead. But he's growing to be a decent human being, which is more than I can say for us."

The insult didn't faze Han, and it no longer surprised him. "You were ten years old when the woman died. You hadn't even known her that long, yet you still harbor tender feelings and resentments, even after all I've done for you."

"Like killing my parent?"

"That was an accident, Den. A moment of rage. We've been through too much for you to keep holding such indiscretions against me. From the day you became an adult, I offered you back your parent's position. You could be king, beneath only me in power."

Den shook his head. "I don't care anymore. Whatever friendship we may have had, it's gone."

"I'll choose the boy. You could come back to the palace with me and remain with him."

"After you're finished with him?" Den gave a dry chuckle. "I don't think so. Choose someone else and let him die with all the others. It's far preferable."

"You'd rather see him dead than watch him ascend to power, glory and divinity? The next Lingdow?"

"You're not divine, Han. You've perpetrated this lie for so long, you've started to believe it."

"I am divine. I have all the qualities of deity and from generation to generation I perfect upon them. I am a god more powerful than the Vasheri legends could ever conjure."

Den stared at Han, unmoving again. How could he hold so much judgment in his young face? He had no right!

Shifting in his seat, Han looked away. "I could make you come back."

"Yes," Den agreed. "Like you made me stay there for so many years after my parent's death? Do you want to go back to that?"

What Han wanted was for everything to be the way it had been. "No. You should forgive me like you've done before. Come back and take your rightful place as the next king."

"Not interested. Now, are you going to kill me or let me go? It's become stifling hot in here."

"You'll change your mind," said Han.

"I doubt it."

Han gestured to the door handle. "Leave. But you will reconsider."

Staring through the window, Han watched Fourteen breathe out a grateful sigh when Den stepped from the car unscathed. There was more to that relationship than Den let on. The man probably didn't even realize the depth of his emotional connection.

Perhaps Han could use the boy. Den had become so very different from his parent, Han wondered if something fundamentally wrong had happened. But Han would fix it. He watched Fourteen's retreating back.

Han had coddled Den and his playthings long enough.

6

Mariessa had prepared an escape from Sando's hut years ago, cutting a hole in the bamboo floor beneath her clothing drawer. But she'd never had to use it, not until now. Dropping through, Mariessa landed in the soft mud beneath. Sandals in hand, she lifted her feet, moving slowly enough to keep the mud from squelching in the silence.

One guard sat against the ladder at the hut's entrance, leaning against the rungs, snoring. The other, standing beneath the open window, shuffled in a tuft of grass. He leaned his head against the bamboo wall, no doubt wishing for a position like his friend so he could fall asleep.

She would have liked to run for the closest expanse of jungle, but she needed a few things first. Wiping the mud from her feet on some weeds, she strapped on her sandals and took silent steps between the sleeping forms of drunken men and women gathered round the dying embers of celebration fires. The bloated moon had reached its peak and started its descent. Its luminescence shone brighter than a lightstone, outlining everything in blue-gray patterns. If anyone woke, her escape would be obvious, but for now one guard slept and the other faced the wrong direction.

After too much liquor, many of the people lay on bare dirt, having shifted off their mats or fallen drunk before getting that far. Mariessa suppressed a wish that they all contract tyan-worms, to infest their stomachs and make them slowly starve. But she didn't mean it. They'd treated her badly, but it was Sando's fault more than theirs. After such spiteful feelings, she'd best hope she hadn't picked up worms herself during her short walk through the mud.

The last man she stepped over was Sando himself. He lay across his mat, well protected from the minuscule worms that milled in moist soil. Mariessa glanced at a thick vine hanging from the branches of a red mango tree at the edge of the bangay. She wished she could cut the vine and use it to strangle his meaty neck. A knife to the heart would be too merciful.

One of the crazy dogs barked and Mariessa scurried behind a hut on the other side of Sando's snoring form. Ter stuck her head from the window above. They stared at each other, the moonlight reflecting in Ter's beautifully straight, dark hair.

"Pshh!" Ter hushed the dog. "Quiet, Londo." She nodded to Mariessa. "Good luck."

"Thank you," Mariessa mouthed.

Ter was one of the few who knew the truth, through her own experience. But Ter hadn't been able to defend herself from Sando. He held her silence by maintaining her fear.

Mariessa placed her fingers to her forehead, letting her friend know that she would always be remembered, even as they parted ways.

After Mariessa filched food from the communal kitchen, she made her way to Dangan's family hut at the bangay edge. This time she had the sense to throw their nearby mutt a scrap of meat, keeping the irritating beast quiet. Inside the door, leaning against the wall, sat Dangan's hunting pack. She grabbed it and started back down the ladder.

"Mariessa."

She froze. Dangan had called out her name. Would he sound the alarm?

Peeking back up the stairs, the moonlight shone through the gap in the door-cloth, illuminating the strong lines of Dangan's face.

"Mariessa," he whispered this time, still asleep.

She shook her head, descending the ladder. It was too late for stolen kisses, too late for what might have been. Shouldering the pack, she disappeared into the dark jungle.

It took longer than anticipated, but she found her long-hidden knives in the crannies of familiar trees and under loose rocks. They were from a time when Sando thought he could confiscate her knives and she'd have no protection. Her mother's refusal to lie with him for weeks had ended his efforts to take the weapons. The woman had sacrificed everything, even her body, to keep Mariessa safe. When she'd died, Mariessa had already learned to sleep light and always have a knife on hand. Sando had learned to keep his distance.

Keeping the blue moon at her back, Mariessa didn't need Dangan's lightstone to illuminate her path. She made her way with the instincts of a leopard and the keen eyesight passed on from her Uradi father, going deeper into the jungle than she'd ever been. She had a knack for traveling through the thick greenery. Despite the arching foliage darkening the inner layers, she was aware of every leaf, every tree and every reaching fern. Her fingers brushed across them as she walked, enjoying the caress of their waxy leaves. If she kept heading east, she'd eventually reach the shoreline. From there, she could make her way north until she found a boat.

No one had ever found her in the jungle unless she wanted to be found. Not as a child playing hide-and-seek, and not when Sando got drunk and sought her out, forgetting her sharp blades. The emperor's men, with their constricting clothes and city ways, wouldn't stand a chance.

She was alone, but she was free.

7

Fourteen tapped his foot on the sterile white tile, waiting for his turn. Eleven was taking way too long, and Fourteen still wanted breakfast.

Finally, the door opened. A woman dressed in a white skirt, wearing a small matching hat with the medical insignia of a heart over a hand embroidered on the front, invited Fourteen into the examination room. Her dark shoulder-length hair bobbed back and forth as she walked, but Fourteen was focused on her long shapely legs, immodestly exposed above the knee.

"You can sit here," she said, gesturing with her hand to an examination table covered with a thin, white sheet.

Fourteen jerked his eyes from her half-exposed bosom to her face, then away, finally noticing the small room with medical posters plastered across the walls, a simple sink in the corner, and various instruments and bottles of supplies strewn across a side-table.

She smiled, making one cheek dimple. "You Numbers. All the same."

"What?" Fourteen said, sitting down.

"As if you don't know what I'm talking about. Every one of you has stared at my legs, my hips, or my chest, before, during, and after the initial examination."

Fourteen blushed. "I didn't mean—"

"It's quite all right. In all honesty, it's part of the test. The emperor wants to know that *everything* works normally on you boys."

His cheeks burned, but she only laughed and continued. She measured his height, checked his blood pressure, and finished taking his temperature.

"You're a cute one," she said, kissing him on the cheek. Her hips swayed back and forth as she exited the room.

Fourteen blinked at her disappearing form. "Paradise," he whispered after her.

"Yes. That tends to be the general reaction."

Swinging his head around, Fourteen saw that the doctor had entered from a side door, coming from another examination room. A green strip on the collar of his white robe identified him as a Numbers physician, while the third-tier tattoo showed his familial connections to those in high government offices. He picked up the clipboard left behind by the nurse and scribbled a quick note.

"Well now." He set the clipboard down again, pen resting on top. "That was the enjoyable part of the exam. Now for the less pleasant side."

He wasn't kidding. The doctor measured every single part of Fourteen's body, from the length of his toes to the length of things Fourteen kept private from the world. He touched, pushed, and prodded outside and inside every square digit, doing things that normally would have provoked Fourteen to violence.

At the end, he sent Fourteen into a bathroom with three cups. "Urine, feces, and semen," the man said. "The feces you can give to me at any time in the next twenty-four hours. You can stay in the little closet as long as you like, but don't come out until there's something in the other two."

Eyes wide, Fourteen allowed the man to usher him into the closed space.

He stared at the wall, stared at the little plastic cups. Maybe emperor wasn't worth it after all.

A couple of hours later, Fourteen was ushered with Twelve, Eleven, and Nine onto the indoor track next to the outdoor training arena. Nine and Eleven were roughly the same size, taller than Fourteen by nearly four digits. Though a good digit shorter than Fourteen, Twelve was broader in the chest with muscles that outdid them all. Fourteen had always thought himself well-developed, at least compared to the servant boys his age. In comparison to his older brothers, he felt like a scrawny twelve-year-old.

One wall of the building was lined with barbells, benches, and free-weights. Two other walls had obstacle courses set up along their lengths, and the black rubber track dominated the building's center.

Master Kurtz, a tall Uradian physical fitness master, flexed his bare chest and fourth-tier arm-tattoo as he held up a clipboard similar to the doctor's. "We'll be testing your physical ability, starting with weights."

On every test, Twelve, Eleven and Nine battled for dominance. Fourteen came close, but never close enough to merit as competition. He'd nearly given up when they moved to running. He raced neck and neck with the others for the sprints, even winning one of the obstacle courses.

"This is your last test of the morning," said Kurtz, pointing to the track.

Fourteen glanced at a clock on the wall. Morning was almost gone. It was ten minutes until noon.

"On your mark, get set."

"Hold on," said Twelve. "From where to where?"

"Round and round, kid. Doesn't matter where you start, doesn't matter where you end, but the moment you start walking, you're finished."

"For how long?" Nine asked, his hands on his knees, still recovering from the obstacle course.

"Until you can't go anymore."

"And we still have one more test today?"

The man nodded. "This evening. Now, on your mark, get set, go."

They each grabbed a lane and took off. Twelve chose the inside track and Fourteen steered clear, staying on the outside. Though Twelve went faster around the oval, it didn't matter. This was an endurance trial. Fourteen started out at the slowest jog he could manage, and set a pace.

This was one of the exercises Master Den had pushed Fourteen to excel in. "There will be fights where you're not the strongest or the most experienced. But if you have the endurance they've never acquired and the smarts to see your options, you can still win."

Twelve went down first, gasping on a mat in the center, burned out. Nine dropped next. A short while later, Eleven finally conceded, actually throwing up in a trash bucket by the doors. Fourteen kept pace, kept his focus, and kept going, a bit nauseous but far from spent.

"Kid. You're done," Master Kurtz eventually yelled across the field.

Fourteen crossed the blue mats. He faced the man while still jogging in place.

"I can...keep going," he said between breaths.

"That's obvious, but there's no point. You've outdone your brothers by more than a fair margin."

"That's because the freak runs every morning before breakfast," Twelve accused, as if Fourteen had somehow anticipated the test.

In a less condemning tone, Eleven added, "He also runs for hours and hours on some of the days we don't have class."

The man with the clipboard narrowed his eyes. "Did you already know about this test?"

Fourteen considered mentioning Master Den's side-training, but the master had never mentioned the tests.

"I like to run," said Fourteen. "I didn't know what our tests would be or when they would happen."

Master Kurtz studied Fourteen for a few minutes, perhaps gauging his honesty, then nodded. "Get yourselves some food, some sleep, then meet back here at twentieth hour this evening."

Twelve glanced at his wristwatch. "Thanks to Fourteen, it's only a couple of hours until dinner."

Fourteen glanced at his own watch. Twelve was right; almost sixteenth hour.

Eleven clapped him on the shoulder. "Let's take the man at his word, aye. Get some grub early from the kitchens and sack out for an hour. I have a feeling this next test isn't going to be any easier."

8

The evening trial appeared to be an opportunity to murder one another. With stiff muscles, Fourteen walked into the auditorium to find a large red circle painted on the mats.

Personal servants and the younger Numbers sat on tiered wooden benches on the other side of the track, waiting for the entertainment to start. Master Den sat immediately behind Aednat, whispering something in her ear. He eyed Fourteen, sitting back again. Aednat waved, a wide smile brightening her worried features, but Fourteen couldn't tell if the happy greeting extended to him, or Eleven.

A small balcony extended from the wall above the door, well above the other spectators. From his superior vantage, the emperor rested his elbows on the banister edge, a pair of gold binoculars to his brow, matching the gold brocade on his voluminous fuchsia robe.

Master Kurtz stood before the Numbers as moderator. "I have four sticks in my hand, shortest to longest. They are the order in which you'll compete. The first two in a match, the next two in a match, then the winners. The youngest Number will choose first."

Fourteen stepped forward, dressed in the white competition hyefu Aednat had ironed for him, a green and yellow strip along the bottom. The hyefu itched along his side, having ties instead of snaps, but at least the loose white pants were comfortable. Not caring when or who he fought as long as he didn't have to face Twelve, Fourteen chose a stick and stepped back.

Twelve's was shorter than Fourteen's by only a quarter of a digit. Eleven chose one longer by the same factor. Depending on the last stick, Fourteen would match Eleven first, or Twelve. He closed his eyes and hoped for Nine's stick to be the short one, not the long. The man opened his hand and offered the stick to Nine, who deflated. He hadn't wanted to match Twelve either.

Twelve, with a green-and-orange-striped hyefu, and Nine, with a green and purple, studied the hardwood sparring rods lined up next to the moderator. The stripes on their shirts seemed silly under the circumstances. Twelve's bizarre dark hair stood out, identifying him more than a stupid stripe. With a malicious grin, Twelve selected a medium-weight stick then stepped into the combat circle. Carrying a shorter but heavier rod, Nine took a deep breath and followed.

Master Kurtz blew a whistle. Twelve attacked.

The sticks swung back and forth, their resounding clashes echoing in the cavernous room. Nine slammed his rod at Twelve's mid-section. Twelve blocked, stepping out of reach, but the heavy impact forced his stick to the side. He used the momentum to flip the stick and whip it across Nine's shoulders. His blow held less power, but met its mark like a whip. They continued like that, Nine's hits echoing against Twelve's stick like strikes of lightning, and Twelve's stick hitting against Nine like pebbles aggravating a mountain. The ten-minute timer ticked to only one minute.

Slapping the rod across Nine's back, Twelve swung it back around, snapping it in the older boy's face. Something cracked. Nine screamed, blood streaming from his nose. Twelve grinned. Sweeping the stick low, he felled Nine to the mat. The rod rose up like a spear, ready to impale the older boy.

"Hold it!" yelled Master Kurtz, running into the circle.

Twelve brought it down. He tapped Nine's ribs hard enough to make him grunt.

"Just so you know," said Twelve, "I could have killed you. Never forget it."

Whether Nine did or not, Fourteen would never forget. Twelve was dangerous in a way he had never seen.

Only a few minutes later, Eleven and Fourteen faced off, blue stripe against yellow, with similar light-weight sticks. As they waited for the whistle, they faced Aednat. She covered her eyes.

"Whichever one of us wins," said Eleven, "it'll make her cry."

Fourteen nodded. "I don't know what we can do about that."

"Just, no blood injuries, aye?"

Fourteen shrugged but didn't comment. He'd do whatever it took.

At the whistle, Fourteen and Eleven's sticks snapped together. Dancing back and forth, they swung and parried, both trying to get a feel for the other. Fourteen's blows came faster, but Eleven's carried more strength. With that recognition, Fourteen devised a plan.

He gave up on any offensive, stepping away from Eleven in an outward spiral. The point was not to gain ground, but to find his moment. With the added space, his sparring rod gained speed. He couldn't stop Eleven's blows, so he knocked them aside.

A forceful swing aimed at Fourteen's shoulder. He sidestepped, knocking the stick point to the mat with one end of his rod. As if part of one motion, the other end slapped against Eleven's ribs, making him stumble.

Fourteen gave him no time to absorb what had happened. He whipped his rod against Eleven's head, foot, stomach, arm. Back and forth, his rod moved as if flying by some will of its own. Eleven blocked, but for every success, Fourteen's next hit was already in motion.

On the offensive now, Fourteen pressed Eleven back. Step by step, his advantage grew. Fourteen grinned, ready to finish the fight.

With an angry grimace, Eleven grabbed his stick in both hands. He swung it like a servant woman wielding a rug paddle. Fourteen might have ducked, if he'd been more prepared and less cocky. It slammed into his hip, sending him to the floor.

But as he went down, he thrust the end of his rod into Eleven's stomach. Eleven stepped back a fraction of a second before Fourteen slid outside the red circle. The whistle blew twice, competition over. Eleven beamed until Fourteen shook his head, pointing at Eleven's left foot.

Following Fourteen's gaze, Eleven swore as he examined his heel extending outside the circle's red line. "You conniving little yenk."

"Brain over brawn," Fourteen quoted Master Den.

"I hate you right now." Eleven glanced at Twelve, now sporting a hungry smile. "You'd better take care of that slick rat or the next time he has you down on the ground, I'll clap for him instead of saving your sorry, wet butt."

Fourteen's face fell. He'd have to face Twelve. He doubted the same tactics would work twice.

Fourteen dragged himself to his feet and without a break, faced his most hated enemy. More agile than Nine, Fourteen avoided Twelve's blows, side-stepping and dancing until he found his moment. Only a couple of minutes into the match, it came. Fourteen danced his rod back and forth, hitting ribs, thigh, shoulder. His momentum lasted all of ten seconds before Twelve stepped out of range, keenly aware of the boundary line. That happened three times, Fourteen wearing himself out, with Twelve showing little damage.

Getting in closer, Fourteen struck. He missed. Twelve pummeled him, forcing Fourteen to the ground. As the sparring rod came down at his ribs. Fourteen rolled away. It slammed into the mat and he jumped to his feet.

Grabbing the end of his rod in both hands, Twelve swung it with all his brute strength. Fourteen jumped high into the air, evading, but still making no real progress.

In the end, the timer ended the match. Fourteen managed to stay on his feet, but every digit of him hurt. He was sure he had a broken rib, blood streamed from his nose, and various bruises had swollen to the point the skin split like an oozing volcano.

Master Kurtz had the boys line up.

"I hate you," Eleven whispered, helping Fourteen stand. "I mean it this time."

"Right now, I hate myself," Fourteen mumbled through a split lip.

"I could have taken him."

"Probably" said Fourteen, leaning on his brother more than he liked. "But look at the frizz-head. The emperor will never pick him. He can't seriously consider him a candidate."

Eleven stared at Fourteen as if meeting a new boy in a master's class. "No, but he's one of the tests. Beating him is probably more important than beating each other."

Fourteen took a sidelong glance at Twelve, the most unscathed of the four of them. Eleven was right, but what chance did Fourteen have against Twelve? He'd never been able to compete with Twelve's mean side, even when they'd been friends.

As if to confirm his thoughts, the moderator announced the day's results. "According to the grading system devised centuries ago to aid the emperor in his selection of a successor, these are the current standings..."

From his private balcony above the other spectators, the emperor leaned forward.

"Nine has 1270 points, Eleven with 1389 points, Twelve—1408, and Fourteen with 1265."

Fourteen deflated. Last place. Making the dejection worse, Aednat's sympathetic expression focused on Eleven. Fourteen would give her extra errands to run tomorrow, keep her so busy she wouldn't have time to make eyes at his stupid brother. But Master Den's frown bothered him even more. For a man who claimed he didn't want Fourteen to become emperor, he appeared sorely displeased.

Master Kurtz spoke up again. "Our candidates have one week to recuperate and prepare themselves. The mental challenge will then commence."

The emperor rose from his seat, stared down at the crowd. Rising with the other spectators, Master Den turned, making eye contact instead of lowering his gaze. No words were spoken but an exchange occurred between them,

Master Den's jaw setting in an angry line. Head held high, the emperor left and the crowd dispersed.

A few minutes later, Aednat helped Fourteen hobble toward their apartment, walking down a brick pathway lined with glowing lightstones dangling from green posts. A group of young Numbers on small bicycles, led front and behind by their maids, passed in front of them, on their way to the nursery and a late bedtime. Fourteen hoped they'd enjoyed the whole bloody show, but some of them looked more traumatized than happy.

Master Den came beside Fourteen, grasping his forearm to help him walk.

"I'm not that incapable," Fourteen said.

Master Den raised his eyebrows, glancing back at the arena. "You sure?"

Fourteen's nostrils flared. "If he hadn't seen my match with Eleven—"

"True," said Master Den, "but coming up with one solution doesn't mean you can't come up with another. You let Twelve intimidate you well before he ever touched you with that stick."

"He's stronger, faster, meaner. What do you expect—?"

"Is this why you joined us, Den?" said Aednat. "So you could tell him all the ways he's not perfect? You know that's not fair."

Master Den went silent. He'd never have accepted such a reprimand from anyone else. Fourteen wondered about that, but still couldn't find an answer. Aednat would only say that Master Den had known her mother.

Master Den took a deep breath. "He's not faster, but Aednat's right. I'm forgetting my purpose."

"I'll do better on the mind tests," Fourteen said. "But I doubt it'll be well enough."

"You could fail all of the challenges. Unless you show yourself to be defective or incompetent, the emperor will choose you. I ask again, let me take you both away from here."

Fourteen glared at Aednat, but she only nodded. "He's right. We need to leave this place. There's a whole other world you don't know about, and it's not as wonderful as you think. If you understood, you wouldn't want to follow the emperor. You wouldn't want to be anything like him."

"I can't believe this." Fourteen pulled his arm from Master Den's. "You've brainwashed *her* now?" He clenched Aednat's hand. "I know there's a whole world out there. If I'm emperor, I can see all of it. If I run away like a fool, I'll be stuck in a tenth tier, seeing only stupid, worthless peasants. Assuming I survive that long." In the umbra of a lightstone, he shook his forearm in front of her eyes. "I have no tier, and it's not like we could just paint one on. You have any jinyo berries on hand? If I go beyond Han City without one, I'll be caught, tried, and executed before they ever figure out I'm a Number."

Master Den barked a laugh. "The way you look now, nobody would ever question you're a Number, if not the emperor himself."

Fourteen ignored him, turning back to Aednat. "That's another reason we'd never survive out there. We'd be caught, and the emperor would be justifiably furious. Besides, I want this. I want the palace, I want the life, and with the emperor's training, I can become a good leader. Even if I fail, I have to try."

Aednat wrapped her other hand around his. "You should trust Den. He says there's another kind of stone—"

"No." Fourteen pushed her hands away, hobbling along on his own. "We should trust our path to the Vasheri. The emperor is Lingdow. Why would I put my faith in a mere mortal over him?"

Aednat sighed, craning her neck around Fourteen to speak to Master Den. "Even if I explained, he wouldn't believe me, would he?"

"No, he believes the only heartstones in existence are those cataloged by the geology master. I think I might have another idea. It's risky, but there's no getting through this ox's stubborn stupidity."

"If you're plotting against the emperor," said Fourteen, "I'll have no choice—"

"It's nothing like that," Master Den assured him.

"Have you ever seen one of these magical heartstones?" Fourteen asked Aednat. "Ever seen anything besides light, strength, and healing?"

"No, but they're rare."

"They're not rare, they're a fairy tale. I would think that old Master Faa knows better than either one of you. He's devoted his life to the study of heartstones."

Aednat opened her mouth to argue, but Master Den held up his hand. "Don't bother. We'll have to let matters run their course. Fourteen will be chosen and then he'll discover the truth."

"I know the truth," he said.

Master Den raised his eyes toward limbo. "You're sixteen. Of course you do."

9

As the sun began to set, Mariessa scrambled through the dense foliage, fat leaves gliding easily to each side as she hurdled and side-stepped ferns, bushes, and undergrowth. Dogs barked in the distance but there was still a chance. They hadn't caught her scent or they'd be howling.

Her legs ached, but she kept moving back and forth between a slow jog and a staggering walk. The dogs' barks grew ever closer. No matter which way she turned, or the false trails she left, they followed. Even imperial hounds shouldn't be that good, but as the next morning dawned, Mariessa limped through the trees, and the creatures' barks turned to baying. She found an open area near the top of a rise, finally sighting her goal. In the distance, the ocean spread out from a sandy beach. Only a few ferns and low-growing plants sprouted from the gritty soil at her feet, evidence of the seashore nearby, but not close enough to outrun those dogs. She could have covered her scent with seaweeds, but the sweet tang of ocean air had come too late.

A little way down the mountain, a single chapnut tree grew straight and tall, similar to the one outside her family's apartment when they'd live in Keran, when father had been alive.

This chapnut had five long trunks stretching toward the sky—a rarity, but not as rare as the seven-trunked tree from her childhood. She shimmied up the hairy bark until she reached the high interlacing branches that formed a multitude of nets from one trunk to the next, interspersed with wide green leaves as big around as her circled arms. It was a frail wish that she might hold off Peder and his men, but it was her only hope.

She balanced on a thin branch, pulling extra knives from her pack and sticking them into the trunk within easy reach. One, she held by its hilt, waiting.

The dogs burst into the clearing first, slobbering as they howled. She ignored the huge cross-bred brutes. Even imperial hounds couldn't climb trees.

The first of Peder's thugs followed, dressed entirely in the deep brown of tilled earth, with pale purple and pink ICRO stripes at their sleeve cuffs.

Even knowing these men were no better than kidnappers, part of a government-approved prostitution business, she hesitated. She'd never killed a man in cold blood before. Even Peder's companion, though murdered by her hand, had not died by her intent.

With trembling hands, she flung the knife. It sank into the ICRO thug's shoulder, nearly two palms from his heart. He slowed, wincing and gritting his teeth, but didn't stop.

Two more entered the clearing.

Her shaking hands continued their betrayal, refusing to find her intended targets. She brought one man to his knees, a blade deep in his thigh. He grunted, yanking the knife from his flesh, but didn't rise. The next whip of her knife struck in an agent's belly. He staggered backward into the dense greenery at the edge of the clearing.

The man with the wounded shoulder had strapped the injury with a thin cloth. He reached Mariessa's trunk and started to climb.

She grabbed her remaining knives, one in her teeth and a hilt in each hand. Scurrying across the tree's thin lattice like a four-legged insect, she reached the opposite side and climbed higher into the branches.

Peder entered the clearing's edge, pocketing a translucent, olive-colored stone in one of the pouches next to his gun holster. Mariessa only caught a brief glimpse, but it seemed a bit dark for a lightstone. Perhaps a seeking stone? But where could he have found such a stone set for her? A person had to spend most of their life intent on finding or keeping a person safe for the xicao worms to turn their heart to a seeking stone when they died. Like most, Mariessa's parents' hearts had become lightstones, collected by the local priest and sold almost immediately for food or debts. Peder's stone didn't make sense.

Taking the blade from between her teeth, she flung it at Peder's chest, hands steady.

Like a cobra, his upper body slid to one side.

She heard a grunt from behind, but the thick foliage hid his other men.

"Come, Mariessa," Peder said. Unlike her father's version of the accent which had given the S a lilt Peder's Uradian tongue slithered across the S like a snake. "You're stuck in a tree, running out of knives. This will be easier if you give up now. Someone might get hurt."

She threw two at once.

Peder leaned back and turned. One knife whizzed by his nose, the other brushed his belt, both disappearing into the dark foliage behind. Another exclamation sounded from the jungle shadows. This time Mariessa recognized the voice.

"No!" she cried.

Limbs snapped near her feet. She'd nearly forgotten the man climbing the tree. He grasped one of the larger limbs, but her confidence in the chapnut was well deserved. With a sudden series of cracks, he landed flat on his back, letting out a short grunt as broken branches rained down.

At the same time, Dangan emerged from the foliage. He dropped to one knee. Shorter than Peder, her blade protruded from his sternum, just below the throat. The other had grazed his thigh. Knowing she carried knives, Peder had purposely placed Dangan in the dark jungle directly behind him. The truth of it was as obvious as the victory in Peder's grin.

Blood gurgled between Dangan's lips.

"No!" Mariessa screamed again, tears burning her eyes.

Dangan's jaw opened and shut, fingers outstretched. His eyes rolled up as he tumbled forward, landing on a small fern. With a twitch, he rolled into the dirt, lying on his side. His open hand clenched shut for the last time, lifeless eyes staring at the blood-stained leaves. Mariessa choked on a sob. Her knives slipped from her shaking fingers. They landed hilt up between the chapnut's roots and the wounded agent's knees.

"You sleth!" Mariessa spat.

Peder made a forward motion with his hand. Two men from her village stepped around Dangan. They brought blow-sticks to their lips.

Climbing higher into the tree's canopy, its wide leaves made interlocking shields. Darts whistled around her, shredding the tender foliage. One finally found its way to the flesh of her calf.

"Stop!" yelled Peder. "She is hit." His last word blurred in her ears, never quite cutting off.

Bark slipped from numb fingers. The leaves' ribbons slapped at her as she fell, though she was only half aware. Arms and legs broke thin branches, cutting her as she tumbled over and around the larger ones. She probably wouldn't survive the fall, but she couldn't seem to focus on why it mattered. As the drug spread, the danger seemed farther and farther away. In her mind she floated, a downy speck of pollen blown from the chapnut tree's yellow blossoms.

Peder caught her as if cradling a child.

Even through the fog in her mind she yearned for her knives, to plunge one between his collarbones and let him die like Dangan. But her hands and arms refused to respond. Her lips quivered, but made no sound.

"*You* have killed him, Mariessa," he hissed, his features blurring back and forth between human and snake. "Not I. Your friend volunteered to stand behind me so as he could talk you down if necessary. You never gave him the chance."

To her blurry vision, a forked tongue slipped between Peder's thin lips. She wanted to respond, tell the sleth that next time she wouldn't miss putting a knife between its eyes. Her swollen tongue tried to hiss the words, but only managed to form a wad of spittle. It ran down her chin.

Peder laid her out, her wet face caked with dirt. She stared at the back of Dangan's head, unable to move. From the corner of her eye, she watched Dangan's father, eyes wet with tears, spit in her direction. Two village women took her remaining knives from their sheaths, trussing her hands with a rope. She didn't care, not in comparison to the horror of Dangan's blood running in a twisted line toward her, pooling at her shoulder and spreading an ever-widening stain across her skin. A xicao worm tickled at her cheek then departed, searching for dead flesh, for Dangan. She wondered at the kind of stone they would make of his heart; a strength-stone, or a simple lightstone like most.

"We are finished," said Tago, Dangan's father, gruff voice cracking with emotion.

"Thank you, Piuno Tago." Peder bowed his head. "I'm sorry about your son, and the strange circumstances of your former leader's death."

Tago shook his head. "To be strangled in such a way. It is sick." He pushed at Mariessa's side with his sandaled foot. "*She* is sick."

In her induced stupor, the words made no sense. Had Ter found her courage and finally taken Sando's life? That seemed the only way for Tago to become piuno.

Twisting his fingers into the sign to ward off evil, Tago returned to the jungle. The other village men lifted Dangan, dislodging xicao grubs then following their new leader home.

Though her body didn't respond, Mariessa cried inside as they took him away. Once, she'd thought Dangan might offer gifts to Sando for an engagement token. If only he had believed her over Sando, trusted her.

Peder gestured to one of his two uninjured men. "Carry the girl. The emperor wants her ready for the ascension ceremony. We have less than six hours to make the landing strip."

The man hoisted Mariessa over his shoulder. Even with the drug, she could sense a far-off pain in her gut.

"We're not taking the boat?" asked the man with the injured shoulder.

Peder shook his head. "The emperor has decided to hurry the choosing, and he wants a new gift ready when the ceremony is finished."

Done with the bandage, the man nodded a head toward his comrades. "Kelbein and Bo Fey are too injured to walk all the way to our truck. Should I leave them?"

"They can keep up, you can carry them, or you can kill them. I care not."

Kelbein tied fabric around his thigh. "Hergen, I can make it." But when he rose, his leg refused to hold his weight. He'd have to hop the entire way or have assistance.

Hergen smiled. Using his good arm, he pulled a pistol from his hip holster. Two cracks echoed through the forest, sending a flock of long-legged king to birds into the air. Kelbein and Trintay's bodies joined the damaged foliage and bloodied dirt.

Peder nodded. "Leave the bodies. We don't have time to wait for Shangsan. Maybe some lucky traveler will find the heartstones when the xicao have finished." He smiled in a flat grin. "There will be fewer men with which to split the emperor's certain reward for such a beautiful prize."

Mariessa watched a few of the rotund iridescent xicao, already called by Dangan's blood, emerge from the soil, latching onto the men's open skin, testing that it was dead. Within a few days, they would consume the corpse, little by little, into the soil. Only the men's heartstones would be left behind somewhere in the dirt, maybe to emerge in time, maybe to be buried forever.

Her head bobbed against her captor's back, still drooling spittle as he carried her into the jungle. They were taking her to a truck—Mariessa had seen the machines before, carrying soldiers from Keran to squelch an uprising in the north, but the rest of the men's words made no sense. She could see no way to get from Kerokos to Zhanda, a whole other continent, without a boat.

10

When Bow Quing requested permission to enter, Han set his stack of dry reports to one side of his black, mangrove desk, giving Quing, foremost among his assassins, his full attention. Little did the man know, the spy assigned to watch *him* had left only twenty minutes before.

Taking a sip of well-aged jiu, he allowed the liquor to slide over his tongue before swallowing, Han leaned back in his chair. "What news?"

With a mere nod of his head, Quing proceeded. There was a time Quing would have kowtowed, bending at the waist if not prostrate on the floor, but they had both become lazy. Han would deal with that...after he chose his successor. "The Keroka girl is in our hands. They are boarding the plane."

A hint of a smile quirked Han's lips. "Good. Is she what I requested?"

"As close as we can hope for, Your Eminence."

Han frowned. Quing always used grandiose titles when he feared Han's anger. "What is *not* as I asked?"

"Peder reported she's a bit smaller than expected."

Rage burned in Han's stomach. He came to his feet, towering over the small man. "I told you the Kerokos are a small people. That they would not suffice! I don't need some random island native for a concubine. I wanted a mother!"

"Her father was unusually tall." Quing kowtowed now, backing toward the door as if he might dare try escape. "Taller than you, Your Holiness. Her genetics fit your request, but not her appearance." At the door, he prostrated himself to the ground, his forehead to the tiles. "Please forgive my failure." He glanced up from the corner of his eye. "I will dispose of her."

Han nearly punished him for his insolence. "Be careful what fire you play with, Bow Quing. A flame once ignited might blow out of your control."

If her ancestry fit his desires, Han wanted to see the girl. Quing had diverted Han's anger by suggesting he might get rid of something Han now wanted. The man played too many games.

"Her skin?" Han asked.

"According to Peder, you will be very pleased. Of course, her hair is necessarily darker, but it's rare for physical appearance to change in your offspring more than minor amounts."

Han held out his hand, gesturing in the general direction of the Numbers Compound, on the other side of the palace wall. "And yet, Twelve."

"An unusual exception," Quing admitted, coming back to his feet. "Unlikely to happen again."

"Such a waste," said Han. "He'd be the best candidate if it not for that unruly, dark hair."

Quing kept his tone neutral, but Han heard the mirth in his voice. "Would you choose him even if he looked different? You seem rather set on Chid Den's favorite."

Han narrowed his eyes, warning Quing that he'd best not push him too far. "I will choose whomever I want, for whatever reasons I deem worthy. Don't forget that, Bow Quing, and don't start thinking you know my mind. No man understands the complexities of who and what I am, even if they think they know some of my other secrets."

Quing bowed so low Han couldn't see the man's features, but he could read the man's tense shoulders and the strain in his voice. "Yes, my master." Defiance or fear? Surely, the latter. "If I may ask, why did you include Twelve if he isn't a candidate? Is it only to challenge the others?"

This time, Han allowed the corners of his mouth to spread upward. "I have my reasons. You need not be privy to all of them."

"The boy doesn't even appear to be a Number," said Quing. "He looks nothing like you."

Han sat in his chair again, relaxed. "Which is why I might allow him to live."

Quing gasped. "Never before—"

"There are reasons for traditions. When the reasons don't apply, sometimes it can be an advantage to disregard them. But I must wait and see. See if he will suit my purpose."

"And the other boy, Fourteen?" Quing asked.

"You were right. The boy's fate is sealed. He will also suit my purposes, but not in the way he expects."

Han glanced up, his brow furrowing as he frowned. He'd let Quing's easy manner, so similar in some ways to the late Beht Den, make him say more than he'd intended. When would he learn to keep his own counsel?

"If I am pleased with the Keroka girl," Han said. "You'll have earned a bonus and a favor. Perhaps a night with one of my extra concubines. Now, I have a meeting with the Public Relations Coordinator regarding the upcoming Betrothal Celebration. You're dismissed."

Quing bowed as he backed again to the door.

"And Quing?" Han said.

"Yes, sir."

Han took another sip of jiu. "Remember, when secrets leak, blood spills. Am I understood?"

"As always, I am your most silent servant."

The door closed. Han sighed, left alone once more. The quiet room grated at him like muted laughter, mocking his inability to lure Den back into his rightful place. Den had had his time to sulk, but the man remained unusually stubborn.

Unwrapping a silver egg-sized stone from its cover of thick cotton, he held it close to his lips. "Fetch Esterelle. I want her in the concubine suite in ten minutes."

"Yes, Your Eminence," a woman's voice responded.

Han grimaced. Having to make his requests to Peder's wife, a woman, was insulting. Wrapping the speaking stone, he placed it in an inside coat pocket, next to something much more valuable.

He threw his half-full glass against the cold grate near his desk. The crashing shards tinkled and bounced across the dark tiles, some settling in the wide rug between door and desk.

Sweeping past the guards outside his study, Han clenched and unclenched his fists, anticipating a more satisfying way to release his tension. "Tell the Public Relations man to wait," he told the secretary in the outside office. "I'll be back soon."

The small man nodded, wisely keeping his eyes to the floor.

Esterelle should be to the room by now, and if not, all the more reason to make her pay for her impudence.

11

Sitting at the low table, lead pencil in hand, Fourteen squinted at the words on the page. He shifted in his wooden chair, wishing it at least had a cushion.

This had to be the stupidest test of them all. History, mathematics, language comprehension, science, blah, blah, blah. What did it matter? At the ascension, whoever became next emperor would receive knowledge from the Vasheri. What could a bunch of young boys know in comparison?

He made a few more marks, solved a simple algebraic equation, and then dropped the stack of papers on Master Den's desk, making a point not to look at the man. The traitor.

Regardless of Aednat's defense in Master Den's favor, it didn't change the facts. His former mentor, the man he thought would support him most in his bid as next emperor, had not only deserted him, but turned more blasphemous than Fourteen had ever expected. Not that Fourteen truly believed his own soul was at risk for not reporting Master Den, but he'd certainly placed them in danger. If a priest found him out, they'd both be in trouble.

Fourteen returned to his seat as the other Numbers, each on the heels of the other, turned in their papers. They poised at the edge of their seats, still and silent as Master Den checked their answers with a red pen. He tapped it between his fingers and the light, bunton-wood desk, rarely bringing it to the paper.

At least, Fourteen consoled himself as he waited, he would not be joining Den in final punishment—drifting with the clouds above, purposeless, lost in limbo until deemed worthy of another chance at mortality.

Yes, Fourteen would stay true to his father, and with luck, be blessed to follow in his footsteps, and see the world.

Thirty minutes later, Master Den rose from his seat. "Your scores are all within one point of one another. This will have no effect on the final evaluation, but it confirms the mental capacity for each of you to learn what is necessary during the ascension. The real test will come later today. You have two hours to rest, eat, and prepare. You are dismissed."

Fourteen sprang from his chair, eager to leave the room and Master Den's disapproving stare.

"Fourteen, if you would wait a moment." Master Den's voice stopped him before he could get two steps from his small desk. "I'd like you to run an errand for me."

The others glanced at Fourteen as if wary the master might be giving him tips for the next section. Twelve outright glared, risking an insolent sniff in Master Den's direction.

The science master laughed out loud. "I've told you all, there is no way I could give you answers to the next section. You'll see when you get here this afternoon. It's not that type of test." He turned to Fourteen as if the other Numbers had already left, but they made their way slowly to the door, intent on eavesdropping. "I have some beads I picked up for Aednat." He pulled a briefcase off the floor, opening it on the desk. "The inner-city vendor ran out of the color she wanted, but I found another shop outside the city walls."

The door shut, cutting off Twelve's derisive snicker. As soon as Fourteen was sure everyone had to be out of hearing range, he turned on Master Den.

"You talk about *me* getting her into trouble. Part of the reason Twelve believes he can have his way with her is that he thinks you're buying services with all your daffing trinkets."

Master Den's mouth dropped open. "That's preposterous. I never—"

"I know that and you know that, but Twelve thinks like the dog he is."

Master Den put a hand through his wavy black hair. "There's a reason for that, you know. I wish you'd left the boy alone. You were friends once."

"I was a little kid and I didn't want to get picked on because I had a freak as a friend. It's a little late to do anything about it now."

"If you apologized—"

"Ha," Fourteen folded his arms. "Not going to happen, not to him. The only thing we have in common now is hating each other."

Master Den searched through his briefcase. "I really do have the beads, but something occurred to me as I watched you take that test. You need to fail some of the questions in the next challenge."

"What?" Fourteen almost turned and walked from the room. "I've told you, I'm not going to sabotage my chances."

"I wish you would, but in this case, it will improve them."

"By getting a lower score?"

"There are two questions you'll be given that no Number has ever solved. I believe you're smart enough to figure them out, but if you do, Han—"

Fourteen gasped. Nobody, not even a master, dared use the emperor's given name.

"Remember, I lived in the palace," Master Den said.

Fourteen's eyes darted around the room as if someone might be listening. "That doesn't make it okay."

Master Den took a deep breath, controlling his obvious frustration. "If you pass those sections, the emperor will question your parentage. Not only would you not become the next emperor, it will be an immediate death sentence."

"That's impossible."

"He's paranoid," Master Den insisted. "Nobody knows that better than I. You must fail the ninth and twenty-third questions. For good measure, I suggest you throw two or three others as well, so you don't score too high above the other Numbers."

"This is crazy." Fourteen turned his back, headed for the door.

"The beads," said Master Den as Fourteen grasped the handle. Fourteen turned with a glare, and Den tossed the small, clinking bag. "I've never done anything, not since I've known you, Gabrick, that wasn't for your own good. Even when angry with you, I've tried to help. I understand your distrust, but please believe me on this. Only this. And I'll stay out of your way for the rest of the contest."

"My name is *Fourteen*." He clenched a smooth bracelet in his pocket while adding the bag of beads. Shoving the door open with his shoulder, he stalked from the building. "I'm Fourteen," he muttered to himself, walking toward his apartment. "Son of an emperor, the sacred Lingdow."

His anger grew as he went, not noticing the chatter of squirrels along the path or the high-pitched calls of the birds. The bricks at his feet passed in a blur as did the well-trimmed bushes and newly-painted lightstone posts. What was Master Den's game, telling him to throw answers on the test? Could he really be looking out for him, or was this another way to prevent him from winning? Questions swirled in his head. He didn't have answers, only a choice. He either believed Master Den or he didn't, a gamble he'd have to take in less than two hours. His nostrils flared as he clenched the sack of beads. He threw open the door to his apartment, not caring that it clanged against the wall, making an indentation.

Aednat stood at a rickety ironing board, running a heavy metal iron over one of his new shirts. The cord swished back and forth like a snake, extending from her hand to a power box on the floor. Only a small one with two outlets, it probably held no more than two or three lightstones, joined together by multiple wires.

Moving in rhythm with the snake at her side, her round hips swayed to some tune in her head. As she turned the shirt, she sang a few notes, "I'll be there for you sugar, mmm, eh-eh mmm..."

No doubt, she was thinking of Eleven again. Fourteen chucked the bag of beads, hitting her in the back.

She nearly dropped the hot iron. "Aye!" She fumbled it into a safe position on the board, turning on him. "That could have hurt, Gabrick."

"Lost in limbo!" he swore. "Not you, too. Fourteen! Is it so hard?"

"It never used to bother you," she muttered, picking up the sack.

"Well it does now. Get me some food. I don't feel like going to the kitchens."

He flopped onto the small sofa dominating the apartment's main living space. Black and white pictures and a few color, of him and Aednat, taken by Master Den on days they'd spent by the waterfall playing games and eating unusual foods, broke up the trinkets and flowers on the small bunton-wood cabinet in front of him. Fourteen bit back the urge to sweep them all to the floor.

"I'll be done in a minute," Aednat said, dropping the beads into a pocket of her skirt and going back to the iron. "What do you want to eat?"

"Nothing too heavy. I need to be alert. Get some bread, an apple."

"You should have some solid energy, too." She paused. "Some meat or cheese."

For some reason, everything about her at that moment set him off. "Don't tell me what I need and don't tell me I have to wait. You're my servant. I'm telling you the food I want and I want it now. Maybe some time with Twelve would teach you—"

She dropped the iron, letting out a cry as it nearly hit her bare foot.

Fourteen flushed, almost apologized, but the more stubborn part—the angry, irrational part—refused to back down. "Get my food. Now."

Aednat, pale and shaking, righted the iron and yanked the cord from the power board. She ran out, slamming the door after her, but it failed to latch. Fourteen heard her sobs as she raced, still barefoot, toward the kitchens.

He ran a hand through his hair like Master Den had earlier. He'd never treated Aednat that way, never even thought to make such a cruel threat. It was Master Den's fault for filling his mind with ridiculous warnings.

Fourteen leaned his head back, pulling out and fingering the bracelet he'd started keeping in his pocket this last week, for good luck. It was the only thing he had from his mother, which was more than any of the other Numbers. Master Den had given the bracelet to Fourteen a few months after he'd arrived, when Fourteen was only ten years old. He hadn't minded being called Gabrick in private then, and he'd carried the bracelet faithfully for years. But he'd put away that part of his life as did all the Numbers. None of them knew their mother.

Small turquoise rocks, veined with silver and separated by silver molds of river dolphins in various playful contortions, slid between his fingers.

He fell asleep, exhaustion winning over his jumbled thoughts, his head still tilted upward toward limbo.

"Gabrick, what time is your next test?" Aednat shook him. "Wake up, It's nearly thirteenth hour."

"What?" Fourteen popped up straight, finding the time on their round wall clock. Ten minutes. The next test was in ten minutes!

"Why'd you let me sleep?! How could you—?" A bruise darkened her high cheekbones and a harsh red line ran the length of Aednat's chin. "What happened?"

"I'm fine. I brought your food, but what time is your test?"

"To limbo with the test. Who did this to you?"

She put one hand on her hip. "Who do you think?"

Fourteen jumped to his feet, one fist clenched as he strode to the door. "Twelve."

Aednat grasped his arm. "Please, let it go. I got in so much trouble last time. I'm fine. Eleven came before..." her voice choked, but she swallowed it down. "...before anything happened."

"You got in trouble last time because I sent you to get me new clothes." Fourteen took in her torn shirt, drooping at one shoulder. "This has to stop."

"Please, don't," she pleaded. "He's bigger than you. Stronger."

Fourteen stared down at her. "You're worried about me? I practically threw you out the door. This is my fault."

She threw her arms around his ribs, her face pressed against his chest. "It's not your fault. You were angry, under too much stress." She looked up at him with her wide green eyes. "You're the most important person in the world to me."

He stroked her back, wishing he could stay, wishing her words were true.

"I'm your owner, Aednat. You have to do everything I say."

"Maybe, but you're also my closest friend, as close to a brother as I've ever had."

Fourteen didn't know whether to be flattered, or offended. Most servants who idolized their owners became infatuated with them, but Aednat gave her real love to Eleven, relegating Fourteen to the role of brother. But he couldn't be angry. Not with her eyes full of tears, holding him tight and wanting to spare him another embarrassing beating.

"I have to go." He pried her fingers loose. "I have my test."

She exhaled with relief. "Good. Focus on the test. That's what matters right now." With a smile, she waved him out the door.

Fourteen ran the entire way to the study hall, barging in as Master Den started speaking. Fourteen ignored the man, walking into the middle of the room without so much as a nod.

"Fourteen?" Master Den questioned.

Evidence of Twelve and Eleven's fight showed in a couple of bruises on their arms and faces, but it looked even. It was time to tip the scales. Looking at Eleven then motioning with his head toward Twelve, he encouraged his brother to follow.

Eleven grinned, a step behind as Fourteen grabbed Twelve's shirt in both fists. He lifted the older boy off his feet, slamming him into the wall. "Don't you ever touch her again."

Twelve sneered, looking to the adults for assistance. Wrong audience. Master Den's lip curled, staring at Twelve like he wanted to lend Fourteen a hand. The other instructors backed away, not wanting anything to do with an altercation between the emperor's precious Numbers.

Twelve knocked Fourteen's arms apart, forcing him to release the shirt. "It's only a matter of time, and there's not a thing you can do about it."

Eleven stepped next to Fourteen. Each of them took a handful of shirt then pinned Twelve's arms against the wall, one of them on each side.

"You ever get near enough to scare her," said Fourteen, "let alone touch her again, and we'll make sure you can't walk for a week." He glanced around the room. "And nobody's going to stop us."

To Fourteen's surprise, Nine stepped forward. "This about Aednat?"

Eleven gave a curt nod.

Nine doubled-up a fist and slugged Twelve in the stomach. Twelve's body tried to double forward, but Fourteen and Eleven held him fast.

"She's a sweet girl," said Nine. "Keep away from her, freak. They'll come to hurt 'ya, but I'll kill 'ya."

One more powerful hit and Nine stepped back. Fourteen and Eleven released Twelve, keeping out of range as he retched on the floor.

Master Den continued as if nothing had happened, but he gave the Numbers an approving smile. "All right, one instructor per student. Pick a seat out of hearing range from one another and set up blinders on each side of the table."

Master Den glanced at Twelve. "Clean up your mess. We'll commence testing in five minutes."

12

In one of the classroom's uncomfortable wooden chairs, Fourteen sat across the desk from his tester, Master Wen. In his mid-forties, with protruding eyes and a touch of gray in his hair, he was one of the less interesting instructors in the compound, and one who hadn't risen in rank since his arrival five years earlier. Possibly because the man smelled funny like wet clothes left in a clothes basket too long—moldy and stale.

It only took one question for Fourteen to realize Master Den was right. It wouldn't be easy to prepare for this kind of test.

"Let's start out simple," Wen said.

He wrote out four numbers on a piece of rough scribbling paper: 1, 35, 79, 1113.

He turned the paper to face Fourteen, offering him the pencil. "What is the next number?"

Fourteen stared at them for a long time, embarrassed when he realized how complicated he'd tried to make the simple challenge. "1517. The next numbers in the sequence of odd numbers."

Wen nodded. "Correct."

When they reached the ninth challenge, one that Master Den had warned him about, Fourteen hesitated. Wen placed a number of slanted sticks in what appeared to be random configurations on top of one another. But as Fourteen stared, mentally replacing the sticks, finding what each set had in common and how they differed, he found the pattern. Only thinking of his victory, he placed the next set, making sure the sticks crossed the exact number of times necessary to be one more than the sticks before.

For the first time since they'd begun, Wen showed some expression. His eyes widened and his hand shook as he set up the next challenge.

Fourteen took a sidelong glance at him. "You all right?"

"Of course," he said, his voice pitched higher. "You're doing admirably."

What would happen to his tester if Fourteen succeeded where the emperor didn't expect? Fourteen had heard once that his father took out his anger on the messenger of bad news in near-equal measures as the person who'd made him angry. Fourteen had never believed that, but maybe it was true.

Wen continued with a series of questions. Fourteen eventually figured most of them out, but he pretended to fail on a couple that proved a serious challenge. Wen relaxed and they reached the twenty-third question.

Fourteen wouldn't make the same mistake twice. He would fail, but he had to know if he could have done it. Taking the blocks handed to him, he manipulated them toward a three-dimensional shape. He could see why the emperor had never mastered this one. Every logical connection took him nowhere, but as he studied their form, getting it wrong over and over again while his eyes darted to the small hourglass keeping time, it all came together. He had to stop himself near the end, making a stupid mistake then dropping the blocks to the table. He pretended to try one more manipulation as the time ran out, but Wen's frightened eyes told Fourteen, the man knew the truth.

"You almost had that one," Wen said. "What happened?"

"Just now?" Fourteen feigned pride. "When the timer went off, I was close?"

Wen's shoulders relaxed. "No, before that. But if you didn't even realize, then it doesn't mean anything. Shall we go on?"

Fourteen nodded, wondering as he addressed the next trial—a relatively simple number challenge—what it meant that he'd figured out both questions no other Number had ever before accomplished. Did being smarter somehow make him unfit? Why would that make the emperor question his heritage when Fourteen looked as much like him as any other Number, besides Eleven? Too many questions and not enough answers.

Master Den knew more than he was telling, but did that make him right? According to him, even if Fourteen was chosen as the next emperor, his life was in danger. But Master Den also talked about bizarre heartstones, and his ideas were ridiculous.

Fourteen put aside his mental meanderings and focused on the next question, another word problem. He had to really think about these.

As the test finally wound to an end, his mental drain more than equaled his physical drain from the week before, but he wasn't done yet. They had a final test later that night. The testing masters handed the test results to Master Den. He looked them over, frowning over one as he raised worried eyes to

Fourteen. As he scanned the rest of the test, he nodded, taking a relieved breath and going over the others.

He raised his eyes, smiling at the tense, expectant Numbers. "You've all done remarkably well, evidence of the skilled masters who have taught you over the years.

"The final results are: Twelve with 148, Nine with 141, Eleven with 150, and Fourteen with 154. Congratulations to you all. You have three hours to rest before the final challenge. Return at the eighteenth hour."

Fourteen and Eleven escorted Twelve from the room, keeping close on his heels.

"Meant what I said, little brother," Nine yelled out before taking long strides to his own apartments. "You touch Fourteen's girl and I'll make you sorry for it."

Twelve made a rude gesture, but he went straight for his own rooms.

Walking alongside Fourteen, Eleven chuckled. "Now I'm scared what will happen if Nine catches me with Aednat."

Fourteen glanced back at their older brother. "With good reason. You'd better be careful."

"Would you mind if we meet at your apartment?"

Seeing the glint in his eye, Fourteen bristled. "Sure. As long as I'm there."

"You're kidding, right? Who knows how much time we have left before the emperor makes his decision?"

"Hey, I've seen what happens to the servants and maids who get pregnant. If she cares for you, that's fabulous, but all you're thinking about is what you'll miss if you have to leave, not what will happen to her."

Eleven's face flushed. For a moment Fourteen thought he might get angry, but he swallowed and took a deep breath. "You're right." He nodded. "Aednat is the sweetest, funniest person I've ever known, and she doesn't deserve that kind of trouble. I'll come when you're there or I'll meet with her in the open. But if I'm chosen as emperor, you should know, she's coming with me."

"I understand. And if I'm chosen," Fourteen paused. This wasn't easy. "I'll let her choose who she wants to stay with."

"That'll be a hard decision," Eleven said, though his grin gave away his predicted outcome. "She adores you so much, it's hard not to be jealous."

"Well, then we're even."

～～～

The final test proved to be one question. Only the emperor, his guards, and a few masters, including Den, stood in the small classroom with them. Each of the Numbers was given a problem to solve, all different, and they had one hour to come up with all aspects of the solution. Den handed them paper and pencil, but their answers would be given verbally.

Fourteen's question read: *On the main road leading into a highly populated area, a truck carrying automotive gasoline overturns, creating an extensive chemical spill. How would you deal with the crisis?* It took him the entire hour to map out the various ways the chemicals could seep into waterways, soil, and spread to individuals and communities and how to minimize the spread as quickly as possible and save populations.

When the hour finished, the emperor approached, his midnight-blue robe brushing the floor behind. "Nine," he said, raising a mocking eyebrow. "What is your solution to a natural disaster ending with mass crop destruction?"

Nine described the ways he would get sufficient food to the starving farmers and their families.

"Why?" asked the emperor. "How would it benefit the empire to use our resources feeding peasants?"

Nine paused. "Because we would want them to plant the next year."

The emperor waved his hand. "There are plenty of peasants eager and able to take their place. What about the economics of the situation? How would the lost crop affect the empire's economy?"

Nine stammered. "I have no idea. I hadn't thought about that."

The emperor sniffed his disdain, his eyes narrowing on Twelve. "And your solution? How would you handle a small group of hidden traitors?"

"Simple," stated Twelve. "I'd kill them."

"Just like that?"

"Depending on the individuals, I may need to become a friend, spy from a distance, or happen to pass them in the street, but the final solution doesn't change. If they are a threat, they must be eliminated."

A thin smile stretched across the emperor's handsome features, the same features he shared with his sons. "And would you enjoy it?" he whispered, so low Fourteen almost didn't hear. Eleven and Nine jerked upright in surprise, but Fourteen kept still, listening closely for the answer.

Twelve stared unflinchingly into their father's eyes. "I don't know." He cocked his head to one side. "It would be interesting to find out."

The emperor nodded, clearly pleased. He'd always had a harsh side. He did whatever was necessary for the empire, but Fourteen saw something else for that brief moment, something that chilled his heart.

Suddenly bored, their father gave his attention to Eleven. "And you? A nation uprising against us...?"

"The best solution," Eleven said, "would be to have a reliable spy network and be aware of the potential for an uprising before it began. As long as status quo is kept, populations will usually not combine against their leader. Keeping people in their respective places, making sure they are respected for their work but not expectant of special privileges, is the best way to keep them tame. If a rebellion did occur, strong force must be used immediately and the population brought into compliance as soon as possible."

The emperor raised his eyebrows. "I think I underestimated you, Eleven. Well answered."

Getting in Fourteen's face, the emperor's breath smelled sharp and sweet. Despite the strong stench of mint, meant to mask the odor, Fourteen recognized liquor. The emperor stared down his nose, seeming angry, but Fourteen could think of no good reason why.

"What are your solutions?" his father asked.

Fourteen pulled out his calculations. "With the soils around most of our populated areas, and the likely terrains, I estimated the spill would start contaminating water supplies in—"

The emperor slammed the scribbled papers to Fourteen's work desk. Clenching them in his fist, they crackled as he wadded them into a ball, which he threw onto the floor. "I don't want your mathematical prowess." He glanced at Master Den, who stood like a rich man's death statue at the edge of the room. "I want your philosophical solutions."

Fourteen bowed his head. "I was getting to that, sir. With my computations, assuming it was a chemical that could be contained and its effects neutralized, it would be advised to evacuate populations in a ten mile radius within the first thirty minutes. If clean-up took longer than that, a twenty-mile radius should be evacuated. No crops should be grown in the affected land for at least two planting cycles."

"Didn't you learn from Nine? Why go to such expense for a population of peasants?"

"Economics," said Fourteen. "Near a populated area, higher-tier professionals would be affected. They're not as easily replaced as the peasants. Also, since the bodies would be contaminated, it's doubtful the bodies would decompose or create heartstones properly, so the cost of postponed clean-up would be higher than the cost of saving the people."

The emperor glanced again at Master Den, giving a half-smile. "You've been taught well, young man. You bring a diversity of ability, along with ruthless calculation." He outright smiled. "This could prove very interesting, interesting indeed."

He turned to the boys, speaking over their heads. From the time Fourteen was a child, he'd rarely seen their father look any of his sons in the eye. "The examination is over."

Sparing a grin for Twelve, he turned on his heel and walked out, surrounded by his guards.

Fourteen threw a confused look at Master Den, but he knew what the man had said about the emperor. Could the master be telling the truth? It didn't seem possible, but then, this test was the closest Fourteen had come to a real conversation with his father. The only one of them he'd seemed pleased with was the least likely candidate for succession—Twelve. What did it say when the emperor favored Fourteen's most hated enemy?

Fourteen shook his head, trying to dispel his doubts and fears, but that night they grew, becoming monsters that stalked his dreams.

Fourteen woke tangled in his silken sheets, covered in sweat.

Aednat rushed into the room, nightgown emphasizing her ample curves.

"Are you all right?" she asked, sitting on the edge of the bed. "You sounded frightened."

"It's nothing," Fourteen snapped.

He didn't want to tell her his doubts. She'd only encourage him to go along with Master Den, which wasn't an option. He'd never find out the truth if he didn't make it into the emperor's palace.

The scent of honey-soap and sweet flowers excited his senses. He reached out a hand, stroking Aednat's arm. He knew she didn't feel that way toward him, but right now he didn't care. He wanted distraction. He let his fingers slide under the sleeve of her nightdress. "Why Eleven? Why not me?"

She flinched away, eyes wide and frightened. "You can't think that way, Gabrick."

"Why not? Most Numbers sleep with their servants at one point or another, including Eleven. He and I look almost the same, you said you loved me, so why not us?"

"His relationship with Aubra was brief, only a curiosity."

"I wouldn't mind a curiosity," Fourteen growled. "At least it would be something."

She bit her lips, tears gathering. "I'm sorry." Fourteen's anger softened only to flare at her next words. "I can't tell you. Not yet."

"You're as bad as Master Den!" Fourteen yelled. "Secrets and more secrets. I thought you, at least, I could trust to be honest."

"People's lives are at stake," she said, eyes pleading. "Why can't you trust us?"

"I can't trust people who don't trust me back."

"If I knew you'd believe—"

Fourteen pushed her off, making her stumble to catch her balance. "Get out."

She opened her mouth to speak, but seemed to change her mind. Her bare feet padded softly against the polished wood as she escaped.

13

The metal bird, an aeroplane they'd called it, landed, barreling down a smooth black trail before braking to a violent stop. Mariessa had heard of these flying metal carriers with twirling spinners on each side that carried their huge bodies into the sky, but she'd never believed. For the hundredth time since they'd left, she wished the thing to limbo.

She held another bag to her face, puking a thin line of yellow bile into the container. She'd lost the food in her stomach hours ago and the smell of it, sealed in paper bags on the seat next to her, made the nausea all the worse.

Outside the small window beside her, flat ground surrounded the roadway they'd landed on. For the most part, the level portion seemed natural, though someone had smoothed the surface. A mountain spire rose into the clouds on one side, a cascade waterfall tumbling between rocks and through crevices. It turned into a river then disappeared out of view. Looking through the windows on the plane's other side, the level portion seemed to drop away. Whether a cliff or more angled mountainside, she couldn't tell.

"Peder," said one of the soldiers. "The escort seems impatient."

Peder growled like an irritated mutt. "They are nothing. Let them wait." He pointed to Mariessa's ankles. "Untie the girl."

The man knelt and removed the ropes binding her feet, but when he touched her wrists Peder stopped him. "Leave those. I have no wish to fight with her again today. It's best she be not overly bruised for the inspection of the emperor."

Mariessa's anger flushed her face, but she had to admit, fear was what made her tremble. Her chances for escape diminished with each leg of their journey. She gave another yank on her wrist ties, but despite her constant tugging, they still held.

A stout man with a short goatee yanked a wheel attached to the airplane's door, spinning it a few times, releasing the lock before pushing the heavy metal outward. Mariessa spied a set of stairs, the top step flush with the open door.

Peder grabbed her by the back of the neck, pushing her forward. "Come. It's time to see your new home."

Mariessa staggered forward, her muscles resisting the movement. She'd sat in the chair too long, and her constant retching had made her weak.

Sunlight blazed above, making her squint as she stepped from the plane's dark interior. Though the air was passably warm, it didn't carry the heat she'd expected. Not like Kerokos. Priest Yosel had explained to her that Dixho revolved around the sun, somehow relating to the seasons, but had refused to tell her more for fear that too much education might put them both in danger.

On the far side of the landing area, the river she'd seen from the window poured over a cliff. The edge of a high white wall in the distance gave the only hint that the city must extend clear to the mountain. On the other side of the wall, well-kept greenery surrounded ornate palaces, everything as clean as if the outdoors had servants—surely the Emperor's palace lay somewhere within that district of rich high-tier nobles. Farther out, a black wall marked another change in tiers, outside of which lay nicely kept buildings, most of them hidden by random foliage. Mariessa couldn't tell where the city ended and the jungle dominated once more, but she suspected it was a good distance away.

Off to one side sat another plane. Behind it, three black autocars with imperial flags waited like a fancy prison transport. From what she'd heard, no one ever left the palace without the emperor's permission, whether alive or dead. As she stepped down the stairs, she gazed out at the barren dirt and rock, honing in on the distant waterfall. This would be her last chance.

Head bowed, she took two steps toward the line of cars, and then stumbled.

The man behind reached out a steadying hand. She shoved her shoulder into him, knocking him into Peder. Hands still strapped awkwardly behind her back, she ran.

"Schisse!" Peder yelled. "That way will only get you killed."

Better dead, she thought. She had no idea what kind of waterfall plunged off that cliff, or what waited beneath. She'd live or die, but she'd not be held prisoner.

Heavy footsteps sounded behind her. Peder gained, his hand touching her arm.

She yanked away, and nearly lost her balance.

His massive hand dug into her bicep. The sudden stop yanked her shoulder, making her gasp. Tears burned her eyes. So close. She'd only needed another length, only five arms from freedom.

He spun her to face him. His foul breath reeked in her face. "What think you be doing, idiot girl? Your risk would gain you nothing but broken bones. No man has ever survived a drop from that waterfall." He took her face in his hand, grating her cheeks against her teeth. "Stupid."

Sando had learned to never touch her face. She lunged forward, clenching the soft skin between fingers and thumb between her teeth, biting down.

He yelped, loosening his grip.

Wrenching away, she stumbled the distance to the waterfall. Unable to regain her balance she tumbled sideways into the river.

It had appeared as docile as a wandering stream, but Mariessa had had enough experience with summer rains to know it might not be true. The river swallowed her in its icy grip, a raging beast. She barely had time to take a breath before the monster swept her into its depths and spat her over the steep cliff.

Legs flailing, she gasped for air, but found water. At the last possible moment, she separated from the torrent enough to manage a brief gasp and remember to straighten out. She tucked her elbows as close to her side as she could manage. The fight to survive had only begun.

Shot into the deep pool, the weight of the water falling from above shoved her downward. Even with her arms clenched tight to her torso, the impact yanked her elbows back. With her exclamation of pain, she lost most of her air. But the force also snapped the last threads of rope. Her arms came loose, buffeted by the wills of conflicting currents.

Mariessa's feet hit bottom, but she let them buckle. Her reaction saved her from broken bones, but she had no chance to push herself away from the waterfall's swirling embrace. It beat her body against the rocks, rolling her like cream in a butter churn. Arms clenched over her head, she shielded her skull. She tried for some sense of direction, but the underground world remained black as a cave.

Her chest burned. She kicked her feet, determined that the effort would take her somewhere. It accomplished nothing. She continued to roll, no sense of up or down, and no escape from the frothing beast which played with her.

As a different darkness closed on her senses, something gripped her tangled hair. She cried out in surprise, swallowing in water. Her lungs screamed. Panicked, she gasped in more water. Whatever had caught her hair, it yanked again.

Mariessa let it pull at her. A strange calm enveloped her senses, the pain in her chest growing distant. She rocked and turned in the water's swift currents, letting it take her where it willed. Closing her eyes, she succumbed to the promise of a warm slumber. She would leave no heartstone, but it wouldn't matter. There was no loved-one to receive it anyway.

14

Birds chittered in the trees and something barked, similar to a dog but higher-pitched. Mariessa coughed, spluttering water across a lush, warm lawn. The water that had burned so badly going down, scraped like sandpaper, making an even more uncomfortable fire coming up. After a few more coughs and splutters, she opened her eyes. Pale, thin ankles wrapped in golden sandals blurred then came into focus. Mariessa turned her head, taking in the whole woman.

She gasped, making her gag and splutter all over again.

The woman standing before her, pale as moonlight, had thick yellow hair flowing in loose waves down to her full breasts. Breasts that showed through the pale pink fabric circling them. Her waist remained bare to her hips. Hanging low, a skirt made of loose pink and white strips covered her to the knees but left little to the imagination. As a light breeze rustled the flakes of cloth, they parted to reveal the full length of one thigh. A dark purple bruise peeked into view, which seemed odd considering her third-tier tattoo, marking her as high-nobility.

It didn't matter. Who knew what customs or morals they had near Han City. She must get herself off these people's land and hide, before Peder found her.

"Are you all right?" the woman asked in Imperium.

"Yes," Mariessa coughed. "Did you save me?"

The woman smiled, shaking her head. "The dolphins caught hold of you. They've learned to bring women to our shore, boys to the opposite side."

Dolphins, in a river? It seemed incredulous to Mariessa, but she didn't have time to think about it.

"Please," she asked. "I need to find a place to hide. There's someone after me."

The woman's eyes turned sad. "You thought to escape Peder? I'm afraid you picked the fastest and most difficult way to arrive exactly where he was taking you. It's hard to believe you survived. I'm Esterelle, one of the imperial concubines."

Mariessa sat up, taking in her surroundings. Inside the luxurious garden, scantily clothed women of every shape, size, age, tier, and type of beauty circled around her with varying expressions of horror and amazement. As a backdrop, nestled against the mountain like a protruding blister, the Emperor's Palace glimmered despite the late afternoon shade.

Mariessa had heard that the stones and mortar were infused with ground heartstones, nearly the entire Yinda nation's worth, gathered after the great genocide. She'd thought the reports an exaggeration, but seeing the palace in all its horrific beauty, she immediately believed. What kind of a man would do such a thing?

And she was stuck here with no way out. Mariessa threw herself back onto the grass, sobbing into the wet soil. She'd held back the tears for so long, always believing she'd have another chance for escape, but the chances had all been used up. In taking the biggest risk of all, she'd landed in the middle of her prison cell.

Esterelle rested a hand on her shoulder, the smell of honeysuckle on her silken skin. "It's not such a horrible life. We have beautiful things, delicious foods, and we want for nothing."

Raising her tear-streaked face, Mariessa glared. "Except freedom."

Esterelle nodded, the sadness returning. "Few people in this world have freedom, even among those who think they do. We're all chained by something. Our circumstances, our beliefs, or our obligations. If I have a bit less freedom than some, at least I'm alive. I can balk at my chains and be miserable, or be happy with what I have. I suggest you choose to be happy, because you won't be going anywhere else."

Mariessa sprang to her feet, staggering as a wave of dizziness threatened to knock her down. She took a few steps forward, then blackness edged her vision and she fell to her knees. Blinking, she forced back the vertigo as she hurled more bilious water onto the lawn.

A pair of large boots came within view, only a few inches from her mess. Shrinking into herself, she raised her gaze to see Peder's grimace.

"Stupid girl."

Grabbing the tattered remains of her wrap, he ripped it away from her body. His thick hands delved into her matted hair, yanking her to her feet.

Mariessa cried out. The toes of one foot landed in her vomit, but Peder didn't seem to care. He turned her this way and that, examining every naked digit of skin.

"Schisse," he said again, his accent growing thick. "You are having luck to be alive, but I am thinking I might you kill anyway. You have bruised yourself. You will not be fit for the emperor for weeks."

He raised a hand, but Esterelle stepped between them. "Please now, Peder. The laurie is here already. She only has bruises for right now, but if you strike her, you might break a bone. Her islander skin will hide the dark spots soon enough, if you let her be."

Peder grunted, throwing Mariessa to the ground. "Make her cleaned up, deloused and dressed. I'll be coming back in an hour."

With a glance at Mariessa, Esterelle stood taller. "Look at all that hair. Please, give us two, so that she may be presentable."

Peder glanced up and down Esterelle appreciatively. "Two," he said. He strode toward the palace, flanked by his men.

"Thank you," Mariessa said. "You don't even know me, but you've given me time. Is there someplace I can go, until I find a way out? You could tell Peder that I escaped."

Esterelle took an exasperated breath. "There is no place on these grounds to hide, and even if I could help with that, I wouldn't. Do you think we should give our lives for your chance at freedom? I think your ability to sacrifice others for your wants is a bit out of balance, laurie."

Esterelle pointed at two middle-aged women dressed in matching mid-calf dresses of coarse gray cloth. "Help her to the indoor baths."

Now that the concubines had dispersed, Mariessa noticed numerous older women in the same gray dresses. One held a cool cloth to a sun-bathing concubine. Another fetched drinks in tall glasses, chunks of ice floating in the amber liquid. Servants. Esterelle had been right. The women wanted for nothing, save their freedom, and ownership of their own bodies.

With graceful purpose, Esterelle strode toward a pair of sliding glass doors that led into a wing of the glittering palace. The servants lifted Mariessa to her feet, helping her stagger in Esterelle's footsteps. Upon entering the sliding doors, Mariessa gasped. Her bare feet slapped slick tiles of marble, the sound echoing against the high ceilings and wide-spaced walls while what appeared to be veins of gold stretched and twisted through the rock under her feet. The corridor needed no lights. Glass bricks lined the hallways, distorting the glow from the palace's exterior blocks while illuminating the passageway. Despite its opulent width, the walls seemed to close in, the light encasing her like a tightening fish-net.

Gold-filigreed fans turned lazily above, creating a cool breeze that smelled of perfumes and teased strands of hair across Mariessa's bare flesh. Strange paintings, a conglomeration of geometric designs twisted and overlaid into vague representations of men and women, some of which made Mariessa blush and turn away, dotted the walls. She set her gaze forward, relieved when they exited the garish hallway into an adjoining one. Though the paintings continued, this corridor had natural lightstones set in elaborate gold lanterns at intervals along the walls. Their illumination felt normal, less frightening, and the cream-painted walls didn't scream of desecration.

A short distance down the hallway, the gray-uniformed women turned, guiding Mariessa down rock-hewn steps. Though they only descended five stairs, the air grew humid. They stepped out into an open, high-ceilinged room, gilt-edged lounge chairs circling a carved-out bath the size of a pond, full of steaming water. The room appeared to have been carved from the mountain's base, the clear water probably tunneled in from the falls.

Stacked on an ornate cabinet in the far corner, voluminous white towels and multi-colored containers of soaps and lotions combined with the other furnishings to give the dungeon-like space an air of opulence. The scents of perfumes and soap grew stronger, overpowering the stale scent of mold.

Mariessa turned in a circle, taking in the high ceiling dotted with lightstones, and noting the top of one wall made entirely of glass.

"Is that a window?" she asked a maid.

The woman bowed, but said nothing.

"Most servants can't speak," said Esterelle, standing at the pool's edge. "That be the emperor's hallway, leading to the pleasure chambers. He often selects his lauries from here or looking out on our garden from his balcony."

"Like dogs on a leash," said Mariessa. "Always at his beck and call, ready for service at his command."

"Watch your tongue," said Esterelle. "Or you'll be as speechless as the servants."

Mariessa bristled, staring at the maid who had bowed. "Open your mouth."

The woman's eyes went wide. She pursed her lips together.

"Please," said Mariessa. "I need to know."

Esterelle nodded and the woman's lips parted. It only took a moment to identify the horrific butcher job.

Mariessa turned away, bile and river water threatening to rise again. "Thank you," she whispered. "I'm sorry."

The servant nodded, going to fetch a towel.

Esterelle's soft hand took Mariessa's callused one. "Let's get you cleaned up and feeling better."

Mariessa glanced up at the window. Her eyes darted around the room in search of unwanted onlookers. Finding none, she allowed Esterelle to lead her to the water's edge. She checked the large window one more time before stepping into the deep pool. Esterelle followed her gaze.

"The emperor is on his way to a challenge for his Numbers. I doubt he'll be back soon."

"Numbers?"

"The emperor's children. They live in a compound outside the palace walls. That's what I've been telling you. Even if you escape the palace grounds, it won't matter. You'll never make it past the Numbers Compound's high white walls, and certainly not past the walls of the inner city."

"So, do you have a child out there?"

Esterelle flushed. "I can't have wee ones, and few of the emperor's mothers become concubines. He has different criteria in his mothers than his pleasure wives."

Mariessa's eyes narrowed. "Did he do something to you like he did to the servants?"

"I'll gather you some bathing soaps," she said, but Mariessa didn't miss Esterelle's anguished look. What kind of a man would risk such a dangerous procedure on a woman, just to keep her barren? She'd been captured by a monster.

She descended into the pool. Esterelle chose a soft jasmine-scented soap that reminded Mariessa of the foreign spice that she'd associated with many of her father's co-workers and their wives.

After washing her bruised and cut skin, cleansing her thick hair with a similar scented shampoo, and smoothing out the snarls with something Esterelle called a conditioner, she emerged from the bath more refreshed than she'd thought possible.

Esterelle rubbed lotion over her damp skin while Mariessa thought through possibilities. "Are there any caves at the back of that waterfall?"

"No. Not like you're thinking."

"Have you been back there? How do you know?"

"One of the Numbers has found a way to get through the turbulent waters to visit us. There's a small cave, but it doesn't go anywhere."

"But maybe—"

"No!" Esterelle held up a finger. "Listen to me, laurie-girl. You've got to stop thinking this way. The longer you do, the more danger for you, and for the rest of us as well."

"You? What does this have to do with you?"

"If one makes him angry, we all pay."

"Like your bruises?"

Esterelle shifted her skirt over her legs. "Aye. And you weren't even here yet."

"Me? How can you possibly blame—"

"I don't blame you." Esterelle opened a cabinet by the door that Mariessa hadn't noticed, holding up a yellow negligee to measure against Mariessa's skin-tones. "There was something about the report on you that the emperor didn't like so well. Maybe because you escaped and had to be captured. But he took his frustration out on me. That's what you have to learn here, laurie. You do something that angers him, everybody pays. Please him, and everyone is rewarded."

"I'm sorry for what he does to you, but I refuse to lie down like a dog and take a punishment I don't deserve." She ripped the flimsy fabric from Esterelle's hand, throwing it into the water.

"You selfish ejit!" Esterelle spat. "Think of someone besides yourself."

"Think of yourself as a person instead of some man's plaything."

Esterelle gasped. "You never call the emperor a mere man, never in the open. He is our Lingdow, granted so by the great Vasheri below."

"He's a brutal, horrible, man who preys on his people like a blood-eel preys on young seals. And I will never bow down to his will, though it be forced upon me and he beat me unconscious."

"Stupid girl," said Esterelle. She put out her hand, gesturing up and down at Mariessa's naked body. "You plan on greeting the emperor like he'll have you in the end? Naked?"

Mariessa grabbed her recently discarded towel. "You sound like Peder. You're such a puppet, you've become an echo."

She deftly wrapped the rectangular fabric like her native clothing. Though thicker, she managed a strong knot to hold it in place.

Esterelle crossed her arms over her barely concealed chest, fuming. She turned to one of the gaping maids. "Fetch Peder."

The woman pointed to her mouth, eyes wide.

"Bow low and point in this direction." Esterelle glared at Mariessa. "He won't punish *you*."

Mariessa stood to her full height, still a good three or four digits smaller than Esterelle. "He'll have to find me first," she said, running from the room.

There had to be a way out of this place.

15

The concubines slept in a communal harem. Lush beds and pillows filled the huge bedroom, but there were bars on the windows, and no secret passageways, at least that she could find. They had rooms to eat, to relax, to do everything they might desire, but every room had bars, or guards, or both. When she reached the end of the concubines' wing, she discovered more soldiers— effeminate ones on her side of the doors, thick-muscled ones on the other.

She made for the gardens.

As she reached the distorted hallway, Peder entered from the other side. A small Zhandanese man accompanied him, unnoticeable in feature from any other one might see on the continent, though his all-black clothing, shaved head, and his silent, powerful stride, suggested danger. The muscles of Peder's jaw popped with anger and surprise. Mariessa sprinted back the way she'd come.

"Return here, or by the holy Vasheri—"

She didn't hear the rest, but she could feel the tiles vibrate with his heavy footsteps.

Thick fingers caught her hair, digging into her scalp. With a firm grip, he yanked her back.

Mariessa yelped like the very hounds she'd compared to the concubines. Knocked off her feet, she hung by her hair, face contorted with pain.

"Let go of me! I was headed into the gardens. Isn't that what you want?"

Peder gave her hair a twist. "You know what it is I be wanting, stupid girl. And you will do it."

"Is that really necessary?" said the small man coming behind.

"You be making your job, Quing, and let me make mine."

"Of course, but the emperor will be angry with me if she doesn't meet his expectations."

"He'll be angry with everyone," said Peder. He went to swat Quing aside, but the man deftly avoided the blow, grabbing Peder's hand in a painful grip. Peder almost lost hold of Mariessa, but not quite.

Quing narrowed his eyes at the larger man. "I respect your authority with the concubines, but don't forget who you're dealing with. I'll not be manhandled like your little protégées."

He released Peder, walking ahead as if nothing had happened. Peder grunted his frustration, his grip tightening on Mariessa's hair. He pulled her through the corridor, half walking and half dragging her back to the bathing pool. He presented Mariessa like a child holding a defective doll. "What is this?"

"The servant didn't find you?" Esterelle asked.

"I have said," Peder bellowed. "What is this?"

"No need to yell, Peder. That is your stubborn little wretch of a mother. I got her bathed, but then she ran off."

He gritted his teeth. "If you weren't his favorite, I would have you pay for making such failure."

"Don't worry." Her eyes flashed with a rebellious flare Mariessa would have guessed long extinguished. "I'll be old soon enough, and then you'll be able to do what you'd like with me. I'm sure you'll make me pay whether I'm competent or not."

Peder fought a grin, pacified by whatever sickening thoughts her words conjured. He turned his focus to Mariessa. Like before, he gripped her wrap in his strong hands and yanked. But this wasn't thin islander fabric. The towel was thick and the knot secure. Every wrench of his hand only served to toss Mariessa back and forth, furthering the impression that she'd become a doll caught in a violent child's grip.

"Please," said Quing. "May I?"

"What are you thinking you can do?" Peder said, his voice heavy with sarcasm.

Quing raised an eyebrow. "Undress her."

"You're not allowed—"

But Quing grabbed the knot at her shoulder. It only took his small but unnaturally strong fingers a few seconds to slip the ties. And there she stood, naked again, stared at by angry men. She didn't attempt to cover herself. There was no point.

Peder gestured for Esterelle to get clothing while Quing's eyes roved up and down her body. "She's perfect," he pronounced. "But we need to get those injuries healed as soon as possible. The emperor doesn't like his merchandise to look used."

"They're in all the wrong places for that," said Peder, his accent under better control "but that's why I grabbed her by that mass of hair."

"And dragged her across the stones," accused Quing.

Peder frowned, but didn't reply. Esterelle handed him a red short-skirt and matching bandeau top as see-through as all the rest, but at least it was a darker color.

"Put this on," Peder said.

Mariessa folded her arms over her breasts. "You put it on. It'll match your demon eyes."

"You are wanting to see me as limbo demon?" He gripped her hair tighter, bringing tears, but she squirmed and fought with him until he released his grip and flung her aside.

"I think the skirt will be the best part," she said, scooting away across the rough floor. "Maybe the emperor will change gender preference and *you* can be his next concubine."

She saw the flash of fear in Peder's eyes and realized the emperor probably had a wide variety of tastes. He just didn't let it be widely known. Face flushed, Peder took the two steps to her side and raised his hand. Mariessa sat up taller. They couldn't hurt her without hurting their cause. That would suit her fine. But despite his rage, he restrained himself.

He threw the clothing onto a divan. "You!" Peder shouted at a maid. "Take all of the towels from here."

Pulling three wrapped wads half the size of a normal heartstone from his inside jacket pocket, he selected one. Unwrapped, Mariessa realized it was a silver communication stone. Very rare, only the ultimate town gossip or gifted orators created such heartstones. They had to be melted or broken in half to be used, but if handled correctly, they were very valuable.

The stone close to his lips, Peder spoke to whoever held the other side. "Be sending me two sets of eunuch guards at the baths immediately."

"Yes, sir," echoed from the stone.

The room was emptied of everything, even the chairs. Only the clothing remained.

"When you have dressed, you can leave," said Peder. "Or, the emperor will be seeing you naked and you may discover yourself his abilities in the area of restraint. Then you'll get the things you deserve, you *stupid* girl."

Mariessa was left, scared and alone, the only sound coming from the gentle swish of water against rock. She cried for a time, but her eyes darted constantly to the observation window, afraid Peder might be right.

As her resolve crumbled, she grabbed the small swaths of fabric. She put the red outfit on, the guards stepped aside, and she made her way to the sleeping rooms with her head held high. They followed her to the ornate drapes of crystal beads that served as doors.

"The concubines are at dinner," said one of the guards. "Would you like us to take you there?"

She hadn't eaten since before the plane ride. Her stomach twisted, demanding food. "No, thank you. I'm not hungry."

She found a thick pallet in the far corner of the room then covered herself with layers upon layers of soft sheets, tears seeping into the lush fabrics until exhaustion let her sleep.

16

The churning water pressed Fourteen farther below the surface, the conflicting currents trying to rip him from the cliff face. Like so many times before, he held to the rocky grooves, using his feet almost as much as his hands. If the roiling waters hadn't worn so much of the rock away, he wouldn't have had a chance at this, but with grit, perseverance, and the ability to hold his breath, he made his way down to the riverbed, behind and to one side of the falls.

His groping foot found the familiar rush of water moving contrary to the other currents. The flow pulled his leg tight against the rocks. Fourteen turned his body, finding the open crevice with his hands. It seemed too small for someone his size, but the lip of rock was deceiving. With one hand gripping the other, he aimed them under the outcropping and dove in. The current sucked him forward like a worm slithering into its burrow. The pressure eased as it released him into a large lake, inside the mountain.

He flung his head above the surface, splashing water, gasping for breath. As he stilled, only dripping water and his heavy breathing echoed against the close walls of the cavern. Though black as the inside of a kettle, Fourteen knew his way well enough by now that he didn't need light.

He climbed out of the underground lake onto a rocky bank, avoiding the stream that funneled water back into the main waterfall. After he fixed his skewed underwear more firmly onto his hips, a familiar stalagmite met his hand on the right. He stood up, walked forward ten paces, ducking his head to the left when he reached the eighth step, then reached his hands forward for the wall. Following it left for four more steps he found a large patch of pale gray light by his toes, leaking through the dense moss and greenery he'd tamped down by numerous excursions, but still muted by the layers of foliage and turns in the tunnel.

On hands and knees he crawled through the narrow space carved by years and years of water seepage. It smelled of mud and layers of decomposing foliage. A narrow stream of water tickled his belly as he switched to a land crawl. Finally, he emerged through a thick mass of greenery that grew in the mountain's dirty crags into mid-day light. A profusion of tall plants at the pool's edge kept Fourteen hidden from the guards. He crawled out, turning a front flip to land on his feet in the shallow eddy of water. It lapped the shore in gentle slaps, well away from the waterfall.

Hunched in the greenery he waddled into deeper water until he could half swim and half float. As he made his way farther down the shore, the swirling tides cleaned the muck from his body. When the trees started giving way to lawn he ducked under the water, turned his position, and came up again as if he'd swum directly beneath the falls—an impossible feat. He covered his tracks well, and this was why nobody, not even Twelve, had ever succeeded in duplicating his trick.

The mud squished between his toes again as he climbed onto the grass. A well-trimmed lechee tree dropped overripe fruit like splattered organs. The sickly smell of it tainted the sweet perfumes wafting from the garden. Fourteen kept close to the trunk where there was less mess and less likelihood of getting hit by an errant glob. He wiped the mud from his feet onto the thick grass, and made his way from tree to bush to tree until he reached the women sun-bathing near the outer hedge. Their shallow pool, in the middle of the garden, lined with concrete and sparkling blue ceramic, reflected the sun's mid-afternoon rays. The garden was large but separated from the rest of the grounds by hedges running perpendicular to the river behind which a wall of glistening palace blocks prevented the women from looking out, and visitors from looking in. Based on the size of the Numbers Compound, Fourteen surmised the rest of the palace grounds to be six times the size of the concubines' space.

Fourteen found Esterelle immediately, lounging on a chair with a wide, pale-yellow umbrella providing shade. She wore a pink chemise and scandalous shorts edged with white lace ruffled against her perfect, pale thighs. Fourteen imagined that if she stood, the strange shorts, a man's style made feminine, might not even cover her buttocks. He hoped she felt inclined to stand; his pulse heightened at the thought of it.

It wasn't until he'd reached the petairi bush directly behind her that he realized someone sat in the chair at her side. A child with unusual golden skin, a multitude of long, dark curls hanging past her waist, and an undeveloped figure, fidgeted in the chair. What in the world was a child doing in the concubines' garden?

"Uh-hmmm," Fourteen cleared his throat softly.

Esterelle turned, a wide grin spreading across her face. "Fourteen!" she whispered. "You've taken your merry time. I despaired of seeing you again."

The girl whipped her head around, searching the bushes like a guard eager to make a capture. With the small hole amid the branches, which he'd slowly cultivated over the last couple of years, Fourteen squirmed his way close. Esterelle's chair concealed him from most of the others, especially the guards at the palace doors, but his head hung out from the bushes so he could see and talk with the women. Usually, Esterelle had quite an entourage, but the girl probably made the more mature women uncomfortable, for they all kept a wide berth.

"I'll always come to see you, Esterelle. Soon, I'll be emperor, and I'll be able to see you whenever I want."

Her happy eyes lost their luster like stars falling from limbo, though she kept the facade of a smile. "You're winning, then?"

"Who are you?" the girl said, staring at him. Her voice went from curious to eager. "How did you get in here?"

Fourteen focused on Esterelle. "Why is there a child in the concubine garden?"

Esterelle choked back a laugh. "Fourteen, this is Mariessa, the emperor's new mother. She's probably close to your age."

"Mother? At her age, her size?"

"I don't think the emperor cares what—"

"Excuse me, you high-stilted look-alike." Mariessa swung her feet to the ground, nearly upsetting a small glass table and their cups of tea. "Don't talk about me like I'm not here. I'm as much a woman as any of these toys stuck in this pretty prison. But more important, I want to know how you came in here."

Esterelle rolled her eyes and sighed. "Not this again."

Fourteen stared, his jaw gone slack. The shock of the unexpected hit him more than the familiar lack of clothing. The girl's red outfit actually hid more than most of the concubines' paler colors, but his initial assessment that she was a child evaporated when she faced him. Though small and thin, her sleek lines reminded him of a mountain cat Master Den had brought in for study. While the other concubines' rounded forms were pleasing, Mariessa's tight muscles lined her graceful curves in a way that felt dangerous. Her wide brown eyes and cat-like pupils shone with the same feral intensity, ready to devour Fourteen whole.

He snapped his jaw shut, shrinking back into the bush. "I don't know why you'd want to leave," he said. "But there's no way out."

"But you got in." She leaned closer to his bush. "That means there has to be a way out."

Fourteen shook his head. "Even if you could follow me across the river, which no girl, especially your size, could do, there's no way out of the Numbers Compound. Believe me, I've tried."

"Numbers Compound?" She looked from Fourteen to Esterelle.

"We've been through this, laurie," said Esterelle. "The palace wall separates the river into the dolphins' keep on the palace side, and a moat of sharks on the other. Even if you make your way past the wall, sharks and the next fence, their compound has another wall and only one exit, heavily guarded. No one escapes."

"You're one of his children." The girl's face twisted in disgust. "Esterelle calls you Fourteen because you're his fourteenth child?"

Fourteen nodded. "It's efficient and keeps our ages in order since sometimes one of us can look older than another, even when we're not."

"Like savages," said Mariessa. A hand dropped to her abdomen. "And he's going to force a child on me so that he can give it a number and throw it into a pen? I thought the concubines were treated like pets, but this is even worse. He treats his own children like livestock, numbered and corralled."

"How dare you!" Fourteen emerged from the bush again, half-crouching, but almost at the girl's eye level. "I'm one of the emperor's consecrated sons, a child of the divine Lingdow, and potential ruler of the entire world."

"And yet you're kept in a pen like a common cow."

"We are taken care of, educated, trained in combat, and we have servants to do our whim."

"A bull is taken care of, taught where to find its feed, trained to stay with the herd, go into its corral, and eventually walk to the slaughterer to have its throat slit and get carved for dinner. What will you be used for?"

"We're not used, we are prepared," said Fourteen, but the girl's words disturbed him more than he let on. Isn't that how he'd felt, and wasn't that one of the reasons he wanted out? "One of us will become the next emperor. The others will be diplomats, carrying the Lingdow's word and mercies throughout the kingdoms of all Dixho."

Mariessa had the audacity to laugh at him. "The diplomats in Keran never looked anything like the emperor. No ruler in his right mind keeps his children around, especially ones that look so much like him. They become a danger. The only way for a leader to stay in power as long as the Zhandanese is to murder potential threats, including his unnamed children. I imagine it makes it easier to sign the order if the offspring don't have names."

She couldn't have struck him harder if she'd slammed the table across his face. It couldn't be possible, yet it made sense. It fit with everything Master Den had said, everything his father had done, and it stung with truth.

Fourteen fell against the bush, branches breaking with loud snaps, stabbing into his bare back. He bent over and ducked through, not wanting to hear any more lies from the strange girl. Heedless of the guards he ran across the moist lawn, toes digging into the soil, cutting the roots and tearing tufts of green from its tangled moorings. He stepped into the cold water. The girl's small hands grabbed his arm, holding tight. She'd followed him?

He pulled at her fingers. "I told you, there's no way out from the compound."

"I'll be closer there than I am here," she said. "You're taking me with you."

Trying to dislodge her, he stumbled too far into the current. His feet shot out from under him, sweeping him deeper. He yanked her off, but she caught hold again. She had the tenacity of a cat, with the grip of a multi-armed demon. The currents whipped them to one side and they entered the edge of the falls. Fourteen kicked away, only to head farther into the river's current, racing downstream. Just past the wall that bisected the river, metal grates extended from above the waterline to the rock below the riverbed. Eventually, the grates would stop their progress, the current pinning them to the bars while they drowned.

The girl still held on as if she believed he was taking her where she wanted to go.

A dolphin swam around them, nudging them back toward the falls, but unsure what to do. They'd learned that females stayed on one side of the river, males on the other. They weren't trained to deal with two stuck together.

"You're going to get us both killed!" Fourteen screamed.

He didn't know if Mariessa heard him, but she held on. "Take me with you!"

He brought up his knee, wedging it between them, prying her off. She grasped onto his calf. Even as he kicked, holding her underwater, she held on and started climbing up his body.

"What in limbo!" he yelled.

He kicked out, his legs flailing until he made contact. She went farther under, but finally released her hold. The struggle had sent him to the other side of the palace wall, the moat side, where vicious sharks waited if he got stuck to the moat's grate.

One foot bumped the wall between rivers. He doubled his efforts, fighting the current and slanting toward the shore. Little by little the water pushed him back. His feet hit the metal bars, just wide enough for his toes to slide through. Fourteen imagined sharks gnawing at them while the current held him under, the salamanders catching whatever bits and pieces the sharks missed. Something brushed beneath him. He groped in the churning water, grabbing hold of a small dolphin's dorsal fin.

Its tail frantically waved back and forth, but the brave creature's slow progress wouldn't last. Fourteen kicked his feet, trying to help. The dolphin had saved him from the grate, but they couldn't seem to make it past the wall dividing the river.

Smooth skin bumped against his legs, sidling up his stomach. Fourteen looked down to find the biggest river dolphin he'd ever seen. It nudged his side, flapping its dorsal fin at him. Fourteen released the smaller dolphin for the larger. As they pulled away, the little one dipped beneath the surface. Fourteen grabbed its fin, trying to bring it with them, but the slick skin slid from between his fingers.

The larger dolphin surged forward. It escaped the plunging current, swimming into the strong eddies at the waterfall's edge. It brought Fourteen as close to the bank as its large body was able. Fourteen released the fin, finding himself in another fight to reach shore. Without the girl, and from a better starting point, he struggled until his feet found mud then crawled onto the bank, legs dangling in the rushing water. After he'd caught his breath, he dragged himself onto the grass. The dolphin gave a quick bark from the calmer side, and then disappeared.

Fourteen gazed across the swirling waters and thick mist. He could just make out the girl who'd nearly drowned them both. Two dolphins barked their displeasure at her as she sat, staring across at him. He couldn't make out her features, but her posture suggested she blamed him for their situation as much as he blamed her. What a daffing selfish, short-sighted—.

The large dolphin surfaced only a few arms in front of Fourteen, keening like a frightened baby. The other dolphins joined in, a cacophony of wailing children.

Fourteen jumped to his feet and ran downriver, pressing his face against the metal-linked fence separating him from the edge of the moat. In the swirling waters of the grate, through the white foam spitting above the metal tines, he found what he'd hoped he wouldn't be able to see.

Further slowing the water's brutal progress, a small shape pressed against the metal bars, fins and tail fluttering in the shark's domain. As Fourteen watched, blood started mixing with the rushing water. The strongest among the sharks, willing to fight the current for such a delicious opportunity, had started its feast.

Fourteen sagged against the fence, his fingers twined in the strands of metal, and bit back tears. The little guy had died saving his life.

With a last glare at the bank where Mariessa sat, he slunk back to the trees to find his clothes, haunted by the dolphins' mournful eulogy.

17

Han watched his concubines, unobserved, from his bedroom balcony. The little one still sat at the riverbank, legs crossed before her chest, arms wrapped around her knees, staring at the opposite bank. She had spunk, but too much determination. That needed to be quelled, and soon.

Esterelle knelt in the soggy grass next to the girl, smoothing her bedraggled hair and trying to coax her away from the river.

As requested, Peder kil Straun entered Han's chambers, his military-style shoes tapping the tile floor on their way to the thick rug. Han nodded to his guards, who then escorted Peder to the balcony, where he lowered himself onto one knee, head down.

Palm up, Han raised his hand, allowing Peder to stand. "My new mother, she nearly killed herself and one of my potential emperors in her attempted escape."

Peder stiffened. "I will have her reprimanded, sir. She is willful, but I'll have her under control before the ceremonies."

Esterelle was done soothing. She stamped a foot at the mother's defiant shake of her head. Servants in gray dresses came forward, grabbing the girl under her arms and hauling her to her feet. She twisted away, her temper requiring the eunuch guards. She fought them like a rabid cat, using nails, teeth, kicking one in the shins. What remained of her wet negligee twisted across her breasts and rode up her muscled thighs.

"No," said Han, his anticipation growing as he watched. Two more guards joined the struggle. "Keep her contained, but nothing more." He rubbed a hand down his thigh. "I'll teach her to behave. Her first lessons anyway."

Peder bowed. "Yes, Your Holiness."

"How far is she into the cleansing process? Have you established she's a virgin?"

"She will see the doctors this afternoon, Your Eminence. It will take three days to run the tests, make sure she's free of disease. Then we must cleanse her body."

"Do it all, now."

"Now?"

Han snapped his head around to face Peder, the fire in his belly seeking an outlet. "Now. I want her prepared in five days."

"Your Holiness, I can hardly be starting the diet cleansing in five days. It is impossible to finish the whole process in such time."

"I don't care about any of that. She's an islander. They eat a diet high in fruits and vegetables. She'll give me a healthy child." His hand rubbed across his thigh again. "Put her through the doctors and make sure she doesn't have any diseases. I want her ready the moment the succession is complete."

Peder bowed, lower this time. "Yes, Most Holy Emperor. It will be done as you command."

"Then go!" Han screamed. "Attend to your tasks!"

Peder kowtowed from the room, a laughable sight like watching a muscle-bound elephant try to bow and walk backwards.

As soon as the door closed, Han pulled a communication stone from his pocket, calling on Bow Quing. When his spy arrived, taking measured steps across Han's red and black rug, Han's anxiety had moved to a near frenzy. He knew it, but didn't care.

"What took you so long?"

Quing bowed his head low, but remained upright. "I came immediately, oh Holiness."

Han turned from the gardens to lean against the side of his dark desk. "Stop your bowing and stupid words of deference. I have tasks."

"Yes, Your—yes."

"I want fences on both sides of that waterfall. All the way from the base of the mountain, until they meet up with the river grates."

"Wouldn't that be under the stewardship of—?"

In two steps, Han stood next to Quing. With an open hand he struck the side of Quing's head. The assassin raised his arm a fraction as if he thought to defend himself.

In a flurry of motion, Han kicked Quing's knees from under him, grabbed the offending arm and twisted it behind his back. Han reached for hair, forgetting Quing's shaved head. Without that leverage, Han wrapped an arm around Quing's neck, yanking the arm up farther, until Quing grimaced in pain.

"How dare you question me?" Han spoke into Quing's ear. "How dare you think to defend yourself from me? If I choose, I will beat you until you cannot stand, and you will thank me for it." He punctuated his sentences with a yank to Quing's arm. "If I choose, I will torture you until you can't walk or speak and yet you will grovel at my feet. And if I choose, I will snap your neck here and now, and in the hereafter as your soul wanders the agonies of Limbo, where it surely will go, you will still sing my praises."

Quing cried out, the sweat of pain dripping down his chin, absorbed in the rug's thick fibers.

"Do you understand your position, spymaster?" Han asked, exacting another cry of pain.

"Yee," was all Quing could manage.

Han released his hold around the man's neck. "What was that?"

"Yes," Quing said, bordering on a sob. "Yes, Your Eminence."

Han stood up, straightening his sash and robe. "Good. Then you will secure the fence within two days. Delegate if you'd like."

He sat at his desk, placing his back to Quing as the man pulled himself up from the floor, but keeping him in his peripheral vision.

"It is a matter of security," said Han, "and thus under the CSO, palace division. Also, you are to speed up the Numbers competition. I want it finished in two days."

"If it pleases Your Highness, would you like the final contest to be held in the mud, oh Most-knowing?"

"Mud?" Han asked, his temper rising again.

"The final contest is outdoors and heavy clouds are gathering. The meteorology master predicts heavy rains this evening."

"How long then?"

"Today is Tingsan. If tomorrow and Lingwu are clear and sunny, then we can have the final competition on Tingkay."

"Fine. Make it happen. But no later than Tingkay."

"If it's not sunny, Your Highness, then it may take another day."

"Another day would be Tingtian, the day of worship," said Han. "I cannot conduct such business the day my subjects worship their Lingdow, but I will give you lenience. As long as the competition takes place by Tingyi, your life will be spared."

"But the weather—"

Han's gaze snapped to Quing's bloody face. He hadn't realized he'd broken the man's nose when he dropped him to the carpet. "Do you question me, spymaster?"

"No, Most Gracious of Lords. It will be done as you request."

"Good." Han's hand rubbed across his thigh again. "We will bring the new emperor to the palace the moment he is chosen."

Quing's face showed surprise, but he had learned enough wisdom in the past fifteen minutes to keep his mouth shut. "As you command," he said, bowing his head.

"And the Erolethan prince," said Han, remembering one of the reports on his desk. "It's time he was dealt with. Order the assassination. If his father gives you any problems, threaten to kill the oldest of his sons living in the Uradi palace. I'll expect news within the week, showing some progress."

"Yes, Holy One."

"Dismissed," said Han. "I'm going to the observation room. While I'm away, get a servant to clean up the mess you've made on my rug."

Han locked his wardrobe, desk, and other belongings, not trusting such things to any servant. He ignored Quing's incessant bows, disgusted by the blood dripping on the rug then across the tiles.

The moment Quing left, Han made his way to the concubine observation room.

He'd taken too long speaking with Bow Quing. The girl had slipped into her outfit already, something Esterelle hadn't picked. It was yellow. The kind of yellow that made the girl's dark skin appear sallow. It must have been made for a much larger woman because though meant to wrap above the breasts and tie in the back, the girl had managed to wrap it around her bust twice, tying it at the side. It billowed to her waist in so many thick folds, it entirely hid her slim curves. She'd wrapped the skirt in the same fashion, hiding her hips and thighs in the fabric.

Han yanked his communication stone for Peder from inside his robes. Before he could call for him, Esterelle entered the bathing room.

She yelled something at the girl, but Han couldn't hear. He needed to install a listening stone in the baths. Usually, he didn't want to hear the women's inane chatter, but now it would have been useful.

The girl screamed back.

When Esterelle reached for the overdone wraps of cloth, the girl swiped the larger woman's hand away. Esterelle tried again and received a kick in the thigh for her trouble.

Han almost put the stone back in its pocket, but changed his mind.

"Peder," he spoke against the smooth silver. "I want a concubine in my rooms in...," he watched the catfight, estimating how long it would take for one of them to prevail, adding the five minutes to reach his concubine suite. "...about twenty minutes."

"Esterelle?" Peder asked.

"No, one of the smaller, dark-skinned ones."

As he watched, he came to another decision. If the girl survived childbirth, he would keep her. Esterelle would be too old soon to be a favorite, though for the sake of devotion he might let her live a bit longer, but he would need someone younger, someone who could give him a challenge. The island girl would suit his needs to perfection. And her golden-brown skin would hide the bruises.

18

Fourteen fidgeted in his seat, waiting for the next doctor while his mind whirled with the questions that had plagued him for the last few days. *That stupid girl!* Mariessa's opinion about Numbers fit with Master Den's far too well. It couldn't be possible, but then, how could it not be? Fourteen had almost approached Master Den, ready to take his advice and run, but there was still a chance he could be made emperor. If so, maybe he could use his higher station to save his brothers, exile them but keep them alive.

"Fourteen," the doctor called.

He entered the man's small office, lined with books and sporting a desk no bigger than a child's. The portly man sat in a rickety chair that threatened to collapse on one side. He raised pieces of paper smeared with black blobs, asking Fourteen's opinion on what they represented. It was crazier than staring at clouds. They did word associations, talked about his childhood, then a timer went off and the strange man ushered him from the room.

"What's my score?" Fourteen asked.

"You passed," said the doctor.

"Well, how did I compare to the others?"

The man cocked his eyebrows. "You either pass or not. You wouldn't move on if you didn't pass, at least for most of you."

"What do you mean, most—?"

"Sorry, I still have one evaluation left."

Eleven winked, slipping into the pale-lit room. The doctor turned away, shutting the door in Fourteen's face.

What in limbo?

The attendant in the room, a severe faced woman with her hair pulled back in a tight bun, took mercy on him. "It was a psychological evaluation." She tapped the side of her head. "To make sure everything works right upstairs."

The telephone on her desk clanged and she picked up the receiver. "From the palace...yes, of course....He's with the last one. We'll have the report ready in two hours....Yes, he'll be finished in ten minutes, but the emperor is having him type up his own notes, won't let me help. The poor doctor doesn't type well. I don't know why..."

Fourteen wouldn't get anything else out of her. Whoever she spoke with at the palace, it was a friend more than a superior. They'd probably rattle on until someone gave her work to do, which would probably be a couple of hours.

He wandered from the room. The emperor compared the Numbers' abilities on everything else, so why didn't he care which of them was more psychologically stable? It didn't make sense.

An announcement boomed from the city, the usual echo making it impossible to decipher. Something about an upcoming celebration, but it would have to be emperor-decreed since there were no holidays coming up. Maybe another betrothal celebration or a military victory on some continent the other side of Dixho. Nothing of any consequence to Fourteen.

They changed the date for the next trial, giving him a note to go to the old storage shed by the staff quarters. At thirteen thirty, he showed up at the squat, metal building. Before he could ask any questions, a burly guard grabbed Fourteen by the arm.

"Try to get out," he said, his voice dull.

He gave Fourteen a shove, making him stagger into the square cement room. The door bolted shut. The place had no windows, only a single lightstone connected to ceiling wiring that kept it charged without having to take it in and out of sunlight. It smelled of old dirt, mold, and urine. He scanned the walls and corners for a hidden exit. The only way possible appeared to be melting into jelly and slipping under the door. Or maybe through a small hole in the side of one wall.

Fourteen took a closer look at the hole, catching movement. On a whim, he pulled a pencil from his pocket, sidled along the wall out of view, and poked his eraser into the niche. A grunt and an exclamation sounded from the other side. Fourteen laughed as the man swore.

He scanned the room again. Poking someone's eye might be entertaining, but it wasn't going to get him out. In the middle of the room, he took everything out of his pockets. Besides the pencil, he only had a few of Aednat's beads. Otherwise, he had his belt, shoes, and clothing.

He unhooked and slid off the belt, letting his pants slide partway down his butt, the hem scuffing under his feet. Eventually he managed to slip the leather between the frame and the door, dislodging the latch, but had no hope with the bolt. Its keyhole went through both sides of the door so he took the buckle prong and tried to pick the lock. He messed with it until the narrow prong finally snapped, the tinny echo bouncing around the close walls, nothing to show for his efforts but low-hung pants.

He considered poking the observer in the eye again, but thought better of it. He needed a way out of this daffing prison. Knocking on walls and looking for lines in the plaster did nothing. The only other object in the room was the lightstone.

Fourteen squatted halfway to the floor, jumping as he aimed for the light's cage. He caught hold, but a piece of wire poked into his palm. He yelled, falling onto his side, shaking his bleeding hand.

"What's going on in there?" screamed the guard from his side of the door.

Fourteen jumped to his feet, pulling up his pants with his good hand. "I tried to grab the lightstone!"

"Stupid kid! Just wait it out like everyone else."

"Holy Vasheri!" said Fourteen, running to stand next to the door. "I must have disconnected something. Help! The wires. Sparks are flying everywhere. I think the ceiling's catching on fire. Help me, please! You can't leave me in here to die."

The bolt wriggled, clanking as it released.

When it burst open, the burly guard ran in before he realized, "There's no fire."

Fourteen slipped behind him, out the door and into the open air. "Maybe not, but it sure feels good to get out of that box."

The man grabbed him by the scruff of the neck. "You get back in there, you conniving little bird."

"But I did what you told me to. I got out."

"That's not how it's supposed to work."

Fourteen struggled but didn't dare actually fight the man. He could get in trouble if he caused injury. "You didn't give rules. You just said to find a way out. And I did."

The guard shoved him back into the box, but a skinny man with an irritated eye under a set of lab glasses came up behind him.

"Let him go," the little guy ordered.

"But," the guard spluttered. "That's not how it's supposed to work."

"Doesn't matter," said the man. "Once he's out, he's out. I have my notes and it's for the emperor to decide."

The guard grumbled but stepped away from the door. "I'll go get the last one."

"Sorry about the eye," Fourteen said, stepping from the box.

The man chuckled, lifting away his goggles. "I'm glad you used the eraser end. You're a smart little chicken. I think you tried almost every reasonable solution and then tricked the guard to boot."

"Will we have the results before the last competition?" Fourteen asked.

"Tonight?" The man nodded. "Yes."

"It's tonight? The ground near the gates has dried out enough?"

"They should have told you after your psychiatric examination. Mister Bow Quing says the area is dry enough, though it still seems a bit sloshy to me. You'd best clean up and get some rest. They say the last test is the most difficult."

At his apartment Fourteen found Aednat setting out his competition uniform, the same as the rod duel—a white hyefu with green and yellow stripes, and loose white trousers.

Fourteen fingered the light-weight fabric. "Why do you think the emperor is in such a hurry to finish the competition?"

"I don't know for sure," Aednat said. "But rumor says he wants the new emperor in place so the new mother can be the boy's ascension bride. They say the emperor is itchy for her and wants the temptation gone."

"His new mother?" Fourteen repeated, unconcerned with the rest.

If he succeeded in the competition, that bratty, beautiful girl who'd nearly gotten them killed would become the mother of his first child. The idea both revolted and intrigued. Of course he'd do his duty to the empire, but after the things she'd said, he doubted she would find duty a sufficient motivator. Then again, he'd seen her eyes evaluating his wet body, and she'd seemed a bit impressed, at first. Maybe if he gave it some time, he could convince her that duty didn't have to be an aggravating chore.

~~~

A few hours later, at the assembly area turned proving grounds, Fourteen cursed his luck, kicking at the soggy turf in front of an elaborate, newly created maze. Fourteen would be entrusting his life, and his success, to Twelve, his teammate for this last competition. He couldn't imagine a worse scenario, and couldn't see the point. Why be forced to finish with their competitor? To test teamwork, coercion, or something else? He suspected that some emperor hundreds of years ago just ran out of ideas and decided to throw this one in for fun. Regardless, this was the place Fourteen needed to redeem himself, and here he was, stuck with Twelve.

"The team which completes their maze first," the announcer roared through a megaphone to the crowd, "will be the victor. They must both cross the finish line. Those seated in the stands will often see the contestants, but if anyone shouts directions or makes any noise, they'll be escorted from the area and receive severe retribution."

The stands went dead silent. Severe consequences didn't mean extra duties or removal of privileges. It could mean anything from losing an appendage to exile.

"I give you, your emperor," the man said.

Standing on a dais, silhouetted by the late afternoon sun and surrounded by guards, their great emperor stood with a brass bell not much bigger than a child's clenched fist.

The people didn't know how to respond, having been warned to remain silent, but knowing they should cheer their great Lingdow. It turned out the emperor didn't care.

He merely glanced at the rumbling crowd and rang the bell. For a moment, no one responded to the tittering clang, then Eleven, Nine, and Fourteen took off into the maze. Twelve jogged between the first set of newly transplanted shrubs then slowed to a walk.

"What are you doing?" said Fourteen. "They'll beat us for sure."

Twelve raised his eyebrows and laughed. "And you think I care? I'm not getting chosen anyway. Making you lose is better than beating some test that isn't going to do me any good."

Fourteen stopped trying to find his way ahead and went back to the daffing idiot. "You can't be serious. While they're in there helping each other figure out the maze, you're going to refuse to even do it?"

"Oh, I'll do it. We have to finish at some point. I'm just going to take my time."

There was only one way Fourteen would have a chance. Quick as a snake, he struck a disabling blow he'd learned from Master Den.

Twelve was ready. He blocked Fourteen's hand, thrusting the base of his palm at Fourteen's nose. Fourteen stepped back. The mud's dry crust gave way beneath his heel. He fell onto his back as Twelve's hand skimmed above his face. Fourteen swept Twelve's legs out from under him. Twelve twisted to one side so Fourteen couldn't land a killing blow to his throat, something Fourteen wouldn't have done anyway. But the movement gave Fourteen the opportunity he'd hoped for. He faked rising on one elbow, but struck out with his other hand, hitting the carotid artery. It was a dangerous move and didn't always work. If he'd missed, he could have killed Twelve, but hours of practice paid off. Twelve's eyes rolled up and he slumped face-down in the mud.

Fourteen tore Twelve's uniform shirt into strips, using them to tie his arms and legs. It only took a couple of minutes, but when Fourteen slung him over his shoulders and hefted him up, Twelve groaned, coming awake.

"Great," said Fourteen. "Now I'm behind, and I have to figure out this maze for myself."

Twelve squirmed against his restraints. "What in —"

"Hold still and shut up or I'll drag you out of here by your daffing hair."

"You're dead, you lost little whang. When I get out of this, I'm gonna kill you!"

Fourteen paused, noticing an unnatural bend in the branch of the corner hedge. "Shut up, freak."

The people who'd planted the bushes hadn't had much time. Only the supervisor had had the map, but Fourteen recognized a pattern he'd cut across the edges like a connect-the-dots or numbered tabs, so the workers could set them up faster.

Fourteen took off, a complaining Twelve bouncing on his shoulders. Running through the maze, Fourteen barely slowed at the junctions, but he doubted it would be enough to beat Nine and Eleven. Carrying Twelve slowed him down and his brothers had a significant lead.

Emerging from the greenery, Fourteen glanced across the open field at the other Numbers' maze. Nine and Eleven ran toward the finish, at least a length ahead. Fourteen came even with Eleven as they converged on the final runway. A narrow white ribbon strung from poles three lengths apart, stood sixty lengths away, about half the distance around the running track. Eleven turned up the speed and with Twelve across his shoulders, Fourteen didn't stand a chance.

"Let me down," said Twelve. "I'll run."

Fourteen didn't have anything to lose. He pulled at the knot around Twelve's ankles. When it came loose, Fourteen dropped Twelve to his feet. As Fourteen had suspected would happen, Twelve swung his tied up hands like a sledgehammer. Fourteen ducked away, sprinting for the finish line. Whether Twelve came with him or not, whether he won or not, he would finish this trial.

He gained some ground, passing Nine, but nowhere close to Eleven. Since Twelve came in last, it meant nothing that Fourteen had beaten Nine. Fourteen had still lost the challenge, making Eleven the most likely next emperor.

19

Han scanned the candidates standing in front of him on the dais. To one side, the setting sun coated the sky and still-billowing clouds in shades of pink, orange, and red. The Numbers' gasping breaths moderated, but tense expectation showed in their tight shoulders and intent gazes. Mud spattered the area, the space around Fourteen and Twelve covered with mounding globs.

Clipboard in hand, Han motioned Bow Quing to a far corner, out of hearing. He extended the papers for Quing's study, glancing around to make sure the conversation would be kept private.

"Here are the results," Han said. "How would you suggest I make Fourteen appear the winner?"

Quing studied the numbers, eyes narrowing. "I suggest, Your Holiness, that you select Twelve. He is the best suited."

"Stupid man!" Han gripped Quing's black hyefu in a tight fist, but brought his voice back down. "That's not what I asked of you."

Quing didn't flinch. "You must discredit Twelve. Then Eleven and Fourteen appear near-equals."

Han glanced at his favorite son, face filthy with mud. "You think that will be enough to quell gossip?"

"I believe so," said Quing.

"Then I'll make sure there's no question." Han returned to the boys, raising his eyebrows at Twelve's bare torso. "Where is your competition shirt?"

Twelve swung his head in Fourteen's direction. "That idiot took it, Your Highness."

"Why?"

"So he could tie me up like some lost-to-limbo kitchen hog."

The emperor sneered. "And you let him?"

Twelve's eyes blazed, jaw clenched.

"Answer me, my son," said the emperor, his voice low and threatening.

Fear sparked in Twelve's eyes. "He got in a lucky shot, sir. Knocked me out."

"Can you explain to me why, since Fourteen was on your team, he felt it necessary to fight you?"

Twelve's fearful eyes narrowed. "I have no idea, Your Highness."

"Fourteen?"

Fourteen swallowed, his fear too obvious. "When we entered the maze, Twelve slowed to a walk and refused to participate. I thought it would be best if I helped him along."

"Helping him meaning knocking him to the ground, tying him up, and making your own way out?"

"Yes, Your Excellency. I apologize if I was wrong." Fourteen winced, as well he should. Under different circumstances, Han would have slapped the boy for acting so contrite.

But Han released his anger on Twelve, lashing a hand across the tall boy's face. The wet smack echoed in the courtyard but Twelve didn't flinch, as if he'd expected it. The boy had a kind of intelligence that kept a man alive when others might crumble. He'd already anticipated Han's actions, and might even understand his motivation for undermining his favorite son. The boy would definitely prove useful.

"You're a disgrace," said Han, his voice slowly rising from a whisper to a roar. "You refuted the task given to you by your father, your Lingdow, then were beaten down like a witless puppy by your younger brother! You're not worthy of my presence, let alone my divine position." He whipped to face Bow Quing. "Deduct marks from Twelve's performance for cowardice. Add those marks to Fourteen for ingenuity and perseverance."

Quing scribbled across the top page, but they both knew that what he wrote didn't matter. He handed the clipboard to Han, bowed, and stepped back.

Han pretended to study the numbers. "In the test this afternoon," he spoke loud enough for those below to hear. "It would appear that Fourteen performed the impossible, not only escaping the prison box, but doing it without wasting any time. With this success, combined with his many other skills, he and Eleven are close in their scores and abilities."

Both Fourteen and Eleven stared at him, the first with greed and hunger, the other with an embarrassing amount of hope, proving Fourteen to truly be the better candidate.

"Based on his scores," said Han, "and by the guidance of the divine, I call him as my successor over all the land of Dixho, from east to west, from north to south, Emperor and Lingdow over the entire world." He turned to his publicity advisor. "Let it be recorded, and tomorrow, spread the announcement over all of Dixho. We will have the celebration in all top-tiered cities, two weeks from tomorrow's betrothal celebration taking place here in Han City."

The man bowed. "Yes, Your Eminence."

"Boy," the emperor pointed to Fourteen. "You have fifteen minutes to get yourself cleaned up and back to my autocar."

"Shouldn't I gather my things?" Fourteen asked with impertinence. "Doesn't it usually take a few days?"

"I have my reasons," said Han, tempted to backhand the boy. "We leave *now*. Make yourself presentable."

Scanning the crowd for the pretty thing who'd watched over Fourteen the last few years, Han finally found her leaning against a post with tears in her eyes. She'd developed quite nicely.

Han's fingers curled along his thigh. "As is custom, we will also bring your servant. She may be of use to you as the new emperor."

Fourteen nodded, tripping lightly down the ladder and toward his apartment. Han barely noticed, his gaze undressing the pretty little servant he'd left behind. She would be suitable as a concubine, to be sure. If Den was right, and she remained untouched, perhaps she might even make an acceptable mother.

He ignored the way Eleven stiffened, staring from Han to the girl. But when Eleven attacked, pulling a knife from an arm sheath and plunging it toward Han's chest, he had his father's full attention.

Bodyguards could stop many attacks, but not all. Not at this close range. Han had survived as emperor because he considered every person within ten arm spans as a potential threat.

Lunging to one side, Han grabbed Eleven's knife hand. The blade struck empty air. Han twisted the hand. Bones in the wrist popped. Eleven cried out, forced to his knees. Han pulled the small dagger from between the boy's stiff fingers, examined it a moment, then thrust it into his son's side.

The servant girl screamed.

"You might survive," Han whispered. "But let this be a lesson to you. If you fight me, *anyone* who fights me, they lose. Accept your fate with the dignity befitting your heritage." He glanced at the servant-girl, sobbing as Den held her back. "And be grateful your Lingdow is all-knowing. I do what's best for you, whether you recognize it or not." He gave the knife a little twist, grinning as Eleven cried out, the girl below echoing his pain. "Let this wound reinforce that knowledge. Find peace in it."

Yanking the knife out, Han dropped it, eyes wide. Had he plunged the blade between the boy's ribs? Blood seeped through Eleven's white hyefu, and for a moment, Han saw himself. The Numbers' uncanny resemblance to himself could be disconcerting, but this one looked more like him than any of the others. But he'd had to teach Eleven a lesson, hadn't he? No one could win against Han. Once everyone accepted the fact, there would be no more need for violence. They could worship him in peace.

Everyone stared while the boy, Han's likeness, bled over and through the dais' wooden slats.

"Don't stand there doing nothing!" Han yelled. "Are you heartless? Get him a doctor. Take him to the compound hospital."

Members of the guard in green and gold uniforms hesitated, but then set to work. The emperor snapped his fingers at the remaining Numbers. "The rest of you, back to your apartments."

As they ushered Eleven away, Fourteen entered the assembly grounds, hair wet and dripping onto his royal blue dress hyefu. He jogged alongside the men transporting Eleven, obviously asking questions, then raised a fearful face toward Han. The boy's glare mattered little. In a few hours, Fourteen's power to judge Han would no longer exist.

Ashen-faced and trembling like he'd witnessed the murder of a beloved pet instead of a competitor for his throne, Fourteen guided his buxom servant to join him in the back seat of Han's new limousine.

Taking his time, Han reached for the door handle, giving Den time to approach. He was stopped five lengths from the car by Han's personal guard. Han gave Den a knowing smirk, calling Quing to his side. "Let Master Den through," Han said. "I'm curious to hear the man."

Den came forward, facing Han. "You think I'm stupid enough to try to knife you like the boy?"

"Of course not, but I'm not sure you didn't put him up to it."

"He's in love with Fourteen's servant as I'm sure you know. You don't need another concubine, and Fourteen won't care about her after you're done with him. Why not leave her here?"

Han shook his head. "You know how this works, Den."

Den took a deep breath, his shoulders slumped. "I know. And since you're taking the boy, I might as well join you. Maybe you were right. I'd rather be with him and Aednat, even on your terms."

Han studied him but gained nothing from it. "You're up to something."

Den smiled that easygoing smile Han hadn't seen since Den left the palace. "I'm always up to something. You know that."

Han grinned. He'd won. It would take time for Den to come back to the old ways. He'd just have to keep a wary eye on him until then.

Den joined Han in his newly constructed limousine, and Han sent Bow Quing to the front with the chauffer. It was a tight fit, the girl having to sit on a small corner seat facing them. Han would have the engineers work on a better design, perhaps lengthening the car.

Across from one another, the pretty servant-girl held Fourteen's hand. She clenched his fingers, large eyes still welling with tears, her face pale with fear.

Han rubbed his fingers across his thigh. She would make a perfect concubine.

"I want to be there," Den said.

Han pulled his gaze from the girl's large breasts. "What?"

"The boy's ascension ritual," said Den. "I want to attend."

Han's eyes narrowed, studying Den for any trace of deceit. "Why?"

"I want to make sure it's done correctly. I won't have him wasted."

This could clinch Den's dedication to him, but Den lied better than any man Han had every known, including himself.

"And if I say no?" Han threatened.

Den shrugged. "Then I suppose I'll find a book to read."

That was how Den had spent his time before he'd left the palace, always lost in a book, always silent, nothing like his parent. Den's lips pursed tight, gripping back disappointment. It was the most real emotion Han had seen from him in a long time.

"You won't try to stop the ascension?" Han asked.

Den bowed his head. "I swear it on Kerise's soul."

Han's sudden anger didn't make sense, even to himself. This was one promise even Den would not dare break. "Then I grant you permission, and you will perform the ritual, under supervision."

"I don't need—"

"I may be crazy, my friend, but I'm not crazy enough to believe I'm back in your good graces. You will still be supervised."

Den hung his head, eyes downcast like a reprimanded child. "Yes, Your Highness. As you wish."

Han stretched his shoulders. A new life would begin, all back in its proper order.

20

Naked and shivering, her skin mottled red from her skin-cleansing treatment, Mariessa startled at the soft swish of an opening door followed by a warm breeze.

"What now?" she said without turning on her bench. "You've studied, poked and prodded me in every humiliating way possible. What is left?"

"In some ways you're lucky." said a soft female voice. Not Peder. Esterelle.

Mariessa dropped her arms from her chest and turned. "Why are they doing this to me?" The tears she'd held back forced their way through.

"Hush," Esterelle said, sitting beside Mariessa and wiping away the moisture with a cotton handkerchief. "You'll redden your eyes and make Peder angry."

"All I've done is make Peder angry. He grabs me by the hair and yanks me around like I'm nothing more than an old sack." Her voice choked. "Has them do awful things."

Esterelle put an arm around Mariessa's bare back as if comforting a younger sister. "I'm sorry it's been so truly hard. On the one side, they've actually done fewer tests and rituals than usual. On the other, they packed the most horrible ones together so you've had no time to recover. And I'm afraid it's not getting better, not for a wee bit yet."

Mariessa raised her head to stare at the woman. "Why? What's next?"

"You're to be pampered and prettied."

"Why is that bad?" Mariessa said, tensing.

"Tonight is your engagement night."

"To the emperor?"

Esterelle nodded. "The *new* emperor."

Mariessa relaxed. "Maybe he'll be kinder."

"Perhaps," said Esterelle, but her expression didn't match her words.

"Can the new one be worse?"

"The emperor picks children who are like him, or so I've been told. But maybe this time will be different. Fourteen might win."

Mariessa clenched a bathing cloth, wringing it between her hands. "I'll kill him."

Esterelle pulled the cloth from her grip. "If the new one be like the old, he'll want some fight from you. He'll like beating you down. The best you can do is resist, but not so much to make him angry. Give him the satisfaction of taking you down a peg. That'll save you from the worst of it."

"I'll escape before then. Somehow. How much time is there between the betrothal and the wedding?"

"Two months, but it doesn't matter. By law, once you're betrothed, he can enter your bed."

Mariessa gasped. "That's savage. No decent man does such a thing. And no decent woman encourages—"

"Do you listen, laurie?" said Esterelle. "No matter. By law he has the right, and by precedent the emperor conceives his first child on his ascension night."

"You mean today? Now?"

"Tonight. We have two hours to prepare, and then Peder will come for you."

"No."

Mariessa pulled away, came to her feet and backed into the corner as if she could somehow melt into the wall and the nightmare would disappear. But she knew it wouldn't. It would haunt her until either she or the emperor died.

"Don't make this more difficult," said Esterelle. "Remember what I told you."

"No!"

Esterelle's soft features turned hard, the way they did each time Mariessa defied her. "Servants," she called at the closed door. Ten women in their drab uniforms filed into the room. "She needs some help to the finishing room."

Mariessa didn't fight the women, at least not as much. She'd been through this before and ten servants could truss her up in soft linens and take her wherever they willed before Mariessa even bolted for the door, and it would be worse if the eunuchs were called to assist. The women dragged her to the room, Esterelle and a dozen concubines following in their wake, all willing to prepare her like a hog for the feast.

They tittered on about how beautiful she would look as if that could be some condolence. All but Esterelle. She, at least, understood that being the emperor's plaything wasn't some kind of perverted blessing from the Vasheri, or the occasional price for an opulent life. To her it was to be endured, with grace, head held high. She seemed to think Mariessa would eventually follow her example, but Esterelle didn't understand. Mariessa was a jungle child, and like most things of the jungle, they plotted or fought, but they never submitted.

Once inside, Mariessa understood the function of the deserted bathing room she'd discovered in her attempts at escape. Designed to turn a woman into the epitome of visual perfection, many concubines served as beauticians, all with a focus on the one—Mariessa.

They tossed her from a scented bath, to a seaweed wrap, to a pearl and ginseng body mask, to some kind of scented grease spread over her body and wrapped with warm towels. When they finished, her unnaturally soft skin smelled like a spring garden, the odors perfectly matched into a sweet, many-faceted perfume.

"Am I done?" Mariessa asked, reaching for a clean towel.

Esterelle whisked the towel from her hand. "We've only started."

"But it's been over an hour," Mariessa complained. "What more can there be?"

With a startled gasp, Esterelle turned to the black and white clock hanging on the wall, its ornate hands marking the time.

"Girls!" She clapped her hands. "We must hurry."

She yelled out names, one after the other, giving them assignments. Three girls finished drying Mariessa's thick hair, using a contraption that looked like an over-sized gun but blew warm air, while another four took charge of her hands and feet, scraping, shaping and painting her nails. Half an hour later, the women working her hair yanked at the frizzy tangles, smoothed some kind of cream through the strands, then used a contraption like scissors, the handles made of ornately carved wood and the scissor-part a long rod of hot metal that they closed against a curved slab, squishing and heating the hair into spiral curls that hung to her shoulder blades. They sprayed a foul concoction over their work then covered the nasty scent with more perfume.

While they finished her hair, Esterelle focused on Mariessa's face. Instead of gaudy blues or purples as Mariessa had seen on the visiting-girls in Keran City, Esterelle painted her eyes with warm tones that brought out the deep browns in her eyes, accented with thick black strokes of eyeliner and copious amounts of mascara. Painted to emphasize the way they curved up at the sides, her eyes and her full, red-lipsticked mouth dominated all else. Mariessa didn't recognize the beautiful girl-made-woman staring at her from the long mirrors covering every wall. She touched her fingers to her chin, needing confirmation that it really was her staring back through the mirror. Nails, the deep brown-red of a woman's first menstruation, warned of the coming pain, from conception to delivery...birth of another horrid Number forced upon her by a man she didn't know.

Esterelle handed her a negligee, the lacy fabric so sparse it would have wadded into Mariessa's fist.

"What's the point?" Mariessa asked.

"Men like to take them off," Esterelle said, at least having the decency to blush.

"And if I refuse?"

Esterelle shrugged. "Then it will be over that much faster, but he may hurt you more instead of taking his anger out on the fabric."

Mariessa put it on, but even with the dark color—a perfect match to the haunting nail polish—it left nothing to the imagination. "What if I don't fight, or at least pretend to go along? Then he won't have any reason to start out angry."

Eyes sadder than Mariessa had ever seen, Esterelle shook her head. "The man is always angry, always feeling the pain of his life. There's nothing anyone can do for that." She handed her a voluminous white robe. "You'll be allowed to wear this to the suite then you must hand it to Peder."

Mariessa snatched it and wrapped it around as far as it would go then tied the strap tight. Peder might have to fight her to get it back.

Esterelle seemed to sense it, and sighed. "Don't fight, laurie. There's no point to it."

"As long as I fight, I haven't given in. *That's* the point."

With another sigh, Esterelle knocked on the door leading to the hallway. Peder opened it, gesturing for Mariessa to come out. She braced her feet, but the servants reached for her and she realized they'd carry her if she didn't comply. At least for the moment, she had her robe.

"Fine," she muttered, stomping from the room. "You're a pig," she said to Peder.

His expression never changed, chiseled from unfeeling rock. "I've heard worse."

He guided her to one of the locked doors, and for a moment Mariessa imagined possibilities. But on the other side of the door, four guards waited. They escorted Mariessa and Peder up three flights of stairs to a room with a gold-gilded door. Inside, though the walls had the same lavish designs, the room only contained a bed. Edged in gold filigree, it was a simple, sturdy thing with two mattresses, no sheets. The only other object was a dim bulb set in an unnaturally high ceiling.

Peder put out a hand. "The robe."

Mariessa swallowed, shook her head.

"Someday girl, I'm going to slap that stubborn jaw so hard you won't be able to speak."

"You can't bruise me." She stuck her chin in the air, not even reaching his chest.

His gargantuan fingers dove into her ringlets at the base of her skull "There are some things the emperor won't notice." He tightened his fist and twisted.

With a cry, her fingers grasped at his wrist, clawing at his boulder of a hand. Her eyes watered, threatening to streak the women's carefully applied make-up. Peder ripped the robe from her body and shoved her into the room. Before she turned around, he'd shut and locked the door.

Mariessa knelt at the base of the bed, found the screws, and discovered they'd been welded to the frame. Every digit of metal had been melded together. No weapons to be found.

She knelt at the bedside and wept, wiping at the black streaks that ran down her cheeks. Hearing movement outside the door, she dropped to her belly and crawled. She went as far under the bed as she could press her small body, ignoring the strong smell of cleaning fluid covering a faint odor of urine and something else.

In the dim light filtering beneath the bed, she recognized a smear across the gold-marbled floor. The crusty dark color, flakes of which had stuck to her negligee, almost made her scream. That was the other smell the cleaning staff had missed, the one emanating from that one telling streak. Blood. Mariessa wasn't the first to hide under this bed, and she didn't doubt her fate would be the same as the poor girl who'd tainted the tiles.

21

Fourteen gazed up at the palace doors with growing awe. They stretched higher than two grown men standing on top of one another. Matched, inlaid-gold carvings of Emperor Beht Han standing with arms outstretched, robes open to the navel, were illuminated by the palace blocks' never-ending glow as well as lighted spheres—something Master Den called lightbulbs. Beneath him were thin wraith-like representations of many Vasheri, palms out as if giving the Lingdow his power.

Beside Fourteen stood the flesh-and-blood man, the one chosen to represent the Vasheri's will on the earth, the Lingdow Fourteen would now become. He would inherit the name, the knowledge, and become the next emperor...and he would stop his father's reign of terror.

So many lights illuminated the driveway, the stairs, and the entryway, that the closing night seemed far away, unable to reach them with its dark fingers.

"This doesn't seem real," Fourteen whispered to Aednat, his excitement making his voice pitch like an eleven-year-old.

"Han's in a hurry," Master Den whispered back. "Not long and you're going to have more reality than you know how to handle."

A sliver of fear slithered up Fourteen's spine, but he suppressed it. He would be emperor. With such power, he could make everything right, even return Aednat to Eleven if she wished. The transfer of power couldn't change him so much that he'd disregard her and his brothers.

Broad-shouldered servants dressed in bright purple and gold livery pulled the doors open as if they weighed no more than a scrap of paper. Armed imperial soldiers in dark gray uniforms, the cuffs striped in the same purple and gold, lined the emperor's path, but he still kept his personal guard, their black and gray uniforms like surrounding shadows. Fourteen, Aednat, and

Master Den followed the emperor, and then more members of the dark-clad guard came behind. The two imperial forces, black and purple, glared at one another as they passed.

Waiting inside, a man with yellow hair, bulky and maybe six digits taller than the emperor, stood at attention. Black slacks and a modern, button-up shirt seemed out of place in the palace full of men in hyefus. The only indications of his station were two thin lines of purple and pink at the shirt's collar and cuffs. Despite the man's size, he seemed to shrink under the emperor's demanding gaze.

"Is she prepared?" the emperor asked.

The man bowed so low Fourteen wondered how he kept from falling over. "Yes, Your Eminence."

Soon, these servants would be bowing to Fourteen, a sixteen-year-old kid who through the miracle of the Vasheri would obtain the knowledge and wisdom of centuries upon centuries of Lingdow. The honor elated him while the responsibility weighed on his soul. And in the back of his mind came the whisper, in Master Den's and then the girl/soon-to-be-mother's voice. "He will kill you all."

The corners of the emperor's lips curved. "We will proceed with the ceremony at once."

"This late?" questioned Master Den. "After such a long day?"

As if sharing a joke, the emperor raised his eyebrows. "I'm sure the boy will have sufficient stamina." He addressed the tall blond man. "Peder, take the servant-girl to the emperor's private suite. She can be there to greet her master when all is finished."

Peder inclined his head, wrapping a muscled hand around Aednat's arm.

"No!" she cried. Her fingers gripped Master Den's sleeve. Though an impressive fighter, even Den couldn't take on a man of such immense size and strength. There was nothing either of them could do. *Until I become emperor*, Fourteen thought.

Master Den turned to Fourteen's father. "Please, Beht Han. Not this girl. Let her remain with me."

Fourteen suppressed a gasp at such outspoken informality, but the emperor didn't even blink. "You come back to the palace on *my* terms. I am master here." He glanced at his guard as if prepared for attack.

Master Den bowed his head. "Go with him, Aednat. I'll come and explain later."

Peder's eyes questioned the emperor, who gave a slight nod of condescending acquiescence, permitting the eventual visit. The emperor's bitter meanness seemed contrary to Vasheri teachings of kindness. As Lingdow, Fourteen would follow a better path.

Aednat went with Peder, tears streaking her face, and the emperor led the rest of them toward a beige-and-white marbled staircase, the white handrails ornamented with gold. Climbing the steps, Fourteen made out Vasheri, in various stages of undress, scattered among the swirls and coils of the filigree. It seemed a desecration, yet it continued to draw his eye. Below them spread the foyer, a large waiting room, and the entrances to hallways, extending out like spokes from a wheel. Lightstones hung from or sat in elaborate sconces on ornate side tables along the walls, or even standing in the middle of a room.

If he'd thought it bright outside the palace, inside surpassed mid-day. Lightbulbs, fueled by some source inside the house, shone like multiple suns embedded in the ceiling, turning the lightstones into mere ornaments. Everything shone, smelling of polish, cleanser, and an overlying scent of fresh-cut flowers. They filled a multitude of finely crafted vases, interspersed among the lights and priceless artifacts so strange, they must have come from foreign countries all over Dixho. And soon, this elaborate temple would become Fourteen's home, his possession.

Down a network of hallways endowed with such overwhelming amounts of rich tapestries, lurid paintings, and embellished furnishings that Fourteen couldn't take it all in, they stopped in front of a solid gold door, the carving in relief shaped into the figure of a dirt-encrusted Vasheri in mid-transformation to a man, a man with the emperor's distinct features, rising from the blessed soil.

Fourteen's mouth opened in awe. It symbolized the ascension, the rebirth of the next Lingdow. A portly man with a protruding gut stood in simple robes by the handle. He prostrated to the floor, taking a nervous glance at Master Den.

"You are prepared?" the emperor asked.

The man nodded, hitting his forehead against the tile with such force that he squeaked. "Yes, Your Holiness." His high-pitched voice didn't match his robust frame. Fourteen had to bite back a laugh.

The emperor pulled a key from deep inside his robes. "No one enters this room but me, the new emperor, and the doctor. Today, I will make an exception. Den may accompany us, Bow Quing, and," he pointed to two guards, "you and you." They appeared surprised, but puffed out their chests and stood a little taller.

Wondering why they needed a doctor, Fourteen stepped into the room after Master Den and the others, the two guards flanking him. He paused at the threshold, but their entrance shoved him forward. The acrid smell of sterilization chemicals replaced the hallway's floral scent; ornate beauty doused by stark white walls. Two beds, white and sterile, identical to those in the doctor's office, jutted out from the side wall. Between them, on a rolling table, lay a jumble of power stones, wires, and two fat syringes filled with a glimmering urine-colored fluid.

"What is this?" said Fourteen. He backed toward the door, but the guards had formed a solid wall.

"Usually," said his father, "we'd have you sedated before you came this far, but I must admit, with Den as your mentor, I was curious at your surprise. Either he didn't tell you, or you refused to believe."

"This isn't really a ceremony, is it?"

"Oh, but it is." His father smiled. "It's just not the kind of ceremony you expected." He turned to Master Den. "Would you like to do the honors?"

Master Den shook his head, "No. I'll be here with him, but I don't want to perform the transfer."

"Transfer?" Fourteen's voice broke on the word. "It's supposed to be an ascension. Vasheri are supposed to appear, prophecies, spiritual messages...I'm gifted the knowledge of past emperors. It's supposed to be sacred."

"Come now," his father said, his soothing voice increasing Fourteen's fear. "All those things will happen; it's just a more medicinal process."

Fourteen shook his head. "I don't believe you."

His father gestured to Master Den. "Maybe you'll believe him?"

But Master Den shook his head. "I'll not lie to him, not in the last minutes of his life. Tell him the truth. We have enough people here to restrain him if it proves necessary."

Fourteen's father smiled as if the prospect brought him pleasure.

"The truth," said the emperor, "is somewhat like you believed. You'll probably see the Vasheri, if they exist, assuming your soul is able to travel below. You see, you'll acquire all my knowledge like you believed, but I'll be coming with it."

Fourteen glanced at Master Den. "He said something about a different kind of stone. He was telling the truth, wasn't he? And whatever stone you have is going to do something to me."

"There are all sorts of stones in the world," his father said. "But I control those made by sorcerers and sorceresses. For centuries I've collected them. There's one in particular that no one in the world knows about but me, Den, and a handful of my most trusted advisers. Some, on whom I bestow favors, know I have the means to give them immortality, but they don't know how I do it. They think I'm magic."

He reached into a pocket of his robe, pulling out an object wrapped in the finest rice paper. "This," he said, peeling away thin layers, "is the most precious and valuable stone in all the world."

It looked as if someone had crystallized blood, removing all impurities, and then polished it to a sheen that only heartstones could obtain. An abomination in his father's hand, Fourteen had never imagined anything like it. Evil emanated from the stone more surely than a vial of poison, yet its profane beauty seemed to promise fulfillment of all desires.

"That's sick," said Fourteen.

"But I haven't even told you how it works."

Fourteen turned on the soldiers. With the strike of his hand he dropped one to the floor, shoved the other aside. He gripped the door handle. A prick, a pain in his arm, and his fingers lost their grip. Edges blurred and the room began to spin.

"Sorry," said Master Den, holding him up by one arm. "I have no choice. There...dozen soldiers...."

As he slumped into Master Den's arms, Fourteen's world went black.

22

"Where am I?"

Fourteen's mouth felt as if lined with cotton, his tongue sticking to the edges, making it hard to form words. Lying on a metal table, the cold seeped into his skin, making him shiver under the thin sheet covering his groin. Someone stood above him, blurred but familiar. The figure started to come into focus and Fourteen recognized his former master. He'd...he'd attacked Fourteen with a syringe!

Fourteen struck out, his movements far too clumsy to be effective. But he continued to flail at the man, determined to find some way to escape the fate his father had threatened.

"Shh!" Den whispered, grabbing Fourteen's weak arms and pinning them to the table. "If the guards outside suspect something has gone amiss, they do have a temporary emergency key. You must remain quiet."

Fourteen stilled, eyes darting from side to side, but he couldn't see anything useful. His arm stung and the room smelled of blood and medicines.

"You stuck me with something. Made me go to sleep."

"It was necessary. Han had to believe I wouldn't interfere. He had to believe it enough that when the medications I slipped in the doctor's drink made his fingers shake, Han would trust me to take over the procedure. His anticipation made him careless."

"Where is he?"

Fourteen tried to sit up, but the room slid sideways. He dropped back down. With another syringe in hand, Den grabbed Fourteen's opposite arm. Fourteen pulled away.

"Do you want to get out of here?" Den asked.

"Yes, but I don't want you knocking me out again."

"If anything, this might make you a bit manic, but we've got no choice if we're going to walk out of here in one piece. You need to trust me, Gabrick."

Gabrick, the name he'd assumed only in his thoughts and private conversations with Den, and only for a short period of time, before he'd become obsessed with becoming the next emperor. He didn't have time to think about it, not now.

Fourteen nodded and put out his arm. "Okay." He blinked, fighting the absurd temptation to sleep. "Go ahead."

The needle plunged into his biceps, the tiniest of pricks, but still uncomfortable. Within a few seconds the room came into stark focus. Fourteen jumped up from the table, taking everything in at once. His father lay on the slab next to him, out cold, a tube of fluid running into his arm. Blood smeared the floor beneath the guards, the doctor, and even the emperor's personal assassin, Bow Quing.

"Are they all dead?" Fourteen asked.

"Close enough," said Den.

Fourteen pulled on his underclothes and reached for his pants. "Let's get away from this place."

"Not yet," Den brought up an elaborate robe in shimmering white, embroidered with silken gray threads depicting again the worshiping Vasheri and the rise of a new emperor. The sight made Fourteen sick. "No shirt, and you must wear this. Appear to be Han."

Fourteen buttoned his pants then slipped his arms into the bulbous sleeves. "He was going to take over my body somehow, wasn't he?"

"Yes, and that's why it's so important that you be a genetic near-replica, so his mind can handle the necessary adjustments. And that's why his wives must be virgins, so the child is conceived with the stone. If a child is altered after conception, the genetic replication is not as accurate." Den strapped some of the emperor's discarded knives and guns onto Fourteen then arranged the robe's folds and ties. "His followers know his stone makes them have look-alike children, but they don't know the same stone is used to transfer their consciousness into their offspring."

"Why didn't you tell me?" Fourteen asked.

Den raised his eyebrows in disbelief. "You never allowed me to explain past the first part. What would you have done if I'd told you the rest?"

What a fool Fourteen had been. "Probably reported you." He stretched his shoulders against the heavy, uncomfortable clothing. "Would I have been trapped inside, aware?"

Den licked at his lips, hesitating. "I'm not sure. I don't think so, but…I don't know."

"Barbaric limbo-demon." Fourteen pulled a knife from an arm-sheath. "We should end this now. He'll go after one of my brothers next."

Den stayed his hand. "He's connected to monitors that will trigger an alarm. We need to be long gone when that happens." Den plunged a syringe into a sac of fluid hanging above the emperor. "This will give us at least twenty minutes. Then he'll start going into a coma."

Disappointment and relief warring in Fourteen's mind, he sheathed the weapon and faced the door.

"Do you remember what I taught you?" Den asked. "How to let a man lead while appearing to be in charge?" Fourteen nodded, nervousness making his stomach clench. "Don't look pained. Hold your head high. Don't smile, but appear as if everything is right with the world and you're looking forward to your next destination. You've seen your father. Be pompous, arrogant, even cruel. Be him."

Fourteen licked his lips, held his head high, and opened the door only wide enough for them to leave, not wide enough for anyone to see the carnage within. Den followed.

"Where are the others?" One of the guards asked as he bowed.

Fourteen waved a hand dismissively as he'd seen his father do. "They're cleaning up. I'll not wait on it. I have business to attend to." Den stood directly behind him, so he swept past the men and straight for the stairs.

"Would you like us to accompany—?"

Fourteen felt a flash of panic. "Stay out of my way," he bellowed. From the corner of his eye, he saw Den give one of his infinitesimal nods.

Sweat beaded across Fourteen's back and neck. He resisted the urge to run down the stairs. Whatever drug Den had pumped into him was doing its work. Every movement, every sound, and every smell seemed amplified. The sweet smell of flowers had grown so strong he would have thought they'd been crushed and left to sit in their vases for days. He longed to jump the steps, take down the guards he passed, attack something, but he forced his steps to remain measured, calm.

As they approached the end of the stairs, Den moved to Fourteen's left, still an appropriate distance behind, but Fourteen sensed the change. He took the hallway to their left. They continued through the palace, Den leading from behind, up another, shorter set of stairs, down multiple hallways, and into the most opulent bedchamber Fourteen had ever imagined.

The bed was big enough for five people, covered with rich swaths of fabric in exotic brown and red designs. Huge closets faced him from the opposite end of the room, an ornate dressing table sat against the wall near the door, and a monstrous fireplace, surrounded by carved granite dragons, took up half the expanse to Fourteen's left. There were trunks, and jewelry cabinets, and a desk, and a variety of chairs, yet the room wasn't cluttered in the slightest. It was so huge, there were rugs and vast open spaces between every object. Huddled in the corner like a discarded doll in a playhouse sat Aednat, crying into her knees.

"Is it done?" she whimpered.

"No," answered Den, using the calm, reassuring voice he reserved for Aednat. "This is *our* Gabrick. Look at him, gawking at his surroundings, wishing it were really his."

Aednat wiped her eyes. "Wearing robes, he looks so much like the emperor. In this light, even the hair is the same. I'd have to stare into his eyes to know the difference."

Den put a hand on Fourteen's shoulder. "You should see the emperor's private chamber."

He laughed as Fourteen's eyes went wide. "He has another one?"

Den nodded. "Smaller bed, since his concubines are never allowed inside, but with a private bath and many more knick-knacks, including a fair number of his stones, kept in an armored vault. He uses this room when he wants a concubine, or concubines, for longer than a diversion, or for other visitors he doesn't want the general household to know about." He gestured to Aednat. "Come. It's time to make our escape."

She ran over, burying her face in Fourteen's robes, hugging him like they'd already succeeded. "I was so frightened."

Den shook his head in exasperation and unfeigned attachment, but spoke to Fourteen. "Here's the story. You've signed the betrothal papers, but decided to spend some time with your new concubine first. You've agreed to allow her see Eleven one more time since you've discovered he may not survive the night, then you'll show her how to behave. Act secretive and devious as if you're being nice because you have a horrible surprise in store for her."

"Will they buy it?"

"Most of the guards don't know him well enough to know any better. I just hope we don't—"

Something moved inside Fourteen's robes. "Aah! What in—" Dancing up and down, Fourteen grabbed at his lapels, determined to get the horrible thing off.

Den grabbed his wrist and felt the vibration at Fourteen's side. "It's a communication stone. I left all of Han's stones in the robe. If someone is trying to contact him, we'd better get moving."

They exited the bedchamber and came face to face with the man holding the other stone—Peder. Fourteen couldn't hide his surprise, not entirely, nor his fear. "What are you doing here?" he asked, but his voice didn't sound as imperious as it should.

Peder's eyes narrowed. "I heard the ascension was complete, but you have yet to visit your betrothed. Is there something wrong?"

"I've decided to spend some time with my new concubine first," said Fourteen, reasserting his father's pompous air. "I'm taking her to the Numbers Compound to see Eleven. It appears I may have dug the knife too deep and he's dying. Then I'll come back and attend to my duties."

Peder stiffened, eying the bottom of Fourteen's robes. Following his gaze, Fourteen looked up from the blood-tinged hem in time to see Peder's fist. He dodged to one side, but not fast enough. The man's gargantuan hand clipped him, sending him spinning into the wall.

In a blur of motion, Den stepped in. Peder had to be a whole arm taller with muscles that bulged against his shirt and trousers, and he was wicked fast. But his ability to fight didn't compare to Den's. Fourteen had seen the master in the practice ring and been impressed, but he must have been holding back. Den ducked and hit with blinding speed. Peder threw him against the wall, but Den only used it as another prop, springing into the air to kick Peder in the chest, the face, somersaulting backward, then landing on his feet.

Though smaller, Den would have beaten Peder, except the commotion brought unwanted attention. The rustle of uniforms and weapons, along with the thrum of multiple feet, converged on the stairs. Den landed a crippling blow to Peder's knee, following up with a hit to the man's neck that should have knocked him out. Instead, Peder gasped, cleared his head, and lunged. Fourteen and Den kicked him in the stomach at the same time, sending him through the bedchamber door.

"Gun," said Den, but he glanced back as soldiers made the top of the stairs. "Never mind," he whispered, grabbing a key from his robes and pressing it into Fourteen's hand. "Hurry, lock the door."

Fourteen did as he was told, the lock clicking as Peder started pounding. "Traitor! You're not the holy emperor!"

The soldiers arrived, glancing from Fourteen, to Den, to Aednat, and back again. Fourteen had no idea what to do, and Den didn't dare tell him. So he puffed out his chest, doing his best to keep his voice steady. "Peder has gone insane. You're to keep him locked behind that door until I return."

Fourteen brushed past them, hoping their confusion would buy some time.

"Come!" he motioned for Den and Aednat to follow, unsure what to call them under the circumstances. The soldiers let them pass, but their eyes darted from him to the door, obviously unsure about what was happening.

When they reached the bottom of the stairs, Den whispered in Fourteen's ear. "We've lost our advantage. That door won't hold Peder, and I suspect he sent someone to the ascension room before he confronted us."

"What'll we do?" Fourteen whispered.

"Move fast. No explanations. At the front door, demand they bring you the Shtedler."

Questions were few, but suspicion seemed to grow with each soldier they confronted. The car pulled up as Peder stormed onto the front steps, limping. "Stop them!" he bellowed.

Den leaped onto the car's bonnet-hood, to the spare tire on the running board, and into the air. He kicked the chauffeur in the face, catching the dropped keys as he landed. Two soldiers brought up guns. Fourteen didn't have time to think. He shoved Aednat toward the open back door with one hand. Using the other, he caught hold of the closest soldier's gun barrel, yanking it up. It shot into the sky as he kicked the other soldier's weapon from his hands. Fourteen pulled the discharged rifle from the first man's fingers and slammed the stock into his face. The soldier slumped to the ground as Fourteen jumped in after Aednat, the other soldier retrieving his weapon as more men came spilling from inside the palace.

As Den squealed the car from the curb, Fourteen fired at the soldiers. He barely managed to close the door as return fire pinged the back fender and shattered their window. Aednat huddled on the other side of the seat, hands over her ears.

"I think I may have killed one of them," said Fourteen, feeling the shock of the situation wash over him. "I've never killed anything before, not even an animal." His voice shook, the high pitch making him sound childish, but he couldn't get over the vision of blood spurting from the soldier's head, the eyes glazing over, stuck open.

"The first time is always a shock," said Den. "But we have a long way yet. For right now, it's them or us. You've got to stay with me, Gabrick."

Fourteen nodded, though the numbness continued to spread.

Den swerved the car toward the gates, illuminated by the guardhouse lightstones. "In fact, I need you to prove your marksmanship right now."

The soldiers weren't the biggest of their problems. One man ran for the lever that would drop a solid metal door between them and the main city.

"Trade me places!" Fourteen yelled to Aednat.

When she didn't move fast enough, Fourteen climbed on top of her. He needed a better view. Opening the door and half sitting on Aednat, he aimed the rifle barrel out the absent window. Bullets pelted into it from the awaiting soldiers, but either they had orders to not kill him or they couldn't stomach shooting a man who looked so much like their emperor. Fourteen took careful aim, trying to adjust for the moving autocar. The man reached for the lever, his heartstone lamp casting garish shadows on the palace walls. Fourteen wished he could wound the man, but it wouldn't be sufficient. It had to be a kill. He resisted the urge to shut his eyes, aimed for a spot just above the man's ear, exhaled, and squeezed the trigger. He was off by a few digits. The bullet shattered the top of the man's skull, above the temple.

Blood sprayed the lever and the gate posts. The gun's kick shoved Fourteen back as the bullet casing clattered to the road. Reaching for the door handle, he missed and the door swung open. As he toppled to the side, he imagined the car's black tires running him over, crushing him.

Aednat gripped the front of his robe. While he dangled half in and half out of the car, they approached the line of guards. One took careful aim, targeting her.

Fourteen scrambled for a grip on the seat. "Pull. Now!" he screamed.

She yanked him in. A bullet pierced the seat pad between their faces, missing them both by less than a digit. He searched for Den, finding him lying nearly flat on the front seat, using side mirrors to drive. Fourteen pulled Aednat onto the floor, covering her body with his own. As they neared the gate, he peeked above the seat.

They reached the soldiers, their bullets leaving gaping holes in the car's body. Fourteen didn't know how the autocar was still running. He kicked his door, tearing it off the hinges, but taking half the soldiers with it. Still, one of them reached the lever. The gate dropped like a giant's knife. The car jerked, cracking Fourteen and Aednat's heads against each other. Caught by the metal slab, part of their bullet-riddled back fender lay on the road, twisted upward toward limbo like an offensive appendage, glittering in the electrical lights atop the palace wall.

"We made it," breathed Fourteen.

Den laughed. "That was the easy part. Even a reinforced car frame isn't likely to get us past the next set."

23

As Han gained consciousness, he first considered shooting the doctor. Han inhaled something putrid and strong, something held to his nose on purpose, an unnecessary waking technique after the simple transfer process. Then it hit him. He knocked the substance away, his eyes flying open. Everything in his vision spun, but not as violently as his anger.

"This is not the right body," he slurred, sounding like a drunkard. Against the spinning room and the nausea in his stomach, he sat up like a sickly man in his late thirties, not a seventeen-year-old in his prime. "What happened?" Quing's face moved in and out of focus.

"I'm so grateful, Your Eminence." The man didn't sound grateful. "As soon as I gained consciousness I started to wake you. Thank the Vasheri you're alive."

"Yes," Han drawled, noting the bruise on Quing's temple, the dried blood trickling down his jaw. "Den outmanned you, my best spy." But how? Den had sworn on that woman, Kerise's, soul. It seemed impossible that he would go against such a vow.

Quing bowed his head in embarrassment. "He caught me by surprise. Then he made easy work of the rest."

Han glanced down, the darkness suddenly clouding his vision almost enough to topple him off the hospital bed. Quing caught him, steadied him, and Han focused on the dead men who littered the tiled floors. His focus moved upward, noting the needle still stuck into his arm, inserting fluids. He yanked it out, ignoring the spurt of blood, letting it run down his arm.

The door unlocked and Peder filled the opening. "Why are you not opening when the soldiers came?"

Quing shrugged, his calculating eyes boring a hole through Peder with their innocence. "Perhaps that's what woke me, the pounding."

Peder grunted. "Matters not. The boy and Den. They have escaped the palace with that servant girl."

"They're in the city?" Han felt his panic rise.

"Ner," Peder grinned. "They won't get past the guards, let alone the wall."

"No!" Han jumped off the table. His knees buckled. If not for Quing, he might have passed out among the dead men. Han had never had such a reaction before, even after a failed transfer. Had Den somehow poisoned him?

"No," he repeated. "I don't care about the girl, but I want the others alive."

Once subdued, rid of his worthless ties to Fourteen and the boy's servant, Den would be pliable again. He had to pay for his treachery, but he would come back.

Han gripped the hard metal slab, regaining his air of authority. "Stop them at the gates, but don't kill them." Before Peder finished relaying the message, Quing had helped Han into new robes, midnight blue, and was trying to help him down the stairs. "Don't touch me. I'm perfectly capable of walking."

"You seem unusually weak, Your Eminence. Are you certain—"

"Indeed!" The man was an imbecile. For some reason, in his drugged state, the falsity of Quing's concern sliced like a sharp knife. The man was not to be trusted.

Near the palace doors, Peder found him again. The news wasn't good.

Han's temper overflowed, "You're all incompetent! You limbo-spawned demons from above." He pulled his gun, one of the few Den hadn't bothered to take. "I'll have all of you lost amongst the clouds for this." He fired. Three guards went down, bullets clean through their hearts, their blood slicking the tiles. Only when it threatened to stain his bare feet did Han come to himself, scanning the open-eyed men. Had he done that? He hefted the warm pistol in his hand, replacing it in a hip sheath. He must have done it, though the memory felt hazy.

"Find them," Han said.

His voice rose as he continued to berate Peder and Quing, but this time he kept the gun in his robe. This was the kind of thing Den could have averted. Fourteen must die or be brought into submission, but Den, Den had to come back. Even if he had to be kept on a chain, he must be found.

24

Mariessa stared at the smear of blood on the floor, disgusted with herself. People were running up and down the halls in a frenzy. Something was happening, maybe an attack of some kind. Nobody would be coming for her anytime soon. Dangan once said she had the ferocity of a jungle cat. But not now. Right now she was acting like a scared, spoiled, fourth-tier.

She scrambled out from under the bed.

"I want them captured!" a man screamed from someplace far away. The words were muted by distance, but their fury carried into her little room. "I want them to pay, and I want to watch them pay. Capture them or I'll give you their suffering. Find them!"

Mariessa shivered. The man sounded as if he might have spittle flying as he raged. She imagined the horrible things a man like that might inflict, but realized her imagination probably didn't do him justice.

And he would eventually make his way to her, and there was nothing, not in the entire room, she could use as a weapon. She stared at her nails, beautifully painted, but not long. She bit at the edges, making the short claws jagged. That wouldn't be enough. It would only anger him, make him more violent. She had no pins in her hair or ornaments on her body. Her hair was long, but not long enough to wrap around his neck.

Her fingers rested on the delicate negligee. Maybe, if she handled it the right way, there might be a small chance. "Small people can have great power," Mariessa's mother used to always say. "Timing and ingenuity are the key." She'd stopped saying it after grandmother had died and Sando had taken her. She'd become a different woman because of him, and Mariessa refused to let any man do such a thing to her. Not even an emperor.

She pulled thin straps from over her shoulders, dropping the negligee to her feet. Picking it up, she sat on the bed, facing the door. Jagged nails ripped at the delicate lacework, intent on their work.

25

The car rumbled its way up the switchbacks to the mountain runway, Den taking the corners at breakneck speed, though how he knew when to turn on the dark road baffled Fourteen. The car's headlights barely illuminated a few lengths in front of them, the rest of their surroundings lost in the darkness.

City alarms blared far below as they barred the area where the city gates had stood, before Den had barreled the car through the ornate metal, leaving them twisted and hanging off their hinges. The guards for the outer city hadn't even tried to stop them, just jumped out of the way. But Den had been right about leaving being the easy part. What awaited them at the airstrip was more than daunting, it was impossible. Two lines of soldiers stood between them and the closer of two aeroplanes, the entire area lit up by multiple lanterns.

"We can't beat this," Fourteen pointed out. "We might as well surrender."

Den chuckled as if Fourteen had made a childish joke. "You only say that because you've never seen what Han can do to his enemies. Trust me when I say our odds here are better. Death is preferable to Beht Han."

Fourteen didn't doubt the man anymore. "We need more guns."

"Well, we'd best convince some soldiers to share."

With that, Den pressed the gas pedal to the floor, aiming for the first line. Some stepped aside, but most didn't. At the last moment, Den yanked the wheel to one side and hit the brake. The car went into an uncontrolled spin. A number of thuds resounded through the car's cabin, bodies ricocheting off the frame. It spun along the line of men, from the center of their ranks, toward the plane. The soldiers no longer tried to hold their ground, but couldn't move fast enough to escape. Metal rattled against metal as their bodies, thrown beneath the tires, rankled the autocar, making it pitch and turn like a frenzied drunkard

Fourteen's rifle flew out his open door and he nearly followed. Aednat grabbed his thick robe in one hand, her other arm wrapped around the front seat. He managed to get a foot on the car's frame, holding him in place. When the car finally lost its momentum, Fourteen slumped back, one leg hanging from the vehicle.

Den shook his head clear as he threw open his door. "Grab a firearm and make for the plane! It's our only chance."

Fourteen stared at him, his world still spinning. Amid the cloud of dirt settling around them, he didn't know what direction to run.

"You want to keep your own brain, boy? Move!"

Sliding out the open door, Fourteen landed on his knees. The ground continued to pitch and turn, but he grabbed a rifle from the grip of a dead man and staggered to his feet. Den had Aednat by the arm, pulling her from the car. Eyes wide, she slumped to the ground like a rag doll.

"I'll carry her!" Fourteen said.

But Den scooped her up, shielding her with his body. "Han will want his revenge on me more than anyone else. He might keep me alive in order to get it, but she'll be expendable."

As if punctuating his statement, a bullet grazed her hair, disappearing with a thud inside the car. Den pulled her tighter behind his body and ran, leaving Fourteen to fend for himself. He tried to get a feel for the terrain while he staggered after, shooting randomly at the soldiers lining up behind the tilted car. A barrage of gunfire exploded to each side, but nothing hit. Den was right; they must have orders to take them alive. Fourteen turned his back on them, running full tilt for the dimly outlined plane. The door was open, the engine rumbling and the propellers spinning. Fourteen was almost there when it started moving away. Den wasn't going to wait.

Fourteen dropped the gun. He swung his arms, running with all he had. The emperor's robes pulled at his legs, nearly making him trip. He yanked the folds apart, popping buttons and ripping the tie-knot inside. Bullets pummeled the garment as he let it slide off his back. He pulled away, dressed only in his dark slacks, but now he could run.

He caught the open doorway, hearing Aednat scream, "Wait for him, Den. You promised!"

Fourteen jumped, getting an elbow wedged at the door opening. Aednat reached out a hand, dragging him over the threshold and inside.

The plane began to lift then shuddered.

Fourteen lay heaving, flat on his back in a small space between the six seats.

An explosion shot a burst of flame from the right propeller, bucking him back to the open door. He caught himself before toppling out, but the plane bucked again, a grinding sputter emanating across its belly. Fourteen slid to the heart of the plane, Aednat beside him, the plane writhing like an old man's writing stick. It slammed to the ground, sending up chunks of soil and wrenched-up weeds. Tilting as it slid, it careened toward the cliff edge, made visible by a line of lanterns. Beyond them loomed an open vacuum of black space with pinpricks of light shining far below.

Debris exploded up into the open cabin. Dirt and smoke filled Fourteen's lungs, but only the inescapable plummet looming before them seemed to matter. He grabbed Aednat around her waist then clenched the closest seat with his other hand. It wouldn't do any good, and he knew it, but at least they might die together. The wing went over, digging into the rough rock at the cliff's edge. They tilted and a large chunk of torn metal wedged into a crevice. The plane lifted, ready to catapult over, then dropped back to the dirt, still at last. From Fourteen's vantage, a long fall was the only way out of the plane.

Aednat buried her face against his chest, her sobs mixing with the distant moans and screams coming from the soldiers on the airfield.

"Den?" Fourteen called out.

A low groan answered him. Something clanked against the plane. Fourteen didn't dare move. If he shifted wrong, the whole thing would go over. He could only hold onto Aednat and wait.

A few minutes later, the plane jerked. Aednat screamed and they both gripped each other and the seats. It jerked again and the cliff's drop became a strip of dirt with deep lines burrowed across. A man stepped in, rifle at the ready. Lantern shadows cast monstrous distortions of him along the plane's seats and walls.

Fourteen stepped in front of Aednat. "You can't shoot me. I know you've got orders."

"Don't flatter yourself, Number. You're on the 'rather not' list. Only Den is truly safe here, and I doubt that's for long." He jerked his head in the direction of the cockpit.

The man behind him scooted around and stepped through the narrow door to Den's unconscious body. "He's alive."

"Get him in cuffs and to the truck," the first soldier responded. He stepped out from the plane, gesturing with his gun barrel for Fourteen to follow. "Don't do anything stupid."

With Aednat gripping his hands, following at his back, they stepped from the plane. Immediately, a soldier grabbed Fourteen and threw him face-down into the dirt. He grunted, struggling to turn his face and see Aednat.

Another soldier had hold of her, handling her roughly, but not abusively. A knee dug into Fourteen's spine and his face was slammed back into the dirt and gravel. The man wrenched Fourteen's shoulders as he pulled his hands behind his back, and then enclosed his wrists in joining metal circles. They must be the cuffs the soldier had spoken of.

Despite his vulnerable position, when the soldier yanked him to his feet, Fourteen stared open-mouthed at the valley spread out before him. He had never seen a city, or any view outside the walls of the Numbers Compound. He was close enough to the edge to see his waterfall, back-lit by garden lights, and beyond it the emperor's palace, glittering like a million crushed stars, its walls almost as bright as the lamplight surrounding it. The town itself could have been mistaken for the night sky, some star-clustered galaxy emanating from the palace's core, a paltry imitation of its blinding presence.

The man dragged a stumbling, awe-struck Fourteen to a square automobile like none he'd ever seen before. The back opened like a door and the soldier tossed him into an open space, a box, but with seats to each side. Aednat tried to help him, but her hands were as useless as his own.

"Move over," a gruff voice told him. Fourteen managed to get to his knees and up to the bench opposite Aednat. Two soldiers stuffed Den into the narrow space between them. His eyes flickered open, he grunted, then they rolled up and closed.

Outside, a man slapped the side of their metal prison. "Take them to the palace, directly to the emperor."

Words were spoken that Fourteen couldn't make out then the motor rumbled, the automobile whined into gear, and they started down the narrow road, back the way they'd come. He should have pushed the plane over the edge, Fourteen realized. Den was right as he'd been since the whole thing started. What awaited them in the hands of his father would certainly be worse than death.

26

"Thanks to you, I'll have to train another doctor to assist with the ascension ceremony," said Han, but Den's expression didn't change. No anger, no remorse; no feeling at all.

Dried blood matted Den's hair and clung to his cheek. He kept catching himself to stay standing, reminding Han of the day he'd killed Den's parent, in this very room.

"It's not an ascension," the Number, Fourteen, said. "It's a murder. You—"

Han slapped him, gratified by the red streak that sprung from the boy's lower lip. He glanced at the soldiers lining the back wall. "You speak another word of that, and I'll have to kill you now."

"What does it matter? Kill me now, possess my body later. I think I like the knife-to-the-heart idea."

Han appealed to the boy's teacher. "Den, tell your protégé to shut up, for his own good."

"Kill him," Den said without expression. "It's because of him I'm here, we're all here."

Han turned his back on them as he stepped across the thick carpet, past the woven bamboo table lined with empty chairs, up the stairs to his dais and his throne. Scratching at his earlobe, he studied Den's placid, uncaring face. Han had to consider what his friend wasn't saying.

"No. I don't need to see your expressions to know you. You want him dead so you'll be free of him, to give me less power and to spare him..." Han glanced at the guards once more, choosing his words carefully. "To release him from his duties. But when he ascends to my glory, you'll be more willing to listen to reason. I'm certain of it."

"I should have killed you," Den said, still expressionless. "I could have. You know that."

Han stiffened. He knew that very well, and he wasn't sure what had stopped Den's hand. "If you had, you wouldn't have escaped. Alarms would have sounded and you'd have never made it down the stairs."

"Do you still think I fear death?" Den said, his flat tone taking on a hint of mockery. "One way or another, I'll eventually be rid of you. Old friend."

Han fingered the hilt of his closest blade, tucked beneath his robe against his forearm. Den was right. Han had offered him immortality through the use of his stone, had even offered him his best concubines and the pick of any woman from any country as wife, but where Beht Den had accepted, his son, taking the name Chid Den, refused. So either Den hadn't been able to kill him because some part of him still cared about Han, or he'd done it for someone else. Han studied the Number, but shook his head. The servant-girl clung to the boy's sleeve, shivering with fear. It was her. The insipid, womanly child.

Han pointed and snapped his fingers. "Bring her to me."

She screamed, cried, all very theatrical, but the guards dragged her to his dais and held Fourteen back. Den didn't move to interfere, but his nostrils flared, a gross show of emotion for him. Han ran his fingers through the dirt crusting the girl's arm, watching Den's muscles clench. The twitch of his nostrils became more pronounced. Han touched other, more delicate areas, enjoying her cries and whimpers as she struggled against the guards. Den still didn't move, but Han hadn't seen that much pain and show of emotion since the upheaval with Kerise. When would Den learn? Han would take care of everything, but Den couldn't allow a woman to become more important than his Lingdow. Han would have to teach him, again.

Han stroked the girl's face. "Don't worry. I don't need a concubine tonight. I have a wife waiting for me. In fact, I'm going to raise your position. I'm making you my new ascension bride. Your beloved master, your Fourteen, is to be the next emperor, and when he takes on this great responsibility, you will be waiting for him to celebrate and conceive his first child." He turned to Den. "And you will watch."

The girl dropped to her knees. "No," she sobbed. "Please, no."

But Han wasn't interested in her reaction. He watched Den. The man visibly paled. For the first time since Han had killed Den's parent, Han saw fear in Den's eyes. He may not fear Han yet, but he feared for the girl. Han would work with that.

"Why?" Den said, and his voice cracked. "Even if you're insane. Why would you do this?"

"I'm not insane!" Han raged, his hand reaching for the pistol, the same one he'd used in this room almost twenty years before. "I told you." Han pried his fingers from the gun's grip and tempered his voice. "Never say that. I'm only doing this for your own good. Once you recognize my divinity and my power, you'll stop working against me. You can stop trying to find women, weak and insubstantial, to be your companion, and understand that you belong at my side. Forever."

"By all the Vasheri," Den whispered. "What kind of monster have you become?"

"Enough of this." Han put out a foot and kicked the servant-girl off his dais. She tumbled down the stairs with a startled cry. In the bedroom, this one might prove to be more fun than he'd expected, if she got some fight in her. At least he wouldn't have to keep her once she gave birth. "Take the girl to Peder," he told the guards. "Den and the Number can go to the dungeons until I have need of them."

The guards dragged the sobbing girl to the concubines' quarters and shoved Den and Fourteen from the room. Han rubbed the front of his thigh, anxious for his new bride-to-be. It was time something went right.

He pulled his communication stone from his pocket. "I've sent a girl for you to clean up and get dressed. I'm going to my marriage suite, ascension or no, and I'm not to be disturbed."

"Yehn, sir."

Han replaced the stone and pulled out his other one, wrapped in expensive rice paper. He smoothed his robes, left the room, and took the stairs two at a time, one hand scratching at his thigh, the other rubbing the blood-red stone.

Han reached the suite's ornate door, throwing it open. He stopped dead-still. Was this to be another disappointment? He'd expected the girl might wait for him under the bed, forcing him to drag her out. He'd expected her in the corner, her nails raised to scratch out his eyes. But this? This, he hadn't expected.

She sat on the bed, lean legs seductively crossed, long hair hanging in ringlets across her breasts, shoulders, and back. She'd removed her negligee, though Han knew she'd been warned against it. His eyes searched for it on the floor, near the bedposts, and landed on the rumpled pillows. There. She must have stashed it there. The Vasheri knew, it wasn't anywhere on her body. Her smile invited, but her eyes flashed a challenge. Maybe this wouldn't be so disappointing after all.

Han removed his robe, hanging it on a hook outside the door, placed his sheaths and weapons into a bin beneath the hook, then stepped inside, allowing the door to lock behind him. He had a key of course, but she'd never have the opportunity to find it.

"I thought I was supposed to get the new one," she said, holding the smile, but he could hear the tremor in her voice. She was afraid.

He rubbed his fingers against the thigh of his underclothing and pocketed the transfer stone in a fold designed for the purpose. "We had some complications, but don't worry. When you're betrothed to one emperor, you're automatically betrothed to his successor."

"I'm not worried," she lied.

Han smirked. Of course, she'd thought Fourteen would be easier to fight. Han still looked forward to taking her with the younger man's body, before she got too far along in her pregnancy.

Han took a confident step forward. "You were told to keep the negligee on."

"It got in my way," she said.

"If you think I believe you won't fight me, you're wrong."

He took another step and she sprung upward, landing on the foot of the bed, lithe as a cat, coiled and ready to spring. As he approached, she retreated toward the pillows. He swiped an arm out, not coming close, but she stepped back, against the wall. Before she could maneuver, he swung around to the side of the bed. She jumped. Her head almost hit the ceiling before she tucked, spun, and landed softly on the other side of Han, in the middle of the room.

He grabbed her forearm, but her smooth skin slipped from his grasp. She ran jagged nails across his biceps, drawing a thin streak of blood as she spun away. The natural direction to run next would have been the corner, but she was smarter than that. She twisted and ducked back the way she'd come, reaching the far side of the bed. But she didn't try for the flimsy negligee beneath the pillows.

Han considered whether to go over the bed or around. "So, it's to be a chase. Haven't had one of those for a while." He licked his lips. "It'll be a nice change."

He lunged to the side then threw himself across the bed, catching hold of one wrist, his body strung across the mattress. "Now you'll find out what happens when I catch my prey. I had expected a longer hunt. And you'll pay for my disappointment."

The girl seemed to have a knack for the unexpected. She didn't try to twist away, didn't reach for her negligee beneath the pillows. She turned in his grip, uncoiling as if she'd flip away again. He kept hold of her, even as she landed on his back. One thin arm wrapped around his neck, the other still in his grip.

He laughed. "You think you can strangle me with a single bare hand, little girl?" Rolling so his weight landed on top of her, she grunted. Thin, shapely legs wrapped tight around his torso. "All right, let's play a little horse and rider. But I warn you, it'll be my turn next."

He stood from the bed, bringing the little parasite with him. She twisted her arm from his grasp, but she couldn't strangle him any better with two little hands than she could with one. He flung his head back, but the little vixen was quick. She jerked to one side, avoiding the blow. He reached for the arm around his neck. It slipped from his grasp. Only one hand held to his shoulder. This was too easy. But when he reached again, fabric slipped around his neck. She hadn't touched the pillows. How had she managed to get hold of the negligee?

"I hate to disappoint you," Han said. "It's the rare girl who makes it this far, but the clothing you whores wear isn't strong enough to strangle a man."

"Of course not," she purred. "But I'm very good at making rope."

The cord tightened and for the first time in over a hundred years, Han feared for his life.

27

Tears of fear and anger ran down Mariessa's face as she tightened the silk-crafted garrote. The emperor bucked, but she kept her legs wrapped tight, increasing the pressure round his neck. He knocked her against the wall, but she'd expected that. She took the abuse, leveraging her elbows against his back, twisting the cord to keep it taut. The vile man would never rape another woman. His reign would end and Mariessa didn't care if she died for her part in it. Her life had meaning if it ended his.

When he went to one knee, she began to hope. Elation warred with disgust and horror. She was killing a monster, but had to act the monster in order to do it.

His fingers scrabbled at the thin cord, but he was weakening.

A knock sounded at the door. "Your Eminence?"

Peder!

Now able to stand behind the emperor, she knocked his legs out from under him, put a knee to his back, and twisted the cord even farther.

"Beht Han!" Peder yelled.

"We're busy!" Mariessa yelled back, not having to pretend that she was out of breath. She should have known better.

The door crashed open, the bolt-lock tearing through the frame, sending bits of shattered wood across the floor and under the bed. The knob crunched into the wall, sticking in the plaster so it didn't quite spring back. Peder wasted almost an entire second staring at Mariessa in disbelief. She kept hold of the cord, her fingers trembling with exertion. So close. She was so close!

Peder slammed his fist into her sternum. Releasing the rope as the air knocked from her lungs, she had no air to scream when her back hit the far wall. Gasping for aa breath she couldn't find, she fought the enveloping darkness.

When she managed to open her eyes and focus, the red garrote was nowhere to be seen. The emperor lay on his back, Peder gently slapping him with his monstrous hands. His vile Eminence gasped and his eyes shot open.

Mariessa dashed for the door.

Peder threw out his arm to catch her. "Noyn, stupid girl."

Vaulting over, Mariessa landed at the open door. It didn't matter that she was naked. This was her only chance.

Peder's meaty hand grasped her ankle and yanked. She pulled free, but his whole body tackled her to the floor. All muscle, he was the size of two men. She couldn't even squirm beneath so much weight. He reached above her head, retrieving the red cord he'd thrown into the hallway. Pulling her hands behind her back, he used it to bind her wrists.

Behind them, a rustle of movement told Mariessa that the emperor was getting to his feet. "The dungeons!" he screeched, his voice hoarse. "Take her to a cell and let the guards have at her. All of them!"

The emperor backhanded Peder, who took the abuse with a head hung low in absolute subservience. Peder might be even more of a crazy fanatic than his master. Did he really believe he served the Lingdow, and not just a madman with unruly appetites? With a wrench on the red rope, the emperor hauled Mariessa to her feet. She cried out in pain.

"If you had done that when I had called," Peder smirked. "I might not have realized something was wrong."

Of course, Mariessa thought, he'd expected to hear frightened pleas and screams of pain, not a woman out of breath.

"If it be pleasing you, Master." Peder bowed. "I will take her to the dungeon as you have asked."

The emperor threw Mariessa's face toward the floor as he swept her feet out from under her. With no way to catch herself her head thudded against the tiles. Her vision blurred again. He dug one foot against the middle of her back. "Where did you hide it?"

"What?" she asked.

He pulled up on the rope. Her shoulder popped with a sound like an opened bottle. Mariessa screamed. They turned to uncontrolled sobs as the emperor pulled a knife.

"There was no place on your body you could have hidden that little rope," he said. "You didn't pull it out from under a pillow. So where?"

"You're not Lingdow," she cried. "You're not even human. You're a demon-pig, and someday, someone is going to kill you. I only wish it had been me."

The thin knife slid into the space between nail and middle finger. She tried to pull away, but the effort only made the pain worse. Bit by excruciating bit, Mariessa screaming and writhing, he severed the nail. She couldn't breathe, couldn't see, couldn't even think to tell him what he wanted. Warm fluid dripped from her hand onto her back and buttocks.

"Where did you hide it?" he whispered like a lover.

Mariessa fought to get the words out between sobs. "In… in my hair."

He reached for the other hand. "Your hair was down! I looked."

"I think the witch may tell true," said Peder. "Her hair is unnaturally thick and the rope was small."

The emperor dug his hands into her hair, finding the knot where she'd tied the rope. Holding the entire wad of curls in his hand, he took his knife and sawed, the blunt edge cold across the middle of her neck. It only took a few seconds for the entire mass to drop to the floor by her face, a mound of dark curls.

"Take her to the dungeon," he said. "You will send someone to fetch Esterelle. I hold her responsible for this. She should have foreseen the possibility."

What have I done? Mariessa thought. *I've accomplished nothing and now Esterelle will pay the price for my rebellion.*

Peder grabbed one of many communication stones from his jacket then dug his fingers into Mariessa's scalp. She had just enough hair left for him to haul her after him like a broken toy. It took a few steps, but she came to her feet.

She fell multiple times as they descended staircase after staircase. He never slowed, but dragged her across the steps until she came to her feet again. When they reached a long set of narrow concrete stairs, farther below ground than even the food pantries, she lost her strength entirely. Her legs bounced painfully against the dull edges, but she couldn't keep up. They reached the bottom and a stench like nothing she'd ever experienced assaulted her senses. Rotten fruit mixed with tobacco, excrement, and redolence of desperate men.

Mariessa stared at her next horror. Ten guards, in filthy uniforms, with pistols and sabers tucked into their belts, stood at some semblance of attention. They took in her nakedness and grinned, most of them missing half or more of their yellow-stained teeth.

"I be bringing a present for you, Cherda," said Peder.

"Been a while since we done had ourselves a treat," replied the largest and most brutish of them all. As tall as Peder, if Cherda had his bulk in muscle instead of fat, they could have contended.

Mariessa found her feet. "No!" She ripped free of Peder's grip, pelting up the stairs.

She only ran a few steps before he brought her down, the side of her face smashing into the concrete, the front of her body scraping against the rough edges. Grabbing her by one arm, he threw her toward her captors. She slid across the filthy floor and into the leg of a rickety table. It teetered, spilling thick coffee across her side followed by the heavy ceramic mug. As it hit the floor it chipped, spinning in front of her face. The men laughed.

Cherda squeezed at her flesh as he wrapped thick arms round her torso. "Let me helpa ya pretty girl." She squirmed, but couldn't escape his beefy grip. She wanted to vomit, scream, even beg. Anything to take these vile men away, but it would do no good.

"She'll be coming back upstairs in a few days or so," said Peder. "I suggest you don't lose your manhood when that happens."

"I was told we could have her as long we like," the man complained.

"Emperor says that now, but he'll be wanting her back, and when he does..." Peder shrugged. "He might not remember the conversation in the same way."

The man grumbled, carrying his prize toward an open cell. "Come boys. Letta open our present."

The emperor was right. She'd take him a million times over what was about to happen. She'd be Esterelle. She'd be anything the wicked man wanted as long as she didn't have to suffer these animals.

"Take me back!" she screamed. "I'll do anything he wants. Anything!"

Peder grinned. "You will, and you'll be grateful."

Cherda hauled her down the dim-lit corridor, kicking aside a half-eaten apple, blackened with rot, as a rodent the size of a small cat scurried across the filthy floor, sweeping at the grime with its mange-ridden tail. One man stared from his cell as they passed, silent and wide-eyed.

She almost screamed, thinking the emperor had come to watch her humiliation, but no, it wasn't him. Too young. It was the boy she'd expected in her room, the emperor's son.

"Fourteen?" she whispered. "Please..." she couldn't finish, her fear choking the words in her throat.

"Gabrick," the boy said. My name is Gabrick."

One of the other Numbers? But no, they didn't have names. Maybe the emperor's bastard? When Cherda threw her in the next cell and slammed the door, Mariessa broke down, the shuddering tears racking her body.

28

"Gabrick," Fourteen had said. A name he'd avoided for years, but the only one left to him that had any meaning. He would never be known as Fourteen again. When the emperor rifled through his mind and memories, for Den had said that would happen, would he laugh at his son's momentous decision that came too late and served no purpose? Probably.

The girl, Mariessa, collapsed in the cell next to theirs into shuddering cries. Solid walls stood between the cells, but the heart-rending whimpers echoed through the corridor, amplifying the sound.

Den squatted in the corner. "She thinks this is worse than what the emperor will do to her, what he'll do in your body, but it isn't. Their atrocity, even multiplied by ten men, will be straightforward. What the emperor will do makes their perversity a slap in the face by comparison." He dropped his head into his hands, staring at the scum on the floor. "And he's going to put Aednat through it. Again and again, until I give in. And even then, it won't stop. It never stops."

The girl's cries turned to wails, screams, and finally she begged. "Please. Please stop," she whimpered over and over again.

Gabrick shuddered. "You told me once, I can never give up unless I'm dead." He gripped the bars facing the prison corridor, leaning into Mariessa's pleading. "I'm not dead."

"Guards!" Gabrick used his most commanding voice, assuming the tone he'd used when ordering men through the palace.

"The emperor," one of the men called out. "He's here. He's down here."

"Don't be daft," said the big one, Cherda. "The emperor never comes down here."

"But--"

"I *am* here," Gabrick said. "You just don't realize it."

Mariessa's wails subsided to choking whimpers. He'd gotten their attention.

Cherda's fat belly moved into Gabrick's line of vision. "Like I thought," he said. "Justa little Number using his grown-up voice."

"You know the emperor is preparing me for ascension."

"So what? You ain't nothing important until then."

"But I will be. And I'll remember." Gabrick straightened his posture, leveling his eyes at the grotesque man, the way his father always did when he made a threat he was about to keep. "And I'll make you pay for your disobedience."

Cherda licked his dry lips, a trickle of fear showing in his eyes. "A new emperor never tooka nothing out on people done wronged him in the past. Ascension takes care of that. Makes him focus on his new enemies. I've been told."

Den joined Gabrick at the bars. "Not true, Cherda. And you know it. Remember Dakka Treiben, or Pel ton Hu? It was subtle, but the memory lingers, and the chosen Number pays back those who have wronged him."

"But I ain't wronging him. It's just a stupid girl."

"I know that girl," said Gabrick. "And if you touch her again, I'll make sure you die very slow, and very painful."

"But me men," the big man whined.

Gabrick resumed the emperor-like stare. "I hold you responsible. You're in charge, and you'll suffer their consequences, only more so. Much more."

"You can't..." Cherda trailed off, but Gabrick could see it in his eyes. He believed that maybe Gabrick could carry out the threat, but he needed one more push.

Gabrick studied Cherda's face, scanning him from half-bald head to stubby feet, memorizing every feature.

"What you doing?" asked Cherda.

"Making sure that no matter what happens, I'll remember you, and remember what I want done."

"Getta you lot out of there!" Cherda screamed at his men, disappearing from Gabrick's sight. "All of you vermin. Out, I say!" They grumbled. It came to blows with a couple of them, but there was enough muscle under Cherda's fat to quell the dissenters. "Go's and feed the prisoners on t'other side. It be past their slop time. Get to it!"

The sound of dangling keys, the grate against a lock, and then the clang as the bolt slid into place. The girl's cries quieted in less than a minute. Aednat would have been in hysterics. And if Gabrick's father would do worse than those stinking guards, they had to find a way out of this putrid cell, some way to get to Aednat before the emperor did.

Cherda returned, his fear making his red face even more mottled than before. "See ya here. I done what you tolda me. No more revenge."

With a curt nod, Gabrick turned away, leaning against the wall near the bars with forced unconcern. "We'll see if you equip yourself as a proper guard. Behave as an emperor's prison man should, the kind of man who'd like to move up in rank, and maybe my memory will be more positive." Gabrick struggled to talk like his crazy, emperor father, using the old accent, haughty tone, and that little edge that made him sound on the verge of losing his temper.

Though it didn't fit with the real him, a teenage Number, in the man's fearful mind, it made sense. "Yes, Your Eminence," Cherda bowed, returning to the foot of the stairs. Gabrick heard him stumble as he plopped his overlarge frame into the small seat.

Den grinned, almost laughed. "That brings back some crazy memories," he said. His expression turned introspective, almost sad, but Gabrick didn't care about the man's reminiscence.

"We've got to find a way out of here," Gabrick said. "We've got to get Aednat away from my daffing father."

"How do you know the girl, the one next to us?" asked Den.

"What? That's the least of our worries. I met her last time I sneaked over to the concubine's garden."

"She's a new concubine?"

Gabrick shook his head. "No, I think she was meant to be a new mother. My first mother."

Den's eyes lit up. "Then there's still hope."

29

A man's voice, refined, with the soft inflections of a highly-educated Zhandanese, reached out to Mariessa. "Girl, are you all right?"

In time, she quieted her remaining sobs and steadied her voice. "If I'd had a knife, I'd have gutted them all. Who's in the cell with you? Is it the boy?"

"I'm not a boy," another voice said. "I'm the guy you nearly daffing killed in the river last week."

"Shush," the other man said. "You're not your father and I'll not have you start acting like him now."

"So, I was right," Mariessa said, going to the edge of the bars so he could hear her clearly. "You're Fourteen, and I'm guessing you didn't make emperor so he's locked you in here until he snaps your head. Can't have lookalikes hanging around."

"Only half right," the emperor's son spat, sounding almost as regal as his demon father. "My real name is Gabrick. My mother gave it to me when I was born. And I was chosen, but Master Den and I tried to escape. As soon as my father trains a new physician, they'll use some sick red heartstone to give the emperor my body. Then I'll come into your room at night, but it won't be me, it'll be my twisted father wearing my face, doing unspeakable things."

Mariessa gasped, she couldn't help it. "Red as blood, smooth as a liar's tongue?"

"Like a bloody promise turned to stone." She heard the shudder in his voice. "You've seen it?"

"He had it in his hand when he entered my room."

"The transfer stone," said the man, the Master Den. "As long as he holds it to the skin of the woman he rapes, she conceives a child that's almost exactly identical to him. Matching genetics are essential for the transfer to work properly." He paused. "But he wouldn't have sent you down here if things had gone his way."

"I nearly killed the demon," Mariessa said. "I would have if his stupid caribou-ox, Peder, hadn't shown up."

"That's impossible," the master said. "I've been through that room myself. There's nothing to use as a weapon."

"They gave me the only weapon I needed, Master Den. String and time."

"Call me Den," the man said. "I have a feeling we're going to become friends before this all ends, or at least allies."

Gabrick barked a laugh. "How's a girl the size of a squirrel going to help us get out of the emperor's dungeons?"

"She nearly killed a man who hasn't been touched in hundreds of years," Den said. "That's more than you or I have accomplished. But how, and where, did you find enough string to make a rope?"

She shouldn't brag, but with that high-stilted boy in the cell, she couldn't quite help herself. "The little see-through outfit they made me wear had enough lace, ribbon, and string to rework it into a good, tight cord. I hid it in my hair, wrapped it around his neck, then held onto him like a flea on a rat."

"That why he cut it off?" Gabrick asked. "All your hair?"

"Yes. I look like a filthy boy."

"I wouldn't say that," Gabrick said with appreciation. The reminder that he'd seen her naked made her shudder with renewed revulsion.

She heard a smack and a soft exclamation.

"What was that for?" Gabrick protested.

"We're lucky he didn't cut off your head for a trick like that," said Den, speaking again to Mariessa. "Did your garrote leave a mark?"

Mariessa grinned, though she knew they couldn't see. "I had it so tight it cut into his skin. He'll have a permanent scar wrapping almost the entire way around his vile neck. Marked forever as the beast that he is."

The yell of complaining men carried from a group of cells at the dungeon's far end. There were some exclamations and threats, then it quieted down again.

Den sighed. "No, not forever. It means he'll be in that much more of a hurry to gain his new body. He'll rush the doctor's training. I doubt we have more than a few days."

"A few days for what?" Gabrick and Mariessa said together. She glared at the wall between them.

"Mariessa, you're a Sorceress of Life Below, a plant sorceress, and I think there's a way for you to get us out of here."

Mariessa scoffed.

The bars clanged. Den had probably leaned his head against them. "They're rare, because the emperor hunts them, manipulates them, then has them killed so he can harvest their heartstones. But there are still a few living, including you."

"How can you know that? You don't even know me."

"My grandmother was a sorceress. Enough of that power was passed down that if I concentrate, I can recognize members of the Vasheri-blessed. And it is a blessing."

"So you think I'm one of them?" Mariessa laughed. "Maybe you should practice your talent more."

"The leader of your village," Den said. "Do you know how he died?"

"Sando?" Mariessa said. "They seemed to blame me, but he was alive when I ran away, sleeping on a cot by the fire like the lazy drunkard that he was."

"Vines came from the jungle, wrapped around his neck, and strangled him in his sleep." Den cleared his throat. "What were your last thoughts toward him before you left?"

"That he should die," whispered Mariessa, shocked. "That I would have liked to strangle him. But I didn't mean—"

"It's not your fault," Den said. "I'm sure he was a very wicked man, and it was only a thought. For whatever reason, you'd stopped drinking your Denke tea, or built up a resistance, and you had no idea of the consequences."

"How can you know?" Mariessa pulled away from the bars, suddenly afraid. "How do you know about me, about Sando, about the tea? Are you a witch?"

"You have your own spy," said Gabrick, the upmost respect in his voice. "Among the emperor's men—"

"Hush," Den reprimanded. "Not here. Even dungeon walls can have ears."

"Then how can you tell her—"

"Most of the information I've given her is known to half the servants and concubines throughout the palace. The emperor already knows what she is. Peder kil Straun found her by using a seeking stone."

"A green one," added Mariessa.

"He let you see it?" Den asked.

"I don't think he meant to, but I saw him slip it into his pocket. I wondered how he could have found a seeking stone specific to me, but it wasn't, was it? It was a sorceress seeking stone."

"Yes." Den sounded relieved that he'd convinced her. "They seek out others of your kind. The emperor created them by torturing your brothers and sisters, making them wish they had Vasheri-blessed to help them. Then he had them killed and harvested their stones, and set out to annihilate them all."

"But why?"

"He saw their power as a threat, so he eliminated it. At first, through stealth. When the groups were too weakened to effectively threaten him, he started a campaign of disinformation and open capture. Despite that there are still many people throughout Dixho who don't believe his lies. True believers, hidden in secret societies, but most consider one of the blessed to be demon spawn."

"Priest Yosel," Mariessa whispered. "He used to tell me stories when we lived near Keran, things he said couldn't be told in open. He knew." She paused. "Why the tea? Esterelle had me drinking it, too."

Den sighed. "Probably on Han's orders."

"The emperor?"

With heavy sarcasm, Gabrick butted in. "He and Den used to be best of friends."

Den continued as if the boy hadn't said anything. "The tea keeps your powers at bay, at least for a time. Eventually, you would have become immune. An advantage of your young age is that the tea still works. He wants a child with a portion of your skill, but he doesn't want to risk your becoming a threat."

The guards filed back from their work, crowding by Mariessa's cell. She huddled in the corner, doing her best to hide herself with her arms and legs. The men chortled, sitting there, stripping away her dignity with their eyes.

"Go ahead," said Gabrick. "Open the cell door."

Cherda joined his men. After a few minutes, shifting from foot to foot, he finally exploded at Gabrick, "Stop looking at me like that!" He kicked one of the men who sat by the cell. "Outta here! All you rats."

"But we're just looking," the man complained picking himself up, but not bothering to wipe the muck from his hands.

Cherda darted looks at Gabrick. "I'll take you to the camps outside the city next day off. Pay for the river-whores myself, but thatta Number done give me the willigers. We're keeping clear of this end. Ya hears?"

The men grumbled but moved away.

"Did you do that?" Mariessa asked.

"You're welcome," Gabrick said, self-congratulatory.

Mariessa sniffed. That boy needed to be brought down a branch or two. "You sound exactly like your father."

He didn't respond, but Den did. "You need to access your powers."

"How? I never knew they existed before now."

"You lived in a jungle, correct? I'm guessing you spent a lot of time there, that you could hide like no one else, find your way when anyone else would be lost."

It seemed so wrong that he could know so much about her, without even knowing her. "Yes, how does that help?"

"You didn't realize it," Den said. "But you were reaching out to the plants when you did that. That's what you need to do now."

Mariessa laughed. "Look around you. This place is a dead, dark, dungeon."

"Dirt," said Den. "Outside these cell walls, all around us, there are roots. We're far down, but some of the trees surrounding the palace have been here for centuries. Their roots run deep. You have to find them, command them."

"I..." she hesitated, "I don't know if I can."

"Which is why it's best to start now," said Den. "Press your fingers into the dirt under your feet, dig them in as far as they'll go, and concentrate. And whatever you do, don't drink any water they give you. We'll exchange with you so they can't slip in the tea."

Mariessa followed his instructions, cringing at the pain of pushing her bloody finger against the soil, using her good nails to scratch at the hard-packed layers. She plunged her hands through the muck, finding her way to what felt clean, almost healthy—the kind of soil a plant would enjoy.

Xicao grubs tickled her flesh, testing if she was alive or dead, then slipped away. She focused, thought of roots and plants. Deep in her heart, she sent her belief, all of her faith toward her goal. Sweat poured down her face, and she felt nothing. No connection, no power, not anything different. Whatever ability she was supposed to have, it wasn't doing them any good.

30

Han held his nose against the smell as he descended the concrete steps, two of his personal guards ahead—disappearing between the heartstone-lamps then reappearing within their muted light—and two following behind. If they turned on him, he could kill them, but they could provide added defense from the unexpected.

As he reached the bottom step, he tied a kerchief round his nose and mouth, addressing the guard. "Where are they?"

A portly monstrosity of neglected flesh and muscle, the man bowed low, almost touching the filth beneath him with his ruddy face. "Who be you seeking, oh mighty emperor?"

"Who do you expect? Chid Den and the Number who came with him two weeks ago."

"I be keeping them close, Your Honorship. On accounts Master Peder tolda me you be wanting them back."

The brute led him a few cells in, but Den started whistling, leading Han to his location. The guard was sent back to his post. Den sat, leaning against the cell wall away from a corner where cockroaches and flies caroused atop bodily waste. The boy stood at the bars, gripping them as if he'd bend them apart, pure hatred in every shadow of his features.

Han waited while Den finished the short tune, a tavern ditty that had gone out of style many years ago. "I can't believe you remember that," Han said.

Den stared at him with accusing eyes. "I remember everything you taught me. Every single lesson."

Han stiffened. He knew to what Den referred, but Han wasn't going to acknowledge it. They'd been over it before. The only thing left was to teach Den his place, and get him to accept it. The doctor had taken longer to train than he'd liked, but after Han had killed the man's daughter, he'd finally learned to stop asking unnecessary questions and focus on learning the steps to accomplish the transfer.

"I came this morning," said Han, "to let you know the doctor will be ready for the Number in two days."

"You number us so you don't get too attached," said the boy. "So you don't have to think of us as your children, but you can't even call me Fourteen. You treat us like cattle, penning us until the slaughter."

Someone shifted in the cell next to theirs. Han glanced over, surprised to see the former mother, Mariessa, huddled in the gray shadows. She was still naked. His hand twitched against his thigh, but the other rubbed at the raised line around his neck. He'd thought of the girl often, vacillating between a desire to own her and the need to kill her.

"Your name no longer matters," Han said, his gaze glued to the girl. "You will be Fourteen for two days, and then you will be me."

"My name is Gabrick. The name my mother gave me."

Han jerked his head to stare at Den. "You gave the boy a name? Even knowing what he is?"

Den had the audacity to laugh at him. "Before you murdered his mother, she insisted on telling me his name."

"My Numbers don't have names," Han insisted, unable to understand his own irrational fear.

"I'm a person," said the boy. "Why does that scare you?"

"Because" said Den. "If he sees you that way, in his heart he'll have to admit that he's not assuming a vessel that belongs to him, but murdering his own flesh-and-blood son."

"I fear nothing," Han insisted, though his hand stretched again to the lesion at his throat.

Both the boy and Den watched his self-betrayal with mocking smiles.

"Guard!" yelled Han. The portly fellow lumbered to his side.

"When the Number is called for, I want you to tie the girl up and clean her as best you can. I'll send some guards to fetch her." He looked toward Den. "Don't worry, your precious niece will still come first."

"I'll kill you, Han," Den whispered, so softly Han almost didn't catch it.

It was the kind of threat a man spoke without inflection but engraved on his heart. Maybe Han was wrong. Maybe he should dispose of Den now rather than risk him finding such an opportunity. But the idea of continuing life on his own, without a confidant, without anyone who could understand him, was too much to bear. He would make Den see reason. He needed time, and he needed these other people, these distractions, to submit.

"It'll all work out," Han assured him. "You'll see." He turned on his heel and walked away.

At the stairs, the fat guard fiddled with his stained uniform, bowed, and worked up the courage to make a request. "Your most, sir Holiness, sir. May I ask you a question?"

Han restrained the desire to kick the guard in the head. "I grant you one."

The man bowed low, maybe sensing Han's angry impatience. "Is it true, when the Number ascends to be like you, he'll get at the people who done crossed him afore?"

Han barked a short laugh at the absurdity. "When the Number ascends, you'll probably be rewarded for your brutality toward him as long as there's no physical damage."

The stupid guard looked confused.

"Adversity makes a person strong. He'll be grateful for that added strength when he understands his new position as Lingdow. But, his body cannot be harmed, understand? We can't have a crippled emperor."

Han took a slow pace up the stairs, straining to hear what they'd planned for the Number.

The guard called out. "We can have our way witha girl, no matter whatta that boy done says. Just so long we don't—"

The man's voice went lower and Han didn't catch the words. There was no question, that little vixen might fight, but she'd never dare try to kill him. Not after those brutes were done with her.

He smiled, whistling Den's tune as he finished his long trek up the stairs. *Two more days.*

31

Mariessa finally recognized a difference as she stretched her hands farther into the overturned soil she'd scratched at for days, digging in up to her forearms. A light bloomed in Mariessa's consciousness and the answer finally flashed with sudden clarity. Gritty tendrils touched each finger and she smiled. All of her work, sitting in the muck of her cell, kicking away the mice and rats, stretching her fingers into the soil and straining her mind for something that didn't make sense, it had done something.

She could sense the life of every plant beneath that prison—the potential of dormant, buried fruit seeds, the small sprouts searching to live but unable to find sufficient light, and the mass network of roots that she'd called to her, all of them waiting on her command.

The emperor left, and she heard his direction to the guard, to bring her back to him, but it came as if from a distance. Her fingers tingled with exertion, imagining a vine, a branch, a root, anything that might wrap around the emperor's smug face and crush it.

From far away, muffled by the plants' vibrant song, she heard the guard calling his friends, their vulgarity and raucous laughter getting louder as they approached.

"Don't touch her!" Gabrick yelled, but the men ignored him.

A heavy key turned the lock on her cell door.

Mariessa kept her eyes closed, calling out to the plants. They slid along her hands, past her wrists.

She ignored Cherda's touch, still reveling in the calm assurance from the plants. "She no care," he said with some disappointment. "Maybe we need to getta— What is that?" His fingers froze, released her.

One of the other guards moved closer. "I don't see— What in limbo?

Something's attacking her."

Cherda shoved one of the men aside, fumbling with the key to open the locked door. He pushed it open, but it clanged shut in his face. Brown roots wrapped around the iron bars, tying them shut.

Gnarly stems encompassed Mariessa's feet and calves, extending up to her shoulders.

"Let us outta here, witch!" Cherda yelled, his voice laced with anger and terror. He lunged for her throat with both hands. Mud-crusted shoots released her legs, shot up and wrapped themselves around Cherda's wrists.

"No!" he yelled. "Please. Letta me go."

Mariessa's eyes popped open, seeing everything through a hazy light. Cherda's mouth gaped. He fell to his knees. "Please." The same words she'd cried at him two weeks ago.

"I've heard you with other prisoners in these dungeons," Mariessa said, her voice lower than usual, unnaturally smooth like a waxen leaf's caress. "The cries of past victims who've been left here to rot; their heartstones beneath me scream for justice. No. You won't hurt anyone again." She turned her glazed eyes to the other men where they pressed themselves to the cold bars and harsh cement walls, struggling in vain to put distance between her and them. "None of you will make them cry ever again."

The floor erupted with roots, forming a protective cage around Mariessa. Lost in her angry daze, she set them to their task. Thick tubers wrapped round Cherda's arms, pulling in separate directions, their grip as relentless as a plant's persistent journey through Dixho's soil. Cherda screamed, the sound going on and on. The men around him joined in his horror. Some died quickly, a head bashed against the wall, a pointed root plunged through the belly and up through the heart. Others took more time.

A grizzled guard's mouth filled with a slithering root, asphyxiating him even as it pushed its way through his torso, down through his flesh, and returned again to its mother soil. It dragged the man's corpse into an unnatural, shallow grave where xicao awaited, swarming up from unknown depths to enjoy the offered feast.

Cherda died last. The plants must have sensed Mariessa's particular dislike toward him. They pulled him apart, piece by piece, ripping his head from his body as a final act of justice.

When the wails finally subsided the roots rested above, beneath and through the men's remains as still and natural as tree roots twining at the surface near a river. The clang of the cell door swinging lazily open to chime against the opposite bars, pulled Mariessa from her trance. She stared at the blood-drenched furrows. Hungry xicao already riddled the men's flesh, swarming the dead bodies, pulling them into the earth with the tenacity of a slow-opening flower. It would take days, but the bodies would eventually disappear, and even as she willed it, Mariessa knew the roots would take the men's heartstones deep into the earth, where whatever poisonous nature they might unleash upon the world would never be seen.

The smell of blood mixed with fresh urine and excrement along with the layers of filth and death that had sunk deep into the soil over hundreds of years. She hurled into the cell's putrid corner, splashing a dismembered leg with vomit.

"Mariessa?" Den's voice whispered. "Is everything okay?"

"Yes," she choked. "I think so, but I've done something horrible."

"Um," he said. "Not quite yet. But do you think you might let us go, before it gets any more uncomfortable?"

She rushed to the corridor, forgetting the nakedness that had become her natural state over the last weeks. Roots crowded Den and Gabrick's cell, lashing them to the wall like a spider preparing its prey. Horrified, she thought to release them, but nothing happened.

"I don't...don't know how to make them let go," she stammered. "I...I"

"Put your fingers in the dirt, calmly request the roots to retreat," said Den, as calmly as if resting beneath a shady tree. "Release your fear and your anger. Let peace and goodwill take its place."

Mariessa knelt down, scraping her nails against the hard earth. Her missing nail had started to grow back, but for now she had to dig without it. At least it wasn't infected, which it should have been. Maybe her connection with the earth and plants somehow helped.

With some effort, she managed to get her fingers into the dirt and made her request. Ever so slowly the twining shoots retreated from the men, though they remained poised above the upturned soil. "They won't go any farther," she said.

Den cocked his head, a worried frown forming. "That's okay. You did well."

"What kind of a daffing stunt was that?" Gabrick accused. One of the shoots twitched and he pressed himself back against the wall and scowled at her. "So, do your magic and get us out of here."

Mariessa stared at him for a moment, suddenly realizing her condition. She crossed her arms across her chest, and ran for the stairs.

"Hey!" Gabrick yelled. "Where do you think you're going?"

"Hush," said Den. "She'll come back, I think."

Mariessa found one of the small scratchy blankets the guards kept on hand for damp evenings. Wrapping it around her body like a Keroka bestit and tying it fast, she rushed back to Den and Gabrick's cell. "I'm feeling dizzy. I don't think I can make the plants open the door."

"It's probably best you don't," said Den.

"Are you crazy?" Gabrick interrupted. "She has to get us out of here."

"Do you think you're up to carrying her if she passes out?" asked Den.

"So, what do we do?"

"The keys." Den addressed Mariessa. "Can you find them?"

Mariessa shook her head. "I'm not going back in there. You don't know..." She trembled, sickened anew by what she'd done.

"We could hear," said Den. "But you have to get the keys and let Gabrick and me out."

She glanced at the open cell and shook her head. "I'm sorry." She turned toward the stairs. "You'll have to find—"

"You'll never get out of this palace, let alone off the grounds, without my help," Den said. "You want out of here, away from the emperor? Then get the keys and open our door. Otherwise, the emperor wins, and you'll be his pet and slave for the rest of your life. And once he's done with you, he'll hand you to Peder for disposal. It's not a pleasant way to die."

Every word he said was true. Even as she trembled under his gaze, unable to force her body to turn, she knew it. Clenching her teeth, she stared at the ground a moment, turned without raising her eyes, and walked back into her open cell. Her bare feet squelched in the dark mud. She kept the bile down in her empty stomach, searching through the cell until she found what was left of Cherda's body. A flash of metal caught her eye. Reaching down she found a throwing knife, not exactly like her own but close. It had fallen from a fat man's thigh-sheath. With trembling hands she detached the sheath, adjusting it to fit round her waist. Choking down another surge in her stomach, she found his arm sheath, the blade still enclosed, and wrapped it on her thigh, then continued to Cherda.

Attached to his belt, lying on top of a face-down guard, rested the keys. Mariessa disentangled them from their hook, stepped on, over, and around more bodies, and reached Den's cell. It took a while to find the right key, her shaking hands making them jangle loudly, but eventually the bolt turned and the door swung open.

Gabrick immediately headed for the stairs. "If you can't keep up, we're leaving you behind."

"Wrong way, boy," said Den, heading in the opposite direction. "And now isn't the time to play emperor. You need to shut up and do as I say."

"But this is the only way—"

"Did I tell you I lived here my whole life?"

"Yes, but—"

"But nothing. I've planned a dozen ways to escape from this place. The planes are faster, easier, and if it hadn't been for Peder, we'd have made it. Now it's time for plan B. Less comfortable, riskier over the long run, but our best option at the moment. And if you don't keep up, I'm leaving you."

Mariessa hurried after the man. Gabrick followed, still complaining. "We're headed into the mountain. How is that going to help us?"

"The other prisoners?" asked Mariessa.

"No, we're not letting them out," said Den. "They'll slow us down, alert Han that we've left, get themselves killed, and some of them are actual thieves and murderers. There are some psychologically unstable ones in there, too, the kind that would playfully kill a baby. The few innocents among them aren't worth that kind of risk."

Den reached an impregnable rock wall, running his hands across its craggy surface. "You did a good job with the guards, especially for your first effort."

"I brutally murdered them."

"And what were they going to do to you?" Den asked.

She quieted, feeling renewed anger burn at her cheeks.

"Exactly," said Den. "They've done it before and they would have continued. You exacted justice in self-defense. Brutal, because you had little control, but nothing more than they, or I, might have deserved."

She wondered at Den's self-accusation, but a sliver of self-righteous pride replaced the guilt. She forced herself to think of the women she'd potentially saved, but something whispered there were plenty more men to take Cherda's place, and the emperor wouldn't have trouble finding them. They'd violated her in ways worse than Sando had every gotten away with, ways she knew would haunt her for the rest of her life, but she pushed the thoughts and emotions away, the way she'd learned she must in order to survive.

Den slipped his fingers into a tiny crevice above a high protrusion of rock. With a wrench to one side, the whole chunk spun as if turning a dial. A click sounded and tiny cracks appeared, thinner than the other hairline fractures around it. Den shoved the makeshift door and it bounced back, pushing at the dirt by their feet. Together, they strained to raise the slab. The invisible hinges attached at the top of the fissure instead of the sides, squeaked from rust and disuse.

"What is this?" asked Gabrick, helping Den hold the rock as Mariessa crawled inside.

Den let the weight rest against his broad shoulders. "A network of tunnels." He grunted, shifting his stance. A small yellow spider crawled across his arm and he shook it off. "They connect the palace to the outside world. The emperor has his own, but these he doesn't know about."

"Well, let's hurry and get out of here." Gabrick crawled into the tunnel, leaving space for Den.

"After we take care of a few things." Den rushed in and the door slammed shut, encasing them in absolute darkness.

"I'm with Gabrick," said Mariessa. "No supplies. Let's just get away from this place."

From a depression in the rock, Den retrieved a lantern. He used small matches tied to its handle to light a length of cloth sticking up from its base where a lightstone should have been. The strange brightness felt unnatural like the emperor's palace. It reflected off the dead heartstones lining the tunnel walls, kept so long from sunlight that they held no power.

Den raised the lantern, flicking shadows back and forth across his somber face. "I'll not leave Aednat."

"Who's Aednat?" Earlier, Mariessa had heard the name from the emperor, but hadn't caught the entire conversation. "What if the emperor catches us trying to get her out?"

Reaching into his back waistband, Den pulled out a pistol, probably lifted off one of the dead guards. "If he catches us again," he waved the pistol in the air, "I'll make sure he can't use people I care about as leverage."

"No assassin has ever killed the emperor," said Mariessa, surprised Den would boast after being stuck in that dungeon. "What makes you think you'll be different."

"I know I can't kill him. He's faster with a gun and every man who guards him is thoroughly brainwashed to give their lives in his defense. No, the gun isn't for him."

"Then what?"

"It's for us."

32

Had it only been two weeks since Gabrick had paced in the exact same cavern, as cocky and unconcerned as a child in the play yard?

After traveling underground from one side of the palace to the other, they'd squeezed through a fissure Gabrick had never seen before, despite his many searches through the cave behind the waterfall. Its crashing thunder reverberated up through the lake, sounding through the hole that led to the concubine's garden and echoing up and against the walls from the ledge that emptied into the river on the Numbers side. Numbers CompoundHe stared at the hole in the rock, his eyes drawn upward to the high ceilings, the lantern reflecting off heartstones in and between stalactites, set like promising gems.

"How do the heartstones get into solid rock?" Gabrick asked. "I thought they descended through dirt toward the Vasheri."

"Vasheri?" Den laughed. "No such thing."

"How and why they go in certain directions is still under study. When you place two heartstones next to one another, what do they do?"

Gabrick blushed at his childhood ignorance of believing in the emperor-created religion. He hoped Den couldn't see. "According to the lying priests who believe my father is divine, they lean into one another, the remnant of the spirits within seeking to commune."

"That's religious supposition. Some element in the heartstones draws them to one another like metal is drawn to a magnet. Little by little, they can travel through wood, or even rock. They leave behind a residue that fills in the gap, so their pathway doesn't compromise the material."

"But you don't know how it's done, or what draws them together?" said Mariessa.

Den shook his head. "No, we haven't figured that out."

She crossed her arms as if to challenge the teacher. "Science doesn't explain everything. Just because priests have been corrupted by that filthy man who calls himself a Lingdow, doesn't mean true Vasheri don't exist."

"Humph." Den muttered next to Gabrick, low enough Mariessa probably didn't hear. "The mind of a simple peasant."

Gabrick moved farther into the room, recognizing the stalactite he had to avoid when he'd come to visit the concubines. It didn't comfort him to see the dark space illuminated. It was larger than he would have thought, and their shadows cast eerie images against the walls and across a swarm of bats hiding amidst the formations stretching from the ceiling.

"You know how to reach her without being seen?" Den asked for the hundredth time.

"I've done this before." Gabrick insisted, slipping out through what he'd always thought was a private hole, never before discovered. But Den had known about it all along. The man knew his way through this mountain with the uncanny certainty of someone who'd spent a lifetime there. And he practically had. If he'd known about them as a child, living in the palace, he'd probably spent many hours and days exploring them.

As Gabrick left the muddy bank and headed toward his first tree, he realized two things. One, he had someone following him. And two, that a fence had been erected from the side of the mountain to the river grate, separating the concubines from much of their river, and from him.

He jerked his head to one side, barely making out the small girl hiding in the thick foliage near the mountain's edge, the water coming up to her knees.

Gabrick put up a hand, indicating for her to stop and stay there. She shook her head in the negative. The little brat! But there was nothing he could do to stop her that wouldn't give him away. He followed the fence, made of brick and mortar, back toward the mountain, hoping for a weak spot. He found it where the wall should have met rock. The builders had neglected to route a small tree, its trunk having broken a space big enough Gabrick could easily fit through.

Staying in the cover of trees and bushes, he made his way to his favorite shrub, where Esterelle lay as usual, surrounded by concubines and a scantily-clothed Aednat. She was probably even more beautiful than Esterelle, and Gabrick felt a wicked desire at seeing so much of her, but more than anything, he wanted to cover her in a robe and get her as far from this place as possible. But this wasn't like before. Peder kil Straun stood watch with the ECRO guards. Plus, Aednat was surrounded by concubines who'd ignored or flirted with Gabrick before, but they wouldn't dare do so now. And the emperor's balcony door was open. He could appear at any moment.

A rustle sounded in the bushes at the far end of the garden.

"Look!" exclaimed one of the women, pointing. "It's one of the rabbits. Oh, and she's had babies," the woman squealed.

All of the women rushed over to fawn over the docile balls of fuzz. Aednat moved to follow, but Gabrick hissed, "Wait. Stay there."

"You came!" Aednat cried, eyes filling with tears. The guards, Peder included, pinned their eyes on her. She turned her head to look for him, but Gabrick had pulled far back, behind the bush.

Esterelle patted her arm as if consoling Aednat. Craning her head to the side in a natural stretch, a greenish bruise marked her cheek and chin, a small gash healing along the jawline.

Gabrick gasped. "What happened?"

"Hush, to the both of you," she whispered "Do you want Fourteen dragged back into the dungeon?" Sipping at one of the fruit drinks on their small table, she spoke in an aside. "You can't take her, loddie-boy. If you do, the emperor will kill me."

"Go over to the rabbits with the others," said Gabrick. "He won't be able to blame you."

"I'm what makes your little hiding place work. I get up from my seat, and the guards will see her slipping away through the bush. I can't help you."

"Gabrick," he said. "My name is Gabrick. I won't be called a Number ever again."

Esterelle gasped, choking on the drink. The guards took no particular notice and Peder, apparently bored, went into the palace. "Where did you hear such a name?"

"Den said my mother told it to him before she died."

"Your mother?" Esterelle asked. "Are you sure?"

"She got the name from someone else, but yes, I'm sure."

Esterelle leaned over, coughing as if from the inhaled drink, but also staring at Gabrick as if seeing him for the first time. "It can't be possible," she muttered to herself. "Beht Han's spitting image, but maybe...." She came to a decision, resting her back into the chair. "Aednat, when the guards stop watching us, slip from your chair, and through the bush with..." She took a deep breath. "...with Gabrick."

"Thank you, Esterelle," Gabrick said. "I know the emperor will make you pay for this. I'm sorry."

"It'll be better this way, at the end of it all."

They waited. The guards watched and the other women were growing bored with the rabbits. A bush on the far side of the compound rippled, a sure indication that someone hid within.

Oh, no, thought Gabrick. *What has that stupid girl done now?*

If Mariessa got herself caught, it would be her own fault. Gabrick wasn't going back for her.

The guards rushed to investigate, giving Gabrick his needed opportunity. He grabbed Aednat by the arm. The table tipped as she scrambled from her seat, but Esterelle adeptly caught it, keeping it and the glasses upright. She took another sip of her fruit drink, closing her eyes with enjoyment as Aednat crunched through the branches and behind the short hedge, tears streaming down her cheeks, eyes wide with fear, but smart enough to stay quiet.

With a grip on Aednat's hand, Gabrick pulled her to the tree, but it wouldn't hide both of them. They had to make a run for it. Gabrick cut a direct path for the fissure between wall and mountain, onto the muddy beach, then to the foliage near the cave entrance. As they reached the last couple of lengths before the opening, he saw the emperor return to the balcony, giving it one last scan. Gabrick's father should have seen them darting under cover, but no one even raised their voice, let alone shouted an alarm.

Gabrick waited a few minutes, keeping low. Something flitted in the water to their left then disappeared; probably a harmless water dragon. After Gabrick was sure they were alone, he led Aednat through the hole and into the cave. She had some trouble fitting through the narrow space, but slipping through the mud had greased her body enough she finally managed. And just in time. Peder showed up, scanning the gardens with a reddening face and a clenched fist.

Gabrick landed next to Aednat. Den had already pulled her into an embrace, holding her in the fervent grip of a family reunited. Even knowing Den was her uncle, or something like it, Gabrick still wanted his hands off.

Gabrick stepped toward the lake, almost tripping over Mariessa, lying on the rock floor, unconscious. "What happened to her? She get scared to death or something?"

Den shook his head at the girl's prone body. "Saving you pushed her too far. She passed out soon after she climbed inside."

"Saving me?"

Den barked a laugh. "You think the hole in the wall happened because of a lazy worker? Or that rabbit family came out of their nest without a plant startling them, or some ghost walked through the bushes to distract the guards at just the right time?"

"And she blocked us from the emperor's view, didn't she?"

Den nodded. "It wasn't a nonexistent wind that made that bunton tree lean to the side at exactly the right moment. With her already exhausted from the ordeal in the dungeon, I'm impressed she made it back into the cave."

Gabrick stared at the girl with new eyes. He'd already experienced her sharp tongue, waiting to strike out like a Hozu with its bristling spines. Yet lying there, she seemed so vulnerable. Her delicate features and slight build hid an intimidating amount of strength and determination.

"Can you carry her?" Den asked.

Gabrick took a step back. "Me?"

"I need to focus if we're to hurry," said Den. "And I should have my hands free in case anyone surprises us in the tunnels."

Gabrick joined Aednat where she'd gone to the cave's shallow lake, both of them trying to rinse the mud from their bodies. "How could anyone possibly know where to look for us? You said none of the guards or soldiers even know the tunnels exist."

"But Han does, and if he was looking for Aednat in the garden, it won't take long for him to figure out that she's disappeared. We have one more stop, and we must hurry."

"Shouldn't we get away from the palace now?" Gabrick said, but he stepped from the lake and scooped up Mariessa. Despite her firm musculature, she was extremely light. If not for her figure, Gabrick could imagine he carried a child.

Den took Aednat by the hand, her other arm crossed over the breasts Gabrick kept averting his eyes from. In single file, they hurried toward the tunnels Gabrick had never found.

"If I don't get what I need in my rooms," said Den. "It won't matter whether we escape or not. We'll never make it out the front gates."

33

The first whisper Han had of disaster niggled at his mind when he noticed Esterelle and the other concubines lounging in the gardens with Den's girl nowhere to be seen. She'd been there ten minutes ago. Perhaps she was sulking in their rooms again. No matter. He had an observation window there, too.

He took his time going down the stairs, unlocked the door, and stepped into a plain room dominated by a one-way mirror. Han stepped around the only furniture, a single lounge chair, and scanned the empty sleeping room. As he did, his temper rose. He fumbled in his robes for the right communication stone.

"Peder," he called. "Where is the new girl, the Number-slave?"

"Aednat?" The tap of quickening steps echoed through the stone. "Last I saw, only a few minutes ago, she relaxed in the garden." A door creaked on its hinges. A pause. "Schisse! She's not being there. I will find her, your Excellency. Do you want her in your pleasure chamber?"

"No," Han left the room, slamming the door behind him. "I need you to check the dungeons."

The sound of a closing door, then Peder's quick steps against the tiles as he retraced his steps. "Were you not just there, Your Highness? Would it not be better to have Bow Quing check the dungeons?" A muffled demand to the Eunuchs filtered in as background noise. Peder must be entering the main palace. "Should I not be finding the girl?"

Han would have reprimanded the man for questioning him, but he was obviously following his orders. "I have another task for Quing. Report to me as soon as you reach the dungeon."

"Yes, Your Excellency."

Taking the stairs leading to the royal suites two at a time, Han pulled a communication stone from another pocket.

"Yes, Holy Emperor?" Quing's voice sounded mocking. Han would deal with that later.

"Meet me in Chid Den's royal suite."

"I wasn't aware he'd been released from the dungeon, Esteemed One." At least the man sounded surprised, suggesting he hadn't assisted an escape.

"You have five minutes," said Han.

"Yes, Your Highness."

Han reached the room ahead of Quing, as he knew he would. A thin layer of dust had settled in Den's quarters while he and the Number sat in their filthy dungeon cell. Han studied the huge bed, the floor, the dresser...there. The topmost drawer was ajar, a thin edge of underclothing wedging it open. Han crossed the room, rifled through Den's old clothes, but he found nothing.

Quing entered. "Your Majesty?" He bowed low, all respect now that Han could see him.

"Come here," Han commanded, opening wide an elaborately carved Erolethan wardrobe made of red berkan wood. The few articles of clothing—remnants belonging to a young man from another decade—had been pushed to either side, suggesting Den had come and gone. "I need you to see what's on the other side of this cabinet."

"Sir?" questioned Quing, taking a step back. "A wall is on the other side."

Han beckoned. "Now! If they've gone through, we don't have much time."

Quing dutifully came forward, but his expression proved he thought his liege truly insane. He stepped into the over-large cabinet and tapped his knuckles against the wood paneling at the back. Nothing happened. Han sighed with relief. The paneling wasn't rigged in any way.

"Move the panel aside," Han instructed Quing. "You can get your fingers around the narrow edge on each side, lift up, and out."

Quing followed his directions, easily removing the thin wood that didn't quite match the rest of the cabinet. He pointed to the cream-colored surface. "It's the wall."

Han smirked, stepping to one side. "Very carefully, punch your hand through it."

"But, Your Highness—"

"Do it!" Han was losing patience with Quing, but he'd rather place his assassin in harm's way than himself.

Quing punched out a tentative fist. The moment it ripped through the camouflaged rice-paper, a trigger snapped and the twang of a bow-string echoed from the interior darkness. Quing jumped back. An assassin's reflexes are hard to surpass, but the trap caught Quing by surprise. Catching in the flesh at his waist, the spearhead's jagged edge ripped through skin and muscle. The bloody arrow sunk into the mattress across the room. Quing clutched at his side, staggering back and tripping through the wardrobe doors, onto the floor. He stared at Han in shock.

"You knew," he accused.

Han reached into his pocket and retrieved a brown stone with elongated striations of greasy, translucent green—an external healing rock. He tossed it in Quing's lap. "I suspected."

"You could have said something," Quing muttered, tearing a strip of cloth from his hyefu so he could tie the rock to his wound.

Han didn't respond. It was his own business if he decided to test his subjects' loyalty on occasion. Quing's surprise proved with finality that he wasn't involved with Den's escape, this time or the last. Han had needed to be sure before he trusted the assassin any further. He pulled a heartstone from his pocket, the pale light illuminating a crude passage tall enough for a man. Two dust-covered panels, sporting gaping holes, leaned on the other side of the passage, along with one devoid of dust, recently used.

Quing came to his knees, wincing, the stone tied over the wound. "It's slowed the bleeding, but I'll still need to get this cleaned and bandaged."

"Later," said Han. "Den is in there. You must find him."

Quing laughed, peering down the dark corridor. He held out both arms. "Shoot me now and save me the suspense."

Han frowned, tempted to give in to the man's request. "You're an imperial assassin."

"Yes, and that's Chid Den, and probably his Number, Fourteen. The boy I could take with my eyes closed. And I might stand a chance against Chid Den, if I caught him by surprise. But both of them, it's a death sentence."

"I'll send Tey-Ran Kep with you."

Quing held his arms out farther. "I've stopped him from putting a knife in my back three times in the last two months. Again, shoot me now if that's your wish."

A communication stone rattled in Han's pocket, sending strange warmth through the cloth and onto his skin. He pulled it out. "Report."

Peder's clear voice sounded as if the man stood next to them. "I don't know how, Your Eminence, but the Keroka girl has her powers. She's murdered the guards, and she, Den and the Number are gone from their cells, but there's no evidence they left the dungeon. The stairwell door was locked and the outside guard is still on duty when I arrived. It's as if they disappeared into the soil itself."

Han's eyes went wide. "He has tunnels I don't know about."

"And you're trying to send me in there alone?" asked Quing. "Against a plant sorceress?"

"I want you to do a job for me, Peder" Han said into the stone.

"Anything, Your Holiness."

Han smiled. Peder would walk through fire for his Lingdow. "I'm going to assign some of the best Perimeter Guard to you, but Peder, after the mission is finished, you'll need to kill the survivors. The only ones who can come back are you, Bow Quing, and Chid Den. Everyone else must die. Do you understand?"

"All that you wish, Your Highness." He paused. "But may I suggest twenty? It is hard being sure, but I believe the witch has already killed ten with little effort."

Han paused. He couldn't let such a woman live, not with such power, or such an excuse for vengeance. "Thirty soldiers," said Han. "But they cannot return. No one but you, Quing, and I can know about those tunnels. Be in Den's bedchamber in ten minutes."

34

"That was close," Gabrick whispered, out of breath from carrying Mariessa. The girl didn't seem quite so light anymore. The last two hours spent twining from Den's old rooms deeper into the mountain, felt like two days. "I hope your little toys are worth it."

Den didn't respond, but continued to hurry them along. While in his old bedchamber, Den had also grabbed three satchels of supplies: two hidden in the tunnel along with another fire-lantern, and one he threw together from items in his room. The leather straps on the strange bags rested over the shoulders, making it easier to carry and still keep hold of Mariessa, but the stiff edges bit into Gabrick's skin. The supplies hadn't seemed near as important to Den as the small bag of items he'd dropped in the front pocket of his trousers. Gabrick wanted to question him on it, but he already regretted wasting breath on his earlier comment.

Aednat, now dressed in clothing she'd found inside the room, loose breeches and a shirt that strained against her chest, put her hand to one of the reflected heartstones lining the walls. It dropped into her palm, offering no actual light, but cradling it seemed to give her comfort. She wouldn't talk much about what had happened during her captivity, only that the experience was horrible and she wouldn't have survived if not for Esterelle.

She continued trying to coerce Den as she'd done almost nonstop since they'd left the cavern. "Couldn't we hide in the city for a time, until Eleven regains his strength, then we could bring him with us?"

Den shook his head. "I'm sorry. I know you care for the boy, but Han will search this city with every soldier he has, and he'll be waiting for us to try something like that."

"But we can't leave him!"

"Shh!" Gabrick hushed her, taking a quick glance behind.

"Once he's healed," Den whispered, "and the emperor doesn't expect a rescue, I have someone who will help him escape. I'm sorry, butterflower, but that's the best we can do."

Gabrick hadn't heard Den use Aednat's nickname in years. It seemed strange now, like the past was colliding with the present, making Gabrick's world unreliable.

A distant rumble echoed down the corridor behind them.

"Are we close?" Gabrick asked.

"Yes," said Den. "But not close enough." They jogged a few minutes more, and the tunnel diverged three ways. "I think I know someplace they won't find us, and it's defensible."

They took the right-most arm, followed by a sudden left that Gabrick wouldn't have seen without the lamplight, then they reached a crevice in the rock. It appeared to be just another fissure, a dark crack going nowhere like the one to the waterfall-cave, but Den directed them to follow him through. Gabrick handed Mariessa through to Den, who dragged her across the rough floor.

Halfway in she started flailing, almost kicking Gabrick in the chin and scraping her legs. "What in—?"

"Shh," hushed Den and Gabrick together.

She stilled, at least having the good sense to realize they might be in a dangerous situation. "What happened?" she whispered. "Where are you dragging me?"

"To safety," said Den.

"We hope," added Gabrick.

On the other side, Gabrick heard her scramble to her feet. He followed her through, surprised to find an open cavern about the size of his apartment. A shelf ran along one side at chest level, wide enough to be a deep bench or a narrow table. The roof extended another two people's height above the lip, at least two and a half lengths, a smattering of stalactites dotting the ceiling, their counterparts littering the floor. The room smelled particularly damp and musty, but other than the formations, there was no evidence of water; not like other places where trickling streams had passed, or stalactites had dropped tears.

Den hoisted Aednat onto the ledge then followed, giving them a height advantage. "They'll have to come in one at a time," he said.

"That would be great if we had more than one gun," said Gabrick, "but I don't want to stand here and try knifing them."

Den pulled an extra pistol from the back of his pants, a package of bullets from his pocket. He handed it to Aednat, whose eyes went wide. "I can't."

"You're a decent shot," said Den. "I've taught you well, and you have to do this. If not for your life, for the lives of the people here that depend on you."

And that would be enough for Aednat. Gabrick saw it in her eyes. That experience among the concubines, preparing to become one of the emperor's mothers, had changed her. She'd hate it, probably fall apart afterward, but she'd shoot if she had to.

"Great for you," said Gabrick. "But they'll have more. It sounded like a lot of soldiers back there." He looked to Mariessa. "Could you kill them before they reach us?"

She shuddered with revulsion and Gabrick was about to lay into her, but Den backed her up. "It's one thing to get plants up through hard soil, but we're surrounded by solid rock. It would take a skilled sorceress weeks of consistent effort to get a single sprout to rise up."

"So we're doomed," said Gabrick.

Den scowled, the lantern shadows making the expression ominous. "We still have a chance. Remember, the fight's not over until you give up."

"Or you're dead," muttered Gabrick, but he took a position a few arms from the entrance, next to one of the larger stalagmites, about thigh height. It was out of the likely trajectory from friendly fire, but close enough to step in when the bullets ran out. The sound of soldiers' feet came closer. It wouldn't be long now.

Mariessa came to his side. She reached inside her strangely wrapped blanket, retrieving a small knife. "You might need this, emperor-boy."

"It's a throwing blade," said Gabrick.

"In hand-to-hand combat, a knife is a knife."

"Not exactly," Gabrick contradicted. "Thank you, but I'll wait until I can snag one of the soldiers' rifles."

"It'll be your death and Shangsan, though I doubt xicao will make it up through this rock to turn our hearts to lightstones."

She re-sheathed the knife, staying by his side. The soldiers' footsteps sounded down the corridor next to them, hit a dead end, and then passed the way they'd come. Gabrick exhaled his relief. Maybe Den's hiding place would work after all.

As the soldiers went in the other direction, Aednat set her gun on the shelf's edge. "Do you think we'll have to wait long before we can get out of here?"

Den relaxed his stance. "At least ten minutes. They'll be in another section of caves then and I'll have time to get us to the mountain's north face, near the east side of the city."

She nodded, studying the rock above them where one area was particularly riddled with a number of useless lightstones. She reached above her head. "This is unusual. Have you ever seen one so beautiful?"

Den jumped to intercept. "Aednat, no."

It was too late. Her fingers touched the stone, exceptional for its discontinuous layers of deep black and brilliant white, punctuated by a few red striations like a thin string of blood. The stone fell from the wall and into her hands. A woman's voice, old but confident, boomed through the cavern.

"From a lonely god, the boy will come.

"The son of none, yet fathered by many, a replica of his enemy.

"The legions beneath the earth gather to his standard, though they despise his unholy visage.

"They will call him—"

Ripping his hyefu off, tearing the snaps, Den wrapped it around the stone, muffling the words. He stuffed the whole thing in Aednat's knapsack. The words continued, but as if someone held a pillow over the speaker's face, muffling and softening the words. The rustle of feet on stone returned. The soldiers had heard.

35

Mariessa pulled her knife again, knowing without doubt that they'd be in for a fight. The time for hiding was over.

Like an imbecile, Gabrick stared at her. "You have any clue how to use those?" he asked.

"Of course I do."

The soldiers milled around the crevice, talking in low voices.

"Are you accurate?" Gabrick whispered.

Mariessa thought of her near-misses in the jungle, her hesitation at taking a life. Yes, she'd killed the dungeon guards, but inadvertently, not by her own hand. But then she thought of the life her hesitation had cost, of Dangan bleeding into the jungle soil.

"They're a little larger than I'm used to, but yes, I can hit any mark within range."

Gabrick pointed her back onto the rock shelf, where Aednat had taken position next to Den. "When the bullets run out, throw your blades."

Mariessa shook her head. "I appreciate you trying to keep me safe, but a couple of throws and then I'm useless. I can help better from here."

"I don't like you well enough to care if you're safe," said Gabrick like a slap to the face. "You'll get in my way here. If you're needed, I'll toss the knives back to you."

"While you fight?" she scoffed. "You think you're that good?"

His return stare was confident. "Against a common soldier? Yes."

"You're so high-stilted," she said.

She had no patience for the boy's conceit, but she went to the shelf where Aednat took her stand next to Den. Let Gabrick get himself killed. What did she care?

As she struggled to hoist herself up, most of her strength sapped by the day's events, the first soldier slipped into the room. Den felled him with a bullet to the forehead. He slumped half in and half out of the hole, his rifle wedged between his body and the wall. Three more soldiers fell that way, each shoving the dead one farther into the room. Someone yelled for them to get back.

The next soldier sent his rifle in first. Stretching it into the room with one hand, a barrage of bullets arced from one side of the cave to the other. As the bullets ranged, they rose. With new impetus, Mariessa dragged herself farther up the shelf. Gunfire sent flakes of shattered rock cutting into her lower legs. Gabrick ducked behind his stalagmite, its top shattering over his hair. The soldier reloaded and prepared to come back the other way.

Den shot. Missed. A bullet nicked the wall next to his ear, ricocheting past Mariessa's shoulder. She dropped back down to the floor. Den's second shot hit its mark. The soldier screamed, dropped his bloodied rifle, and pulled a bullet-shattered hand to his chest.

In the same moment, someone shoved the wounded soldier over his comrade, into the room. Den shot the falling man through the heart. All went silent. Gabrick ran forward, snatching one of the dead soldier's rifles then returning to cover.

"Back!" Den yelled out, running for the darkness in the cave's deepest recesses. He grabbed Aednat, jumping off the shelf then leading her by the hand.

With a quick glance at the dead soldiers, Gabrick followed after Den, toward the fading lamplight at the back of the cave. He only took a couple of steps when he stopped to stare at Mariessa. She knew she should listen to Den, that he must have some reason for what he said, but they needed to defend that hole.

Before she could realize his intention, Gabrick dropped his rifle, arms wrapping around her torso like a child grabbing a bundle of sticks. He followed Den, running for the back of the cave. A deafening explosion reverberated in the enclosed space like the roar of a hundred dragons. The concussion knocked them to the ground, propelling them toward the wall. Cave formations—stalactites, stalagmites, soda straws and full columns— ruptured from the pressure. Debris rained in the form of pebbles and rough-edged shards.

She and Gabrick huddled together, an arm from the back wall, a broken stalagmite under Mariessa's side, another pressed against her back. Thick clouds smelling of dust, sulfur, and gunpowder started to settle. A number of approaching lightstones grew brighter as minute particles of grit descended to the cave floor like a spring drizzle. As the air cleared, the stones came closer. Through the haze, Mariessa counted nearly twenty-five soldiers. She recognized Bow Quing, the assassin, and Peder kil Straun. All of them held guns at the ready. This was it. Their defense had become an inescapable trap.

Even knowing the real reason Den had brought the gun, Mariessa was still shocked when he held it to Aednat's head. "You're not taking them back there. I'll kill them first."

Peder replied, obviously in charge. "Go ahead, Chid Den. It will save me the trouble."

Tears running down her dirt-encrusted cheeks, Aednat nodded. Den's finger tightened on the trigger.

Mariessa scooted forward. She couldn't help herself. The idea of the girl's blood splattering across her face was too much. Her hand scraped across the hole left by the razed stalagmite, cutting her palm as it fell into the shallow well. To her surprise, a thin crust cracked beneath her weight. Underneath, her fingers found soil, surprisingly soft, bordering on thick mud. There wasn't much in the way of plant life there, and she didn't have time to gather more than what was directly beneath them, but it might be enough.

Digging her fingers into the mud, she shook her head. "Den, don't do it. There's another way."

"No," Den insisted. "I won't let—"

The first of the roots shot up like geysers, sprouting from myriad holes left devoid of their sentinel appendages. She asked the plants for protection while also sending a message to kill the attacking men coming toward them. She fought to retain control this time like she had in the concubine garden, but the haze that had clouded and protected her mind in the dungeons vied for dominance. She didn't dare let it win. Without her control, everyone in the room might be killed, including Gabrick and Den, maybe even Aednat.

Bullets drilled into the tubers as they formed a protective cage around them. The painful destruction enraged the newly-awakened sentience in the trees and bushes. Mariessa's anger merged with theirs, making the flame grow. Roots pressed upward at the rock floor's thinnest points. She joined in their struggle to break through and fight. A thick root wriggled close and suddenly, soil crumbled beneath Mariessa's hand, landing in rushing water—an underground stream. It nurtured a dense root system, much more than she would have expected. With a loud series of resounding cracks, a trench opened up, bisecting the cave. Plant roots exploded from the easy opening, reaching for men like angry tentacles.

The rock beneath Mariessa's body collapsed. She fell, managing to keep hold of her connection, but losing her focus, her mind drawn into the comforting haze. A painful grip on her wrist jerked her upright, before she could fall in. Gabrick struggled, but managed to catch hold of her under both arms.

"Mari—!" he yelled, but was cut off.

Legs dangling in the water, her hands scrambled for contact with the ever-changing soil. But Gabrick just lay there, holding her over the edge. She looked up. Face pale from lack of oxygen, tubers wrapped around Gabrick's torso and neck. Shocked, Mariessa forced herself to regain control, differentiating in her mind between the soldiers and the men in her group. The roots released their hold on Gabrick and Den, but now Mariessa experienced the attacks on the soldiers as if her hands reached down men's throats, suffocating, plunging into their beating hearts, and ripping them limb from limb. She cried out in horror, wishing to die rather than commit such atrocities, but then her friends would die, and what the emperor would do to her and Aednat would be worse. So she kept on, joining in the plants' carnage.

But it wasn't all one-sided. Bullets discharged, exploding roots like an axe chipping at wood. Mariessa shared in the plants' sudden flashes of pain. The steady slash of a machete, like the ticking of a clock, made her twitch.

Gabrick pulled Mariessa up from the water, but she couldn't let her fingers leave the soil. They scraped along the surface, her connection diminishing.

"The soldiers are getting around!" Gabrick yelled at her. "The plants aren't reaching far enough!"

"I need my fingers in the dirt!"

Gabrick twisted her, making her head, shoulder, and one arm dangle over the edge. He sat on her legs near the drop-off as a counterbalance.

Mariessa dug her hand into rising water and into the gooey muck that had once been the river's shore. She didn't need to see the soldiers. Through her connection with the plants, she sensed their location.

A handful of men, no more than five, had evaded the roots by running to the far side of the cavern. Constrained by their origins near the river, strings of brown lashed back and forth, unable to reach. Once the men crept far enough along that wall, they'd be in range to put a bullet through Gabrick and the others.

Mariessa sifted through the plants' newfound consciousness. Most of them were bushes or small trees, but one...one surpassed them all.

Outside the mountain, on a deep ridge with plenty of sunlight, it longed for her request. Mariessa worried the beautiful tree might not survive, but she expressed their need, trying to somehow channel her vision of the soldiers into the tree's simple and new understanding of events. Like a grind within her chest, Mariessa felt the roots yank through soil, gripping rock and other trees in order to pull itself to the very edge of the cave's mouth, on the brink of the small waterfall struggling to escape the mountain and its disruptive debris.

A bullet ricocheted off a root protecting Mariessa's head. Pain lanced across her cheek, the bullet burning skin. Another one discharged. Gabrick yelled, clenching his arm. The fabric blossomed red beneath his fingers.

Mariessa's anger spiked. The mother-tree pressed its trunk into the river, clogging its exit. The water around Mariessa's wrist rose, making its way toward her elbow. So much closer, the tree's roots stretched farther through the soil. Selecting its longest branch, Mariessa encouraged it through the narrow water passage, extraneous limbs breaking as it plunged its golden near-autumn plumage against the river's current to rise in front of Mariessa's face. It stretched and bent. Unable to reach the soldiers, it formed a semi-circle around Mariessa and her companions. With the trunk so much closer to the cavern, its roots took care of the rest, lashing the evading men to the floor by their necks. They gurgled, thrashing against the hard rock as they died. Mariessa sobbed, slumping against the damp soil, the water pulling at the ends of her short hair. The trees and roots started to retreat.

Still, a machete whistled and tore, making Mariessa flinch, but she couldn't catch a sense of the man, only his sharp blade. She raised her head, resting it on the cavern floor. Peder kil Straun appeared amid the wreckage.

"How?" Mariessa gasped. If anyone should have died a more painful death, it should have been Peder. The plants had to have sensed her particular hatred for the man.

"He gave you the protection stone." Den said it as a statement, not a question.

Peder merely raised an eyebrow, raising his pistol to aim at Mariessa's skull. The tree branch surrounding them quivered, but didn't move, unable to attack the man holding the stone.

Mariessa slipped a knife from the sheath on her leg. Even lying down, she could still throw.

The man's mocking laughter, familiar from the last few weeks, echoed in the room. His finger rested on the trigger, his aim sure. "You think you can hit me with a knife before I am making your brains scatter?"

From behind a remaining mass of roots, a man's hand jutted out. The butt of a gun struck the back of Peder's head then clattered across the stone floor.

Peder's eyes rolled up and he collapsed.

Mariessa sent the roots into full retreat, too exhausted to hold them any longer. The limb protecting them ran along the length of Mariessa's body as it pulled away, a devoted pet rubbing against its master. In a rush, the water level sank, the river suddenly draining like a basket pierced with a sharp stick. Her sense of the tree disappeared as it tumbled from its mountain ledge, taking debris and rocks with it. Mariessa mourned its loss, thanking it for its sacrifice. The plants slipped back into their normal state of simple existence, free from the burden of understanding the world around them. Her sight blurred toward blackness as she tumbled forward, toward the rushing stream.

Water splashed in her face. She gasped, her eyes opening with a start. Somehow she was lying face-up on the rock.

Gabrick's stern scowl stared down at her. "I know you're tired, but you can't pass out, not now."

"Emp-boy?" She shook her head and sat up. "How long was I asleep?"

"Only a few minutes," said Den. He pointed to the wide rock-strewn hole the soldiers had blown from the cave entrance. "We'd best hurry."

"Are there more?" asked Mariessa.

"Somebody dragged Peder out of here while our backs were turned," said Den. "My guess is the assassin, Quing. There will be more men on our tail in less than half an hour.

"Who saved us?" Mariessa asked, looking from Gabrick to Den.

Gabrick shrugged, and a small voice in her mind reminded her he had. Not from Peder, but from the explosion, and from falling into the river. The boy didn't even know her, and he'd risked his life. She could think of no good reason why.

She scanned the carnage in the room, plant and human, then turned back to the river and vomited. Holding her head in her hands, she rested it on her knees. "What have I done? What have I let myself become?"

With his good arm, Gabrick gripped her shoulder. She noted that they'd already bandaged the other one. "If you hadn't acted quickly, if you hadn't used the plants, we'd all be dead or on our way back to Han City. You saved our lives."

"But I massacred them all. I'm a witch. I'm evil!"

"Pah!" said Den. "There is no such thing as good and evil. Your ridiculous religious notions--"

"Please," interrupted Aednat. "*She* believes in the Vasheri and *she* believes in good and evil. I don't think you're helping."

Gabrick's hand gripped harder. "Look, you saved us from people trying to kill us. That's not evil. It's survival."

She brushed off his hand. "I don't care." She thought of the five soldiers, jerking in their last throes of death. "It was wrong and I don't want to use it ever again."

"You're right about one thing," said Den. "You have a right to choose your own path."

Gabrick came to his feet. "But—"

"We'll get well away from the city. Then, Mariessa, I'll give you some money and directions for how to get home to Kerokos. You can go your own way, never use your power again if that's what you want."

She nodded

"Now," said Den. "No more time for talk. Let's go."

Aednat hoisted her pack over one shoulder.

"Get rid of the stone," ordered Gabrick. "It's heavy and that stupid thing gave us away.

Mariessa rose, a little unsteady, but she shook a finger in the emp-boy's pompous face. "Don't tell her what to do."

Den gently pushed them apart, but spoke to Aednat. "It's a useless stone, but Han wants it badly. And anything he wants, is something he shouldn't have. Go ahead and keep it, Aednat, but make sure it doesn't come out of that bag."

Mariessa gave Gabrick a smug smile, resisting the impulse to stick out her tongue. The high-stilted brat deserved a swat across his backside.

They started out again, moving slower than before, all of them exhausted but knowing the end was far from over. Mariessa leaned against the cavern walls as she stumbled forward. How much longer could they keep going? Her vision swam, and as much as she hated it, she had to reach out to Gabrick more than once to keep the blackness from reclaiming her. This time, a little splash of water wouldn't bring her back.

They turned a corner, slid through a thin crevice into another cave, and Mariessa saw an opening, greenery spilling in at the edges, reflecting natural sunlight.

36

Han wrung his hands, his silken slippers padding back and forth in front of his desk. Quing and Peder had sent their message that they'd found Den nearly twenty minutes ago. What was taking them so long? He fingered the hilt of one of his knives, part of him wishing to go into the caves himself, but it wasn't worth the risk, and if Den wanted to go on the offensive, the tunnels could be rigged with all kinds of traps.

A knock sounded, faint but unmistakable. His personal guard wouldn't allow anyone to request entrance without Han's approval. Unless, Den had come back into the palace and killed his personal guard.

The door began to open. Han's grip on his knife tightened. Quing staggered in, dragging Peder's massive bulk along with him. What remained of Quing's clothing was in tatters. Lacerations marked every surface of his skin, from the brow of his forehead, to his unclad, bloody feet. Splotchy patches of red trailed behind them, outlining Quing's footprints on the tile and leaving spots in the rug. The acrid smell of their blood mixed with the faint odor of fresh dirt.

"What in limbo happened?" roared Han.

He would have liked to strike Quing, but the assassin was already too damaged to make the effort worth his while. Instead, he struck Peder, backhanding him hard enough that his eyes rolled back. Quing shook the man to keep him from losing consciousness. He must be worse off than he appeared.

Han resumed his pacing. "I gave you the protection stone, and you still couldn't win against a little girl?"

Quing held the porous, beige protection stone out to him.

Han stopped his pacing, turning slowly to face Quing. "How did you get hold of it?"

"I found it," said Quing. "About an arm from Peder's body."

"Body?" yelled Han. "He appears alive to me."

"He was passed out, Your Highness. I secreted him from the room when the plants were retreating."

Han stalked over to Quing, close enough to get personal, but remaining far enough off that the man couldn't surprise him with a weapon. "If their backs were turned, why didn't you kill them?"

Quing bowed his head toward the floor, probably hoping Han wouldn't strike out at him. "They had multiple guns by then. My weapons had been stripped from me and I wouldn't have survived."

"You should be willing to sacrifice your life for—"

"Also," interrupted Quing, "I knew you would need to be informed of what had happened. Peder appeared dead when I found him, so I was the only one who could give you that information; but not if I died."

Han struck him across an oozing cheek wound. "Never interrupt your Lingdow."

Quing bowed deeper.

"I never took the stone from my pocket, Omniscient One," said Peder, managing despite his greater height and his necessity of leaning on Quing, to bow lower.

Han gripped the man's hyefu in his fist, pulling Peder upright. "Then what happened?"

"I was having a gun trained on the girl, the little Keroka. Something struck my head. The world became black and then I was waking over Quing's shoulders. I don't know what happened."

Han tightened his grip. "Do neither one of you have real answers?" He turned to Quing. "You saw nothing?"

"Movement in the roots' shadows," he said. "I think there was someone else in there, someone unharmed by the plants, but definitely human."

Han dropped Peder. He rubbed his suddenly sweaty hands on the outside of his red robe. "Someone else knows about the tunnels?"

"Perhaps there's some kind of hermit living inside," Quing offered. "He probably doesn't even know the tunnels connect to the palace."

"If he didn't, he does now," whispered Han. "As soon this is over, I leave it to you, Quing, to find this intruder. You may use some soldiers, but afterward you must dispose of them."

Quing's eyebrows rose in surprise. "You want me to assassinate an entire search-party of soldiers? That will take time."

"We have a gas chamber near the dungeons for that express purpose," said

Han, dismissing the problem with a wave of his hand. "Tell them they need to accompany you to a special room with rewards. When they're all assembled, kill them. Peder can show you how it's done."

Quing nodded, his eyes hard and unreadable. "Yes, Your Holiness."

Han returned to his pacing, from the tiles near his desk, across the rug, and back again. The men before him looked ready to collapse, but this day was far from finished.

"Something has bothered me," said Han. "How did they get the servant-girl from the gardens and back into the caves without any of us seeing something? It had to have happened around the time that we were all there. One minute she sat next to Esterelle, the next moment she was gone. How?"

Peder bowed low, his composure restored, his Uradi accent reduced to an occasional mispronunciation. "If I may, Your Highness, many things seemed to have worked in their favor. The rabbits came out of the bush at the right moment to gain the women's attention, gathering them to one end of the gardens. Not much time later, there was a disturbance at the opposite end, which drew away the guards. I don't know how they managed such things, but—"

"A powerful little witch indeed," said Han. "The Keroka girl. She orchestrated the entire thing and then Fourteen pulled his slave-girl away." Han's brow furrowed and he stopped his pacing. "Didn't Esterelle stay in her chair? How could she have not noticed?"

The silence in the room grew heavy as Han strode to a nearby shelf, pressed a lever, and a door opened to reveal an immaculate dual-edged sword, dating back to the reign of the first emperor, which was actually Han's second body. It had been over sixteen years since he'd last used the blade. He pushed it back in favor of a newer style, a sharp single-edged, broad-bladed, short sword. It performed well as an executioner's weapon, to slit a man's throat, or chop off his head. The grip was still somewhat stiff, not fully accustomed to his hand. It could use some handling.

"If I may speak, oh Omniscient Lingdow," said Peder.

Han turned as Quing finished rolling his eyes. No doubt he found Peder's fanatic attachment tiring, though that was what had always endeared Peder to Han.

Han inclined his head.

"Esterelle would never sacrifice herself, or the other concubines, for a newcomer, however..."

"Yes, it's the however, isn't it?"

"If she stayed where she was," Peder continued. "She would have blocked the guards' view of the new mother. Is it possible she was a willing accomplice, maybe because she liked the boy?"

"When it comes to treachery, Peder, all things are possible. Fetch the woman here. You may send an errand boy to tell one of the guards, so you don't have to walk the distance, but wait outside until she comes."

After they left, Han caressed the hilt of the executioner sword. Deep in his heart, he knew Esterelle, his favorite concubine, had betrayed him. But why, after all these years? She always forgave his violent ways, actually played with locks of his hair or traced his chin-line, afterward. She was one of the few concubines he actually talked to. He could tell her some of his problems, because she never shared his words with another soul. So, why? Yes, she'd been fond of Den, and fond of his little tramp, Kerise, but that was years ago. Was it for Fourteen? He doubted it. At his request, she'd replayed every conversation she'd had with the boy—every look, hope, and dream the boy had ever divulged. She'd acted as Han's spy, but now, something had changed.

Much too soon, a knock sounded on Han's door. Peder hobbled in, without Quing, guiding Esterelle by her elbow. She stood with her head held high, a slight tremble in her darkened pink lips. Despite the bruises and faint scars, her body was still gorgeous beneath the iridescent white negligee. Her full breasts had barely begun to sag, and the whisper of wrinkles at her eyes and mouth would have gone unnoticed, if not accented by her recent, well-deserved beating. Yes, she was due to be retired soon, but Han wouldn't have let Peder have her. He would have sent her to one of his other palaces.

"Why?" he asked, swallowing to keep emotion from his voice.

She tried to act as if nothing was amiss. "Why what, Your Holiness?"

In two strides, Han was across the room. With a closed fist, he struck her across the face. She went to the ground, but Peder hauled her up, grasping both arms and pushing her forward to receive more punishment.

Han turned his back, going to his desk and leaning on it, his shoulders sagging. "After all I've given you, all the ways I favored you, you helped a servant-girl escape? Why?"

"You beat and rape me more than any other. To you that seems a favor, but it isn't right. You know that, deep down. You've taken everyone who mattered to me, reduced me to a frightened slave, then taught me to be grateful for any scrap of kindness. I didn't help them out of spite, but there was a chance for justice, and I took it."

Han's head whipped around. "Justice? What are you talking about?" He turned from the desk, leaning against it and folding his arms. "Is Den planning to take some kind of revenge?"

Esterelle dropped to her knees, and Peder let her. "If you leave them alone, they'll go in peace. There will be no need for revenge or justice. You'll be safe." She hobbled toward Han. "I'll stay with you. Despite everything that's happened, you still have some small amount of decency. It's been damaged. You've been hurting so much for so long, but we can make it better. We can grow old together like normal people, happy people."

She smelled of sweet perfumes and soft nights. Han saw the sincerity in her eyes, knew that she cared for him, and a very small part of him, a part he thought he'd long ago crushed, was compelled by her dream. But he had a divine calling, one that required sacrifice. Love only resulted in betrayal. Esterelle was one more proof of that.

He placed a foot between her breasts and shoved, sending her to the floor at Peder's feet. She cried out, but Han refused to hear. "Have her taken to the dungeon. I'll sign her execution order when the rest of this mess is finished."

The distant pang in Han's chest shouldn't be there. He grabbed a second century Tehkxyayen vase from a side table, watching its swirling colors turn as it flew from his hand to the far corner, behind his desk. It shattered, the glittering pieces catching the heartstone-lights as the shards bounced across the floor.

The only more dangerous emotion than love, was trust. Han had drilled that fact into his mind and soul over and over, and yet the pain of betrayal reappeared when he least expected. Esterelle must pay, and the emotions must be extinguished.

37

They hid in the mountain foliage whenever possible, making their own trail the rest of the way down the mountain. This time, Gabrick didn't even mention the possibility of Mariessa using her strange ability to help them hide. She barely seemed to be keeping herself upright, and he wasn't doing much better.

Nearing the mountain's base, in a well-concealed copse of trees, Den revealed a rickshaw. Gabrick had only seen one a few times within the Numbers Compound, on the rare occasions when the emperor showed his Numbers off to a dignitary, but wouldn't allow the man inside his car. The thing was pulled by a servant or a slave, while the passengers sat in the shaded seats set above the wheels. The ones from the palace were ornate, open, and had padded seats. This thing looked ready to fall apart. Made of old lumber, with a worn wooden seat, it was enclosed halfway up, more an uncomfortable pen than a passenger transport.

Gabrick pointed at it with distaste. "We're riding in that?"

"Once we get closer to a road, yes," said Den. "Help me get it out and down the hill."

The terrain wasn't made for people, let alone anything with wheels. By the time they reached a near-deserted pathway Gabrick's wound had bled through his bandage.

Mariessa shielded her eyes from the sun, dipping low in the sky. "It'll be dusk soon."

Den pulled out a folded, vermin-chewed cloth, big as a blanket, purple on one side and black on the other. He shook it out then laid it over the rickshaw's canopy, black side out. "We need to get through the inner-city gate before the emperor figures out we've escaped the tunnels. He'll close the gates, and he won't open them again until we're found, or he's certain we're not here. This city will become a death trap for anyone left inside who doesn't have at least two months' worth of provisions."

He adjusted the black shroud to envelop the rickshaw's passengers. Gabrick fingered the filthy fabric. "What's this?"

"It marks a leper carriage. Whenever lepers are found within the city, they're carried to the closest tenth tier and dumped." Den gestured to the empty seat next to Aednat and the packs piled at her feet and lap. He donned a black circular cap. "I'll get us out of the city and find someplace we can make further plans."

Gabrick stashed the rifle he'd picked up off a dead soldier under the seat before sitting down. "And the concubine?"

Mariessa's slap came so hard and sudden it nearly knocked Gabrick off the seat. "Don't you dare call me one of the emperor's whores." She pulled one of her knives, angling it toward his neck.

He put up both hands. "What in limbo?"

Den chuckled. "You're in a different world now, Gabrick. And I wouldn't mess with this little cat, were I you. Outside Han City, being a concubine is not a good thing. Any woman who gives herself to a man without marriage is someone who lacks character and morals. For some, the emperor is an exception, but I don't think our Mariessa fits into that category."

"Royal pigs," Mariessa muttered under her breath, but she sheathed the knife.

Den pulled out the small satchel that had been so important that they'd risked their lives going to his room to retrieve it. From it, he extracted an ink pot and a delicate brush. With practiced strokes, he placed a design on his bare forearm, near his wrist.

Gabrick sat back in his seat. "Eighth tier?"

"It's the highest tier that ever does leper duty. For most, it's not worth the money." He wiped off one of the lines. "Maybe you're right. A lower tier will be better. Ninth, but not quite tenth."

Gabrick shrugged. He had no frame of reference for any of this. Other than a few of the concubines, he'd never seen anyone below fifth tier in his entire life.

"Do I walk beside you then?" Mariessa asked Den.

"Dressed like that, with your skin, and curly black hair? No, you'll have to ride with them. At least you don't weigh much."

Mariessa shifted into a wide stance, fists on hips. "Where? There's no space for another person."

Den lifted her up like a small child, dropping her on Gabrick's lap. "Right there." He pulled the curtain over them. "And we don't have time to argue."

The rickshaw jolted over the dirt path, and they started forward. Gabrick held on with one hand, but the other extended into mid-air. He didn't know what to do with it. He didn't dare touch Mariessa, even as she fought to stay seated, so he helped Aednat keep hold of the packs. Aednat grunted and groaned as they jostled from side to side. Perhaps it was expected that lepers might make some noise. Gabrick had never seen one, so he didn't know.

Other than Aednat's noises, they rode in uncomfortable silence, Mariessa's jostling against his thighs proving a constant distraction. He focused on the slivers poking up from the rickshaw seat, but that only brought another kind of misery. He was grateful when they reached a main road that was relatively free from holes or unexpected dips.

Every few lengths, Den yelled with a heavy low-tier accent, "Lepers coming through!"

Gabrick peeked through a hole in the curtain, noticing that people gave them a wide berth. Den had always said the best way to hide was in plain sight, but Gabrick had never understood before now. He lifted the edge of the canopy, hoping for a better view.

Mariessa slapped his hand and the curtain fell. "What're you thinking?"

He reached for the fabric. "I want to see my city."

She held the corner down as he tugged it up, turning on his lap to face him. "It's a city like any other, a little richer, but basically the same."

He glared into her big, round eyes, noting that their exotic flare stemmed from her Kerokan heritage, making them tilt at the outside edges. She also had a Uradi pupil, tall and thin like a cat's, nearly encompassing her deep brown iris in the darkness under the black tarp.

He blinked, reminding himself that they were arguing. "I've never seen a city," he said. "I've never been allowed away from the palace and when Den and I tried to escape last time, it was night."

She leaned in, her whisper fierce. "If we get caught, you'll get to see the city from here all the way back to the stinking palace. It can be your last memory before he takes over your body. Find another city to gawk at when we're safe from that insane, demon-emperor father of yours!"

Mariessa came closer as she punctuated her words and Gabrick caught something enticingly spicy, a remnant from the concubines' perfumes perhaps.

"She's right," said Aednat.

With a huff, he dropped the curtain and they continued in their former silence. Now that he recognized Mariessa's exotic smell amid the rickshaw's grime, it made her uncomfortable dance across his knees even more difficult.

After a moment, she inspected his arm. "It's still bleeding," she whispered.

He sneered. "That happens when a person gets shot."

Without any warning, she yanked at what remained of his shirt, leaving a ragged sleeve that barely came past his shoulder. A few rips and tears later and she'd changed the bandage.

"We'll need something clean later," said Mariessa. "But at least you won't leave a suspicious trail of blood."

"Lepers don't bleed?" Gabrick asked.

"If Den is transporting lepers who've reached the stage of nose-bleeds, they're likely to pull him off the side of the road and burn the rickshaw. I saw that happen once, in Kerokos."

Aednat nodded. "I've seen it happen here, too. The lepers' screams were horrible."

Half an hour later, as the sun was dipping toward the horizon, they stood in line at the city gates, people giving them a wide berth in every direction. A bellowing announcement echoed across the city, sounding so similar to the speakers in the Numbers Compound, Gabrick almost jumped in fright.

"Your emperor, the holy Lingdow of the Vasheri, speaks to the citizens of his holy city. Still yourselves and attend his divine words."

His father's voice came so loud, it was as if he stood outside the rickshaw, the background static the only giveaway that the man didn't address them from one of his towers. Gabrick had heard of the newly-erected screen near the city gates, the only one of its kind in all of Dixho. Tempted to look, Gabrick clenched his hands into fists. Mariessa was right, he mustn't give them away.

The emperor's deep voice, so smooth yet menacing, sent shivers up Gabrick's arms. "My message today goes out to the one in our city who has taken something from me. I would rather not lock the city gates, thus depriving many citizens of food, and I would like to give this individual the opportunity to come forward, repent, and be welcomed into the Vasheri's loving arms once again, through me, their divine Lingdow."

The crowd shuffled, their discomfort evident. Through his peephole, Gabrick saw a few of them eying the gate.

"In case you can't see the screen, I have a lovely woman kneeling at my feet. She was drawn into this web of sin by those who have fled from me. Tell them your name, my dear."

A whimper sounded through the speakers then a woman cried out.

Through her subsequent sobs, she whispered her name. "Esterelle."

Gabrick turned toward the voice, clenching the backboard and almost knocking Mariessa off his lap. "No," he whispered, raising the rickshaw curtain just enough he could see.

Mariessa gasped, but all eyes were focused on the black-and-white picture screen. Blurry, scratchy, the sound a bit ahead of the picture, the images were well enough defined to be unmistakable. Esterelle knelt at the emperor's feet dressed in a dirt-stained negligee that left little to the imagination. Gabrick suspected that displaying her was part of the humiliation. Smudged make-up made her pale eyes even larger, coloring the tears coursing down her corpse-like face.

His father's fist clenched a single-edged short sword, the hand guard and dull edge gilded. He stood in one of his most illustrious white robes, one hand buried deep in Esterelle's hair. The lighting made the strands light up like a Vasheri's halo, a symbol often drawn to represent their origins from the light of life hidden deep in the planet's core. Gabrick's father looked like the demon Mariessa called him, clothed in the billowing white clouds that drifted through limbo. He appeared to be hovering over a Vasheri rising from the earth, still stained with the blessed soil that marked her divine origins. If he'd realized the religious import of their appearance, he certainly would have thought to take more care.

He moved the communication stone from in front of her lips, yanking her hair to keep her upright, her face next to his thigh. "If those escaped sinners will proclaim themselves now, let one of the royal guard bring them in, then I can grant them means for repentance, along with the woman they've tainted. But if they refuse, then she must pay the price for all of their sins, until I find them and—"

Esterelle's high, clear voice superseded his low bass. Despite the communication stone's distance, her sweet tones boomed through the speakers.

"From a lonely god, the boy will come."

Mariessa leaned forward with Gabrick. "That's from the stone Aednat found. In the cave."

The emperor hissed something in Esterelle's ear. Tears still streaming down her face, she sobbed as she continued.

"The son of none, yet fathered by many, a replica of his enemy."

The emperor yanked her head back, twisting his fingers to pull the hair from her scalp.

Her features tightened in pain, her eyes squinting shut, yet she continued.

"The legions beneath the earth gather to his standard, though they despise his unholy visage."

Raising the sword, the emperor yelled at someone outside of their view, "Turn it off, I say! Disconnect the system."

Esterelle's eyes shot open, filled with a light Gabrick had never seen in her before. It was as if, for the first time, she was truly alive, maybe even happy. "They will call him..."

The sword came down.

"...Savior."

Blood spurted from her neck, spraying across his father's white robe.

"No!" Gabrick screamed, but the sound was muffled by a small hand.

Gabrick's last view was of Esterelle's wet, darkened negligee clinging to her full figure, her head still held high in his father's angry grip. The image burned behind Gabrick's eyes even as he squinted them shut, the picture of his father, standing in the blood of the woman Gabrick had lusted after, and yet been the closest to a mother as he'd ever known. Were they disparate feelings? Yes. Maybe even sick in a way. But his life hadn't been entirely normal and the two desires had clashed together, that of a pubescent boy and the needs of an orphan. Esterelle's role had slowly progressed from an object of desire, to confidante, to nurturer. And his father had humiliated and murdered her.

The city alarms blared for the second time in a week.

"Gates are closed," Gabrick heard a guardsman say in front of them.

"As you wish," stuttered Den, his accent so like Cherda's it made Gabrick's skin crawl. "Then I need the likes of a script, telling them law-men I can stay in thissa city. Being ninth tier."

"Are you crazy, Dett?" another gruffer voice said. "You want a pack of dying lepers wandering the city while they infect people until they die? And a ninth-tier thief? I've known the gates to stay shut a month or more if the emperor demands it. Get this filth out, and then we can lock up the gates."

"Yes, sir," said the guard. The rickshaw struggled forward. "You heard the man, move it quick or I'll shut the bars on your backside, you old crete."

The wooden wheels clattered over the bridge cobbles, and Gabrick peeked through one of the front holes. If the man leading them didn't wear the same stained clothes as he had in the dungeon, Gabrick wouldn't have believed it was Den. He slumped over the bars, his neck forward and back arched. The hair under his cap, still wavy, was almost entirely white. Gabrick couldn't see his face, but everything else indicated an eighty-year-old man.

They made it over a shining, metal bridge, and past some close-standing homes. Den pulled off the road, into a deserted back alley. Instead of raising their black cloth, he leaned against a grimy building, turning his back to them, his face in his hands. A brief glimpse showed Gabrick the wetness in his eyes, the sadness he held back.

"Why?" he heard Den whisper to himself. "Why would she repeat that forsaken prophecy?"

Mariessa faced Gabrick as he struggled to hold back his grief. To his surprise, tears ran down her cheeks.

"Sometimes, I hated her." She choked back a sob. "But she protected me when she could, and was kind when I wasn't being a brat. She didn't deserve to die like that. No more than Dangan did."

He didn't know who Dangan was, but Gabrick pushed back the moisture on his cheeks and placed a hand on Mariessa's shoulder. She flinched, pushing his hand away. Slumping to the floor at his feet, she curled up with her head to her knees, crying into the blanket she was still using as clothing. Her quiet sobs could hardly be heard, but her shoulders shook against his legs.

Aednat wrapped him in her arms, holding him. He let the tears come, let them stream down his cheek until Den raised the canopy. Gabrick pulled himself together, wiping away the wetness.

The alarms stopped blaring behind them, a monotone announcement declaring the gates closed and early curfews enforced until the criminals were found. The citizens were to stay indoors for the rest of the day or risk getting shot.

Gabrick was out of Han City, but they still had a long way to go before they'd reach a place his father couldn't find them.

38

They left the rickshaw, taking what weapons they could conceal, which meant Mariessa's knives, a knife for Den, and no guns. According to the others, getting caught with a firearm would be an immediate death sentence.

"Why are their homes so dirty?" Gabrick asked, touching the peeling paint along a building's back wall. "Don't the people every clean or repair anything?"

Mariessa stared at him as if he'd turned into a daffing chicken while Aednat and Den shook their heads.

"What?" Gabrick asked, going on the defensive.

"These aren't inner-city folk," Aednat said kindly. "They have no servants, they work all day every day in order to keep their tier status, and they don't have the money of the third and fourth tiers."

"So they can't keep things clean?"

Den frowned at him. "Don't be a dolt, boy. They are clean, they're just not scrubbed to the point they glitter in the sunlight, which is what the emperor requires near his residences. These are normal, actually rather well-off people. You know nothing about the world around you, so I suggest you keep your judgments to yourself until you know something of which you speak."

Gabrick ducked his head, feeling his face heat with shame and anger. "So I'm to be mute rather than learn anything. That'll help."

"Don't give me your uppity, I'm-a-Number tone out here. You're—"

Defense came from an unexpected source. "He has a point," said Mariessa. "I'd have never believed the things I've seen if I hadn't been thrown in that polished cage of a palace. And I made a lot of judgments, said a lot of things that were stupid. But if you don't say them, and you don't ask, how are you supposed to know better?" She lessened his shock at her generosity by looking at him and adding. "You are stupid, and definitely high-stilted, but I guess you'll never be able to help that." She said the insult as a simple matter of fact.

Gabrick sneered back. "What a daffing little imp you're turning out to be."

Mariessa swung back her little arm and slapped him. "Don't you dare curse at me!"

"Curse?" Gabrick rubbed his stinging cheek. "What are you talking about, you little crete?"

Den stepped between them, facing Mariessa. "You defend him for what he doesn't know then punish him for it. In most of Zhanda and about the fourth tier up to the first, calling someone a minion of limbo is rude, but not a vulgarity."

He knew it was childish, but Gabrick stuck his tongue out at her, over Den's back.

She glared and looked ready to hit him again, but Den's patience was wearing thin. "We have things to do tonight, before we find a place to sleep, and I don't want another word from either of you."

He dragged them down the street, casually reaching down and grabbing a small plastic bucket resting near the stoop of someone's home. The gesture meant nothing to Gabrick; of course they would take whatever they needed, that was something he was used to, but Mariessa scanned frantically up and down the avenue.

"Calm down," said Den. "If you keep looking for someone to notice, they will. I won't take what we don't need, but we must survive."

"And a bucket will help?" she asked.

"Yes," said Den.

They reached a large fountain spraying water into a round tub and Den dipped the bucket. They made their way to another small alleyway, pilfering a dim lightstone on their way. Den started pulling items from his pack, including a stiff brush. He dipped it in the water and scrubbed at the ink on his arm. It faded but remained. He glanced up at Gabrick's worried expression.

"It takes a couple of days to completely erase, but that's not a problem. It looks like someone did a poor job when it was updated. We can work around it. As long as one of us has an arm with the right tier on it, I have forged documents for the rest." He studied each of them and sighed. "No help for it. Gabrick and Aednat will be our owners."

"Owners?" Mariessa's voice rose.

"It's just a cover," Den said. "Don't worry."

"Easy for you to act like it's nothing." She snorted derisively. "You've never been at risk of becoming a slave."

Den's expression darkened. "You might be surprised."

He grabbed Gabrick's arm, drawing a fifth-tier mark as he began explaining their cover story and ordering Aednat to pull out hair-styling supplies from their packs.

Sometime around midnight they reached a bright yellow hotel, tall and narrow, crammed between two businesses, only a few streets from the looming factory district. Entering the main room, flooded with the light from multiple lightstone lamps, Gabrick caught a good look at everyone for the first time since Den's makeover in the alley, their faces clean and scratches concealed.

Den's wavy hair was now straight and scraggly while Mariessa's hair, also straightened, had been transformed from mid-neck to a boy's cut that barely reached her ears. He'd replaced her blanket-dress with stolen pants and a double layer of tunics—a tight one to flatten her breasts, and a long, loose one to hide her figure. The reddish tints in Aednat's hair were darkened to near-black. They'd changed her boy clothes for a modest ankle length skirt and sky-blue blouse, a matching ribbon taken from the shirt weaved into her hair. Den had dyed Gabrick's blond hair black. The tie holding it back at the base of his neck itched and didn't accomplish much. Multiple loose pieces fell around his face, getting in the way. Aednat had nodded her approval, saying he looked like a fifth tier from a small city.

All four of them wore their shirts cinched up to the elbow. Gabrick hadn't had to do so in the Numbers Compound, but servants, soldiers, and most masters had. In the city, apparently, to do otherwise was to ask for an enforcer's beating and a fine.

Gabrick approached the small polished desk that dominated the lobby, trying not to sneer at the multiple rivets scarring the wood. He stuck out his chin, prepared to do his imperial voice, but Den kicked his ankle. With a glance, he saw Den lower his chin and direct his eyes at the attendant approaching the desk.

Yes, Gabrick remembered, *I must treat him as an equal.* He pasted on a smile, then lost it again as Den tensed.

Straight-faced, looking into the man's eyes, Gabrick said. "We'd like a room for the evening." Mariessa had wanted two, but Den insisted they stay together.

"How many in the room?" the man inquired.

"Four," Gabrick answered, though he didn't see why he should. Den had said these places charged by the room, not the number of people.

The man poised a simple ink quill above a plain piece of paper. "Um...three men and a woman, correct?"

This was getting irritating. Fifth tier or not, this couldn't be normal. "Two men," said Gabrick sharply. "Myself and a hired companion." The man tensed. "We have our cousin, who is merely a boy, and my sister, and we would like *one* room for three nights."

The man inclined his head. "Please excuse me, sir. With the trouble in the inner-city, everyone has been instructed to ask for details." He wrote down the information. "I'm to detain any group of two men and two women, regardless of station." He breathed a sigh of relief. "I'm glad we don't have to bother with the kinds of problems that would bring. Even then, I'm required to get your names."

The emperor already had hotel staff on the lookout, probably store owners, maybe even rickshaw drivers and market vendors as well. Sweat broke out on Gabrick's forehead as he spit out all the names and relations Den had made him memorize.

Finished fulfilling the emperor's latest decree, the man visibly relaxed, though his forced smile suggested he thought Gabrick strange. He pulled a key from a board hanging on the wall behind him. "I gave you the lowest floor we have available, room 303. You're required to pre-pay for the first two nights, pay the other when you leave. That'll be two emps and a king."

Gabrick dug into the pouch Den had attached to his waistband. Though he knew the coin denominations, he'd never actually had to pay anyone before. The attendant didn't notice his discomfiture, chattering on. "So, I assume you're here for the postponed celebration. What kind of business do you run that gives you the funds to travel to the capital?"

Gabrick almost dropped the coins on the floor. He fumbled with them, catching one as it slipped from his fingers, and slapping them onto the counter. "Wh-what?" Den hadn't prepared him for a question like this.

The man's eyes narrowed suspiciously. "What kind of business?"

Aednat chuckled, though it sounded strained. "I'm afraid my brother's exhausted and a bit slow this evening. We run a baublery."

"Like beads, feathers, hairpins and such?" the man questioned.

"Yes, very similar to our auntie's near the main wall, Patai's Baublery."

"Keng Patai?" he asked. "We send each other business. She's never mentioned any family. Where did you say you're from?"

"Hang Dezi," supplied Gabrick, finally knowing a right answer.

"I'm not surprised Aunt Patai doesn't mention us." Aednat blushed as if the whole story was real. "My mother was seventh tier before she married my father." She pointed to Mariessa. "Hence, our lower-tier cousin."

The attendant relaxed. "Keng Patai is a bit touchy about station. To me, a coin's a coin as long as it's legal and proper. Don't want no trouble with the emperor." He cocked his head. "Did she show you any of her new supplies? I pick up writing quills from her now and again."

"Oh," Aednat looked truly disappointed. "We didn't grab any quills. She pulled out a small satchel—their reserve coins—and gave them a quick, short shake, enough to make sound, but nothing distinguishable. "Auntie gave us a few of her latest bead samples to take home with us." She slipped the coins back into her travel-sack. "Show him the bracelet we put together while we were there, Pai. The one with the dolphins."

Gabrick froze, then nodded dumbly. Yes, he still had his mother's bracelet in his pocket. He yanked it out and held it on his palm, standing as dumb and mute as a toddler Number newly arrived at the compound.

"That's a nice piece," agreed the man, though not really interested, which was exactly what they wanted. With a tired glance at the door from which he'd come, he recited the hotel's amenities. "Breakfast is between seven and eight thirty, served in the kitchen through the door to my left. Other meals cost extra. The bathhouses are through that door behind the stairs, across the green to the back of the property. There are four private toilets. A communal hot bath for three people or more costs two magers each, cold is one each, a private hot bath is four magers, and cold is three. Any questions, ring the front bell."

With a quick nod, he scurried through the door. As soon as he was out of sight, Aednat leaned her forehead on his shoulder, expressing a sigh of relief.

Gabrick put an arm around her and they started up the stairs. "I'd have never guessed you could pull that off."

Aednat gave a weak laugh. "I'm not as useless as you think, but I am exhausted."

Each of the hotel's five levels only had four rooms. It didn't take long to reach theirs. Aednat took the key from his hand, unlocking the door and pushing open the rickety wooden slab on creaking hinges. Two beds, covered in white sheets and plain black blankets, with frames not much more than polished posts, reached out from the wall. A small towel, a ceramic basin, and a matching pitcher of water sat on an equally plain table between them. Aside from a strange pot in the corner and a streaked window with plain black drapes, there was nothing else in the room.

"This is a nice hotel," said Mariessa, running her hand along the bed linens. "We can afford this?"

"We'll be fine," said Den.

Aednat lay down on the closest bed. "Softer than the one in our apartment, to be sure."

Mariessa's face paled. "You and Gabrick lived together?"

"Of course," said Gabrick. "Aednat is my servant."

"Was," corrected Aednat. "Now, I'm your friend."

Den tried to explain. "They lived in separate rooms, separate beds, because she took care of cooking, cleaning, and errands at all times, day or night. Nothing more."

"As if it's any business of yours," Gabrick muttered, but pointed to the pot before she could retaliate. "What is that thing for?"

The girls chuckled, but Den laughed out loud. "Only fourth tier and above are likely to have indoor plumbing, and it's much too expensive for a small hotel such as this."

Gabrick cocked his head, still confused.

"The pot is in case you have to relieve yourself in the middle of the night, since the bathhouses will be locked." Den laughed again as Gabrick finally understood. Pulling two small blankets from the bottom of their packs, Den kept one and tossed the other to Gabrick. "We all need sleep. We'll discuss plans tomorrow."

Gabrick pointed at Mariessa. "Why should she sleep in the bed? She's a seventh-tier little crete."

"Because she's a lady and one of the Vasheri-blessed." Den shoved Gabrick to the floor, his eyes hard. "And you are as spoiled as she claims. Get used to it, boy. This will be our last hotel stop before we reach our destination."

"But—" Gabrick tried one more time.

"Quiet," said Den, wrapping his blanket round him and lying on the floor near Aednat's bed.

Gabrick took the corner well away from the disgusting pot. He didn't think he'd be able to sleep on the hard floor with thoughts of the last week running through his brain, but within seconds his eyes closed and his breathing steadied.

He awoke to a high-pitched scream.

39

Within seconds, the quick tap of shoes sounded from the stairwell. Mariessa snapped her mouth closed, still shivering from images she'd revisited in her nightmare.

Outside the door, the attendant paused as a number of voices overran one another.

"Don't worry," the man responded. "Go back to your beds and I'll take care of it. You won't be disturbed again."

A firm knock rapped against their door.

Den cracked it open. "Just a bad dream. I'm sorry."

"Keep it quiet or I'll have enforcers at my door," the man said, turning back toward the stairs.

"Gather everything," said Den. "Time to leave."

"I thought we were staying three days," said Gabrick, stuffing their bags.

Den shook his head. "That was only to waylay suspicion. And now that we've drawn the hotel attendant's attention, we need to leave. Now."

After using the hotel's fancy toilets in the bathhouse, Mariessa and Aednat waited in the hotel's front entry while Gabrick and Den went to the kitchen, interrupting the cook as she prepared breakfast. They returned with food for their satchels: bread, fruits, and dried meat; and they handed out pastries, fresh from the oven. Before now, they hadn't been able to eat much, just stale granola and rice bars filled with rock-like bits of fruit. The filling wrap, made with rice flower and filled with diced pork, fluffy cooked eggs, and aromatic spices, was like a bit of warm paradise. Each bite seemed to melt in Mariessa's mouth. She'd never tasted anything so good.

Gabrick screwed up his face. "What is this thing? It's so coarse."

Den frowned. "It's food, and it's the best you're going to get for the next few weeks. Eat it."

"Spoiled terdo," Mariessa mumbled under her breath.

Gabrick glared at her, but didn't say anything. He chewed the food as if it was made of rocks then appeared ready to vomit every time he swallowed.

They'd only walked a few paces in the gray pre-dawn when Den flagged down a strange, horse-drawn rickshaw. It had a large, elaborate canopy, a door and windows with raised curtains. On the narrow wooden bench attached to the passenger box sat a thin sixth-tier man. A fifth-tier license was displayed prominently on the bench's edge, explaining how the man could be moving freely in a district above his tier. That was a rule Mariessa had had drilled into her as a child, to never travel above tier.

"Is the cart safe?" Mariessa asked, ignoring Gabrick's subsequent laugh.

In Keran there were carts pulled by Caribou, but horses were extremely rare. They seemed much too fast and frisky for pulling people.

"It's called a carriage," Den explained. "And the man guiding the horse has to be very capable to be allowed in the tier."

"Read his license," Gabrick added. "He's earned a number of commendations so he must know what he's doing."

Mariessa gave a stiff nod, agreeing as if she understood the scribbles on the paper, but even a palace-bred brat like him should know she couldn't read. Born an eighth tier, even when becoming Sando's step-daughter had raised her tier level, it still wasn't enough to allow her an education.

Den gave the man directions to a local stable then ushered them up a little step attached to the side and onto the seats. Instead of one, the carriage had two padded seats, covered with soft fabric, facing one another. Gabrick and Aednat sat side by side. Mariessa had to face Gabrick, whose face screwed up again as soon as he sat down.

"What's the point of padding a seat if you're going to feel the board underneath?"

Mariessa rolled her eyes, laughing inside at Aednat's identical reaction. She only wished Gabrick had seen it. He'd be much less likely to sneer at his precious Aednat.

As they traveled, the sun rose, giving color to the landscape and more bustle to the city. Mariessa watched with interest. Though the buildings were shaped different from Keran, people had different clothing styles, and the air smelled of spicier food and lacked the underlying stench of sewage, the cities had similarities.

Tables and benches sat outside the homes and establishments, waiting to be filled with heartstones to charge in the sunlight. Men still gathered to gossip, children laughed inside their homes as they ate breakfast and prepared for their day, vendors moved across the streets as they prepared to sell their wares, and a few men and women, dressed in finer clothing than the rest— some riding horses and a sparse few in sputtering, crank-style automobiles— rushed to the upper-tier jobs they'd acquired. Of course, they'd be told the gates were locked shut, but the news must not have reached everyone yet. Mariessa wondered how many, unable to reach their jobs and steady pay, would be left in destitute circumstances. How long would it take them, without work, before the children started to go hungry? Before Mariessa had seen the palace and the fine way the upper-tier citizens lived, she'd thought starvation a potential hazard of any normal life. It seemed ridiculous now, that a person should live in opulence or hunger based on a number tattooed to their arm as an infant.

Gabrick scrunched up his face again, about to throw his half-eaten pastry from the carriage. Mariessa snatched it up, gobbling it down in three large bites. This earned another sneer, but Mariessa didn't care. A person learned to take food whenever they could find it.

They reached the stables. Though the owner appeared surprised at their little group, he seemed to know Den. They conversed in low whispers then the man left his stable as if they weren't standing there.

Gabrick made to stop him, but Den pulled the boy back. "For a number of reasons, we don't need to worry about the man. It's taken care of."

Den refused to say more than that. He readied two horses, took bedrolls and a few extra supplies, transferring one of the knapsack's contents to the packs on the horses' backs, then he placed Aednat on the tallest of the two mounts.

"You'll ride the bay gelding," he said to her, though it looked the same as most of the horses in their pens. He pointed to the other horse. "Gabrick, you lead the gray mare."

Mariessa kept her distance from both. They walked from the stable as if picking up their property rather than stealing a man's livelihood.

As soon as they were away from the building, Gabrick sidled up to Den. "Won't he report these stolen?"

"Not for an hour," said Den. "There will be streams of people leaving the outer city now that the betrothal celebration has been postponed and the inner city is closed, but in the off-chance the man at the hotel has called in the authorities, we must split up. Han will never suspect us to be traveling in pairs, not so soon. I will stay with Aednat, but you must keep Mariessa. Change your names, but have her continue acting the boy cousin, come along for the ride so you won't be alone."

"Why doesn't my father lock the gates like in the inner city?"

"Too many gates," said Den. "Too many people from other districts, and too many other ways out if he makes us desperate."

Gabrick nodded.

Den squeezed his shoulder. "Keep at least three groups between us, and follow. If we get separated, take the road north until you reach the bridge. Go east along the bank for about ten lengths. We'll wait for you there."

"I'm not walking after this high-stilted boy on his fancy horse like I'm some paid slave," Mariessa interrupted.

Gabrick started, making the horse side-step. He glared down on her as if his height was supposed to be intimidating. "What is that supposed to even mean? You insult me with words that make no sense."

"It's a person who thinks they're community chief, who thinks too much of themselves."

Gabrick blinked in surprise. "Are you crazy? Why would I want to be chief of a little jungle community of savages? I was nearly emperor, you daffing idiot."

"It's an expression, terdo." Her fingers curled as her anger grew. "And terdo is Kerokan, too. It's a leaf we clean with after we relieve ourselves." She smirked, knowing the term was crude, even by male terms, but she'd had enough of this imperial brat.

"You little crete," Gabrick swore. Mariessa didn't need that term explained. It meant she had no value above that of a goat or a pig. "You respect your position, little concubine, or I'm going to have to show you where you belong."

That was it. Mariessa didn't care where she was or who might be watching. She still had a knife tucked inside her boy clothes, and this over-stuffed demon had been warned. She arced the knife in a wide swipe, forcing him to jump back then deal with the horse as it clomped its dangerous feet and pulled at the reins, wide-eyed and snorting.

Gabrick put out a hand. "Hey," he whispered. "Put that thing away before you get us both—"

"Is there a problem?" An enforcer in a blue uniform, cuffs striped in gold, stood in front of them, his rank and name stitched in red thread above his left breast pocket, Lieutenant Xey Betan.

Mariessa froze for a moment, realizing the trouble she'd gotten them into. She put the knife back in its sheath, smoothing her shirt and standing wide like she'd seen the men in the village do when on the defensive. She went to fold her arms over her stomach, but Gabrick reached out and pulled one to her side. She didn't understand why, but let the other drop with it, not daring to say anything in her defense. Like Den had said, her accent was too strong.

"Hold out your brands," the officer demanded.

Gabrick blinked a few times, but didn't move. As higher tier, he should take the lead, but Mariessa extended her forearm, her tattoo turned upward. Gabrick awkwardly followed her example. His eyes swept over the man's head, going wide with panic. Mariessa didn't have his view, so had no idea what caused such a scare that Gabrick's forehead beaded with sweat despite the cool morning air.

The man waved a lightstone over the swirls and curves of Mariessa's seven, making sparkles of purple appear within the dark ink. He passed the stone over Gabrick's and frowned. "How old are you?"

Gabrick looked to Mariessa, but she didn't dare say anything. She could only raise her eyebrows and hope he got the message.

"Uh...nineteen?" he said.

She almost rolled her eyes. It was supposed to be an answer, not a question, but he'd gotten the message, at least close enough.

"Had a growing spurt lately?" The lieutenant watched Mariessa as he asked the question.

Mariessa thanked the Vasheri that the stonehead of a boy picked up on the Lieutenant's suspicion. Gabrick pulled himself together, calmed his expression, and looked a little too regal, but at least confident. He watched Mariessa lower her eyelids, once, as if nodding her head, then Gabrick turned away and back again as if he'd been bored and was now focusing on what was going on. "Yes, I guess. In the last couple of years or so."

Lieutenant Xey seemed satisfied, or at least, less suspicious. "You need to get your tattoo updated. It gets those funny discolorations and cracks when you've grown too much." He pulled out a pad of paper and started writing. "Your name?"

Mariessa choked back a gasp as the idiot gave the family name. "Chid...um, Chid...Fen." She wanted to strangle him. Could he have come any closer to completely giving them away? This man's superiors would see that name and report to the emperor where she and Gabrick had been and at what time, and probably remember their descriptions.

But the lieutenant didn't blink. He wrote down the information—Gabrick gave him the same city they'd given at the hotel—and tore off the yellow sheet beneath the carbon paper and original white copy. He handed the yellow slip to Gabrick.

"You have sixty days to get the tattoo updated," he said. "If you won't reach your home province by then, I suggest you do it before you leave. There are a number of government offices near the main road, on your way to the gate." He looked up from his paper and took a deep breath like he really had better things to do. "Now, are you together, or do I have a renegade seventh tier to deal with today?"

Mariessa held her breath. With one word, Gabrick could be rid of her. If he said no, the guard would take her into custody and haul her away. She could tell the lieutenant about Gabrick, but there was a good chance, with the tattoo and Gabrick's appearance, that the man wouldn't believe her. It would depend on how much the emperor had told his military, and how much they'd shared with their lower-rank officers, which would probably be very little.

"Yes, we're together," he said, then ruined his good acting by almost messing up. "Sh—*see*, *he's* my cousin."

He rifled through his pack until he found the paper Den had given him, allowing for a seventh-tier companion.

The lieutenant glanced over it then handed it back. "No more fighting in the streets." He looked down his nose at Mariessa, "You, boy, had better learn how to respect your betters. If you'd actually cut your older cousin, by law, I'd have to take you in for flogging. If not for other business, I'd do it anyway, but I don't have time for you ordinary yenks."

He caught Gabrick searching the growing crowd and narrowed his eyes. "Are you traveling with someone else? You are a little young to be on your own."

"No," he laughed. "I've been traveling these roads since I was young, accompanying my father." His head drooped a bit. "Before he passed away." He replaced the slight frown with a knowing smile. "I was looking for a girl I saw earlier, traveling with an escort. I thought she might want some company."

The lieutenant returned the knowing smile, the way all men did when discussing women. "I'd suggest you wait to join her after you leave the checkpoint. We've been instructed to detain anyone traveling in groups of four."

Gabrick nodded. "Thank you, officer."

Lieutenant Xey sent one last glare at Mariessa then turned back into the crowd.

She turned to Gabrick. "Where's Den?"

He shook his head. "As soon as the enforcer showed up, he disappeared. We've been left to fend for ourselves."

40

By the look on Gabrick's face, he felt as scared as she did.

"I assume we were headed toward the checkpoint," he said. "We just need to continue forward."

Mariessa looked out at the ever-growing throng and swallowed. Even during a Keran festival, she'd never been in a crowd like this. Workers from the sixth tier, special bands wrapped on their arms, some of them holding their license so it couldn't be pilfered, made their way into the city. At the same time, multiple people of fourth and fifth tiers were making their way back to the places they'd come from, many of them grumpy about their wasted trip for a Han City betrothal celebration that had never happened. To gather this many people, from cities all over the region, the emperor must provide quite a spectacle when he took himself a wife.

Gabrick started forward, but Mariessa put a hand on his arm. "You're fifth tier. You should ride."

"Oh, right." Gabrick swung up on the huge animal as naturally as a fisherman throwing a net, then urged it forward.

Keeping her distance, Mariessa walked beside him. The animal's long legs danced up and down, going nowhere but pounding the pavement with its mallet-like feet. The way it threw its head up, pulling at the piece of metal in its mouth, showed its impatience. At first, she'd thought it couldn't be that different from a Caribou. The horse pulling their carriage had seemed almost docile, but this one's movements were erratic, unpredictable. It could sidestep or rise up on two legs, or who knew what, ending with her crushed beneath its heavy, fast-moving feet.

"Move it, kid."

A wide man carrying a huge bag across his back shoved Mariessa aside. She stumbled, landing in the dirt. Before she could apologize, Gabrick pulled a small riding whip from the edge of his pack. He smacked the man across the neck.

Nearly as tall as Gabrick had he not been on the horse, and twice as wide, the man turned, the arm with his sixth-tier tattoo ending in a balled fist. "Hey! What do you—"

His face paled when he realized he'd been struck by someone on a horse. Gabrick casually rested the hand with the whip on his knee, his fake fifth-tier tattoo facing out.

"Watch who you push around, crete," said Gabrick. "He's with me."

The man cast his eyes to the dirt. "I be sorry to ya sir. The boy walked so far from the horse. I didn't realize."

"So you shove everyone out of your way who isn't your better?"

Coming to her feet, Mariessa wanted to scream at him to let it go, but she didn't dare say a word.

The man swallowed hard, his eyes shifting around for enforcers. "Just in a hurry, sir. I was to be out of the city by eight bells, but the merchant I carries for, he was late."

He sounded scared and desperate, the poor man.

Gabrick shifted uncomfortably in his saddle, as if he looked down at a dog with mange. "Be off with you then. And watch where you're going."

Mariessa scooted as close to Gabrick and the horse as she dared. "Poor man."

"Are you afraid of the horse?" Gabrick asked. "Have you never seen one before?"

"Of course I have. I lived in Keran when I was young."

"Then put your hand on her withers and stay with me."

Mariessa stared at the thing, wondering where to touch. On a hunch, she placed her fingers to its side, behind their bags of supplies. The hairs were surprisingly soft, not coarse and wiry like a caribou. Still, she kept a wary eye on its feet. But the horse didn't move. Mariessa looked up and Gabrick raised his eyebrows, mocking her.

"What?" she asked, dropping her hand and putting it on her hip. "So, I've never touched one before."

Rude as ever, he laughed.

She stood to her full height, which felt even smaller than usual. "You're such a sleth."

Gabrick covered his mouth as if trying to flatten his grin. "A sleth?"

"A long reptile with small legs and poisonous, needle-teeth. They hide in mud pits." She glared up at him. "They ambush their victims and can't be trusted."

Gabrick's laugh turned to a poisonous glare like a sleth, but he gave a condescending smile. "You had your hand on her flank, not withers, and you touch her like the poor mare has a disease. We'll never get through the crowd at this pace." He stretched out his left hand. "Come on."

Mariessa stepped back. "What do you mean?" He couldn't expect her to get up on that beast.

Gabrick shook his head and took a calming breath. "You're small. You can fit between the supplies and the edge of the saddle."

That would put her up against his back. If she rode like that for very long, what would he expect when they made camp later? She shook her head.

"You're causing a scene," Gabrick hissed. "Get over here now, or I'll leave you behind, cousin or not."

Mariessa felt tears come to her eyes, the fear of getting close to Gabrick and the horse almost as intense as the fear of getting caught and taken back to the emperor.

"Come on, Bahn," he urged, his hard eyes reminding her of his father. "Don't start acting like your *sisters*."

Was she acting like a girl? Was every boy, even a seventh-tier, accustomed to horses in this country? She didn't know, but if she didn't do as he asked, they'd have another enforcer asking questions.

Ignoring the sudden perspiration on her forehead, she scooted forward and took his hand. Gabrick gripped her forearm instead, dislodging his foot from a hoop dangling on one side of his chair; then once her foot was in the hoop, he hoisted her up. It felt like she was being thrown. She stopped herself mid-screech, knowing she couldn't make that kind of scene, and settled on the tall animal's back, nudging the supplies back a few digits with her bottom. Her hands grasped at the bags, but they were too full to grip, so she rested them on her thighs.

This was nothing like a caribou with its broad back and slow gait. The horse even smelled different, similar to a dog but sweeter, less repulsive; nothing like the earthy caribou. Gabrick urged the horse forward and Mariessa panicked, gripping the back of the strange seat. As the horse moved, Gabrick's buttocks rolled against her fingers. She released the seat, but had nothing to hold. Her momentum combined with the horse's shifting gait, sent her sliding to one side. Gabrick shot an arm back, circling her. He pushed her upright.

"What's your problem?" he whispered.

"There's nothing to hold onto."

"You can hold onto the saddle or to me."

He had to be joking. The situation was already bad enough. "But—"

"Or fall off," he threatened.

Mariessa rested her hands on the fabric of his shirt, careful not to touch his muscular back. The horse suddenly stopped, making Mariessa's face hit Gabrick between the shoulder blades. She gripped the sides of his shirt, terrified the horse was about to rear, or worse, run. A child ran from in front of the horse, through the crowd, and to the other side. The horse sidestepped, but nothing more, then started forward again. Mariessa made to put her hands back the way they'd been, but Gabrick pressed a palm against one of her knuckles.

"Keep them there," he said. "It's obvious you don't know what you're doing on a horse, and a boy cousin in the same situation would hold on tight."

"But—" Mariessa tried again.

"It's a cover, Mariessa," he whispered. "A disguise. Make it work or we're both dead."

And so Mariessa did. After a while, the horse's steady rhythm began to feel natural, the occasional sudden stops, less jolting. The guards practically waved them through the check point, making a snide comment about Gabrick letting a seventh-tier ride with him.

"Believe me," he said. "As soon as we're out of this crowd, he's on the ground walking. Stupid crete of a cousin."

He'd mastered the superior tone needed for a tier insult, sounding like the nobles in Keran. As they passed between the guards, Mariessa noticed the setting on the wire fence dividing the tiers was set to full voltage. How many people would be hurt or die in the emperor's efforts to find them? Could she really consider herself and Gabrick, or Den and Aednat, worth so many other people's lives?

But no, she couldn't take that road. Priest Yosel, in Keran, had always told her that people's decisions were their own. To do good or evil, regardless of the influences in a person's life, was an individual choice. Her decisions would decide her fate in the afterworld—the blessed paradise of the Vasheri below, or the mindless wanderings in limbo above. Perhaps she was already doomed because of the men she'd killed in the dungeon and the caves, but Emperor Beht's actions belonged to him. She wouldn't carry his sins along with her own.

Still, as she glanced around at the apartments of the sixth tier—two and three-story white-washed buildings consisting largely of families that performed duties for the tier above them, provided services within their own communities, or worked in the factories unfit for higher tiers—she hoped none of them would be hurt today because of her escape. She closed her eyes, trying to think of something else.

Mariessa wasn't sure how long they traveled, but she kept her tight grip on Gabrick, figuring what was done was done. She stopped her cheek from resting on his warm back a number of times, but exhaustion finally won out and she dozed. Sometime later, the clatter of hooves on wood jerked them both awake. The bridge. She only hoped this was the first bridge they'd crossed, assuming Den really intended to meet with them.

41

Gabrick jerked awake, the horse's clopping like a sudden thunderstorm. It amazed him, the little things he came across that he'd never experienced, having lived in the Numbers Compound all his life. He'd never heard horses' hooves on wood. On dirt, on grass, and even on the road, yes, but never that jarring sound of hooves striking boards.

They still had travelers around them, but some had diverted east at an earlier junction, some had taken alternate routes, and the rest had spread out, putting space between one another. Gabrick glanced around. The tight apartment housing had given way to the occasional small home, no bigger than a bathing room, with just enough land for a garden and a few chickens or pigs. The world outside was nothing like he'd expected. Dirty, crude, these people moved around like beaten dogs searching for food scraps.

Behind him, Mariessa startled and took her weight off his back, though she kept a grip on the sides of his shirt. A wet line ran down his spine, either sweat or the girl's drool. With a gentle tug on the reins, he directed the mare down the bank, weaving between trees.

At first, most of the undergrowth was tamped down from others who'd stopped to rest, stay the night, or taken water from the river. As they continued, the grasses and undergrowth became more dominant, until they were traveling an ever-narrowing trail. Gabrick took the horse nearly twenty lengths, hoping Den hadn't completely deserted them, his eyes searching up and down the riverbank.

"Do you think we went far enough?" asked Mariessa.

"More than." Gabrick tried to hide the worry in his voice, but it cracked with fear. "I'm sure they went through the gates before us, so they should have arrived first."

Mariessa's grip tightened, straining his shirt across his back. "So we're on our own. Great friends."

Gabrick swung his leg over the mare's head. Mariessa scrambled to hold onto him but he slid down, forcing her to clamp onto the saddle. "Aednat would never leave me," he said. "But she's not strong enough to defy Den." Noting Mariessa's white-knuckled grip on the saddle, he stepped on the reins and reached up. "Let's stretch our legs for a few minutes then we can figure out how to find them."

The girl acted like she was going to be physically ill. She stared in horror at his outstretched hands. They were a bit dirty, but not any worse than hers.

Gabrick gave her a mocking smile. "You can put your leg around, and slide down the horse's side, but it might be kind of hard between the supplies and the saddle."

Of course, he could have brought the stirrup closer to her foot and helped her make a proper dismount, but Gabrick relished the chance to take her down a peg. As if testing the heat in a pot of water, she touched his shoulders, released, then gripped again, sliding toward him. When he wrapped his hands around her thin waist, she flinched. She'd gone halfway to the ground like a loose saddle angling round a horse's girth, before Gabrick was able to dislodge her foot from between the pack and the saddle. It was a good thing she was so small and thin, or they'd have ended up toppled to the ground.

He held to the slim curve of her waist, making sure she'd found her balance. With fire in her eyes she slapped his hands away, stepped back, and poised to grab a knife.

Gabrick raised his eyes to limbo. "Not this again."

She took a few more steps back then eased her hands onto her hips. "Don't think that because I rode on the horse with you that you can touch me."

With a shake of his head, Gabrick picked up the reins, though the horse didn't seem eager to go anywhere, happy to nibble at the long grasses growing along the river.

A sultry voice came from farther down the bank. "It appears we have company. Next time, boys, you need to go a little farther down. We're not supposed to be this close to the road."

Gabrick turned, wishing for some kind of weapon in his hand. But the two women who approached didn't look dangerous, anything but. They dressed different than the other women he'd seen as they traveled. Instead of long earthy-colored skirts that reached to mid-calf, these women wore bright, form-fitting dresses that barely reached their knees. One hung off the shoulders and swooped low, to show generous cleavage. The other had no sleeves, went high around the neck, but had a raindrop-shaped hole that revealed even more of her breasts than the other woman. Their faces were unnaturally pale, with bright color spread above their eyes and stretching toward their temples, all outlined in thick black lines that curved at each side. Their lips shone a bright red.

Though their faces and figures didn't compare to the women Gabrick had seen in the concubine garden, their smiles invited his trust, and maybe something else.

"I'm LiChu, and my friend is Sang. Usually we're visited by soldiers from the city," said the bare-shouldered one. "But they've been a bit scarce lately. If you'd like a turn, we could give you boys a discount."

She stepped closer and Gabrick smelled strong perfume like flowers mixed with overripe fruit. He tied the horse to a nearby branch, giving LiChu his whole attention. "Discount?"

The girls twittered a laugh. "First-timers, huh?" LiChu stepped close, running fingers up Gabrick's thigh. "Don't worry. We can handle any level of experience."

Gabrick didn't know the women or understand them, but he wasn't completely daft. Though complete strangers, they were offering some kind of intimate favor, probably in return for money. He'd heard soldiers in the Numbers Compound talk and laugh about going to the river, but he'd never realized they paid for the women's attention.

Mariessa stepped next to him. Sang stretched a hand toward her flattened chest, but she slapped it away. Her attempt at a low, male voice made her sound like a sick donkey with an accent. "Whoring isn't allowed outside a licensed house, at least for sixth tier and above."

"Don't worry, little boy." Sang reached down the front of her dress. The deliberate way she stretched the fabric had Gabrick breathing a little quicker and wishing Mariessa to limbo. Sang pulled out a slip of paper. "We have a license. Most of the soldiers in the outer city and dungeons can't afford the house-girls, so they come here." She turned away from Mariessa with a sneer. "If he's too young, you could leave him here to watch the horse. We've got a quiet place down the river where we won't be disturbed. Maybe we can even give you a two for the price of one special."

With an embarrassed chuckle, Gabrick took a step back. "I'm afraid I'll have to pass."

LiChu raised her eyebrows as if questioning his sanity. A part of him agreed with her.

"Well then," she turned away and spoke over her shoulder. "If you ever change your mind, you know where to find us."

Fluid as a snake, Mariessa slipped behind the woman and pressed a knife to her ribs.

42

"What are you doing?" Gabrick yelled at Mariessa.

She spoke in her strange tenor, with a stronger accent. "Give it back."

LiChu made a slow turn. "I don't know what you're talking about, Keroko boy."

Great, thought Gabrick, they've recognized where she's from. This whole situation was getting out of hand. "Let them go."

But Mariessa moved the knife to the fabric between LiChu's breasts. "Are you going to give him back his money, or shall I let him see it for himself."

Though not close to Mariessa, Sang took a step back.

Mariessa pulled another knife, poised to throw. "I don't know which one of you has it, but I can hit a chapfruit from twenty lengths away. I'll kill and strip you if I must."

Gabrick patted his waist. She was right. The women had taken the entire money purse.

With a shove, LiChu knocked away the knife at her ribs and turned. Sang lifted her dress, already running away at full stride.

"I've got her," Gabrick yelled to Mariessa, running after Sang.

In his peripheral vision, he saw Mariessa tackle LiChu, the altercation disintegrating to the womanly grunts and squeals of a catfight. He reached Sang, grabbed her waist and threw her to the thick grass. She struggled, but he turned her over, sitting on her thighs and holding her wrists in one hand. With the other he reached a hand between her legs, pulled at a lacy band, and retrieved his money.

Gabrick raised a fist. "You will be beaten for this." In the Numbers Compound, theft by a slave meant certain death, but it seemed too cruel. A beating would have to be sufficient.

"No!" Mariessa yelled at him, not even attempting to hide her feminine voice or her strong Keroka accent. "Don't hurt her."

He glanced back, thinking the statement rather hypocritical since she held a knife to LiChu's throat.

"Please," said Sang, eyes filling with tears. "If you beat us we won't get work for at least a week. We're already near to starving."

Gabrick pushed off from the woman and rose to his feet. Sang remained on the ground, sobbing for some reason Gabrick couldn't understand.

"I have the money," he said, tying it back around his waist and tucking it *inside* his trousers.

Mariessa eased away from LiChu, retrieving her other knife and sheathing them both.

"You're not Keroko," said LiChu, her eyes suspicious. "You're Keroka, a girl."

Mariessa took a deep breath, glaring at Gabrick as if to say this was his fault. She went to the horse, reached into their saddlebags, and took out a roll, a piece of fruit and a small chunk of cheese. She handed it to LiChu. "This isn't much, but we don't have enough for our journey as it is."

With a slight incline of her head, LiChu accepted the offering. "Thank you, whoever you are."

Mariessa returned the nod. "When the soldiers come, they will be looking for us. They will promise you money, but if they know you've seen us, they'll kill you, no matter what you tell them."

The woman smirked and nodded as if she'd heard this before, knew better, but pretended she would keep their secret.

"This isn't like an escaped slave or a broken law," said Gabrick. "The emperor doesn't want anyone to know about us. He will issue the order, and his soldiers will follow it. Do you understand?"

Something in his manner or his voice must have affected the girl, because her eyes went wide and her mouth dropped open. "You..." she didn't finish the sentence, but shook her head as if staring at an apparition. "Go. Please, go."

With that, she tucked the food to her chest and ran. Sang joined her and they disappeared into the woods.

"Will they tell?" asked Gabrick.

Mariessa shrugged. "I don't know. If the emperor's men flash enough coins in front of them, then yes, probably. Low-tier whores near a city have reached such a level of desperation in their lives, the gamble might seem worth it, especially to those who are addicted like Sang."

"Addicted? To what? How could you know?" He gathered up the horse's reins and started them walking back up the river, toward the road.

Mariessa walked beside him, not as wary of the horse as before. "Pyium. You've never heard of it?"

Gabrick only shook his head.

"They really did keep you sheltered in that little pen of yours."

"It was a large and illustrious pen," said Gabrick, "but yes, they did. I know history, culture, and languages, but almost nothing of life in the real world. I didn't realize how stupid I was until I stepped outside those walls."

Mariessa put a hand on his arm. "Not stupid. Ignorant." With a start, she dropped the hand and moved away. "I'm beginning to think that all of us are ignorant of something. If we don't know it, we haven't seen enough of the world to understand."

"So the Pyium?" Gabrick asked.

"Sang's eyes were too wide, the eyelids and tear ducts too red, and her hand had a slight tremor to it. She also had disease. Did you notice the rash at her ankles, her neck, and probably other places? If you'd gone with her, you'd have had the same itching problems for months, if not the rest of your life. Though I'm not sure you wouldn't deserve it."

Gabrick stopped the horse, turning to stare at her. "Why should I deserve it? I didn't do anything, didn't even hit her, though it would have served her right."

"Men are so stupidly selfish," said Mariessa, placing her hands on her hips as if that somehow made her taller. "Those women are the way they are because of men like you. Men who have the money and the power to hold it over their heads unless the women give them their bodies, give up their dignity. Do you think that's really how they want to earn a living?"

"Then why don't they do something else?"

"Because they don't know anything else. Either their mothers lived that life, so they were born into it, or something happened so they never learned other skills. And then men," she spit the word, "took advantage."

"You can't know that," said Gabrick.

Mariessa gave an insufferable sigh. "You think someone says, 'I think I want to be a whore or an addict?' Sang was probably eased into her addiction by some man who wanted her, and then when he left her she had no place to go, felt worthy of nothing better. Women become the whores, but it's the men who treat them like animals of pleasure who make them that way."

Gabrick shook his head. "How did you get to be so bitter?"

"I saw women like that where I grew up. And I saw men like you."

"I didn't go with them," Gabrick pointed out.

Mariessa sniffed with disdain. "You would have."

"And so what? They're already selling themselves. What difference does it make if I'm the buyer?"

At this Mariessa went to her full height and tried to get in his face, staring up at him from somewhere near the middle of his chest. "Do you ever want a woman to care about you, maybe marry you, have your children? Or do you only want the concubines like the emperor's—women you own but who're afraid of you?"

"I'll never be emperor," Gabrick said, resisting the urge to grit his teeth. "You know that."

"But which type of love do you want?" She peered into his eyes as if she could see into his soul. "You didn't cry for Esterelle because you would never have her, you cried for her because you cared about her, the person."

"What's your point?" Gabrick just wanted her to shut up.

"When that day comes, that you want a woman by your side, not just in your bed, will you marry a whore?"

He scrunched up his face. "Of course not."

As if she'd somehow won, Mariessa smiled. "And yet you think it should be okay for you to treat women like objects to look at, lust after, and play with. Go from one to another for as long as you'd like. You do that, then *you're* the whore, whether you get paid, you put out the money, or it's all for free. And I don't see why any decent woman should want anything to do with you."

Gabrick was left speechless. She'd turned his words against him, but she wasn't right. It was different for men than it was for women. That kind of comparison couldn't be made.

She turned away, smug in her supposed victory, and Gabrick wanted to turn her around and shake her until...until, he didn't know what.

He tugged the reins and caught up with her. "You're an acid-tongued little crete."

"And you're an ignorant emp-boy who still thinks you have tier, when you really have nothing."

The words slapped him harder than if she'd struck him with a board. She was right. He only had a painted arm that would last him a few days before it needed to be refreshed. And once they reached the next tier district, Mariessa would be in a better position to survive than he would, even with her accent. Why hadn't he left her in the city when he'd had the chance?

He regretted the thought immediately. She'd saved their lives, retrieved their money, and though bitter and angry, she was the only companion he had.

As if reading his mind, she asked. "Do you want me to make my own way? I might be a hazard for you if LiChu tells the emperor's men what she knows. You'd be better off without me."

Though Gabrick could see her point, and he only foresaw more arguments in their future, the idea of going it alone scared him more than he'd admit. "I still think we're better off if we go together," he said. "Unless you really can't stand my company anymore."

"As long as you remember that I'm not like the women in the palace or the women you just met, and you keep your hands to yourself, then I think we might be able to help each other. Only, no more fighting in public."

"Then you've got to do as I say."

"No," she countered. "We make plans together, and if we disagree, we talk until we find an answer. No more treating me like one of your stupid slaves."

"Then you can't get your back up and refuse to do what needs to be done, like riding a horse or putting up with being close to a boy you don't like."

She paused, her cheeks reddening. "I'm sorry. I was afraid, but I should know better than to let fear have control." If her apology shocked him, her next words nearly felled him to his knees. "And I don't dislike you. I don't like where you're from, and I have trouble with the way you treat people. No one should think they're so much better than others."

"I can't help where I'm from, how I was raised, or..." some of his own bitterness crept into his voice, "...who my father is. I'll try to do better." He still wasn't sure what he was supposed to change, but it seemed like the right thing to say.

It must have been, because as they reached the dirt path by the bridge, she smiled. "Deal. Do you think you might teach me how to read? Maybe at night, when no one is looking?"

Gabrick came up short. "You don't know how—?"

Pointing to the other side of the bridge, where a man led a blood-splattered bay, Mariessa squinted. "Is that Den?"

The synchronized movements of the woman draped across the gelding's neck were a bit too perfect to be natural, like a tied corpse.

Gabrick dropped their horse's reins. "Aednat!"

He ran across the bridge, screaming her name again. But she didn't raise her head. She didn't even stir.

43

"Master Den, what happened?"

Den stopped the horse, leaning against it. "Don't ever call me that, boy. Never again. Master is an archaic title that's only used in the emperor's city. Den is a common first name. Use it."

Gabrick reached a hand to Aednat's face. It was cool, but not the stiff chill of death. "Is she going to be okay?"

Den nodded, handing Gabrick the reins. "I knocked her out, but she'll be fine."

"You what?" He inspected her face and neck for bruises.

"I didn't hit her, you blistering stonehead. I used a simple concoction that only put her to sleep. It was necessary."

The clop of hooves approached from the far side of the river. To Gabrick's surprise, Mariessa led their horse. She walked too far ahead, but she had a firm hold on the reins. Considering how afraid she'd been of the sweet mare, to be leading it must have taken some grit.

Den didn't notice, just continued with his horse toward the river. "We'll get cleaned up and be on our way."

At the riverbank, Gabrick worked the blood off the horse as Den waded into the cool water and stripped. Tying a rock to the stained clothes, Den tossed them into the middle of the river. He rummaged in their bags until he found another set of clothes, completely unconcerned as he strode around naked.

Mariessa averted her eyes until Den cleared his throat. "Let's get going."

"What happened to Aednat?" Gabrick asked.

Den hopped onto the mare and grabbed the gelding's reins. "We need to keep moving. When we stop, then we'll talk."

As Gabrick and Mariessa walked beside the horses, Mariessa pointed out plants and animals that were the same as those on Kerokos, and asked about those that weren't. Some of them, Gabrick had seen before, but others he only knew from textbooks. Mariessa was much more knowledgeable, if not formally educated, than he'd expected.

They passed a sign indicating they'd entered the eighth tier, but there was no checkpoint, no enforcers, and the travelers on the road continued to thin even as the foliage to each side of them thickened.

As they followed a bend in the road, stepping around the deep crevices caused by years of wagon travel, Gabrick laughed at her stories about climbing a chapnut tree that had grown outside her childhood home, hiding in the leaves and dropping unpleasant surprises on people she didn't like.

"I think you may know as much about plants, especially your native ones, as the botany master at the compound."

"That's not right," she scoffed. "I never even went to school."

Gabrick shrugged. "You still know more than I do, and I had to take classes on it."

Engrossed in their conversation, the changing shadows of late afternoon snuck up on Gabrick.

Rubbing at bleary eyes, Den sat up on his horse. "Not that he ever paid much attention in class." After scanning the area around them, he pointed to a small nook between tall trees and crowding brush, where knee-deep grass could be tamped down into makeshift beds. "Take us in there and we'll set up camp for the night."

It didn't take long, finding a comfortable place to lay Aednat, tying up the horses and setting up a fire ring. In the midst of their work, Aednat woke up, screaming for Den and fighting at the ropes still tied on her hands and feet. As soon as Den untied them, she slugged him full in the jaw, making her knuckles crack. It was hard to tell who looked more pained, she or Den.

Gabrick ran to her side. "Careful. You could break your knuckles hitting a man in the face."

She pointed an accusing finger at her supposed uncle. "He was going to leave you."

"But look, Gabrick's here," said Den, holding the end of his tunic to his nose. "And the Keroka is with him. So you can relax."

"You were really going to leave me behind?" asked Gabrick.

Den turned his back on them, going to the fire ring they'd nearly finished. "How'd you get past the enforcer?" he asked over his shoulder.

Since Den continued to work as if nothing had happened, Gabrick told his and Mariessa's story while cutting back the grass and finding more rocks. Den set fire to a crumpled piece of paper covered in damp tinder, making Mariessa gasp. The lighter was an invention Gabrick had seen multiple times, but it must seem like magic to her.

Finally, Gabrick found the opportunity to pose his accusation. "So you thought we didn't stand a chance and instead of sticking around to help, you left us?"

The tinder started to burn and Den stared over the faint flames at Gabrick. "What sense would there be in all of us getting caught? I had to get Aednat out of there."

"I never saw the enforcer stop you," added Aednat. "And Den didn't bother to tell me until we'd left the city."

"Shouldn't have told you then, either, but you wouldn't stop asking."

"Is that why you knocked her out?" asked Mariessa, sounding as upset about Den's solution as Gabrick felt. "You didn't want to deal with an angry female?"

The flames took hold and Den fed in some larger pieces. "Beyond angry. She was hysterical. I led the horse off the main road so I could try to talk her down, but an enforcer followed us. He heard us talking, put two and two together, and...I didn't have much choice."

"You killed him," said Gabrick matter-of-factly.

Den nodded. "I hid the body well and made it look like a thug killing. Han won't realize it was me. I'd rather he not know the road we're taking. He might figure out our destination."

"Which is?"

"Haigang. We have a boat waiting and when we reach it, Mariessa can go her own way."

Gabrick sneered. "Unless it becomes convenient to leave us again."

"Not unless I'm dead," said Aednat, turning to confront Den. "We went through this in the Numbers Compound, and I thought you understood. I'm not going anywhere without Gabrick. I wouldn't have let you leave Eleven behind either, if he wasn't wounded. You're sure you have someone who can get him out?"

Den nodded. "They won't be watching Eleven for escape. As soon as he's able to travel, my friend will fake his death and sneak him out of the city. They'll meet us at our final destination, assuming we get that far."

Gabrick didn't know why this conversation pained him, but it did. No, Den had never particularly liked him. He knew that. But he'd taken a special interest at least, or so Gabrick had thought. Was it entirely for Aednat's benefit? Would the man really so callously discard him as if he were one more soldier to dispose of?

As if reading his thoughts, Den answered him. "I like you, boy. I know I don't always act like it, but I do. But if I ever have to choose between Aednat and you, it'll be her. And don't you pretend it would be otherwise for you, because we both know you'd slit my throat in a second if it somehow saved her life."

Gabrick couldn't argue that. It was a truth they both understood. "You're right. And I'd rather you save her and let me die than risk her life for me."

"Enough of this!" Aednat cried. "Nobody is going to die for me, or kill for me, or any of this. We're in this together, all of us. Understand?"

"All right, Aednat. We won't leave him again."

"Gabrick?" she said.

"Yeah, no sacrificing Den to save you. Though I think he might look better with a slit across his throat than that bruise you gave him. Don't you think?"

Aednat laughed, releasing some of the tension. "Sorry, Den."

Leave it to Mariessa to make everything uncomfortable again. "You could probably do better without me now. If those river whores talk, they'll know where to find us."

Den pulled out their sleeping rolls. "What's this?"

Gabrick had hoped Mariessa wouldn't say anything. He sighed. "We were looking for you by the river, and ran into some women."

"They made Gabrick some interesting offers."

"I was curious, but I wouldn't have gone with them," he assured Aednat, hoping she believed him, though he wasn't sure he believed himself.

Den stopped unrolling the bedding. "How stupid can you be? Why would you talk to anyone when we're on the run?"

"I was looking for you! And we were about to leave, but one of them stole our money and we had to get it back."

"You fought with them?" Den dropped the bedding, turning on Gabrick. "Don't you realize, a boy who can fight like you will be noticed."

"I never hit them, either one."

"It wasn't his fault they figured out who we were," said Mariessa. "My accent—"

"You stone-headed yenk!" Den kicked the bedding, nearly knocking a corner of it into the fire. "If they recognized you, we don't stand a chance!"

"We gave them food," said Gabrick, backing away from the fury in Den's eyes. He'd never seen the master like this. "They promised they wouldn't say anything."

"Are you a child?" Den scoffed. "At the first flash of a gold emp that promise will mean nothing. Absolutely nothing!"

Gabrick faced Den like he'd learned to face his father. "I'm sorry."

"Sorry?" Den descended on Gabrick. "Do you know how many times I've heard that word? Sorry doesn't get us down these roads, get us away from enforcers. A blistering apology doesn't bring people back from the dead!"

"Den," said Aednat, hobbling around the fire. "You need to calm down."

He backhanded Gabrick, sending him to the dirt. One arm hit the edge of the fire. Gabrick rolled away, swatting at the smoking fabric. But that was the least of his problems. Den's eyes had glossed over with murderous rage.

"Don't you try to get out of this," he said, going after Gabrick like a dog on the hunt. He gripped the front of Gabrick's shirt, holding him half up. This time he used his fist. Gabrick's head flew to one side.

"You traitorous demon!" Den hit again.

Aednat pulled on his arm. "Stop! You're—"

Den shoved her aside. She stumbled, dropping to the grass.

Den struck again. "I'll kill you, Han!"

Blood seeped across Gabrick's eyes. He brought up his arms, breaking Den's hold, but the man dropped with him to the ground. Den straddled him; hit again. Gabrick's cheek scraped across broken stems of thick grass. His vision blurred. Den brought up another fist, but Gabrick saw echoes of it on either side. Then Den disappeared.

Standing above Gabrick was a boy. No, Mariessa dressed as a boy. She had knives in each hand. One poised to fight, the other poised to throw. "You take one more step, you crazy sleth, and I'll stick this knife in your chest."

Despite the pain, Gabrick turned his head, making out Den on the other side of the crushed embers, his sleeve and half of one side smoking as Gabrick's clothing had a moment before.

Aednat rushed over, placing her palm on Den's stomach. "Calm down."

His hand struck out. He stopped mid-motion, staring at her as if seeing her for the first time. He dropped the fist, shoulders slumped. "My butterflower. So much like your mother."

Taking in his surroundings, Den's eyes darted from side to side like a man coming awake. He hugged Aednat to him, and Gabrick frowned. Den was too young to be her parent. Maybe he really was an uncle like he'd said, or maybe not related at all. Maybe the rumors around the Numbers Compound had been true and there was more to their relationship than either of them let on.

Releasing Aednat at last and slapping the last traces of smoldering fabric on his tunic, Den approached Gabrick. Mariessa threatened with the knives, but Den help up his hands in surrender. If the girl had known what those hands could do, and how fast, she might not have relaxed, but she stepped back and Den didn't try anything. He knelt at Gabrick's side, tenderly touching his bruised and broken skin, checking Gabrick's burns.

"They're minor," Gabrick said. "I'll be fine."

Tears welled in Den's eyes, more frightening than his anger, because it was something Gabrick had never seen in the ten years he'd known the man.

"I'm so sorry," Den said. "I never believed I could do this, that I would ever lose control like that again."

Mariessa sheathed her knives. "I saw some yiro plant near the road. It'll help with the swelling and maybe heal his cuts. We need some for his bullet wound anyway."

And she disappeared. Aednat went to a nearby stream to get water, leaving Gabrick alone with Den, though Gabrick wasn't sure he shared their sudden trust.

"I guess I should have said something sooner," Gabrick said, though his heart wasn't in it. Den had had no right.

"Yes, but it's not the end of the world." Den hung his head and placed a hand on Gabrick's chest. "My reaction really had nothing to do with you. No, boy, you're not the one to be sorry. I am."

He glanced around to make sure the girls were still gone. "This isn't a huge secret, but it's hard for me to talk about. I've mentioned Kerise."

"Yes. The woman who was so nice to you when you lived in the palace. The one you're always saying Aednat looks like. She's not really your niece is she?"

"No. She's Kerise's niece, her sister's daughter. Her real father is dead, but she thinks the emperor is her father." Den cocked his head. "You hope to win her from Eleven?"

Gabrick ignored the question, more focused on the lie. "Why would you tell her something like that? My father is twisted, evil. Nobody who truly knows him could want him as a parent."

"I had to tell Aednat something so she'd keep her distance from you as your servant. I didn't want the same thing happening to her as happens to so many of the others." Den shook his head, dismissing the subject. "Anyway, your mother was taken as one of his wives and conceived weeks before the emperor took Kerise, so you should have been born the thirteenth child."

"The cursed one," said Gabrick automatically. He'd been raised to believe the number was declared evil by the Vasheri, but now he remembered Den's words at the compound. "But only because the emperor decided?"

"Because of that prophecy that Aednat found."

"So, I'm guessing I wasn't born thirteenth," said Gabrick, "or I'd be the one dead."

"Because you came late, and Kerise went into labor early, she had the thirteenth son. The emperor plunged his sword through the baby and into Kerise's heart so he could nullify the prophecy. I know it's not your fault, when you were born, but it's hard not to see that moment every time I look at you. And as you get older, it's hard not to see the emperor in that moment. He was in his early twenties then, close to my age and not much older than you."

It was a relief, to finally understand how Den had liked him for all these years, yet hated him at the same time. It wasn't right, but at least Gabrick understood. Judging by the relieved expression on Den's face, it must have been a relief to finally tell him the truth, to explain himself.

Gabrick grinned. "So, as far as Aednat, do I have—"

"What about me?" Both of them jerked their heads up, surprised that she'd returned sooner than Mariessa.

Gabrick turned a worried frown on Den. "Do you think something happened?"

But in that moment, Mariessa eased into the clearing, her feet as silent on the thick grass as socks on carpet. "There's something coming over the far hill," she whispered. "Someone with a glowing heartstone."

"Green?" Den asked.

Mariessa nodded.

"Lost demons of limbo!" Den swore. "A seeker. Leave the fire. Grab what you can and get on the horses. We'll walk them over the next rise then run them for all they're worth."

Aednat already sat astride one horse and Gabrick grabbed the sleeping roll and went to join her.

Den grabbed his arm, stopping him. "We need to get as far from here as we can tonight. Putting me with Aednat and you with Mariessa will equalize the weight on both horses." In an undertone, he whispered. "See what you can do to teach her to ride."

With the clothing tied to the back of their horse, Den hopped onto it behind Aednat. She held the reins with confidence, having taken many of the same lessons Den had inflicted on Gabrick.

Turning to their smaller mount, Gabrick wrapped his hands round Mariessa's skinny waist, making her gasp. She almost squealed as he lifted her off the ground and onto the saddle of their mare. Despite the gravity of the situation, he had to choke back a laugh.

"What?" she protested. "I can't—"

The horse pranced and Mariessa gripped the pommel. Her knuckles shone pink in the dimming shades of sunset. It would be dark soon.

Gabrick kept hold of the horse's reins, slipping his foot into the stirrup. "I'm going to teach you to ride, and this is the best way."

He swung up behind her, his arms encircling her in order to keep hold of the reins. Her back fit perfectly against his chest, and if she let it, her head might nestle under his chin.

She shivered in the evening air, making the skin beneath his shirt tingle as if she shared the chill of the night with him. Despite the weather, the prospect of being chased seemed to be keeping him warm. His size probably helped, too. Being so small, and from a warmer climate, Mariessa suffered more.

He wrapped one arm around her waist, holding both reins with his right hand. "Lean into me."

She tried to pull away. "What are you doing?"

"You're cold and it's only going to get worse as we ride."

She sat straight as a stick.

Gabrick chuckled. "What is it with you and horses? Every time we're on one, you think I'm trying to attack you. I'm interested in someone else if you haven't noticed, so relax."

"I wouldn't put it past you to want both," she said, but she leaned back.

As they began moving forward, Gabrick hugged her tight against him, realizing the lie in his words. Yes, he wanted Aednat, but having Mariessa pressed close against him, smelling her earthy scent, brought unbidden thoughts and desires that had nothing to do with his former servant.

He swallowed back the thoughts and tried to make conversation. "Thank you for defending me, with Den."

"I didn't really," said Mariessa, contentious as usual. "If he'd asked, I would have agreed that you were an idiot." She laughed, and he realized she was teasing him.

The girl was completely unpredictable. And with the banter, she relaxed. Like he'd suspected, when she leaned her head back, it nestled almost completely under his chin. He resisted the temptation to lay his cheek against her short hair, and resisted more the temptation to move his hand from her waist and let it explore. He was grateful when they made the next rise and it was time to run.

"Feel how the horse moves and try to move with her," Gabrick told Mariessa before clucking at the mare and giving a light kick. "Try to move with me as I move with the horse."

And she did, much more than Gabrick had expected. And having her so close, synchronized with him as the horse went from trot to canter to gallop, did nothing to alleviate the desires he was trying so hard to tamp down.

"It's great, isn't it?" he said, the huskiness in his voice and the way he'd gone out of breath having little to do with the ride.

She was equally out of breath, but surely not for the same reason. "This is horrible."

"Ah, come on. This is daffing fabulous! The wind on your face, through your hair, the speed and sense of freedom."

"The wind is making my hair stick out like a hut caught in a hurricane, the air is cold, and it's full of bugs."

Her hair did flap around a bit, but it was short now, so it didn't bother him. The tie on his braid had flown out and he'd be the one with knots to untangle when they came to a stop.

A gnat landed in his mouth and he choked, spitting it to the side. "Yeah, sometimes it's not a bad idea to keep your head down a bit. You never see a rider smiling wide when they're running a horse, not unless they're hungry."

Mariessa's laugh rumbled against his chest. "Maybe I should open my mouth wider. I feel like I've not eaten in days."

"Not since a lousy breakfast," said Gabrick. "But I think we'll like our meal in the next town better without the bug aftertaste."

They both laughed, continuing the ride in companionable silence, but the thought that tugged at Gabrick's mind, was the reminder that as soon as they reached Haigang, Mariessa would go her own way.

44

Division reports littered Han's desk, which he systematically reviewed. He longed for the days when he'd had someone at his side to assist with the never-ending pile, someone who could add insights into what wasn't written on the page, who had a finger on the pulse of the empire. Den was supposed to take that space, but now Han wondered if his threats and coercions might not work. Den was willing to die, embraced the concept, and that diminished Han's leverage.

He stared at the stack of papers: the new science coordinator lacked foresight and passion. There hadn't been a significant scientific advancement since the aeroplane, which Han refused to let them mass produce. He didn't want such technology to be used against him. He had stones and loyal soldiers to withstand any warfare on land, but just one rogue aeroplane could cause unforeseeable havoc. Now, the scientists played with some theory based on how space and time related to one another. They also claimed all creation consisted of some kind of small constructs they called atoms, but without some realistic benefit from the knowledge, he didn't see the point in their research. Den would have understood it, known how best to use it, but Den had abandoned him.

Useless reports by Quing and his underlings from the CSO gave no indication of Den's whereabouts. Quing didn't even know if the four of them had stayed together. Han's small force of seekers focused in the area north and east of Han City, but the Sorceress Tracking Agency director indicated they'd found no hint of the Keroka girl other than a false sighting. He didn't like the idea of having so powerful a sorceress roaming the whole of Dixho. Maybe they should patrol that little nothing of a country, Kerokos. If the group had separated, she might go home.

Even Peder's support was absent, he having gone to Eroleth in search of Han's new ascension bride. The reports from the local ICRO officer were near useless, even worse than Xo's had been.

An urgent knock sounded, followed by Bow Quing's quick-spoken request. "I have news, Your Highness. May I enter?"

Han jumped to his feet, a few of the papers fluttering off the desk like falling leaves. "Yes. Enter." He stepped on them, meeting Quing in the middle of the room. "What do you have?"

"A report from the enforcers came through the telegraph service, but one of the stupid cretes merely filed it instead of passing it on. We should have known about this two days ago."

Another knock sounded.

"What is it?" Han yelled.

The guard cracked the door. "Tey-Ran Kep requests entrance, Your Holiness."

"Your assistant?" Han asked.

Quing nodded. "Whatever Kep has, it can wait."

Han would decide who entered his office and who was kept without. Quing supposed too much. "Let him approach."

The door swung open and Kep came to Quing's side, bowing so low he nearly folded in half. "I have urgent news, Your Eminence."

Quing bristled, casting a quick sideways glare at his assistant. "Mine takes precedence, Kep. With your permission, oh Holy Lingdow."

Impatient for the news, this time Han let the impertinence slide. "Go on."

Quing held out the telegraph. "Enforcers found a couple of river whores willing to talk for a few coins. They recognized the boy, Fourteen, and the Keroka girl."

Han turned to the assistant. "And you?"

The man blushed. "I'm sorry to disturb you, Your Eminence. I have a copy of the enforcer's report. It came in the overland mail this morning."

Han furrowed his brow. "When did they find these girls?"

"Three days ago," the men said in unison.

Han backhanded Quing. "And I find out about it now?"

Quing went to one knee as if in supplication, but he'd kept himself from falling to the floor. "As I said, the telegraph operators claim they put it in the urgent pile, but since they were unaware of the magnitude of the escape, they just thought it was another case of a random child who looks like you who needs to be found and eliminated." Quing raised his face. "The women met the boy and Keroka-girl almost two weeks ago, but we should still be able to catch them if we use cars."

"No," said Han. "Den is smart enough to know we'd eventually get that report. He'll count on beating us to Haigang, so we have to stop him."

"How?"

"The two of you have two days to find the ship and receive a large bonus, or I'm having you executed."

The assistant gasped, but Quing came to his feet. "Executed?"

Han fiddled with the gun at his waist. "You've failed me too many times of late."

Quing had the audacity to sneer. "Three lifetimes of service aren't sufficient to gain me some flexibility when dealing with a man such as Chid Den? It means nothing to you that the man can fight better than any other man on Dixho, that he was your science director until he chose to become a Numbers master, and that he's the best strategist our world has ever known?"

"No." Han stared down at the man, suppressing an insane desire to press his gun to Quing's head, to pull the trigger and watch his fiery eyes go dull. "You do your job, or you die trying."

"You might as well give in and shoot me," Quing challenged. "Haigang is far enough from here that without the rail system you denied, I'm dependent on information from my network in the city and the telegraphs. Even if I took an autocar, Den and his friends will be well gone before I reach the edge of the city, or they'll be alerted by the imperial automobile's arrival. Are you sure you don't want to send seekers? It would be equally reliable."

Han considered their dilemma. He hated to admit it, but Quing was right. An autocar would alert Den to go in another direction, even an impossible one, and the CSO network in a port town like Haigang would not only be clumsy, but susceptible to bribery. If Han left it to them, Den would slip through their fingers.

Han released the pistol. "You know how to fly a plane, correct?"

Quing's eyes lit up, but if the man thought he'd be sent off on his own with one of Han's prize machines, he was crazy. "I and my personal guard will accompany you."

"There's no airfield in Haigang," said Quing. "I can't land on the ocean."

"There's one east of the city."

Quing scowled. "I didn't know—"

"You didn't need to, nor will either of you ever mention it to anyone. The regional governor can pick us up in his car and we'll be inside the city within eight hours. That will give you six hours to find the boat."

"Six hours isn't much time." Quing said. "It will be evening when we arrive."

Han pulled the pistol from his waistband, holding it loose at his side. "If you don't find it by then, the two of you," he waved the gun, "will be dead."

They arrived in Haigang behind schedule, but Han wasn't about to give the men any leeway. "If you could have found the boat in six hours, you can find it in five."

Han had an ICRO man stationed in Haigang pay for a room in the nicest hotel available, though in a dump-town like Haigang it would still be unsatisfactory. Han snuck in unnoticed. Nothing would tip Den off about their presence. He'd made sure of that. Of course, it was possible Den had come and gone, but he'd be hard-pressed, even changing horses often, to reach the port city in under two weeks.

Haggard, with a crumpled paper in his fist, Quing returned just before midnight. "I think this is it."

His assistant, Tey-Ran Kep, was on his heels ten minutes later, confirming the same boat. It seemed strange that Quing didn't have more of an advantage over his young assistant, especially since Quing had had three lifetimes to hone his skills.

"Shall we gather the soldiers and board tonight?" Quing asked.

Han shook his head. "No. There will be no warning, not for the men on the boat, and not for Den. This time, he cannot escape."

Quing gripped the paper in his hand a bit tighter. "You want him dead then? Not captured."

"If he's captured, all the better, but if he attempts to run, kill them all." Han couldn't afford to let old sentimentality govern his decisions, not anymore.

45

It was past midnight, after two weeks of horse travel, when Gabrick and the others finally reached the Haigang harbor, each riding a fine, but not particularly well-groomed steed. Gabrick had lost track of what horse he rode. They'd changed mounts in every town that had had a stable.

An autocar passed and Gabrick's palms went sweaty, sure the emperor had found them, but it was merely the district's governor. None of the other citizens raised their eyes with any interest apart from idle curiosity. In Haigang, the tier districts resembled slices of pie with the harbor as an epicenter, rather than the concentric circles like Han City. The affluent sections flowed from the outside slices to the small mid-tier sections down to the largest slice, the seventh to ninth tiers, with no definitive lines between them. As a prosperous city, even the lowest citizen didn't descend to a tenth tier. Den explained that if one was caught in a higher tier without proper paperwork the laws still applied, but unless someone went two or three tiers above their station, the authorities weren't likely to notice.

"Will we leave tonight?" Gabrick asked as they slipped into the seventh tier section of the harbor district.

They turned down a smaller avenue. Sewage ran in partially covered canals down the side of the street, making Gabrick gag intermittently. He'd seen worse in the eighth and ninth districts, where sewage ran down the streets, or the tenth district of the last city they'd gone through, where it piled up in alleys and back corners between buildings, waiting for rain to wash it away. But having seen worse didn't make it smell any better.

The stench forced even Den to raise a neckerchief to his nose, muffling his words. "No, we'll go before daybreak. There's an inn here where we can get some food, board the horses, and get a few hours of sleep."

"But what if—"

"There's nothing we can do until the boat can legally leave harbor."

Gabrick nodded, glancing at the girls riding behind them. He'd only shared a horse with Mariessa that first night. In the morning, Den had purchased two more horses and despite her fears, Mariessa had insisted she finish her training on her own. She'd mounted up, put her heels to her new gelding's flank, and figured out how to make the beast follow her instructions.

She no longer wore the façade of a boy. There was no point since the river whores had found her out. Under Aednat's persuasion, the short haircut had gone feminine. She'd coaxed the ends to turn under and pulled the thick mass back from Mariessa's face with a wide ribbon, emphasizing Mariessa's high cheekbones and distinctive eyes. Den had found her a dress of burnt orange and warm browns that flared out from her hips, allowing her to straddle the horse without looking completely unfeminine. The tight bodice emphasized the small but shapely figure she'd kept hidden, a direct contrast to Aednat's voluptuous curves.

Sitting side-saddle in a long, pale pink number that strained in all the right places, many boys and men had given Aednat second glances as they passed, though a few seemed equally taken with Mariessa. Gabrick wanted to strangle each one.

Den led them to a small wooden building next to a little store. Beyond it, a wooden sign read, *Traveler's Inn*.

"Take the horses into the stable." Den pointed to the wooden building's wide doors. "I'll get us some food and rooms."

Gabrick dismounted, taking Den's horse as Aednat slipped down from her sidesaddle as gracefully as a third-tier. Mariessa swung her leg from over the saddle, and stood there for a moment, foot in the stirrup, trying to figure out how to stretch her leg the long distance to the ground without giving the world a very dramatic view of what was under her skirt. Finally, she leaned over the saddle, slipped her foot free, then pushed away from the horse to land on her feet, the dismount of an acrobat. Her skirt lifted like a parasol in the wind, but she patted it down. Gabrick suspected a blush beneath her sun-darkened skin.

Walking into the squat stable, barely tall enough to fit the horses, they found narrow stalls lining one side and part of the other. The remaining space held a mound of hay, some grains, and extra horse tackle. Unlike most of the stables they'd been in over the previous two weeks, the place smelled more of hay and leather than sweat and horse manure.

A boy about Gabrick's age, broad in the shoulders, with dark hair pulled back into a short tuft, approached from the far end of the room. "I'm Teipen. Can I help you?" He sized Gabrick up with his eyes, puffing out his wide chest, probably to compensate for what he lacked in height.

The stable boy's tattoo showed him to be eighth tier. Gabrick raised his chin a little, so it leveled above the stable boy's head. "You're to board our horses until morning."

"Yes, sir," said Teipen, reaching for the closest one. The words came out right, but the tone held a hint of mockery.

Mariessa stifled a giggle and Teipen gave her a very different once over. He winked at her as he led Den's horse to a pen. It was no surprise when Teipen reached for Mariessa's chestnut, but Gabrick maneuvered himself ahead. Another mocking smile, and Teipen led the horse away. He went to Aednat next, saving Mariessa for last. When he took her gelding's reins, he made a point of pausing as he touched her hand. She blushed as prettily as a serving maid, and the boy flashed a triumphant grin.

"Take care of my *sister's* horse," Gabrick said. "My uncle is particularly fond of it, as I am of my sister."

He'd meant it as a warning, but the boy turned with a quizzical expression. "You feel toward your sister as if she's a horse, sir?"

Gabrick's temper flared to the surface. "Low profile," Aednat whispered into his ear.

"Of course not," Gabrick said with a stiff jaw. "I wouldn't kill someone if they touched my horse."

The boy seemed unimpressed by Gabrick's blatant threat, merely raising an eyebrow.

They turned to go, but from the far end of the stable, Teipen called out, "Miss, can I ask you a quick question, about your mount?"

Gabrick moved forward to speak with the daffing crete, but Mariessa placed a hand on his arm and stepped forward. "I can handle it."

Though they talked for a few minutes in the stall's deeper shadows, Gabrick never saw either one of them even glance at the horse.

"Question about the horse like limbo." Gabrick said under his breath.

Aednat leaned close and put her chin on his shoulder, the way she'd done when they were kids and she had something special to tell him. "I think it's kind of cute. Who knew Mariessa had such a feminine side?"

And she very obviously did. The boy gazed down at her with a rogue smile, the kind that always won Gabrick extra helpings in the kitchens, but usually caught him rude remarks from Mariessa. She giggled, put her hands behind her back and shifted her hips from one side to the next, looking at him from under her lashes, shy yet inviting. What did she think she was doing?

"Uncle is waiting for us," Gabrick called out. "Come on!"

Mariessa shifted a bit more, nodded her head, then hurried to join them.

"What was that about?" Gabrick whispered as they left the stable.

"Don't you know anything?" she said. "If you wanted to know what was happening in the palace, who did you ask?"

"The only ones I ever talked to from the palace were the concubines."

Mariessa sniffed with condescending disdain. She'd already made it more than clear that she thought his association with the concubines, even though he'd never done more than look and talk, made him a horrible example of the male species.

"Well, the concubines picked up most of their information from the servants, at least they would have if the emperor hadn't cut their tongues out, because servants are rarely seen, hear everything, go everywhere, and gossip even more than old ladies."

"What does that—"

They stepped into the inn, and Gabrick let the conversation drop. Unlike the hotel in Han City, this place was more like a bar than a reception area. Thick wooden tables stood on a dirty concrete floor, most of them empty. A fair number of men sat on stools at a bar on the far end of the room, drinking. Den sat at one of the tables near a crude, empty stage, guarding four plates of steaming fish, vegetables, and rice covered with green sauce along with a hard biscuit, and some tall glasses of water.

Gabrick weaved through the room to the table. "I'd rather have something stronger for once."

"Liquor dulls the mind and should only be used when a man wants to be stupid," replied Den. "How often in life do you think it will ever benefit you to be stupid?"

As the girls joined them, Gabrick glanced at the men on the stools, wondering if they were aware of this seemingly well-known adage. "Never?"

A shadow passed over Den's features. "You can only hope."

Gabrick shook his head and went to his food. He'd gone from one confusing conversation with Mariessa to an equally baffling one with Den. He'd best stick with Aednat. She didn't always have much to say, but at least she usually made sense.

With only two-thirds of her food eaten, Mariessa declared herself finished. She pushed her plate toward Gabrick who was wiping up any remaining specks with his biscuit.

"Would you like to do more reading lessons tonight?" he asked. He'd been helping her whenever they walked the horses or took a break to eat or sleep.

"Not tonight." Mariessa winked at Aednat. "I'm going to check on my horse for a minute. See what news he has for me." And she was gone.

"What's this?" Den asked.

"The stable boy showed interest and seems to like to talk," said Aednat, as if that explained everything.

"Mm," was all he said.

Gabrick wolfed down his biscuit, watching the door Mariessa had disappeared through, then pushed the plate away. "Where can I find a decent toilet instead of a stinking pot?"

"Decent?" said Den. "Back where you were born. Sufficient would be a small shack behind the stables, made out of wood or mud, with a hole in the ground. We don't want to get separated, so come right back."

"If you don't want us separated," said Gabrick, "what about Mariessa?"

"She's on her own starting tomorrow. It's up to her to figure out how to survive from this point on."

Gabrick's food turned heavy in his stomach. He'd seen Mariessa call plants into living monsters that could rip a man into unrecognizable pieces, but she still seemed so small and vulnerable, so lonely. How could they be leaving her to fend for herself?

He found the inn's back exit, but instead of making his way toward the rickety shed that could be smelled from across the courtyard, he went to the small door ajar at the back of the stable. Without moving it more than a digit or two, he slipped in, hiding in the dark shadows at the very back of the squat building.

What he saw dissolved the knot in his stomach and set his blood on fire.

46

Mariessa had her back against one of the beams between two empty stalls. Leaning close, Teipen's elbow rested against the nearest slats, his fingers fiddling with the ruffle at Mariessa's shoulder. Gabrick couldn't hear what they whispered to one another, but he recognized their smiles and the seductive, low tones.

Other hand on her waist, Teipen gave her a teasing yank forward. She pushed him away, saying something.

As a horse shuffled in its stall, Gabrick moved a little closer, the straw hiding the soft step of his boots.

"Give me a kiss, and I'll tell you," Teipen said.

Mariessa still had hold of his arm. "I already gave you a kiss, but you're not telling me anything interesting."

She'd kissed him? Some stable boy?

"I like your curls." Teipen's voice grew husky. "Your eyes reflect the gold of the lamps, only brighter." He touched her mouth. "Lips as full and inviting as morning dew, dark like sweet molasses."

Mariessa gave his finger a light kiss. "I want to know about this city I wandered into. Not hear vain flatteries."

The warning in her voice seemed obvious, but Teipen dropped his free arm from the stall, pushing himself against her. His hand ran across her hip.

Mariessa's startled gasp, not directed at Teipen, cued Gabrick that he'd risen from his hiding place. Not only had he stood up, but he'd taken several paces toward the daffing stable hand. Gabrick hesitated, but he'd gone too far to stop now. He'd have to carry through.

Sticking out his wide-as-a-horse chest, Teipen faced him. "She's old enough to do as she chooses, big brother. Why don't you go away and mind your own business?" He caressed Mariessa's arm, but she pulled it away.

The rage that flared through Gabrick didn't make sense, but he couldn't tamp it down. "Don't touch her, you filthy crete."

"Crete?" The boy took a step forward. "You think you're fourth-tier or something?" He pushed his rolled-up sleeves past his elbows and onto his thick biceps, gesturing Gabrick forward. "Why don't you see if you can stop me?"

A part of Gabrick knew he should walk away. Mariessa was more than capable of taking care of herself. But another part, where the anger bubbled, wanted to rip the boy to shreds.

"Gabrick, no," said Mariessa. "Nobody needs to get hurt."

Glancing back at her, Teipen's confident grin suggested he knew his way in a fist fight. "Don't worry, miss. I think I can handle your scrawny brother without marring his pretty face."

Gabrick had gotten rather lean the last few weeks. With little to eat, a lot of travel, and the digit he'd added to his height, he'd gone beyond thin, but that hadn't made him scrawny, not even close. With a sneer, he punched at the boy's stomach.

Teipen blocked. Gabrick had expected he would. With a quick double-thrust to the neck, Teipen's eyes rolled up in his head and he slumped to the hard dirt. Gabrick stepped over him to Mariessa.

"Are you crazy?" she asked.

"He's fine. Just passed out for a minute or two."

She sneered up at him. "We're not supposed to draw attention."

"You not only had his attention, you were getting yourself in trouble." Gabrick knew better than to goad her, but he couldn't seem to help himself. "What do you think he would have done after you quit leading him on and finally told him no."

"I'm not defenseless, you high-stilted stonehead." She pulled a knife through a rip she'd hidden beneath her dress sash. "I can take care of myself."

The fire that had ignited as soon as he'd stepped into the stable refused to be quenched. Watching her pull the blade from beneath her clothes only made it worse. Her flushed face turned the little scar from the bullet-graze in the caves a contrasting white, and her chest continued its rapid rise and fall...from anger, exertion... or excitement?

With a chop of his hand, Gabrick hit her wrist. The knife landed, hilt up, in the dirt. He slipped behind her, running his hand up her thigh, beneath the dress, stealing the other blade.

The same huskiness in his voice as he'd heard from Teipen, he whispered against her ear. "I don't know why you always go for the one at your waist. It seems that this one would be much easier to unsheathe." He threw it down into the dirt, where it slid on its side next to the other one.

Mariessa swung around, leading with her fist.

Catching it, he held out her arm, staring at the fiery light in her eyes. He didn't think about it, didn't know why he did it, but suddenly his lips pressed against hers. They tasted sweet, of winter squash and honey. She opened her mouth to him and the fire burst into an inferno, his hands coursing across her back. Lifting her up, he pressed her body against him, his tongue exploring every recess as if he could consume her essence, press them so close together they would meld into one being.

And she responded. He couldn't have gone so blind with desire if she hadn't. One arm wrapped up his back, gripping his shoulder from behind, pulling herself up. Fingers from her other hand slid into the hair at the nape of his neck. His loose braid unraveled as she pressed his mouth harder against her own. She matched his intensity like a wild cat seeking purchase on its prey. Leg wrapped around his lower thigh, she released his shoulder to find a gap beneath his shirt. She widened it, allowing her cool hand to slide up his ribs, across his back.

Gabrick went feverish, frenzied. It didn't matter that they were in a horse stable. He didn't think it would have mattered if they'd been in a mud pit.

"Mari," he whispered against her cheek, his mouth trailing down her neck, to her throat. She smelled of woods, and nature, and if wonder had a smell, it was ingrained in her skin.

She groaned in response, a pleading sound, a wanting that not only gave him permission, but demanded he act. He lifted her small frame so that both legs wrapped around him. His hand pushed against the door of an empty stall, lined with fresh straw.

Movement to one side caught his eye. Mariessa turned her face and gasped. Suddenly her hand was out from beneath his shirt and she was pushing Gabrick away. She dropped to the floor, half in and half out of the empty stall. Hands that a moment ago had coursed over his body, smoothed at the skirt of her dress, straightening it out to appear respectable. Gabrick didn't see the point. If Teipen had witnessed any part of what had taken place, respectable was so far gone an aeroplane couldn't catch it.

"Definitely not your brother," Teipen said.

"I'd think that's obvious," Gabrick sauntered next to the stable boy, leaning on the same stall Teipen had been at with Mariessa. "Do your friends consider you very smart?"

Teipen narrowed his eyes. "Smart enough."

"That's what I figured." Gabrick jumped forward, knocking him out again. "You figured out enough to get us into trouble, but not enough to get away."

Checking Teipen's head where it'd banged against the hard-packed dirt for a second time, Mariessa huffed. "That can't be good for him."

"It's better for him than being dead, which would be the smart thing to do."

"You wouldn't."

The fact that she considered him more than capable of cold-blooded murder showed what she really thought of him. Gabrick shrugged. "I would, but I know you'd throw a fit, so we'll just tie him up and hope nobody finds him before we leave."

They trussed Teipen with rope, wrapped a thick piece of fabric around his mouth, and propped him up in one of the back stables, locking it behind them.

When they finished, Gabrick stared at Mariessa, part of him wanting to continue where they'd left off, but knowing she wouldn't let him get that close. Besides, if he wanted Aednat, this was something he couldn't do. But he wanted to, and Mariessa knew it.

She moved out of reach and picked up her knives. "Don't you ever touch me again, you filthy-minded—"

"Me?" Gabrick asked incredulous. "You seemed pretty willing for someone who's always spouting off about Vasheri, and treating women with respect, and...," he sputtered off like a little kid, wanting to hit himself for it.

"You caught me by surprise," she said. "Which will never happen again, believe me."

She sheathed her thigh-knife, but kept the other one pointed at his chest, as if he were his father and planned to throw her to the floor and rape her. The insult burned more than her thinking him a murderer.

"You'll be gone tomorrow," he reminded her. "So you won't have to worry about me. Besides, I have Aednat, and believe me, you don't compare."

Mariessa laughed. "If you really had Aednat, you wouldn't try to distract yourself with me, but she doesn't love you that way. Any fool can see it."

"She will. And when we're together, with children and grandchildren, you'll be a lonely, bitter, old woman with no one to care about, and no one who will give a daffing thought for you. Including me."

"I know men like you, Beht Fourteen." Mariessa waved the knife like pointing a finger. "Even if you convince her, you'll get tired after a while and want someone new, someone more exciting, and then she'll be left at home, taking care of the kids, and pretending that she doesn't know you run around with other women."

Gabrick took a step toward her. "My name is not Beht Fourteen" his low voice held no passion this time, only a cold threat. "You'd do well to remember it, you little whore."

"I warned you."

She had, and he'd believed she'd meant it. So when the knife whisked from her fingers, aimed for his right shoulder, he was ready. He turned to one side and bent backwards, the knife whizzing past. It landed in the back door with a thud, and then the resounding echo of reverberating metal.

Gabrick descended on her, grabbing both of her clenched fists by the wrists. "And let me warn you. No matter what I say...stupid, insulting, or wrong...if you ever threaten me with a knife again, I *will* throw you to the ground, and I'll make you sorry for the day we met."

Her voice cracked, on the edge of tears, but the ever-tough Mariessa would never give in to something so feeble and weak. "I'm already sorry." She lifted her chin, defiant and unafraid.

And the flame sparked again. Gabrick wanted to keep to his promise and throw her to the ground, but not to teach her a lesson. He wanted to bring out the cat again, make her groan with a desire that begged for release.

He dropped her hands and turned on his heel. "Remember, I've saved your life at least as many times as you've saved mine. You wouldn't be alive without me."

He stalked from the room without turning back. A couple of arms from the stable door, he heard another knife land in the thick wood.

"I hate you!" she screamed after him.

A few horses whinnied, but Gabrick continued to the inn, leaving her to wallow in her rage alone. He regretted what he'd done, but he couldn't take it back now, not any of it. And there was no point in trying. He'd never see her again anyway.

"Good-bye, Mari," he whispered.

47

The thoughts that kept Mariessa awake were not the ones she'd have expected. She shared a room with Aednat, Den and Gabrick in the one next door. Since they still had plenty of money from the magistrate, they'd ordered two. Once her anger with Gabrick faded, her fascination had remained. She lay on a blanket next to Aednat's uncomfortable mattress— why the others preferred the horrible things she didn't know— trying to rekindle her disgust, her fury. But the feel of Gabrick's demanding lips and the ripple of his hard muscles against her palms, had come back again and again.

When she finally fell asleep, despite Aednat's soft snores, the thoughts multiplied in her dreams. Her name repeated over and over as if no one had ever spoken it before. Some of her childhood friends had tried to shorten her name to Mari, but it had always sounded flat and nasal. The way she heard it in her dreams, the way Gabrick had whispered it against her cheek, made it rich and exotic, the *A* drawn out as if there were two of them instead of one, the *R* rolled along his tongue and guttural, reminding her of the deep kiss that had invaded her senses and exploded a passion she'd never known existed. Even the short clip of the last syllable fell off his tongue like a tease, a nip of teeth on bare skin. That a word, just her name, could leave her so breathless was uncanny and unfair. She'd never escape Gabrick, no matter how far she ran, because every time someone said her name she'd think of how it had sounded from his lips.

When she woke the next morning, the memory still fresh, the unwanted desire to repeat the experience lingered. She'd kissed other boys before, but she'd never experienced anything like last night. Such mindless abandon, especially with someone she so detested and knew she could never trust, was beyond reason. Maybe, deep down, she was everything Sando had claimed, if not by action then in her heart.

Before Den came to knock on their door, Mariessa had already awoken, washed her face, and used the chamber pot in the corner. She shook Aednat until her unwilling eyes fluttered and focused.

"So tired," she muttered.

"You'll get plenty of sleep on the boat," Mariessa promised. "Being on the sea is like being rocked by a loving mother."

Aednat groaned and gathered her things, but Mariessa didn't follow suit.

"You'll come down with us?" Aednat asked. "To say goodbye?"

Mariessa knew she should. "Give Den my thanks, but I'll stay here a little longer then find a boat when the harbor gets busier."

"If you gave him a chance, Gabrick is a good person. He's going to be an amazing man someday."

"I'm glad you think so." The attempt at a smile made Mariessa's mouth feel twisted. "He certainly thinks you're more amazing and beautiful than the Vasheri themselves. I think he plans on marrying you someday."

Aednat laughed, the sound beautiful and kind, not at all mocking, and Mariessa couldn't feel any ill will toward her. "If you're thinking of Gabrick and me together, it'll never happen. Not only do I love Eleven, and Den has promised he'll get him back to me, but there are other reasons. And even if there weren't, he's like a brother."

"Does he know that?"

Aednat shook her head. "Gabrick is good in a lot of ways, but he's stubborn and he's ambitious. I represent some achievement he thinks he must have, but he doesn't know what he really wants. He'll figure it out, given time."

Mariessa's cheeks grew warm. "Well, I'm grateful he doesn't want me and I don't have to deal with him anymore. So tell them both goodbye for me, and that will have to be good enough."

"We're leaving the horses. If you sell them, you might have enough coin to get you set up when you reach Kerokos." To Mariessa's surprise, Aednat stretched out her arms and enfolded her in a hug. "I'll always think of you as a sister. Take care of yourself and be careful going home. I hope you have a glorious life."

Unbidden tears pushed at the corners of Mariessa's eyes, but she forced them back. She returned the hug, awkwardly patting Aednat's back. "You, too," she managed.

And then Aednat grabbed her things, gave Mariessa one last encouraging glance, and was gone.

When the door to the inn opened and shut, Mariessa gathered her scant belongings and went downstairs. Boards squeaked every third or fourth step, alerting anyone interested to her presence. The deep gray of early morning, right before sunlight peeks over the horizon, muted everything in the tavern. The cooks could be heard bustling in the kitchen behind doors near the bar, the smell of fresh-baked breads cleansing the odor of stale beer and sweaty customers. Another early riser sat in a corner drinking a steaming mug of morning tea and eating an old roll leftover from the night before. Otherwise, the room was deserted.

Mariessa hadn't wanted to talk to Gabrick and the others, but she still wanted to see them one last time. Not Gabrick in particular, but all of them together.

As her hand touched the door it swung inward, forcing Mariessa to jump out of the way. A visiting-girl, a strange sight at this time of the morning, walked into the room as if she belonged there. She was an uptown version of the women she and Gabrick had met by the river, with high-tier clothes, genuine jewelry, and no signs of disease. But the generous amount of cleavage shown, the tight skirt, the high and narrow heels, and the hard look in her eyes, marked her as sure as any tattoo. She scanned the room as if Mariessa didn't exist. Not finding what she was looking for, she directed her gaze downward.

"One of your customers, a Chid Den."

Mariessa hid the shock at hearing Den's real name. Who could have found him here, and what would happen to Mariessa by association? "I don't work here, but I think I heard a man going by that name leave a few minutes ago, toward the edge of town."

The woman breathed a put-out sigh. "Well, that's great. I hurry all this way to deliver a message, and the sweets is already gone. To limbo with it all. Now I won't get me payment."

"I think I might catch him," Mariessa offered, wondering more and more what kind of a message a visiting-girl would have. "I could take it to him."

"Then you's get paid and gets the pleasure? I'm thinking that doesn't help me none."

"How much?" Mariessa offered, pulling out the small coin satchel Den had given her the day before.

The girl immediately stretched out her hand. "The message was supposed to earn me an emp, but I'd had hopes of getting me a job, if you knows what I mean?"

Mariessa held up a gold emperor. "I'm not giving you a job, if you know what I mean, so it's this or nothing."

She frowned, but took the coin. "I was to tell him, specifically mind you, that I's was here to give him a royally good time."

"What's that supposed to mean?"

The woman shrugged. "Likes I know that?" She pulled out a folded piece of paper from the bosom of her dress. "Thens I was supposed to give him this."

Only one word was written on the piece of paper, in smeared black, as if a sooty ember was used rather than a pencil: A-M-B-U-S-H. It took Mariessa a moment to sound out the letters, but when she did her insides turned hollow. "By all that's holy below."

She crumpled the paper and handed it back to the woman, along with the gold emperor. "Burn that note. And for your life's sake, you were never here." She turned to the wide-eyed man staring from the bar. "Same for you."

He nodded dumbly, dropping his mug and shooting up the stairs two at a time.

Bursting from the inn, Mariessa scanned the street toward the harbor. It wasn't hard to make out the three figures, especially Gabrick's tall frame, but they were far down the street. Nor was it difficult to see the man standing some distance behind them, outside a bakery with steam and warm smells of comfort wafting from its open door, a rifle held behind his back.

She was too late. Using her evil power wasn't an option. But what could Mariessa do? They were already surrounded. The trap waited like steel jaws, the trigger only another step forward.

She stared at the buildings, the street, the boats, and then she turned tail and ran.

48

Han watched from the top of a woman's parlor, hidden by the garish pink and teal sign. His personal guard waited in various positions nearby, their first assignment to keep him protected. Coming from an establishment farther down the street, Den appeared with two companions, all wearing fine upper-tier clothing.

He watched Den with a heavy heart. Did he really want to kill this man? After all Den had done, it had to happen, but still Han couldn't imagine it. Maybe once they'd reached the heart of the trap, the obvious futility of running would convince Den to admit defeat. He wouldn't let the children be massacred to be sure, especially his dear Aednat.

"The sorceress girl isn't with him," one of his soldiers whispered.

Han waved the matter aside. "She is nothing. We'll find her later."

In the moment it took him to answer the guard, everything changed. From the prow of the ship, barely within clear sight of Den and his companions, Bow Quing stood on a crate waving his arms. There was no question Den would recognize him. The traitor!

Den turned the youngsters beside him back the way they'd come, urging them to run.

Han pulled his pistol, aimed, and fired. Red blossomed across Quing's shoulder. He tumbled off the crate and out of sight. In the same instant, Han gave the signal, waving a yellow neckerchief high in the air. The attack order was passed on via communication stones, electronic talking boxes and manual flags. Men rushed from alleys, storefronts, behind crates, boxes, holding pens, and on the ship itself.

Den and the others ran only a few steps then stopped. Surrounded by soldiers, they had nowhere to run, they had no weapons, and they had no defense. It was over.

Den had said he'd die before he went back. He'd even threatened to kill his supposed niece, though Han had never believed he would go through with it. But in an act of suicide, Den grabbed the children's hands, running toward the closest line of soldiers.

The men took aim. Han gripped his pistol, the tension making his eyes water. But no shots fired. Instead, one by one, the soldiers dropped their guns, falling face forward on the packed dirt. Knives of various sizes, some appearing to be nothing more than kitchen cutlery, protruded from their backs.

It took eight dead soldiers before their comrades turned to face their new threat. But the knives were nothing. Han hadn't seen anything like this in hundreds of years. He'd known the girl could be dangerous, but even with Peder and Quing's descriptions, he hadn't realized she posed such a monumental threat.

49

When Den pulled them forward, Gabrick knew they were heading to their deaths. He'd told Mari he would never be called Fourteen again, that he'd die first, but he hadn't imagined the opportunity would be presented the very next day. Still, the decision had been made, not only in his mind, but in his heart, and there was no turning back.

Soldiers aimed. Gabrick ran toward them, steeled for the worst. But it didn't come. One by one, in rapid succession, the men fell, knives plunged deep into their backs. Searching beyond their bleeding and twitching forms, Gabrick found her, Mari. Three more soldiers went down as they turned and then Mari disappeared behind a herd of saddled horses. They barreled down the street and Gabrick realized it wasn't a herd, only the horses that had been in the inn's stables. How had she saddled them all and sent them down the street at just the right time? How—

At the far corner, a burly-shouldered boy turned a dark roan stallion as if limbo demons themselves had given chase. Teipen. After what Gabrick and Mariessa had done, somehow she'd still convinced the stable boy to help.

The horses forced the soldiers aside, but Gabrick, Den, and Aednat took the opportunity Mari had presented, grabbing reins. More soldiers pressed in from the harbor and its piers, coming after them from the other side.

A far-away voice, so like his own it sent chills down Gabrick's spine, screaming in deranged fury, "Kill them! All of them!"

Gabrick jumped onto a horse. Artillery fired. The smell of gunpowder and smoke filled the small thoroughfare. A horse whinnied in pain. Aednat screamed. Turning to save her, Gabrick's horse circled but found nothing. Den rode from the thickening smoke, Aednat thrown over his saddle. Gabrick gripped his reins, about to follow, but the sight from the harbor dropped his mouth in open awe. The smell of brine washed over him, more powerful than the smoke.

Men screamed. Not from surprise, or fear, but the kind of horror that can never be erased. If any of them survived this, they would have nightmares for life. Roots plunged up through the road, grasping at men and firearms. From the greenery lining the thoroughfare, branches shook off their autumn leaves, reached out their gnarly hands, and grabbed at men's limbs, wrapped around their necks, or pierced through their mouths, eyes, or ears before plunging into their skulls. Though unbelievable, Gabrick had seen these things before. But what rose above them all, dwarfing the horror on the streets, shocked even him.

Similar to the vines growing outside his apartment in the Numbers Compound, only a hundred times larger, brownish-green ropes with thick leaves larger than a grown man's arms, came up from the water like hungry snakes. Some wrapped over and around the boat, crushing it as they dragged it to the ocean's depths. Others lashed out at the soldiers near the pier.

A rifle fired, pulling Gabrick from his trance. Long lengths of seaweed crawled across the piers toward land, reaching for more prey, but he forced his attention away from the gruesome scene.

Kicking his heels into the horse's flank, he encouraged it to flee. Then he found Mari. Slipping ever closer to her, holding an olive-green stone that shone like sunlight through a stained-glass window, a seeker raised a pistol.

"Mari!" Gabrick screamed. "Behind you!"

She turned, the action pulling her from the soil. A small branch slapped the gun from the man's hand, but without Mari's connection, it slowed then stilled. No knives left, her connection with the land broken, she had no way to defend herself. She staggered, and Gabrick saw what the attack had cost her. She could barely remain upright.

"I'm coming!" he yelled.

The seeker ran for her, pulling a long dagger.

Gabrick urged the horse faster. They closed in at the same moment. Mariessa reached her hands up to Gabrick like a child supplicating a parent. Her legs buckled. Gabrick caught her under the arm and heaved. As he swung her up, intending to lay her across his lap, the dagger sliced across her right hip. It cut through her dress, into the flesh, before the blade's tip pulled free.

The horse reared as the seeker grabbed hold of the reins. It was all Gabrick could do to keep Mari and him in the saddle. She wrapped herself round his waist, gripping him round the back like the clamp of a river shark. When they landed, her firm hold freed up both Gabrick's hands.

The seeker thrust the dagger in Mari's back, the blade long enough to pierce her and Gabrick together. Gabrick caught the man's wrist. Using his height and superior strength, he retracted the blade. The morning sun glinted off Mari's blood.

Gabrick pressed fingers into the man's wrist, forcing the knife to clatter against the cobblestones. The seeker reached up with his other hand, thinking to unhorse Gabrick.

With a twist and a quick change in grip, Gabrick sprained the man's wrist, breaking three fingers in the process. The seeker cried out in pain. Though Gabrick's restless steed sidestepped, he managed a solid kick to the man's stomach, leaving him gasping. Dropping the horse's rein, Gabrick leaned over, gripping the man's head in both hands.

Eyes suddenly wide, the man clenched Gabrick's pant leg with his good hand. Gabrick pulled free, placing a foot on the seeker's shoulder. With a yank and twist the multiple pops of the man's breaking neck resounded in Gabrick's ears. The seeker's eyes went still.

Gabrick dropped him, sickened at what Den had made him capable of, but with no feelings of remorse. The man had deserved to die.

The pounding of approaching boots reminded Gabrick of their situation. He glanced back to see what was left of the soldiers, no more than five, raising their rifles as they approached.

Gunfire sent his horse into an uncontrolled run, the reins dragging at either side. If the horse turned its head it was likely to catch them under its hooves, then they'd be a tumbling heap.

He pulled at Mari. "You've got to get behind me, so I can reach the reins."

She didn't move, but stayed clamped to his stomach.

"Mari?"

He pushed at one knee, but it remained stiff like a long-dead corpse. "Mari!" he yelled.

The soldiers would follow, he was sure. But he couldn't continue the way they were going. He had to get the horse under control.

"Whoa," he coaxed, trying to hide the strain in his voice. He stroked the russet neck, calming the beast. Its run relaxed to a canter, then a trot.

Den emerged from the shadows of an alleyway. "You can't slow down, boy! They'll be on our tail in seconds."

Aednat straddled the back of the saddle, wincing in pain. A spot of blood soaked through the dress she'd pulled up to her knees, and ran down her leg.

"What happen—?"

But Den gathered Gabrick's reins, pulling the horse after him, sending them again into a run.

"Den!" Gabrick yelled into the wind. "I think Mari might be dead."

Den didn't answer, probably didn't hear. Gripping the horse with his thighs, still encouraging it to run, Gabrick squeezed one arm across the slice along Mari's hip, his sleeve cuff against the cut in her back. There was no point in it, considering they'd be burying her when they stopped, but it was something to do, something to help him not think about what had happened.

Gabrick held back his sobs, determined to be strong like Mari had been. A knot built up in his chest, a weight that seemed to press at his heart and stifle his lungs. He let it hang there, let the city pass in a blur, turning to outlying farms, to countryside, and finally to a deep crevice in a mountain that formed a long canyon. Through it all, he kept his arm to Mari's hip, the heel of his palm to her back, watching his surroundings pass in a watery blend of dull color.

50

In growing horror and fear, Han watched the troops of the city die or flee, half of his imperial guard crushed, and the imperial forces he kept garrisoned near Haigang decimated. Five soldiers remained of three-hundred. Only two of Han's personal guard still lived, the rest dead from their efforts against groping tree limbs.

And all because of Bow Quing.

Han went to the opposite edge of the building, the part still intact, his heavy blue robes rustling chips of stone and block around his feet. So much destruction in so little time. He'd been wrong. He'd never seen a sorceress this powerful, not in all his lifetimes combined. Den and the boy were petty threats compared to that petite little Keroka child.

He pointed to one of his bodyguards. "You. Get down there and tell the remaining soldiers to find troops. Induct farmers if necessary. They have two hours to find where that girl went or they're all dead. If they turn coward and refuse to come back, then their families and loved ones die."

"But Your Eminence," the man said. "You saw what she did."

Han gave a curt nod. "Which means she'll be exhausted and vulnerable. If we find her now, she'll be easy to kill."

The man hesitated, bowed low, and went to fulfill his order.

"You," Han said to another. "Go to the harbor. Find out if Bow Quing is alive. That girl had remarkable control over the plants' targets. Other than a few fishermen with minor injuries, I didn't see one civilian harmed."

It took them almost an hour to find the man, half-dead, clinging to the back of a fishing boat, waiting for his chance to emerge and escape. Ironically, it was his assistant, Tey-Ran Kep, who captured and brought Quing to Han. Kep may have not realized it, but in doing so he'd saved his own life.

While Kep and the others searched, Han had moved to the higher-tier end of the harbor, where the piers were well-kept, and the establishments had glass windows and clean floors. He'd routed a man and his lower-tier employees out of their restaurant, commandeering on behalf of the empire.

Hand wrapped in the back of Bow Quing's shirt, Kep brought Quing through the glass doors, between tables, to Han's chair, forcing Quing to shuffle as he walked. Quing's hands were not only tied behind his back, but tied to his back by a rope that stretched around his torso and attached to his ankles, also reaching up and around his neck. It chafed as he walked, forming an ever-reddening line, but it ensured that he couldn't strike at anyone. Shirtless, revealing the musculature of a very fit man in his early thirties, Quing's face and body were crisscrossed with scrapes and bruises. It appeared there had been a struggle, and by the bruising and profuse amount of blood around the bullet hole in Quing's shoulder, Kep must have used the wound against him. It couldn't have been easy. Quing was the best assassin Han had ever had, almost as capable as himself or Den.

Kep kicked Quing's legs out from under him, forcing him to kneel, then shoved his head forward, choking Quing with subservience. His body jerked as a natural reaction to the rope's suffocation, but he didn't resist. Han nodded to Kep, who then brought Quing upright, kneeling red-faced and breathing hard.

Drawing one of his daggers, Han rose. "Why?"

Quing gasped a moment longer then spat blood on the floor near Han's feet. "Why what? Why Chid Den over you? Why guarantee my death by coming out in the open? Or why didn't I try to kill you the many times I've had a chance?"

"Why betray me? I've given you three lives, made you the director of the entire CSO, let you have your own concubines, given you money, provided you with a lavish mansion in Han City's top district."

Quing's bitter laugh surprised Han. He'd never, in over a hundred years, seen this side of the man. "You belittle me at every turn, risk my life without thought, curse and abuse me at your whim, but for the money and the sake of the empire I still would have held on, if you hadn't destroyed my daughter."

"Daughter?"

Quing sneered. "You don't even remember."

Han went back in his memory. He'd had five lives to Quing's three, but he remembered nothing about Quing having a daughter. "Was she pretty?"

"Not particularly," said Quing. "Not like the concubines and mothers, not pretty enough for you to steal, abuse, and murder, but pretty enough to fall in love."

Han stared at Quing, unsure what he could have done that would merit such hatred.

"The man she loved was good" said Quing. "Intelligent, capable, but he was eighth tier. I requested you raise the boy's status, so they could live with me in the city, and I'd help them start a life."

"Eighth to fourth tier is quite a jump," said Han. "He'd have had to learn to read."

Quing lifted his eyes and glared. "You didn't want my focus divided by concerns with a daughter, and who knew, maybe grandchildren. She went to him, living in the squalor of a hut the size of an outhouse, her husband gutting bass, salmon, and perkay in a fishery, right here in Haigang. When the cholera epidemic swept the seaboard, you refused medical help for anyone under seventh tier. Before I could get to them, her entire family had died, even their little two-year-old boy, Ger Quing."

"You have children near the palace," said Han. "I let them live in the Numbers Compound. What does another one matter?"

"My copies. Three Bow Quings, parentless, raised without conscience, so I can pick and destroy whichever you deem most healthy. And the horror they experience when I take over their minds. You never told me it would be like that. You never told me I would have their memories, that I would lie awake at night wondering at that dark place in the back of my mind, if that might be where they were hiding, watching me, hating me."

Han brandished the knife at Quing's face. "I gave you immortality! They are dust, ants beneath our feet, born one day and dead the next, but I let you taste godhood, more eternal than the Vasheri themselves."

"You heartless yenk." Quing lunged for him, choking himself and landing on his side. Kep backhanded him as he brought Quing back to his knees.

Leaning forward, Han grabbed Quing by the throat. "How dare you? I am the holy Lingdow, chosen of the Vasheri."

"Den used to call you that, a yenk, behind your back. He said you were a nobody. Born to a wealthy family, but with no true skills other than wealth and privilege."

"I'll kill him." This time Han meant it. "I'll take away everything dear to him, and then I'll kill him."

"Not if he kills you first."

"What do you mean?"

Han's grip tightened on Quing's throat, making the man's eyes bulge even as he grinned. Han threw him aside.

Blood dribbling from his lip, Quing laughed. "Every attempt on your life in the last ten years has been orchestrated by us."

Han gestured for Kep to pull Quing back to his knees. "You could have killed me a number of times."

"Your hand is always on a knife or a gun." Quing winced and gritted his teeth as Kep pulled him up by an ear. It took him a moment to catch his breath. "If I'd failed, I couldn't try again, but if I appeared to have no involvement, if it seemed that I tried to save you, then I could hope for a flawless opportunity, and keep trying."

Han rose, turning his knife between his fingers. "I will torture you until you beg to die. I will torture and brutalize your children then distribute them as tenth-tier slaves."

"I've been tortured for the last eighty years of my service, and I have no love for the replicas you call children. They were tainted at conception. There is nothing left you can do to me." He raised his head, looking straight into Han's eyes. "But I know about the prophecy. Somehow, somewhere, a thirteenth child will rise up. Perhaps Fourteen will follow your example, have many wives or lovers, and one of them will be the thirteenth. I don't know. But it will happen, and that child will come for you. He'll destroy you and everything you've built."

Rage surged over Han. Quing's features blurred. With a roar, the battle cry Han had screamed in the days of chieftains and clans, his knife sliced forward.

The mouths of those standing around him hung open, fear in their eyes. Following their gaze, Han found blood coating his soft shoes, seeping inside and running between his toes. Quing's split-open neck rested on them like a dog lying at its master's feet, his eyes staring up, the shadow of a grin creasing his lips. Two guards lay next to him, murdered for no reason other than Han's rage. He shifted his gaze to his blood-coated dagger, the hand holding it spattered red, his sleeve cuffs soaked with it.

Kep stood motionless, eyes wide. It wasn't right for an assassin to be afraid. Han thrust the knife again, piercing Kep through the heart. No more trusted assassins.

He pulled a stone from his pocket. "Peder, I need you to return. You must come to Haigang."

"Your Eminence," Peder's voice returned through the stone. "I have not yet found the type of mother you requested."

"It doesn't matter. You're the only one who can kill that sorceress. Grab the prettiest girl at hand, and come."

"The prettiest one is young, very young."

"Is she old enough to bear children?"

There was some distant mumbling. "Just, but I'm not sure how reliable her cycles."

"It doesn't matter. If the ability is there, the stone will make it happen. Bring her, and hurry."

A high-pitched scream and the rustle of feet erupted from the stone as Han wiped his hand over it. Half a second later it stopped as the connection on Peder's end closed.

Han swept outside to his remaining personal guard. "Have they come back yet? Did they find the sorceress?"

"It hasn't been two hours yet, Your Eminence."

"I don't care. If they haven't returned, they've failed. Tell the governor's personal guard to kill their families and associates. You will take me to the governor's mansion."

"Yes, Your Holiness." The man bowed and ran toward a clump of newly arrived soldiers a few lengths away.

Han pulled another communication stone from his robe. "Spread the description of Chid Den, the Number, and the Keroka girl to every enforcement agent in every city, town and way-station over all of Zhanda. Information leading to their discovery will be rewarded with five-thousand gold emperors. A dead body is ten-thousand. Any enforcer or soldier who earns the reward, will also receive a position in the royal palace in Han City. I want every one of those traitors dead, and their corpses at my feet."

51

The canyon continued to narrow and steepen, the trees holding less and less of their autumn foliage as they ascended, a greater number of evergreens taking their place. Eventually, the horses couldn't go any further up the steep and rocky hill. Den helped Aednat to the ground, grabbing the pack he'd somehow kept during the attack. Gabrick struggled getting off his mount with Mariessa's cold fingers still gripped in his shirt, her knees pressed against the back of his ribcage. He cradled her awkwardly, looking to Den in desperation.

Reaching around Gabrick to grab their supplies, Den slapped both horses, sending them running back the way they'd come. He pulled clean bandaging cloth from a pack, ignoring Aednat's protests of modesty as he lifted her skirt and wrapped a gaping bullet wound.

"Is it still there?"

Den nodded. "There's nothing we can do about it. They'll still be coming after us." Den strapped everything together and onto his back then lifted Aednat into his arms. "Let's go."

"But, Mari." Gabrick gestured at her in exasperation.

Aednat's pale face lifted from Den's shoulder, creased by a half-smile. "When did you start calling her that?"

Gabrick flushed, hoping Mari hadn't shared any part of their experience from the night before. Had it only been yesterday? "I don't know," said Gabrick. "I...I think I said it to bug her." Not that she'd ever hear him say it again.

She wiped at the tears on her cheeks. "I'm sorry."

"Me, too," He glanced behind him, sure that soldiers would be barreling down the canyon at any moment. "I know it'd be easier, but I don't think we should leave her here."

Den stared a moment, his normally blank expression shifting to confused surprise. Gabrick expected him to argue, but he only cocked his head. "If you stroke the muscles, she might relax. You'll have an easier time carrying her." Then he started up the hill.

At least he hadn't told Gabrick to leave the body. It was the practical thing to do, but the idea of her lying there, discovered by soldiers and dragged back to the emperor, made him sick inside. She was dead. She'd never know. But it bothered Gabrick.

He set to stroking her arms as he walked. He rubbed along her thighs as well, but it felt awkward. Sure, she was a dead body now, but it still felt like an invasion, touching her like that without her awareness. But Den was right. The stiff hold gradually relaxed and Gabrick was able to drape her over his back. After putting her hands together a number of times, shifting between holding one leg then another, some of the rigor mortis returned, her hands clasping in front of his neck, her legs stiffening round his hips.

The climb was steep, the terrain rocky despite the dense foliage. They'd only gone a couple of hours when the skies darkened with gray clouds and the temperature dropped. Gabrick had been cold before but until now, exertion had kept back thoughts of freezing. The chill of autumn in the mountains was far different from what it had been in the city. Den pulled out two blankets, draping one around Mari and Gabrick, the other around himself and Aednat. Huddled under the blankets, both men tripped over rocks and fought to pass through grasping shrubs.

They continued their climb, fighting the biting wind and sharing the small amount of water they'd carried. It was halfway gone when Gabrick realized water wouldn't be a problem. A stream, about as wide across as Gabrick was tall, intercepted their path. Den refilled their container, they both carried their charges across the rocks jutting above the surface, and they continued their climb. Gabrick's shoes, made for cold weather in the city, but not rough terrain, felt every pebble.

"Shouldn't we stop for the night?" he asked.

"Too cold without better supplies," said Den. "It's been a long time, but I was up in these mountains once. There's a trapper's cabin, if I can find it."

The sun dipped below the horizon, the temperature dropping again. Den pulled a heartstone the size of a child's fist from his pack, something from a small animal and hardly charged, but it provided enough pale light to illuminate their path.

Gabrick stumbled, falling to one knee. He fought to bring more frigid air into his aching lungs. "I can't do this."

Den stood there, staring at him. "You have to do this."

With a groan, Gabrick came back to his feet, but he knew he wouldn't last much longer. The next time he went down, he might just huddle with Mari and die.

They topped a rise and Gabrick saw it. Made of crossed logs, the edge of a rising moon silhouetted the squat structure, and no bigger than his closet back in the Numbers Compound. "Will we even fit?"

"It'll be tight," said Den, "but that much warmer because of it."

Gabrick managed to push himself the rest of the distance, but only because he had a goal in sight. When they reached the little building, it wasn't quite the shelter he'd hoped. The spaces between logs were mortared with mud, but large chunks of it had fallen away, leaving huge gaps in the walls. The logs were rotting, and along one edge some had come loose, making the corner sag, along with what was left of the roof. It had no door, just a gaping hole.

Den leaned Aednat against one of the walls, pulling a knife from his pack. He entered the hut, one side of it clogged with branches, debris, and a good share of the roof. Gabrick leaned in after him. An owl screeched, spread its wide wings, and flew up into the night. Den threw the knife, but missed. It bounced off the open roof, slid across a section lying askew on the floor, and landed an arm away. No other sounds indicated anything else lived in the cabin, probably because the owl would have eaten them. Den reached to retrieve his knife. An animal lunged from beneath the slanted remains of the roof.

"Den!" Gabrick yelled, stepping forward to kick at it. But the animal didn't strike at Den. It veered for Gabrick.

Leaping with its cat-like legs, the hozu's bulbous body kept it from gaining much height, but it was enough to aim its flat-edged teeth at Gabrick's thigh. He stumbled back and the beast landed at his feet.

Needles round its neck and shoulders rose like a collar of thin spikes. Gabrick peddle-stepped away. The beast rushed.

Mari's weight offset his balance. He tripped, landing in a bed of pine needles. Mari's body fell beside him. The hozu shifted its focus.

Spines brushed the bottom of Gabrick's shoe as it lunged at her exposed ankle. He kicked its non-quilled haunches, nearly impaling his leg and sending it back half an arm. But the beast refused to back down. It ran for Mari's blood-covered hip.

With a downward plunge of his knife, Den pinned the beast to the ground. The hozu screamed, a high-pitched wail like a child bereft of its mother. Its quills shot backward, but Den released the hilt before they could brush his knuckles. To Gabrick's surprise, it was Aednat who scooted close and committed the final blow. A piece of wood hefted in both hands, she brought it down on top of the Hozu's head. Something cracked, the neck or the skull. The wreath of needles raised a digit then fell, limp and still.

Breathing hard, Den gestured to Mariessa's body. "Let's get them both inside. We'll build a fire to get us warm, then we'll get everything situated so we can cook that thing, eat, and pull the bullet from Aednat's leg. I'll try to find a pan to cook a broth for Mariessa."

"Broth?" Gabrick asked, angry at Den's cruel joke. "What are you talking about?"

Den's brow creased with disbelief. "You carried her all the way here, and you don't want to bother keeping her alive?"

Why was he doing this? "You know she's not alive. She's stiff as an old corpse. There's nothing alive about her."

Den stared.

Aednat scooted to Mari's side, touching her cold cheeks. "What are you saying, Den? You think she's still breathing?"

"All that time, you thought you were carrying a dead body?" Den said. "Why would you do that? Why would you risk yourself for someone who's not even alive?"

Gabrick shrugged. "I felt like we owed her that much, so she could have a decent Shangsan."

"Why would she care? If she's dead, she's gone."

"But she believed in the Vasheri," Aednat said. "A proper Shangsan would be important to her. A Liwu-shijan ceremony, honoring her life and presenting her heartstone to..." but Aednat couldn't think who the girl would want to have the stone.

"To who?" Den accused. "The girl doesn't even have any living family."

"I don't know! To someone. She would have wanted that."

"Who cares what she wanted if she's already dead?"

"We do," Gabrick and Aednat said together. "But you think she's alive?" Gabrick added.

Den raised his hands into the air as if they'd lost their minds. "Bring her into the shed. I'm cold."

Gabrick brought both of the girls inside while Den searched for supplies. Near a crude stone fireplace, Aednat massaged Mari's muscles until she lay flat on their thin blanket, then collapsed beside her. Gabrick and Den cleared the flue of birds' nests and debris so the smoke would rise, but their work left

Gabrick covered in dirt and droppings and he longed for a bath like never before. He and Den moved the broken section of roof thatching, leaning it against the wall above the fire and shrinking what little space they'd had by two-thirds. They'd be sleeping on top of each other like a litter of pups, but at least they'd be warm. For now, their blankets went to the girls, as did the majority of the hozu cooked above the fire. To one side, a piece of its leg and some water sat in a pot Den had found, waiting for its turn to boil in the coals.

Gabrick glanced at Mari, shivering despite the close blaze and the blankets. "So, you still haven't explained. Why is she all stiff like that?"

Den stared at her so long, with such a somber expression, Gabrick started to wonder if he'd heard. When Den finally spoke, it was as if he held the conversation with the flames. "Usually a sorceress would have to work at her abilities for a long time before they might learn to trance. I can't even guess at Mariessa's power to have fallen into it so soon."

"How can going stiff as a corpse be a defense?"

"Did you take zoology?" Den asked with blatant sarcasm.

"That's not the same."

"But it is. On a battlefield, if she merely passed out, an enemy would recognize that she's alive. Like this, with her breathing so shallow and her body stiff as death, unless a person is familiar with a plant sorceress, they'd assume she's dead."

"Then why did you think I knew?"

"You kept her with you instead of trying to dump the bodyI thought you had some sense."

They sat in tense silence, the snap of the damp, burning wood in odd syncopation with the pops of the cooking Hozu.

"How did she hold onto me like that?" Gabrick asked.

Den went back to staring at Mariessa, that same look of concern on his face. "She's more aware than you realize. When she wakes, she'll remember everything since the trance as if it was a dream."

"Then why do we have to coax her into changing position?"

Den used Mariessa's blanket to grab the end of the spit, pulling the finished Hozu off the fire. "The other thing a trance is good for is helping a sorceress hide. She can climb a tree, have the branches obscure her, and they'll stay that way with minimal effort on her part, while she holds her grip, in the trance. The tree will even give some of its energy and life to her as she recovers. Every branch and bush you waded through tonight transferred a bit of its life and energy. If not for her wounds, she'd be in better shape than any of the rest of us come morning."

While the hozu cooled, Den placed the pot at the edge of the fire, starting Mari's broth.

Gabrick huddled closer to the warmth. "I guess none of it matters anyway. We left an obvious trail. It'll lead them straight here."

"It would have, if they'd stayed after us." Den poked at the hozu, but quickly withdrew and blew on his finger. "Han can be impatient. Knowing him, he gave them a time limit to find us, and when they couldn't catch up, they were forced to turn around. By the time someone picks up the chase, the trail will be cold. We have a chance now, but we'll need to start moving by first light."

"Move to where?" asked Gabrick. "We can't survive out there with only two thin blankets and a couple of knives. You said so yourself."

"We have a bit more than that. When it's light I can find some of the supplies hidden here. They might be enough to get us across these mountains and back to the seashore."

"Then what?"

"Then..." Den paused and Gabrick realized he'd completely run out of back-up plans. "Then we hope we can find a ship."

His frowning gaze returned to Mari.

Gabrick tucked the blanket around her neck. "What are you so worried about?"

Den hesitated before he answered. "She's more powerful than any sorceress I've ever seen or heard of."

Den offered Aednat a piece of the steaming hozu, but she set it aside. "Is that bad?"

"Han's seen what she can do firsthand. In his mind, we'll be a nuisance compared to her."

Eating at the hozu's front leg, Gabrick spoke between bites. "So he'll go after her."

"Every resource, every seeker, will be focused on seeing her dead. And even on such short notice, Han can find at least a handful of seekers."

"We're not leaving her behind," Gabrick said. "Even if it will save our lives."

"I know," said Den. "But I wonder if she shouldn't have let us die today and saved herself. Surviving this wilderness may be merely a postponement of the inevitable."

"We'll make it," Aednat said. "We have to."

Neither Den nor Gabrick contradicted her optimism. They ate the hozu, engrossed in their own thoughts. Survival had never appeared likely, but now it seemed entirely impossible.

After they finished their meal, Den heated his knife in the fire. "Aednat, we have to take care of that wound." He pulled a small bottle from one of the packs. "I have the same anesthetic I gave you outside Han City. It will knock you out while I extract the bullet and cauterize the wound." He glanced at her uneaten hozu. "Maybe it's best you saved that for later."

She nodded as Den poured some foul-smelling liquid on a piece of cloth, torn from the bottom of his shirt. Within seconds of placing the cloth to Aednat's nose, she lay back, asleep.

Den handed the concoction to Gabrick. "The pain will wake her. When it does, bring the fabric to her face again, but only long enough to put her out."

Gabrick scooted close to Aednat's side, his kneeling position rather uncomfortable in the small space.

Raising her dress enough to reveal the wound, Den set to work. She only woke once, early on in the procedure. Before she could scream, Gabrick covered her mouth and nose with the cloth until her eyes rolled up again. Still, she whimpered in her sleep, obviously feeling the pain.

More than anything at that moment, he wished he could take her place. He'd never seen Aednat in pain, not any real pain, and he never imagined that it could be so hard to watch. If only he could shoot himself and spare her, he would.

Once it was finished, the blood cleaned, and the gaping hole in her thigh wrapped, Gabrick asked the obvious question. "Will she be able to travel like this?"

Den shook his head. "No. We'll have to take turns carrying her, and if Mariessa's wounds are too bad for her to walk then we don't stand a chance. I can't see us getting through this wilderness if we both have to carry another person the entire way."

Gabrick rubbed at Mari's feet through the blanket, trying to warm them. "Let's hope her wounds aren't as bad as they look."

Den grimaced. "Hope is about the only card we have left to play."

52

When Mariessa woke the next morning, two people in burly fur coats stared down at her. She startled, about to scramble for cover, then realized the small patches of face inside the fur hoods were Gabrick and Aednat.

"Hungry?" Gabrick asked.

Mariessa nodded. "Starving."

Gabrick handed her a boiled leg of hozu in a shallow pan, now as cold as the frigid air around them. She'd never seen a hozu, never heard of them and had no idea what they looked like, but in a hazy way she remembered that they'd saved her from one, killed it, cooked it, and fed her some broth. She pushed herself up, every part of her body protesting at the movement, leaned on her left arm, and dug into the meaty haunch with a ravenous appetite.

Den's voice came from the other side of the partition. "I'm afraid that's all there is that will be of any use to us." He appeared, giving her a wan smile. "We'll have to make use of the blankets, trade off the boots, and let the girls keep the fur leggings."

Mari reached a hand under her blankets, realizing something was different. Beneath the remains of her dress skirt, her legs were covered with sewn animal skins. "How—"

Gabrick blushed. "I had no choice. Sorry."

Mariessa's mouth dropped and she was sure she easily out-blushed Gabrick, remembering how he'd massaged her arms and thighs so she would hang on his back as they traveled. She also had a vague recollection of him wrapped around her calves last night as she slept. Mariessa focused on the last of the hozu's meat, snapped the bones and sucked at the marrow.

Gabrick scrunched up his lip, but Den nodded. "I should have had all of us eating like that. We're going to need the nutrients." He extended a hand to Mari. "Can you stand?"

She reached up, but only made it halfway. "Aah," she half-groaned, half-screamed. "I can't lift my right arm."

Den knelt at her side, pushing at her shoulder and moving it in a multitude of excruciating positions. Tears came to her eyes, and she released a few choice words.

"You're hurting her," said Aednat.

Den let her arm rest. "It doesn't appear broken or dislocated, but I think it's a nasty sprain."

He moved to the other side and extended his hand. Mariessa took it, but when she started to rise, a pain shot through her hip, another one up her back. Before she could fall, Gabrick had his arm around her waist, helping her upright.

Den watched her move as if evaluating a caribou for farm work. "That seeker sliced you up pretty well. You're lucky you didn't bleed out more." He turned to Gabrick. "You're going to have to help her."

"No," she said. "I'll manage on my own."

"Don't be stupid," Gabrick said. "Is this because of the other night? I promise, I won't—"

"No!" She didn't know if he was referring to carrying her, having his hands underneath her dress trying to work out her legs, or their kiss in the stable, but she didn't want to remember any of it let alone talk about it. "That has nothing to do with it, but I'm sure I'm no worse off than Aednat."

Aednat stood, her weight entirely centered on her good leg. "I'll be fine. I can walk on it."

Den grabbed a bulky pack crammed with various supplies, others hanging to the sides. "We'll trade off carrying both of you, but you're right, you'll have to walk when you can."

Mariessa felt at the wound on her hip, looked at their mismatched clothing, and peered through a gap in the cabin walls at the bare trees and rough terrain. "Den, can we even survive out there?"

He followed her gaze, the muscles in his face tightening into a determined grimace. "I don't know, but we're sure as limbo going to try."

They hiked until midday, morning clouds clearing out and a brittle wind setting in. Gabrick insisted on carrying Mariessa as much as Den carried Aednat, no matter how Mariessa argued. As they traveled, she brushed her cold fingers across the crowding plants. Gabrick insisted that compared to yesterday, it was as if the plants moved aside, clearing the way, but the going was still difficult.

After a while, she gained a feel for the unusual species, figured out which plants had edible seeds and discovered some bitter stalks and leaves. She had no idea how she knew, but she even discovered a medicinal plant, using it during one of their rests to dress her wounds, as well as Aednat's, and what remained of Gabrick's.

"The leaves will help," Mariessa told Aednat, "but this wound is deep. It doesn't look quite right."

Grasping her hand, Aednat looked her in the eye. "Thank you. You've been the best of friends, better than a sister."

Mariessa dropped her eyes to the ground. "At least I can be that." She tried to smile, but didn't quite manage.

"What do you mean?"

"Nothing," said Mariessa. She didn't need to talk about yesterday's events to know what kind of person she'd become.

Aednat squeezed her fingers, almost making them warm. "What you did was right. You saved our lives."

Shaking her head, Mariessa struggled against tears. "I feel what the plants do to them, Aednat. They come alive, but without conscience, and I'm there with them while they kill. I swore I wouldn't let it happen again, but I murdered those men, every one. I'm a monster." She looked into Aednat's caring face, the girl's tearful eyes reflecting Mariessa's pain. "And I'd do it all again. I have no family left, no one who cares anything for me. I heard what you and Gabrick said, about my wanting a Shangsan ritual and the Liwu-shijan ceremony to present my heartstone. I would want you to have it, Aednat. If anything happens..."

"No," Aednat cut her off. "Nothing is going to happen to you. And you're not a monster. You saved us from monsters, and somehow, whether or not the plants feel any remorse, none of the civilians died. *You* did that. *You* kept them safe. We're in a war, Mariessa, and you fought like a soldier, except you let the innocent live while the emperor will have had them slaughtered."

Pained at the many murders their escape must have initiated, Mariessa still raised hopeful eyes. She wanted to believe Aednat, wanted to believe she'd done the right thing, but there were so many deaths, so much destruction.

"She's right," said Gabrick. "One thing you can always count on from Aednat, she tells the whole truth, even when you don't want to hear it."

Mariessa nodded, wiping the moisture from her eyes and turning away from Gabrick, not wanting him to see her weakness. Maybe there was some truth to what Aednat had said. This was a war, and she'd had to act or let her friends die. But Mariessa doubted the images of what she'd done would ever leave her in peace again. Peace of soul seemed even more impossible than their survival.

Den called from a few lengths away. "Let's get going."

Gabrick remained silent while she contemplated Aednat's words. Peace may have not come, but Mariessa found a sliver of acceptance. Whether she'd wanted it or not, she was everything Den had claimed, a sorceress of life below, either Vasheri-blessed or cursed. And whether good or evil, she would use that power to defend her friends. She'd let the Vasheri figure out the final consequences.

They continued in silence, Gabrick's fingers turning blue as they went, while he blew on them and stamped his legs so they wouldn't freeze. The more they walked, the more frigid the wind became. After three attempts to give Gabrick her heavy leggings, Mariessa finally convinced him to at least cut off the over-hanging hem, making a kind of sock for his hands.

Mariessa lost all thought of decency or worrying about physical contact as they traveled. As Gabrick carried her, Mariessa pressed her chest against his strong back, wrapped her hands in the blanket's edge, and made a kind of shared hood that she warmed with her breath.

But soon, Gabrick's steps began to falter. She could sense the quiver in his legs and the way his breathing went from strained to gasping.

"Let me down," she told him.

"No, I'm all right," he wheezed.

"I don't want to end up face down in the dirt. Besides, I'm getting cramps in my legs." It was a complete lie. If anything, she wasn't sure she could feel her legs.

He put her down, but wrapped an arm around her, still helping her walk. They ended up with the blanket draped over their heads, arms wrapped around each other with fingers tucked under the other's armpit for warmth. Crystal slivers clouded the air with every breath, and little by little their forward struggle slowed.

Nearing dusk, they set up camp beneath a tall pine with wide branches. Mariessa coaxed the tree to release the life in its lowest limbs, making it easy for Gabrick and Den to snap them off. They laid the still-green foliage down as bedding, leaving space for a small fire-pit. While Den set animal traps, Gabrick, Mariessa, and Aednat gathered large rocks, and small pieces of dry wood.

The pine complied easily when Mariessa directed it to stretch its limbs toward the earth, creating a type of living tent, but it balked at the fire.

Mariessa had never had a plant resist her urging, but the newly-sentient tree had an understandable fear of burning. She finally convinced it to create a passageway for the smoke, but they had to keep the fire small while Mariessa soothed the tree into a sleepy complacence. Den killed an owl stalking them from the next tree over. Combined with some edible tubers, they had food. The stringy roots didn't taste fantastic and smelled worse, but they would keep them alive.

After they'd eaten, Gabrick filled the silence. "What day is it?"

Den thought for a moment. "Tingisi." He gave a faint half-smile. "The nineteenth day of Shiyu and a week after the official beginning of autumn. Happy belated birthday, Gabrick."

"How old are you?" Mariessa asked.

"Seventeen." Gabrick said. "Aednat turned seventeen a few days ago. How about you?"

Mariessa shrugged. "I'd guess more than fifteen, less than eighteen, but I don't know. I haven't kept track for a long time."

"Your bangay chief knew," said Den. You were sixteen when they took you to the palace."

"Then I'm still sixteen. My birthday is in the middle of winter."

"You don't know the day?" Gabrick asked.

"A simple crete doesn't have time or energy to worry about keeping track of what day they came into the world. We're too busy trying to survive it."

As the mood returned to uncomfortable silence, Mariessa heard something that hadn't haunted her nightmares for weeks. Imperial Hounds.

"They've found me," Mariessa whispered over the crackling fire.

"Who? A seeker?" Gabrick peered through the branches. "Can you see him somewhere?"

"Not a seeker, though they may be out there somewhere as well. No, it's Peder. I can hear the imperial hounds."

Gabrick turned to Den. "Can you hear them? Where do we go?"

Den strained as Gabrick had, his shoulders slumping with an exhaustion that went beyond bone and muscle, into a man's heart. "If Peder's here with the hounds, I guarantee he has seekers arranged to each side of him, forming a noose."

"Then there's no way to the seashore." Mariessa said.

"Not unless you can either get rid of the dogs, or we can slip between seekers. Our chances might be as good with that plan as the alternative."

"Which is what?" Aednat whispered, her voice weak.

Den wrapped an arm around her in a futile effort to provide warmth. "The desert. Our only escape is across the continent to the seashore on the other side through the desert."

Gabrick frowned, his expression confused. "But won't Peder follow us there? He'd be able to see us for miles."

Den shook his head. "The only drinkable water to be found in the desert might be a thin layer of snow, if we're lucky. It won't be enough for Peder to survive, and he knows it won't be enough for us. No, he'll monitor the border and if we don't come back, he'll assume we're dead. And rightly so. The weather won't be the only thing likely to kill us there. The natives are less than friendly."

Mariessa wrapped her thin blanket tighter across her shoulders. "It can't be worse than this."

"Yes," said Den. "It can be much worse, but as long as he's got those dogs, I don't see any other choice."

And so they decided to get a few hours of sleep then head northwest, away from the seashore, hoping for a miracle.

53

Rustling branches didn't mean anything to Gabrick at first, nothing more than another whisper at the edge of his dreams. They'd been on the run for days, sleeping little, pushing themselves hard. Animals scurried out in the woods from time to time, usually getting themselves caught in Den's traps and becoming breakfast or a delayed dinner. But this one was different. Not the soft step-thump of a snow hare, or the pattering feet of a hozu, but something quieter, bigger, accustomed to the art of surprising prey.

In his half-sleep he snuggled closer to Mari on their side of the tree trunk, as close to the fire as they dared place their bedding. Den and Aednat slept on the other side. Not that Den needed to worry. Gabrick did nothing more than think about the possibility of draping his arm over Mari before exhaustion forced him to sleep each night.

Mari had pulled the blanket over again. One of these days she'd catch it on the embers. As he'd done in his sleep a dozen times, he yanked it from her curled fingers, settling it over them both. A slight rustle, so quiet he shouldn't have noticed, jerked Gabrick awake. He sat up.

Eyes a luminous yellow, a wolf bigger than Gabrick had ever imagined shot through the limbs at the tree's edge. Its hind feet had just touched ground when it leapt forward again.

"Wolf!" Gabrick screamed.

Everyone shot awake, but the wolf's body already glided in mid-air, its paws aimed to land between Mari and the stones ringing the fire. Gabrick jumped to the side, shoving the wolf into the ragged limb stubs protruding from the trunk's base.

It whined, snarled and snapped its teeth at Gabrick, missing his face by less than a digit. He grabbed Mari's injured arm and she cried out as Gabrick yanked her close, out of the wolf's path. Its jaws snapped for her legs. She jerked them back, but the wolf caught a foot encased in the heavy boots Gabrick had given her for the night. The wolf's head thrashed back and forth as if stunning a frightened rabbit. Mari screamed. Grabbing a sharp limb, Gabrick stabbed at the wolf's neck and shoulders but it paid no attention. Aednat kicked embers at it, singeing its fur. It cringed, but still wouldn't let go. Den came at it with a knife. About to thrust it to the wolf's side, he ducked. A limb missed his head, batting the wolf.

Looking down, Gabrick saw Mari had worked her fingers into the soil. Limbs beat at the wolf, hit it repeatedly on its side, the green needles turning a bright red. Still, it held on. Roots began to rise, but they were slow, half-dormant for the approaching winter.

"Stop!" yelled Den. "Let me reach it!"

But Mari was terrified, not listening. Gabrick grabbed her arms, pulled her fingers from the ground. She struggled, but he held both wrists, wrapping his arms around her as he pinned them to her waist.

The wolf saw his chance. It released her foot, going for something more vital—the throat.

Holding Mari to his chest, Gabrick kicked. His foot slammed into the wolf's jaw, pushing it away but inflicting no damage. It whipped its head back, sinking sharp teeth into Gabrick's calf. He screamed, releasing his hold on Mariessa. She thrust her fingers back into the soil.

Den's knife skewered the beast, straight to the heart. It faltered then fell over, still holding Gabrick's leg in its clamped jaw.

A tree limb beat at its corpse.

It took some yanking, but Den pulled the wolf's jaws wide enough to release Gabrick's leg. Blood immediately seeped into his pants, even as Den jerked the fabric up to his knee. Aednat pulled out Mari's leaves and she and Den wrapped the wounds. His leg felt more bruised than cut, though the amount of blood suggested otherwise.

Mariessa huddled near the fire's dying embers, watching Aednat and Den with concern and a lingering fear.

"Can you move it?" Den asked Gabrick.

Gabrick pumped his leg a couple of times, pressed it against the ground and half stood up. "It's sore, but I should be able to walk."

"Good," said Den. "Because that was our last night of sleep. I can hear those hounds getting closer. We're going to have to walk every moment we have light, even if it's only by moonlight."

Legs to her chest, her arms wrapped around her knees, Mari stared at the gray ash.

"Is your foot going to be okay?" Aednat asked, reaching out for Mari but then pulling back, thinking better of it.

All of them had learned that Mari didn't appreciate people entering her space uninvited. According to Den, her personality required a certain amount of alone time. Gabrick didn't know if that was true, if the events of the last few weeks had traumatized her, or if she still didn't trust them.

She watched Aednat pull her hand back, but didn't acknowledge it with more than a glance. "Why?" Mari turned her eyes to Den, demanding an answer. "The wolf only bit Gabrick when it realized he was an obstacle to reaching me. First the hozu and now this."

Gabrick nodded. "I bet that owl that had seemed to be stalking us was really after Mari."

"Don't call me that," Mari said, and not for the first time. Because she hated the nickname, he continued to use it. He was pretty sure that every time he said it, she thought of their kiss in the stable. Why he wanted to keep reminding her of their terrible mistake, he wasn't sure, but he liked watching her blush and squirm.

Den nudged the dead wolf with his foot, leaning over it with his knife. "I've never seen this happen before, never even heard of it." He dragged the carcass a few arms away then started cutting the hide from the body. Soon, a good-sized river of blood started running toward an outside bush.

"Gabrick," he said. "Go get the animals from their traps. You know where I laid them. Take a knife so you can kill them and gut them outside. Aednat, build up that fire again so we can be warm for a short while and cook the smaller animals. Mariessa, I know you're tired, but we'll need you to disperse the smoke. We're going to cook as much of our meat as possible. We won't stop to hunt again."

Gabrick returned with three rabbits, a hozu, a deer that required Den's help to drag near the tree, and a breed of wild cat called a fexai—a nasty piece of work between wolf and fox in size, but with long, spindly fangs. As Den had trained him, Gabrick started butchering the animals, from smallest to largest.

"I've given this some thought," said Den, still working on the wolf. "It's common for a sorcerer of one element to repel the subjects of another. So a sorcerer of life above—an animal sorcerer—might have more trouble walking through this forest than the average person. A weather sorceress might have trouble in water or difficulty climbing rocky mountains. There aren't definite opposites, but just as a sorceress of sight usually loses the use of her eyes, each area of sorcery puts them at odds with either some sense of their body or at odds with another element they don't control."

Mari helped Aednat with a makeshift spit for their fire. "So mine is obviously the animals. No wonder I never liked pets."

"Yes." Den nodded, finishing with the wolf pelt. He left its meat, moving to the tastier deer. "The thing is," Den held up his bloody knife as an index finger. "That's all it should be." He sunk the knife into the deer's belly, slitting it open and releasing its steaming entrails outside their branch perimeter.

"Won't that lead Peder to our trail?" Gabrick asked.

"Between the seekers and the hounds, he's already on our trail."

"What do you mean," Mari continued, grabbing a knife and starting on a rabbit. "You said, 'all it should be.' I shouldn't like pets?"

"You naturally don't like pets, and they don't particularly like you either, but their instincts shouldn't be strong enough to attack."

"Then why?"

Den shrugged and continued to dress out the deer, as careful with its hide as he had been with the wolf, though taking time with this carcass to preserve some of the meat. "Maybe because you're so powerful. I'm sure you didn't make full use of your power until you called up almost an entire city's worth of plants including those in the harbor, so maybe that's what set them off. I do know that the only way to stop it is with a guardian given to you by an animal sorcerer."

Mari closed her eyes as if she could shut out his bad news. "So I'm stuck with animals trying to kill me unless we survive this wilderness and find an animal sorcerer."

Den cringed. "I know of only one animal sorcerer in all of Dixho."

"Where is he?" Mari asked.

"On the other side of the world."

Mari felt the last of her hope die. She might as well die with it. "You should leave me here. Peder will find me, I can kill myself, and then he won't be able to track you."

Den shook his head. "As Aednat has said before…we're all in this together now. Besides, you're still strong. You're as much a protection to us as a beacon for him."

"But the animals…"

As Aednat pulled their cooked rabbit from the fire, Den finished the deer. "The attacks seem fairly random and only happen if an aggressive animal gets close. We know to look out for them now. I can set traps specific to predators. We may not have as many other animals to eat, but we'll be okay. And when we somehow survive this whole ordeal, as Aednat insists that we will, our eventual destination is that strange country on the other side of the world, where the animal sorcerer lives. He can help you."

"It'll be all right." Gabrick said.

Though she nodded, she couldn't catch their optimism. It would be better for them if she left the group, but she couldn't make herself do it. She didn't want to be alone, left to face Peder and his hounds.

When they started out again, the dressed skins lay fleshy-side-out over the blankets on Gabrick's and Den's backs, giving some extra warmth. Aednat and Mariessa took the fur coats they'd been wearing and everyone had chunks of meat hanging across their backs, exposed to the cold to keep them fresh. The smell was nauseating, but not as bad as it would have been in warmer weather. When the sun set, a bright moon would be their light until near morning. They'd have no more than a couple of hours to cook the remaining meat while they slept, and then they'd eat it as they walked.

The hounds' barks echoed from mountain to mountain, ever-threatening, ever closer. "We are coming," they seemed to say. "We will find you. We will rend you."

Mariessa picked up the pace, the limp from her healing wounds nothing compared to Gabrick's inflamed calf and Aednat's leg. The only one not wounded was Den so he helped Aednat, and Mariessa went to Gabrick. She couldn't carry him, but she could be a crutch. He protested, but she ignored him the same as he'd ignored her the week before. Their pace didn't improve much, but at least he didn't have to suffer as much as hobbling on his own.

54

They discovered Peder's location two days later, as they left the cover of their tree after three hours of sleep, eating a breakfast of meat, bitter plants and shriveled seeds. Despite Mariessa's affinity to plant-life, perhaps because of her fear of the beasts, she noticed the change in the hounds' echoing bark.

She hobbled the couple of arms distance up to Aednat and Gabrick, her half-eaten rabbit between her sleeve-covered hands. Mariessa walked on her own now.

Nearer in height than anyone else, opposite legs injured, Aednat and Gabrick had become one another's crutch when Den was busy or needed a break. The situation was surely to Gabrick's liking, finally close to the girl he'd been trying so hard to win. And they fit together well, arm in arm, sometimes with Aednat's head on Gabrick's shoulder, or his leaned on top of hers. It was a bit revolting how they whispered together, laughed, and were constantly holding onto one another, but at least he'd been right. Aednat was perfect-- Mariessa couldn't deny the truth in that--and she was perfect for him.

Watching the rising sun, Den scrunched up his face as he forced down his bitter plant and a few tasteless seeds, following it with cold venison. He cast a worried glance at Aednat then turned around. "Come on. We need to move faster."

"But the hounds aren't any closer," said Aednat. Her breath came out in heaving gasps, though they'd only been walking a few minutes. Each day, she slowed more and her limp became worse. "Walking half the night, we should be able to stay ahead of them, right?"

Gabrick hesitated, obviously wanting to agree with Aednat, but not sure. "I think we have to trust that Den knows what he's talking about. He wouldn't put you through this if it wasn't our only way to survive."

"If Peder has our trail," said Mariessa. "He'll push his remaining men and his hounds that much harder. I know, I've been in this situation before. There's no question he'll find us, only a question of whether or not we can get far enough ahead that he isn't willing to follow. I still doubt Den on that, but I hope he's right."

Aednat's chin quivered beneath the strip of cloth she'd wrapped around her face. She appeared ready to cry, but tucked her head down and continued forward.

At nightfall, Den declared it time to stop. As he worked with some kindling, Mariessa pulled out the herbs she'd gathered, dressing her hip wound and ignoring her nearly-healed back, then moved to Aednat. She pulled down the fur pants, gasping lightly at the blackened plants clinging to Aednat's leg. The poor girl slept through Mariessa's care, letting out a quiet groan. The damaged area bulged, brighter red than before. Mariessa tenderly laid the new leaves onto the fevered area, but she must have applied more pressure than she thought. An explosion of yellow pus burst from the constricted hole, spraying over Mariessa's hand. The foul smell sent a new surge of bile to her throat. She turned away, swallowing it down.

Den left the smoking tinder and joined her, his quivering voice betraying emotions Mariessa had rarely seen. "It's infected. I must not have lanced it well enough. She's going to lose that leg."

"Cut it off?" Mariessa shuffled back as if he intended to start the procedure at that very moment.

Den's face contorted with the effort of suppressing his emotions, but tears rolled from the corners of his eyes. He wiped an angry hand against both sides of his cheeks, took a deep breath, and got a hold of himself.

He bent down and stroked Aednat's cheek. "She's the only connection I have left to Kerise, and she's going to die." Den plunged his fingers into his wild hair, the curly strands grown near to his shoulders. His palms covered his face as he hunched over and fought the tears anew.

"She's not going to die." Mariessa wouldn't let her, not without a fight. "Dressing the wound is helping, I'm sure of it, so we just need to change the leaves more often. At least that will slow down the infection until we get out of Peder's reach. Then, if we have to perform surgery, we'll do it, but not until we're someplace we can set up camp for a few days."

Den raised his eyes to her, a faint spark of hope returned. "If it appears we might survive, we'll take care of it in the desert. You know, her chances still won't be good. Keeping off infection from the surgery itself will be difficult."

"But not impossible." Mariessa paused, hoping for the best. "She believes we'll make it. We have to believe, too."

Den shook his head. "The reasons for her hope are ridiculous. It's not—"

"It doesn't matter." Mariessa's voice strained on the verge of screaming. "We need to have faith like she does, keep trying no matter what."

She saw the determination slip back over his features. He nodded, mostly to himself, and went back to his fire. Mariessa cleaned up her hand and returned to Aednat. She cleaned and dressed the wound, using extra leaves, then laid a hand over the girl's sweating brow. The fever had become worse, much worse. They'd have to carry her from now on, but Gabrick wouldn't be able to help. His leg wound needed more time to heal, at least a couple of days, but none of them had that, and exhaustion haunted them as much as their injuries. At what point would they collapse, unable to support one another?

Finished with Aednat, Mariessa moved to Gabrick's calf. His moan as she lifted his pant-leg softened her touch. He wasn't the high-stilted boy she'd met in the palace, not anymore. He treated her as an equal and often accepted her opinions above Aednat's, though it obviously didn't change his feelings for the beautiful girl.

Maybe there were still some trustworthy men in the world. A weight left her shoulders, and despite their circumstances a part of her felt more free than she had since a child, if only for a short time.

Come morning, the dogs sounded like they bayed outside their tree. Their echoes had always seemed closer than farther away, their actual distance distorted, but Mariessa recognized the clear sound of dogs that would be there in less than an hour. For a moment, she wished for her chapnut tree, but that hadn't done her much good last time. Peder had still brought her down, captured her, and this time they wanted her dead. Maybe Peder even wanted to kill her as much as she wanted to kill him.

She looked at the charred snow pheasant lying in the fire. It had come loose as they slept, burning the back, and leaving the rest half-raw. Still, they'd eat it. Gabrick's haggard face rose up, a wish to die rather than face that icy wind again evident in his pain-filled eyes. Aednat attempted to rise, but fell back to the pine branches. Her glazed eyes and shivering body suggested a worsening fever. They couldn't go on like this. They couldn't outrun Peder and those demon hounds. It was fight, or die trying.

Mariessa grabbed the end of the spit, thrust the pheasant outside and rolled it over the cold ground, steam rising as if she'd stuck fire into a bucket of water. She didn't care.

"What are you doing?" Gabrick asked.

Den placed a restraining hand on his arm.

Mariessa pulled the dirt-coated carcass back under the tree. "I'm eating."

The hounds bayed closer. She didn't have time to explain. Ignoring Gabrick's protests, which calmed soon after Den started whispering in his ear, Mariessa picked at the cooler sections, eventually devouring all the edible meat. She would need every bit of strength the animal could give her.

A look of desperate understanding passed between her and Den. He nodded as she tunneled her fingers into the warm soil near the fire. The hounds were gaining. She had to assume that Peder still had the protection stone, but maybe she could rid him of his seekers and hounds.

She shook with the effort of searching for them, such a distance from herself and someplace she couldn't see. Her furrowed brow dripped sweat. But she found them—the men, their guns, and their knives—and she ordered the plants nearest them into action.

Her consciousness shared with the distant trees, she participated as thick limbs beat and broke bones, impaled men and dogs through their soft tissues, invading through any accessible orifice. Distant screams washed over her, carried by the piercing wind, muffled by the encircling pine boughs, but clear inside her mind.

The wail of injured dogs, confused and in pain, mingled with the shrieks of their vicious trainers. Bushes twined their branches around beasts and men, encircling and strangling them. Guns fired. Mariessa lost contact with some plants, but she loosened the roots of others from winter's encroaching hold, urging them up through the binding dirt. Hot blood warmed the soil, reviving more grasping plants to help their brothers, arousing sleeping xicao to move alongside the plants, in search of dead flesh. One man stood immune to her. No matter how she tried, she couldn't touch him—Peder.

Blinding white pain burst in Mariessa's skull, but she wasn't finished, she couldn't let go yet. She ordered every tree, every plant, every bush, to crush, bury, and dismantle the weapons the men carried, even the ones by the man they couldn't harm. He was immune, but not his metal. She'd learned enough control to differentiate between the two. When she'd finished, Mariessa pulled her consciousness back, but the white light wouldn't let go.

She fell into the trance she'd experienced before, but it was different this time. No awareness flitted through her mind as people spoke and moved around her. Everything was white, piercing, and painful. Stabs of electricity pulsed in her mind, telling her to let go and let the light claim her, but she knew if she did, the dirt from which her precious plants sprang would become her home. Embracing that warm light would be a peaceful death, but she refused to abandon her friends.

55

A low, faint moan drifted through the trees. At first, Gabrick didn't recognize the noise, thinking it another rise and fall of the winter winds. Then his mouth fell open and fear stabbed at his gut.

"I hear hounds."

"It's the wind," said Den, but he strained to listen. The sound was faint, much fainter than before, but it was the bay of an imperial hound.

Gabrick was already massaging Mari's legs and arms, preparing her to travel. "Mari killed them. How'd they get more?"

For the first time Gabrick ever remembered, Den appeared confused. "I don't know, but it doesn't sound right. Could one of them have survived, refused to give up the hunt?"

It seemed the only explanation. The beast sounded close, but still faint. Den didn't move.

"We need to hurry," Gabrick urged him. "Seekers might pass by us while Mari's in a coma, but a hound won't. It doesn't need a stone to smell us out."

Den shook his head as if thinking Gabrick the greatest fool, but he bundled Aednat's feverish body across his back. They wrapped the girls as best they could, tying them to their backs. It would have made more sense for Den, so much smaller than Gabrick, to take Mari, but Gabrick knew that the man's devotion to his niece wouldn't allow it. They set off into blinding swirls of ice and new snow, the beginnings of an early winter, the bay of the hound approaching in the distance.

They knew the route Peder had taken and veered farther north, hoping they wouldn't step between a couple of trees and find themselves face to face with him.

The ridges ahead grew higher and higher. A thin layer of snow dropped, leaving the wind bits of ice with which to slice at their skin and tattered clothing. Come nightfall, the baying of the hound ceased, and they took their customary refuge under a tree. Aednat's fever and delirium grew worse. Mari's unnatural trance remained the same. Gabrick had no sense of time. Was it two days or ten? He didn't know. He worried over Aednat, knowing they needed to take her leg, but knowing she'd not survive their journey if they did. And he worried over Mari. If she woke, Peder and the seekers would surely find them, but if she didn't return to herself soon, at least long enough to eat, she would starve. They fed the girls any broth they could convince them to swallow, but it wouldn't sustain life for very long.

At the last ridge, it began to snow in earnest. Icy wind found its way to Gabrick's skin as if scraping the meat from his bones. And then they were past the peak, coming down the other side, the biting wind even more severe, the snow swirling like water going down a drain. In the distance, the foliage thinned to a barren waste of dirt and rock.

On a ridge to the south stood a man, well-covered from the cold, outlined only here and again by the ebb and flow of the racing snow. Gabrick felt an envy at that moment like none he'd ever experienced. To stand in this nightmare and be warm, truly warm, would be a paradise beyond anything the Vasheri could ever promise.

The man strode purposefully in their direction. Den picked up the pace and Gabrick followed. They skidded down steep stretches of dirt and gathering snow, sliding on the loose gravel. Gabrick watched Den go down, maneuvering himself to take the brunt of the fall, sliding several lengths on his belly, trying to protect his precious cargo. And then Gabrick followed suit. As Den had, he twisted in mid-fall, landing on his face. Loose gravel and sharp rocks scraped at his arms, hands and legs. When they finally stopped, Gabrick pushed himself up, ignored the blood, and staggered on. There was nothing else to do. It was move or die.

As they reached the plateau stretching from the mountain's base, the dog's hoarse baying crested the peak above them. It ran on three legs, a front one twisted at an unnatural angle from its body. Frozen blood matted its fur, especially around a shriveled eye socket, out of which hung a limp, frost-bitten twig.

With its impaired eyesight, its paw entirely missed the trail. It rolled down the hill like a barrel, much faster than Gabrick and Den. As it went, it cried so piteously Gabrick almost felt sorry for the beast, but he remembered how the imperial hounds were raised. They had no compassion; only obedience, a keen sense of smell, and a lust for the hunt.

Despite its painful descent, it rested for only a moment. Raising its nose to the piercing wind, it staggered onto its three legs, whimpers turning to a growl. And it came on. It would catch them. Even injured, the scent of its prey so close made it frenzied. Its hackles rose and it moved into a strange, sideways lope. Bloodied paw prints stained rocks, patches of barren dirt, and growing drifts of snow as it ran.

Gabrick unlashed Mari and lay her down. He faced the beast.

Den came behind him, breathing hard. "We can't face a hound, boy. Not in our condition."

Gabrick's breathing was almost as labored, and he knew it shouldn't have been. Mari weighed much less than Aednat. He held out his hand. "Give me the knife. I'd rather fight here than have it come at me from behind."

"I should...I should—" but Den's heart wasn't in it.

Gabrick stretched his hand farther. "I choose how I will live or die, but you stay with Aednat until the very end. There's no shame in that."

The way Den bowed his head, Gabrick knew the man didn't believe him, but he handed Gabrick the knife. Den picked up Mari as if cradling a broken doll. With Aednat still strapped to his back and shoulders, he stumbled on.

The hound approached with his lopsided run, less than ten lengths away. It tried to run past Gabrick, its true lust reserved for Mari, but Gabrick stepped in front of it. Exhausted and hungry, Gabrick's frozen fingers so tight on the hilt that the knife moved as an extension of his hand, he took a swipe at the beast. The knife slit through it broad nose.

It skidded to a halt, pulling its head back, whining. Blood ran into its mouth. It bared its teeth and lunged at Gabrick. Pink icicles formed down its snout like an extra set of fangs. The beast circled—a step and a hop, a step and a hop—like some overgrown, deformed rabbit.

Already exhausted, Gabrick knew he had to make this encounter short. If he didn't, he'd wear out before he could make a move.

He lunged toward the beast's blind side, stretching forward with his knife. The hound stretched its head too far, trying to see the attack. Gabrick kicked. His boot connected with the twisted front leg. A crack, a whine, and the hound fell. Its broad haunches stuck up in the air, its stub tail tucked tight in pain while its shoulder lay in the drifting snow. It scrambled to rise.

Even an injured hound could turn its head to catch an enemy aiming at its neck, so Gabrick didn't try. He came under the injured leg, angling the knife into the hound's chest. It wasn't an immediate kill. He'd missed the heart, but he'd sliced an artery. Yanking back on the knife, blood spilled onto the new snow, forming a shallow trench at Gabrick's feet. It warmed his toes through a hole in the boots.

The beast snapped at Gabrick and he scurried back, fell, then half-scooted, half-rolled. The hound crawled after him, but slowed like a wind-up toy running out of tension. Each snap came a little later than the one before, missing its mark by a few more digits. Finally, the animal stopped, its legs twitched, and it lay still, remaining eye staring up at the thinning clouds.

Scanning the horizon, Gabrick spotted Peder at the plateau less than fifty lengths away.

Gabrick stumbled to his feet, turning toward the desert. Amid the swirling dirt and ice, Den's dark form had disappeared. Telling himself he only had to reach Den, then he could stop, Gabrick followed.

The man had more stamina than Gabrick had expected. As the sun began to set, its last rays reflected off an unwrapped sliver of Aednat's stupid prophecy stone, still strapped to her waist. The three of them were huddled together, an outcropping of black rock serving as their only shelter from the wind.

Den had placed Mari between himself and Aednat. As Gabrick came close, he half-opened his eyes. "Aednat and I will die, but perhaps you and Mariessa can live." He angled his body over one side of the small girl, pressing his face to her forehead.

Gabrick pulled Aednat's skirt over her animal-skin pants, concealing the stone again, then he squeezed himself between Aednat and Mari, almost on top of the small girl. He added his thin blanket and animal skin over the three of them. It wouldn't reach Den, but Aednat and Mari were his priority. Though he knew, as did Den, dying of cold might be a mercy to Aednat rather than dying of the infection.

He didn't know whether exhaustion would claim him or the freezing temperatures, but it didn't matter. In the end, the result would be the same. Tonight, he would either discover the Vasheri, and the pain of this violent world would finally be over. He smiled, wrapped his arms around Mari and Aednat, and let the darkness take him.

56

To Mariessa, only aware of her fight with the burning white light, no time had passed. It continued to sear at her mind and she continued to push it back. But now, the light faded, withdrew, and with a final force of willpower, Mariessa snuffed it out. She found herself standing in a white expanse, not the white that had burned at her mind, not even bright, just a dull white that stretched in both directions. In the distance, her mother's voice called to her. She ran toward it, suddenly on a path, flowering greenery to either side, the vivid blossoms filling the air with sweet scent. The whiteness of her path turned dull, changed to a light beige, then eventually darkened to rich earth. She continued to a simple white gate. A canopy of vines with delicate lavender flowers arched above it. From their open petals rained a white mist, obscuring the scenery beyond.

Her mother's voice seemed to sigh from the other side. "It's time for you to fulfill your destiny, my Essa," she said. "Come through the gate so I may guide you."

Mariessa entered the cleansing mist, refreshed as if rising from a much-needed sleep. She turned the latch, and stepped into darkness. A hand clasped hers, small as her own and obviously a woman's, then suddenly it was gone. Alone in the darkness, Mariessa gasped for air.

Heavy weight pressed down, stifling her. Another gasp, and her eyes popped open. She flailed, but her body didn't respond. Encased in something soft, it created a stifling cocoon. The smell of animal hides, similar to the odor of Den's make-shift blankets in the mountains but less putrid, filled her nostrils. She willed her body to move, but it protested. After repeated efforts, her stiff arms raised. Using her elbows more than her hands, she pushed back the covering. Cold air washed over her naked body. She yanked the furs back up to her neck, taking in her surroundings. Lying atop large cushions, she was surrounded by a mound of furs, some sewn together and some made from beasts big enough to have covered her twice.

She blinked a few times, adjusting to the dim glow of two failing lightstones. The small structure in which she slept appeared to be a latticework of hollow plants, similar to the bamboo in her country and Gabrick's lower Zhanda, but larger and pockmarked with holes. They'd filled the holes and gaps between the framework with a hard mixture of mud and dry grass, similar to the stepping stones made in Kerokos, or perhaps a rough version of the material around the emperor's palace, the stuff they'd called cement.

Other than the furs and the lamp, the room held little. Until Mariessa craned her neck to see what lay behind her, she believed herself alone. An older boy sat slumped on the floor, his bare chest arched across his folded knees. Mariessa squealed in surprise.

He straightened, alert and holding a knife, their knife.

"How'd you get that?" she asked. "That belongs to Chid Den."

The boy kept it between them, but ran to a slab of mud-cement fitted into the hut's side like a removable door. He pushed it out and the whistle of wind mixed with his babble of words to someone on the outside.

A man not much bigger than the first, but broader in the shoulders, joined them and shut the door. His straight black hair lay flat over his ears then evolved into a wide, intricate braid he'd wrapped across his face and around his neck, leaving only his ice-blue eyes visible. Eyelids similar to most Zhandians, but with a much more prominent skin-fold, made his eyes appear smaller than they really were. Both men's noses lay so flat to their broad cheeks they seemed made of melting wax. Thin lips took their place above chins almost as broad as their cheeks, held up by a thick neck a caribou might envy, as well as broad shoulders and a sturdy build. Her guard wore only a pair of thin calf-length breeches while the second man was dressed in thick furs and boots.

The second man spoke, the sound like more babbling in the wind. He finished, awaiting a response, but she could only stare like a tree lepur mesmerized by a heartstone.

He released a heavy sigh, pointing to himself. "Kxeichya." He pointed to his bare-chested companion. "Ptzekeera." Gesturing his hand to them both, then sweeping it around the room, and gesturing outside the hut, he said. "Our people, Tehkxyay."

She pointed to herself. "Mariessa."

They pronounced it "Myezza," but it seemed close enough. "Where are Gabrick, Chid Den, and Aednat?"

Kxeichya nodded. "They open," he said mimicking his eyes opening up. "They die. The prophet-girl, very sick. Soon, you all die." And with that, he mimicked taking a knife across his throat.

Tears stung her eyes. Gabrick and Den's necks slit, or waiting for Aednat's recovery? "Are they dead?" she asked. "If you kill us, then why help us?"

The man seemed confused. "So you hear," he pointed to his head instead of his ears, "why must die. You go with smile and good heart." He pressed his hand against his chest. This didn't make any sense. He pointed to what appeared to be a smaller pile of rugs. "You make ready. We go to pen, with others."

Holding the furs to her chest, Mariessa reached for the pile. Thinner garments lay wrapped inside what appeared to be fur pants and a long-sleeved shirt. Both men stood, staring, waiting. She hadn't understood everything Kxeichya had said, but she knew he wanted her dressed and thought he might be taking her to the others, if they weren't already dead.

"Please turn around while I put them on."

They stood, continuing to stare. If he knew enough to speak some form of Zhandian, the idiot men knew enough to turn around when a woman was naked. She glared at them, rotating her finger in a circle. "Turn away."

A hint of a smile played at Ptzekeera's mouth.

Her eyes narrowed further and she crossed her hands over her fur-covered chest. "No. I will dress when you are gone," and she pointed to the door.

With a laugh, the men turned, Ptzekeera grabbing some similar clothing. Watching him dress gave her some idea of how to layer the various shirts and pants. She wasn't sure they wouldn't turn back around, but the cold compelled her to keep up with Ptzekeera's pace regardless of their presence.

Kxeichya and Ptzekeera led her outside where the wind whipped at her clothing and stung her eyes. Still, she was warmer than she'd been in the last few weeks. Ptzekeera wrapped a cloth round her face, leaving only her eyes exposed. She could scarcely breathe, but it kept back the biting cold. She'd thought the mountains unbearable. At least there they'd had trees and foliage shielding them from the wind's vicious temper. Here there was nothing, or at least it seemed so. When Mariessa took a closer look, she realized it would be even worse outside the gathered huts and away from the rocky hill gathering their homes in a semi-circle.

Ptzekeera guided her toward one of the many identical huts near the black rocks. He said something to Kxeichya, but the man shook his head in response, answering in their strange language. Ptzekeera's shoulders dropped with disappointment, and he ushered Mariessa into the hut. She expected the men to follow, but they pulled the door shut by yanking it snugly into place behind her. Unlike the hut in which she'd awoken, the handles on this door were only on the outside, making it a prison.

A small fire warmed the hut and cast a faint glow on the mud-pitch walls. The floor was covered in furs, blankets, and cushions of various colors and sizes. The furs moved and a face emerged.

"Den!" Mariessa exclaimed, falling to her knees and scrambling over a red cushion to hug him. "You're alive." She sat back on her haunches, and immediately searched the other furs. "Ptzekeera said something about killing us. I couldn't tell if he meant you were dead, or that he plans on doing it later." Den seemed alone, and a new panic struck Mariessa. "Where's Gabrick?"

Den lay a hand on her arm, the ends of two fingers gone black, his others a sickly gray. "He's okay. They take him every day to warm his feet and ears, trying to counteract the frostbite. They only work on one of us at a time. I finished and Gabrick will be back soon." He gestured to a far corner. "There's food. You haven't eaten anything but broth for going on two weeks. I imagine you're famished."

And she was. The mention of food made her stomach clench with a hunger that won out over her fear. She scrambled up and over another pile of blankets, took a woven cover from off the short table no bigger around than one of the emperor's fancy plates and found it piled high with salted meats, dried fruits, and soft cheeses. She dove in, talking to Den between bites.

"Aednat?" she asked Den.

His expression fell. "She's alive, but not well. They're arguing whether to take her leg before the execution so she'll be 'healed' or to save her the pain."

"So they're really going to kill us?"

Den nodded. "I've tried to talk them out of it, but Han made an agreement centuries ago that he would leave them in peace if they promised to never let any stranger cross their borders. I even explained that they've only been safe from him these last thirty years because I hid a report about the oil in this desert, but they don't believe me."

"Why do they want us healed then? Why not simply let us die?"

"So we can understand that they do this for the good of their tribe and hold no ill will against us. So we can be at peace with it."

"Peace?" Mariessa dropped the food in her hand back to the plate. "I'm not at peace with surviving everything we've been through just so we can have our throats slit for trespassing on some bangay's hunting range!"

Den sighed and Mariessa feared that if Aednat didn't survive, which seemed likely, then Den wouldn't care what happened to him, or to the rest of them.

The door rattled against the side of the hut, the wind whistling at its edges, then Gabrick scrunched his tall frame through the space that opened, his long hair pulled back in a shorter version of the natives', hiding the tips of his ears but not the gray lobe of his left one. The hair wrapped around his neck, but only made it halfway. Ptzekeera followed.

Mariessa dropped the food lid among the blankets, tripping over them as she made her way toward them. "Gabrick!"

"You're alive," he said with relief. He met her halfway, scooping her up and holding her so tight she thought he might crack a rib. His cold coats made her shiver. "Oh." He dropped her to the cushions and started undressing. To her surprise, he didn't stop until he stood in only his long underpants.

He laughed at her wide eyes. "They told me I would stay warmer in the huts if I don't wear clothing from outside. At night, they tell us to sleep under the blankets in our baby-skin. Believe it or not, it works."

Mariessa had stopped listening, not only because she refused to pay attention as he laughed at her, but because she caught sight of his calf above a number of blackened toes. "Did you even bother to change that dressing at all after I went into a trance?"

"We were kind of busy surviving."

"Let me see it." She pulled at his arm, making him sit down as she untangled the crudely packed poultice, and inspected the wound. "This is horrible."

"They've been putting some foul-smelling cream on it, and a leaf, different than the ones you had in the mountains, but the daffing thing isn't getting any better."

Mariessa glanced at Den. He spoke with the tribesman at the door as if he'd been raised in this frigid desert.

"How does Den know their language?" she asked Gabrick.

He shrugged. "It has some similarities to old-Zhandese, but I can only catch a word here and there. He's able to hold entire conversations."

"So he can tell them anything?"

"Seems to."

"Den," Mariessa changed her attention to the other man. "Tell the men we need more of their healing plants. I'll dress Gabrick's wound myself from now on."

Den passed Mariessa's words to Ptzekeera. His response was not what she'd have expected. His broad form stiffened. He gestured a fist in Mariessa's direction and judging by the cadence, asked a clipped question.

After Den's response, Ptzekeera's babbling rose in pitch and speed. With a quick wrap of his hair, he was out the door, not even bothering to stop it up behind him.

"What was that about?" asked Gabrick.

Den shook his head, as confused as they. "The boy asked if Mariessa was a healer. I told him no, but as a sorceress below she has a knack with plants and herbs. He went crazy, talking so fast I had no hope of understanding."

Chief Kxeichya returned with Ptzekeera, three women, and the plants and cloths needed to redress Gabrick's wound. Ignoring the others, Mariessa set to work, replacing the leaves she'd removed then adding more, creating a healing poultice. She'd never thought about it before, but she knew squeezing them before placing them on the skin would make a difference.

One of the women placed a hand to her cheek as Mariessa finished. The woman nodded to the others, saying some word Mariessa didn't understand.

With a huge grin Ptzekeera slapped the chief's—probably his father's—chest. He rambled off something in their language.

Den chuckled. "I guess the chief's son has been trying to talk them into keeping you. He says you're small and as long as you never go into the city, the emperor will never know. Besides, they cannot kill a sorceress, not a potential...something. I don't know the meaning of the last word."

But Kxeichya removed his son's hand, and babbled something somber. A look of joy and frustration crossed Den's face in rapid succession. "He says you might be able to heal Aednat, using the desert plants which are much better than those found in the forest."

Mariessa shook her head. "But if it wasn't enough before, what hope will I have now?"

"When you were able to change the dressing often," said Den, "it started to help."

For a brief moment, hope swelled in Mariessa. She rubbed a leaf between her fingers. "These are better, I can tell."

Den gave a half-laugh. "And yet it doesn't matter. As soon as she's healed, they're still planning to slit our throats."

57

Aednat took weeks to begin to mend. The infection had spread far, gone deep. But little by little, the black lines shooting from the wound like forks of lightning turned gray, the red areas softened to a paler pink, swelling diminished, and her golden skin regained its color. The weeks passed, the cold grew worse, and the day of their execution drew near.

If the Tehkxyay people thought she would let them kill her and her friends without a fight, they were mistaken. But when the time came, Mariessa had still found no way to defend them. The ground was too frozen for her fingers and there was nothing with which to make a decent weapon.

In only a thin layer of knitted underclothing, with equally thin stockings, they walked out into the late morning. Ptzekeera had them leave their winter gear behind, explaining the need to keep it clean so it could be used by another. Ropes tied their ankles together, held by warriors walking at a distance. Thin patches of snow gathered in corners where the wind had blown it against structures of rock, dirt, and sand, but everything else around the huts was barren.

Den whispered to Aednat. "Stay calm, butterflower. It'll be easier that way." He paused. "I'm so sorry."

In the center of the community of huts a deep pit had been dug, rocks piled around the edge. Inside, roared a blazing fire, hot enough to warm the ground beneath Mariessa's socks.

"The fire grows to honor what you give," said Kxeichya, standing before a line of warriors. "To remind you that your bodies die, but your souls will return to warm paradise, in the company of our brothers and sisters, the Vasheri."

Mariessa used her toes to pull the socks from her feet. The ground was still chill, but it was the cold of a Kerokan winter, not the cold of frozen soil. Not for the first time, she wondered at her undamaged flesh. Gabrick and the others had sacrificed much in that wilderness to keep her alive. It was time to return the favor.

At a command from Kxeichya, the tribesmen pulled their knives.

Mariessa dug her toes into the warming dirt. Gabrick glanced her way, but remained silent, as did Den. Aednat stood with her head hung forward, arms folded over her chest, tears falling on them in silent sobs.

Kxeichya approached with his knife, continuing his praise for their sacrifice, but Mariessa no longer listened. The tribe didn't deserve to die, but neither did they, and even a Vasheri-forsaken land such as this had to have plants somewhere.

She sent her senses in search of roots, but only found small weeds, desert shrubs, and nothing large enough to reach them. She found an oasis full of plant life, though the water they fed on was brackish and unfit for humans. Still, even the longest roots, plunging deep into the desert soil, weren't enough to reach the huts and the men poised with their knives.

What motivated her to search downward she didn't know—desperation or inspiration. Through layers of dry dirt and sand, between broken rock and centuries-old fossils, she found a single seed resting less than a digit above the water table that stretched from the mountain range to this spot. The ancient seed should have been dead, if not from time, from the pressure. But it wasn't. And it needed only to grow the tiniest roots to have water.

Mariessa had never made a plant grow, never even considered it, but something inside of her said it could be done. She hoped her power could substitute as sunlight, but would she have the strength to call the ancient foliage through centuries of barren land and bring it almost instantly to full bloom? She must. It was their only hope.

She focused, straining, commanding.

Kxeichya raised his knife. Though Mariessa saw, she didn't acknowledge anything but water, dirt, and the efforts of a seed. She dropped to the ground, seeking more contact with the soil. As she dug in her fingers, the ground rumbled.

Kxeichya's knife landed, blade down, between Mariessa's hands.

Her plant fought the link between them. That piercing light, a pinpoint at the back of her mind, began to blossom, getting larger the more the plant refused to cooperate. Reaching to its temporary consciousness, she commanded, *Grow now or you will never live. This is your only chance.*

It submitted to her will. The painful light at the edge of her mind disappeared, replaced by peace and purpose.

Hold me in your embrace, and I will live, the tree spoke to her. She almost lost hold of it. No matter what she'd felt from the consciousness she gave a plant, none had ever spoken to her.

The ground continued to shake. Ptzekeera babbled something to his men. They stuck their knives into the dirt, prostrated themselves to the ground, and began a chant.

At first, Mariessa assumed they were attempting to call forth some power from the Vasheri, trying to stop her, but then Kxeichya knelt at her side when he could have picked up the knife. Though the tree—and she knew now that it was a tree—continued to grow, the effort required by her became less and less. When the ground in front of them erupted, Kxeichya was thrown to the side, and Mariessa landed in a heap with Gabrick, Den, and Aednat. She lost her connection, but this had been no ordinary seed.

A sapling shot up from the ground, its green bark and limbs shimmering in the winter sun. It twined itself around Kxeichya's knife, though the blade should have been thrown back with the rest of them, enveloping the blade and hilt as its trunk became sturdy, branches shot out, and white leaves began to bud. Every part of the tree glowed; the trunk and limbs, a combination of translucent white and pale rose, swirled and twined around dominating shades of green.

It rose larger than the old oak trees on Zhanda, larger even than the giant pettung trees in southern Kerokos. It shoved dirt into the bonfire, making it smoke and then burying it to nothing, but the warmth in the air didn't dissipate. If anything, it increased.

Mariessa glanced at Ptzekeera's warriors, their knives in front of them, their chants somehow drawing the tree upward. Somehow, she'd given birth to this hoped-for monstrosity, and as soon as they finished raising it, the blood of her and her friends would be the first nourishment it received. She couldn't let that happen. It was still a plant, and she could take control.

Again, she dug her toes and fingers into the dirt, surprised at how warm it had become. She reached her consciousness to the tree, ordering it to protect her, to protect her friends. She hesitated, but she had no choice. She ordered it to kill Kxeichya and the other warriors.

The tree shook, branches flailing. A particularly long and slender limb stretched outward, wrapping around Mariessa's waist. She screamed. Gabrick tore at the slick bark, to no effect. The tree yanked her into the air, pulling her through its tall canopy.

She'd spent her life in trees, clambering through their branches. They'd never dropped her, never hurt her. But now she was terrified. Not only had the tree not responded, it had attacked. She opened her mouth to warn the others, "R—"

Shush, the tree said into her mind. *Your friends are safe, as are you, as are the Tehkxyay warriors.*

The tree deposited her on a thick limb, near the tree's center. She placed her hand on the trunk as smooth as a heartstone and warm to the touch. The cold wind didn't wind between the branches, the tree somehow keeping it at bay. Warmth spread from Mariessa's hand throughout her body like a warm tea.

They're planning to murder us, Mariessa told the tree, sounding like a petulant child.

And if they had not, their entire village—men, women and children—would have died at the emperor's hands. A brutal, long-suffering death. Are your lives more valuable than all of theirs?

Mariessa's fingernails bit at the clear bark, though they didn't leave the slightest indentation. *I will not sit back and let them murder us. These people talk of honor, but they cower to the emperor rather than rise up and fight. If they died, at least it would be for a cause.*

Remember those words when it is your turn to make the same choices. A white leaf as cold as the limbs were warm, caressed Mariessa's cheek. *They have suffered long, both in numbers and in pride. They are nearing the final sacrifice.*

The branch wrapped around her waist again. *I will release you. Do not try to turn me against them for I am their protector. You have killed many because you lack control. That is forgiven. There is much you will learn, but you will kill none here. Do I have your promise?* The branch, with its icy leaves, gave a gentle yet threatening squeeze.

Mariessa had no choice. *As long as they don't try to harm my friends....* She took a deep breath.

The humor in the tree's voice was like a rustle of spring leaves. *That will be sufficient.*

The tree deposited Mariessa back at Gabrick's side. He reached for her and a twig curled around his hand. "No," she yelled. "You promised."

Three of the twig's white leaves turned black and fell to the ground. As it released him, his blackened ear and toes healed, fully restored. Another branch touched Aednat, losing more leaves, healing the frostbite and her damaged thigh. One by one, it touched the members of the Tehkxyay tribe, losing leaves and healing wounds, new and old. It reached for Den, shuddered, and retracted, unwilling to make contact.

Finally, the branches retreated and the tree stood still.

Ptzekeera left his brothers, and rushed toward them. Gabrick stepped forward, in his way, but Mariessa put a hand on Gabrick's arm, bringing him back. She'd promised the tree, and she couldn't go back or all their lives would be forfeit.

But Ptzekeera dropped his knife. He wrapped Mariessa in an embrace, lifting her off the ground and babbling in his language.

"What is he saying?" she asked Den.

He shook his head. "Too fast. I don't understand." He grabbed the boy's shoulder, speaking in slow Tehkxyayen.

The boy responded, but again, much too fast. Den tried again and this time Ptzekeera slowed down. As he spoke, a surprised smile spread across Den's face.

"Somehow, your power played into a prophecy of theirs, one I've never heard about."

Aednat stepped forward. It was so good to see her move without a limp. "Like the prophecy stone they took from me?"

"You still have that thing?"

She shrugged. "It doesn't matter now. What did the boy say?"

"According to the chief's son, a prophetess lived with them for many years, many centuries ago. She's the reason they quit fighting with Han and agreed to his terms. She told them that someday a sorceress would come and revive a sorcery tree, that it would herald a revival of magic in the land, and become their protector. 'The tribes will rise up, along with the earth, water, and sky, and defeat their eternal enemy,' whatever that's supposed to mean."

Ptzekeera said something else and Den translated. "To seal the prophecy, and to appease the angry emperor, the sorceress gave herself up as a sacrifice." With the last few words, Den's eyes went wide. He stared at Ptzekeera as if he'd grown demon wings. "The emperor had her killed on the spot, but her heartstone had no power, no value whatsoever. He threw it back at the chief and killed seven of his best warriors, including the man's oldest son, to make up for the insult. He took their heartstones, but threw the one from the useless prophetess into their fire pit."

Kxeichya, who had been waiting outside their circle, joined them, placing an arm around his son's shoulders. "I am a descendant of that chief's youngest son. His father grieved, but the son dug deep in the fire pit's center, burying the heartstone. For a week, he fasted and prayed to the Vasheri to change the stone, to make it a tool to fulfill the prophecy. Eventually he gave up, but he told the story to his descendants, always telling us we should never trust a sorceress."

"I can't believe it." Den seemed overcome, not with emotion, but surprise. "Her heart was a seed." He walked over to the tree, laying his hand on the trunk. "And now, it's this."

The tree rustled and brightened.

"Aah," Den pulled his hand back, bright red and blistering.

A limb slapped him in the chest, throwing him across the clearing. He slammed into one of the huts, sliding to the frozen ground. It took him a moment to breathe, and then his gasp turned to a groan.

Mariessa, along with the others, rushed to his side.

"Are you all right?" Aednat cried, checking him for broken bones then grasping the wrist of his red and blistered hand.

"It's all right," said Den. "A little balm and some wrapping, in a few days it'll be fine." His last words were said between chattering teeth.

Away from the tree, the brutal cold returned.

Kxeichya's eyes narrowed to thin lines as he turned his gaze from the tree. "You," he pointed at Den, "we kill. Others go far from evil Beht Den."

Den came to his feet. "I am *not* Beht Den! That man is dead."

Mariessa joined Gabrick and Aednat in standing between the chief and their friend. "You'll have to kill us first," she said.

Snatching a nearby warrior's knife, Kxeichya said, "So be it."

A tree root shot up through the soil, clear as ice. It wrapped itself around Kxeichya's ankle, yanking him back.

He dropped the knife and the root retreated. "You not should give trust. He is evil friend." When they didn't respond, he sneered and turned away.

Ptzekeera took his place, babbling again to Den, who nodded understanding for whatever apology the boy gave, then turned to the rest of them to translate. "I told him to take us to Janxia, a port west of the desert. We'll catch a boat there."

"At least the emperor won't think to look for us, right?" asked Gabrick. "Since he'll think we're dead."

Placing his hand against the hut for leverage, Den groaned as he stood. "We can only hope, boy. But hope has taken us this far, so maybe it will finally see us through."

58

Glass shattered against the wall, a red stain running down the governor's blue and white wallpaper to join similar dark spots in the gray carpet. Han paced in front of the oak wood desk. "You told me they were dead."

Skirting the bits of glass and spreading wine, Han moved his pacing to the center of the room. "We're readying ourselves to return to Han City, and now you tell me you were *wrong*?"

Peder trembled with his own anger. "I was seeing the Tehkxyay take them away. They have never let an intruder live. Never. They should be all dead."

For a moment, Han wondered if Peder had allowed Den and the others to escape. Could he be another accomplice?

As Han spoke his next words, he studied Peder's reactions. "And yet informants have spotted them in Janxia?"

"They could be wrong," said Peder. "One family claims to have seen them, based on the description we sent around Zhanda when they escaped the palace."

Peder seemed as devout as before, but that didn't mean he could be trusted. Han rubbed at his stone-smoothed palms. When alone, he'd taken to caressing the transfer stone, to help him think.

"Den is capable of anything," said Han. "As long as he's alive, he's unpredictable."

Han studied the stains along the wall. There were quite a few. The red jiu had soaked into the paper, into the carpet fibers; layer upon layer, long fingers of red and brown spilling to the floor like remnants of a tortured man.

"Your Eminence. Would you like me to go there?"

Han's gaze held Peder's. "I will have you send a decree to Zhanda's high general. He's responsible for the continent's security, and he'll be held responsible for cleaning up this mess. Every enforcer who spoke with Den and his children is to be killed, everyone who knows of them or of their movements, every person Den or the others talked with or might have seen them; I want all of them killed. Every memory of their travel from the palace to Janxia is to be eliminated."

"And the tribe, Your Holiness?"

Han almost smiled. "We'll massacre every nomad in that desert as soon as we've dealt with Den and the witch at Janxia."

"It might not—" Peder tried again.

"It is," said Han. "They're there. I can feel it in my blood like poison."

"I will find them at once," said Peder.

Han pulled a matchstick as long as his hand off the desk, striking it along the side. As it flared into life, it left a long gauge in the polished wood. "I'll be accompanying you. We'll take the plane and our land soldiers can join us as soon as they are able. I want to watch Den die." The flame ate away at the long stick of wood. "It's no longer appropriate for the governor to have this home, not after the holy Lingdow has lived and breathed between these walls."

He tossed the burning match onto the brown-stained carpet. Without a care, Han sauntered from the room and out the front door, toward one of the many waiting cars ready to escort him home. Behind him the carpet burst into flame, the fire racing up the wall and licking at the drapes and ceiling.

Screams of servants and cleaning staff melded with the growing blaze behind him. Curious, he thought, how much people could sound like horses when truly frightened. They were all animals really, with their short life-spans, limited vision, and limited abilities. Their purpose seemed clear now that he'd had centuries to observe. They must learn to live out their pitiful existence in order and obedience, or be squashed before they could infect others. And when they died, there would always be more to take their place, like insects, made to populate the planet and bring pleasure to higher beings. And there was none higher, nor would there ever be anyone greater, than Han.

Den's death would bring freedom to them both. It would be a good thing, a sealing of their destinies, not the painful separation Han had imagined.

He stepped into the governor's former autocar and Peder drove for the makeshift aeroplane strip. The shrieking of men and women, and the spread of the fire, faded in the distance. A high-tier fire engine, similar to those in Han city, raced past them toward the blaze. It was very fortunate for the city that Han had allowed the governor to have one. He wondered if the small supply of water on its back would be sufficient, then dismissed his flicker of concern.

Han rubbed his hand along his thigh, imagining Den with a knife plunged to the hilt in his chest, blood spilling onto Han's fingers, dripping to the ground beneath his feet. The sound of suction when Han pulled the knife from Den's chest and he started bleeding in earnest, would be the sound of final victory. It would be a delightful day.

He spoke to Peder, loud enough for him to hear above the engine. "Den deserves some honor. I will declare the day of his death a national holiday throughout every continent, region and country...on all of Dixho. What should we call it?"

"Traitor's day," Peder said with a grunt.

"No, no. Much too dull." Han leaned back into the comfortable cushions. "Day of Remorse, maybe? We'll require the sacrifice of a prominent figure, maybe in every region, or maybe the cities. I don't know." He ran one hand along his leg as the other tapped his chin. "We'll have to build altars outside the churches, something ornate but functional, so a priest can tie the sacrifice down. It will need some kind of funnel to gather the blood." A slow smile creased his smooth face, crinkling it with the first hints of age. "It will be a fine day, a day when everyone can feel of my remorse."

59

Gabrick watched as Chuluun, weary from his long day sluicing fish, brought his youngest son into his arms, close to the meager fire in the fireplace, and began a story. The few coals and sparse sticks of wood cast red flickers over his tenth-tier scar, yet the man seemed more happy and content than any person Gabrick had ever seen.

Mariessa had gone to use the communal privy, wearing some of the younger daughter's clothes plus a thick gray scarf over her unnaturally curly hair. The dark mop reached past her shoulders now, and when tame, it was like a tumultuous waterfall.

Den snored in the corner, his fingers gripping the edge of his thin blanket, highlighting the consequences of the surgery they'd had to perform three weeks before. Because of the frostbite, they'd been forced to cut off the top of his pointing finger on his right hand, along with his pinkie and the top digit of the middle and ring fingers from his left. Sometimes he woke up clenching his missing appendages, his face contorted by pain. But for right now, he slept in peace.

Gabrick waved his hand in Chuluun's direction. "Why are they doing this for us? Especially after the emperor's decree."

Aednat turned her beautiful big eyes on him, lashes longer than Mari's and almost as thick. "Because they're good people, they know the decree is wrong, and they believe Den."

It still didn't make sense. Chuluun was risking his wife, and his seven children's lives. Gabrick brought his voice even lower. "Den only talked about the possibility of a revolution so he could get us a safe place to hide while he found us a way out of here. In over a thousand years, no army has ever reached the palace, let alone come close to killing Beht Han."

With a glassy look in her eye, the kind of look Mari got when she talked about the Vasheri, Aednat said, "That's all about to change. There's a prophecy about a savior coming, someone who will destroy the emperor."

Gabrick ran a hand through his wavy hair, recently unraveled from its braid. "Den says prophecies are some sorceresses' ability to see the way events might go, then people believing her and making it happen. He says there are no Vasheri watching over us."

Aednat leaned away and gaped at him. "You saw what happened in that desert. Mariessa said the tree talked to her, with its own personality and completely separate from her giving it any consciousness."

Not wanting to argue with her right now, Gabrick didn't say anything more, but Den claimed those trees, though not common, had dotted the continents here and there centuries ago. According to him, Mariessa had just found an old seed.

Chuluun left his chair, tucking his son into a blanket next to the other children by the fire, then joining his wife on their pallet in the far corner.

"Have you ever wondered," Gabrick ventured, "if the emperor really is your father, why weren't you born a boy? You know, one of the Numbers?"

Aednat shifted her weight, moving away and fully facing him. "Den says my mother knocked the stone from his hand, when he...when he attacked her."

"What if she was already pregnant?"

Ever since they'd been kids Aednat had always known when he purposefully hid information. She eyed him like a hunter's falcon. "Out with it."

Gabrick hesitated, wondering if she'd be angry he hadn't said anything sooner, or maybe angry at him for saying anything at all, destroying her image of her mother. But he'd gone too far to back down now.

"Den told me your mother was already pregnant when Beht Han raped her." He closed the distance between them. "You and I aren't related."

"That's hard to imagine. My mother was very pious and virtuous, but I guess anything is possible." She smiled, but not the kind of smile he'd hoped for. "So, you're thinking...you and I..."

If she out and out laughed at him, he didn't think he could take the humiliation. He pulled away, trying to hide his disappointment. "I wasn't saying anything."

She placed a hand on his arm, the way she always did when apologizing or trying to get him to see reason. "I'm sorry. You know I love Eleven, and even if I didn't—"

"He's never coming back." Gabrick didn't know why he said it. He tried to tell himself it wasn't a sudden urge to be vindictive.

"What do you mean?"

"Never mind," Gabrick muttered. "I thought you knew, but I shouldn't—"

"What do you mean," she whispered.

Because Aednat never yelled at him. She always gave him the benefit of the doubt and she never blamed him, even when he deserved it. He couldn't believe he'd done this to her.

"I deserve to know the truth," she pleaded, tears burning her eyes. "Please, tell me."

"The man who warned us at the docks." Gabrick dropped his gaze, too much a coward to watch her face. "Den told me he was the one who was supposed to get Eleven out. Without his spy, Den has no other way to reach any of the Numbers."

"He promised."

She choked on her tears and couldn't say anything more. Gabrick put his arms around her, and she broke down, crying into the thick leenta-hair shirt the Tehkxyay people had given him. He rubbed one hand along her back, soothing her.

She didn't cry long, but dried her eyes. "Have you been hoping all this time, thinking that you and I...?"

She wasn't laughing now, but Gabrick still didn't want to say anything. He couldn't deny it, but that didn't mean he had to admit it.

With a shake of her head, that amused smile returned, laced with grief. "You can be so determined, Gabrick. Put the sun in front of you and as long as you're focused on finding a candle, you'll refuse to see what's already lighting your way."

"What in limbo is that supposed to mean?"

"You decided that you and I should be together, so you've been courting me, trying to convince me to let go of Eleven, or so you think. Really, you're trying to convince yourself."

"You're wrong," Gabrick said. She wasn't even making sense. "I've wanted this for a long time."

"Perhaps, and I know you love me as I love you, but you saw so many Numbers get involved with their servants that you think that's where this should go. It would be a perversion, whether we're related or not, because deep down our feelings are those of brother and sister."

She gave his arm a gentle squeeze. "When you calm down, think about what I've said. We get along, but you only find half of what I say remotely interesting. You'd much rather talk science with Den or philosophy and religion with Mariessa. You think I'm sweet and you're protective, but you have too much fire to be satisfied with someone like me." She leaned close. "Quit focusing on what isn't going to happen, and look around you. Find a girl who can be your equal, who can fight and love as passionately as you do."

He would have railed against her for telling him to look for someone else when he'd just declared that he wanted her, but as always, Aednat was so sincere, she cared so daffing much, he couldn't hold onto his anger.

She changed the subject before he could dwell on his thoughts for too long. "Did Den say he knew the father, my father? Could he still be alive?"

The bark of the only dog still left in the community, a little yapping pest owned by a stubborn old crone who sneered at everyone whenever they passed, announced Mari's return. The others had been sent away or made into stew, though the thought still made Gabrick a little queasy. Considering what the dogs here ate—feces and garbage scraps—to eat one seemed almost as bad as eating a prison rat.

Mari came in, shaking snow from her hair and shoulders. The clothes she'd borrowed made her look like an over-developed child. Her breasts, though small, were much too big for the eleven-year-old's dress, making it stretch unnaturally then hang at the shoulders and waist. She discarded it as soon as she walked through the door, standing in the breeches and shirt the desert tribesmen had given her for their journey to Janxia. She scooped up the dress, hanging it with the family's few items of clothing, in a simple cupboard in the corner.

Gabrick realized he'd only seen her twice in clothes that fit: the dress she'd been wearing when he kissed her in the stable, and the clothes she wore now. Made of soft leenta-hair, the creamy pants hung loose from her hips, but flowed against her thighs and calves as she walked. The shirt followed a similar design, hugging her subtle but definite curves, tight around her small waist, then tucked into the pants. She reached to a hook on the door and slipped a long-haired tunic over the shirt. The small fire at the far end of the room did little to dispel the cold.

She joined them, folding her knees to her chest and sitting like a wrapped package. If Gabrick tried something like that he'd fall over or end up rolling around like a stranded turtle, but it came naturally to Mari. The distant fire played with her features, clear of scars since the Tehkxyay tree had touched her and healed them all—all but Den.

She rocked forward then settled back into her tight squat. "I heard you say something about Aednat's father. Are you finished or should I come back later?"

"He told me everything," said Aednat. "But even if he hadn't, you'd be welcome to stay. And he told me they can't reach Eleven. He's stuck there, until the emperor takes him or kills him." Her eyes started to tear again, but she brushed them away. "I'm going to lie down. I have a lot to think about."

Poor Aednat. She'd have a night of little sleep and a lot of tears, all because of him. She went to the mat the family had set out for her, turned to the wall and pretended to sleep. Her shoulders trembled as she cried in silence.

"Will she be okay?" Mari whispered.

Gabrick could only shrug. They sat there a moment, the silence uncomfortable. Sometimes he almost wished he and Mari could go back to the time when they'd exchanged insults. When they were alone like this, neither of them seemed able to say anything. That night in the stable had been a stupid, stupid mistake.

"It's winter already," Mariessa said, an obvious attempt to fill the silence. "I guess we missed celebrating Whisper's Night while I was in my trance."

"On Zhanda we call it The Rising, when Vasheri supposedly come close to the surface and whisper secrets to the pure in heart." His expression darkened. "The emperor would pretend to receive spiritual guidance and then send decrees telling the people to be happy with their station in life or more diligent in their worship, which only meant their worship of him. I can't believe I swallowed those lies."

Mariessa released her knees, folding her legs and sitting on the dirt floor. "In Keran, I would sometimes go to the church, to sit and think. I became friends with the priest there and learned that the sermons he taught on Tingtian were often monitored by the emperor's men. Priest Yosel knew how to spot observers and newcomers and those were the days when he preached what he called, 'the emperor's gospel.' But the other days, he taught the 'old gospel,' the way the Vasheri had intended. He said that just because the emperor twisted things that were good, it didn't mean the good was never there to begin with."

"So you still believe in the Vasheri?" Gabrick asked, unable to contain the bitterness in his voice. "After all that you've seen and all that has happened?"

"They didn't make those things happen."

"But if they're so powerful, and loving, and everything they're supposed to be, then why do they allow it?"

"Gabrick, *we* are the Vasheri," she pointed out. "Every person living is a Vasheri who entered a Dixhoan, a mortal body, away from warm paradise and our perfect life below, releasing our memories at birth so we could test and refine our basic natures. We wanted to see what we are when we must survive in an imperfect world, and to learn from it. If our Vasheri brothers and sisters interfere with our choices and control them, then what can we ever learn?"

"Then what's the point?" asked Gabrick. "Why should we try to commune with the Vasheri below, or listen to their supposed guidance and principles if they're not going to do anything to help us?"

Mariessa sighed. "I said the same thing to Priest Yosel, and I struggled with it after my father and then my mother died. I think the Vasheri help guide people toward good choices, but pain is part of our learning. They help where they can. I don't think we ended up in those dungeons, together, by chance."

"So they helped us get nearly killed, thrown into a stinking prison, you nearly raped more than once, all so we could meet?" His voice rose as he spoke, his anger growing. "And with what happened to Esterelle, thanks, but I don't think I appreciate their version of help."

"I knew Esterelle," said Mariessa. "She was taken from a man she loved and forced to become the emperor's plaything, but she believed in the Vasheri and she prayed—in the old way, not through the supposed Lingdow—every day. She even learned to find the good points about your father, and care for him and pray for his soul. Regardless of what she was, or what happened to her, I'm sure that she is in the warm, loving arms of her brothers and sisters below, and she cares for us as we struggle here."

Gabrick shook his head. "I'm glad you believe it, but I'm afraid I don't know what to believe anymore."

"If you pray,—"

"No. I've tried, but I can't make the words come. I touch the earth, but as soon as I think about the Vasheri, as soon as I close my eyes, I get angry. Sometimes I wish they were as lost in their paradise below as I am in this torture on Dixho. Sometimes, I wish them all to limbo."

Mariessa released a small gasp. "You're stubborn, and if you don't control your pride, you'll end up like your father."

"Who's to say I won't anyway?" He stared into her dark eyes. "That's why you hate me, isn't it? You see in me, the man who hurt and tried to rape you. You see the emperor when you look at me."

She touched his arm, her first willing contact since she'd hugged him in the Tehkxyayen hut. "I don't hate you. I think your sex is flawed with a tendency to be abusive and self-serving. And yes, there are little things sometimes, like the way you talk about lower tiers, that make me think you're too much like your father."

Gabrick leaned back, feeling like he'd been slapped. Well, at least she was honest. "Maybe while you're judging fifty percent of the human race you should consider the fact that you're a hypocrite."

Mariessa bristled, but he went on.

"You just called half of the supposed Vasheri 'innately flawed.' We can't be divine and finding the good in ourselves if we're already doomed by being born the wrong sex."

"That wasn't what I said. All I meant—"

"It doesn't matter." He grabbed a sharp stick off the ground. "You've decided who and what I am, and for all I know, maybe you're right."

Chuluun's daughter, Satsral, walked by with a couple of dresses she'd mended and one of the boy's breeches. A year older than Gabrick, though not of the same caliber as Aednat and Mari, she was fairly pretty.

Gabrick jumped to his feet. "I'm going to talk to Satsral."

"Of course," Mari said, shaking her head as she went to her own mat, near the fire with the children. They'd insisted that her size meant she needed more warmth like the young ones. He'd almost laughed at her embarrassed and angry expression, even as she'd swallowed it down for the sake of good manners.

"Satsral," said Gabrick, sidling up next to her. "What do you believe about the Vasheri?"

She returned his question with a blank expression. "What do you mean? The priests tell us they live in paradise below. What more is there?"

"That's all right," he said. "I'm feeling tired. I think I'll get my mat and go to sleep."

She glanced at her father, arms wrapped around her mother, their thick blanket barely covering them both. "In a few minutes, we could go outside and talk, if you'd like."

The invitation was obvious, and Gabrick wouldn't have minded taking her up on it, but he thought of the family's kindnesses, the parents' risk in letting Gabrick and the others stay in their home. He couldn't betray them like that, and though he might press the girl into giving herself to him, he was fairly sure that her idea of sneaking away was to get a kiss, and not much more.

"Your father is a good man," said Gabrick. "You shouldn't betray his trust like that."

He ignored her hurt expression and went to his mat, falling asleep much more quickly than he would have expected.

60

Scooping up the last mouthful of watery rice-porridge from his bowl, a food Gabrick now appreciated since he'd spent weeks starving in the woods, he reached for a chunk of bread to mop up any last bits.

Suddenly the door banged into the wall, Chuluun's thirteen-year-old son, Kushi, rushing in. "They're coming! Enforcers, from every direction."

Gabrick jumped up from the table, eyes darting around the small room in search of an escape. Nowhere to go, and no question of what would happen to the family who'd harbored them.

But in less than ten seconds, Satsral and her mother had all the dirty dishes thrown into a bag along with the few clean ones not in use. The older boys cleaned out the clothes from the small closet, and the small children had picked up all of the mats. Chuluun stood at the far end of the small home, a piece of the wall held open like a door. Gabrick smiled. Despite all the cracks in the splintered boards, most of them from washed-up ship wrecks, he would never have guessed it was a false wall. And neither would the enforcers, not in a little hut like this. The men would assume the family heard they were coming and already deserted their home. Even better, Gabrick saw a trap door, leading into an underground cellar. The women filed down first, taking the rickety wooden stairway as if they'd done it a hundred times, and by the way they moved, they'd probably practiced.

Chuluun turned to Kushi. "You know what to do?"

The boy nodded. "I'll close up the wall, slip out, and hide with the other street boys. We'll meet at our rock north of the docks in three days."

Aednat stepped carefully into the darkness, guided by Den. When Mari gestured for Gabrick to go first, he took a close look at her eyes. They darted from side to side like hunted prey.

"It's okay." Gabrick put a hand to her waist, nudging her forward. "They'll never find us down there."

She stopped fidgeting and focused on him. "They'll have a seeking stone. There's no place deep or far enough away that I can ever hide."

Curse it all to limbo, she was right! As if he'd agreed with her, she spun away from his hand and darted out the door, the edge the green dress she'd borrowed trailing after.

"No!" Gabrick cried. Against all reason, he followed.

Chuluun caught up with him halfway down a thin stretch of waste-encrusted alley. He stopped Gabrick with a yank on his arm. "You can't help her, boy."

Gabrick pulled free of the man's grip. "I have to try."

A table of animal-sized lightstones, all these simple people could afford, turned over in the street, the old ones shattering as they hit against one another. An enforcer's yell followed. "There. I see one."

Chuluun shoved Gabrick into the house next to them. The person inside spun him out the far door to another alley. A door opened, another hand reaching to grab and hide him.

Why? Why would these people do this? They were all tenth-tier, living in hovels, lucky to have the most menial of jobs that didn't pay enough to decently feed or clothe their families. Why would they risk their lives for a seventeen-year-old boy they didn't even know? The guards would kill Chuluun, for the only crime of having been seen with Gabrick.

He let the man pull him in, but grasped his shoulders before getting shuffled further. "Get me back to the alley, behind the enforcers going after Chuluun."

The man shook his head. "He asked us to keep you safe."

"Why?" said Gabrick. "He's risking his whole family, the whole community."

"He's saved many of us from starvation and worse." The man tapped his head. "He's smart. He believes that some things are worth sacrifice, and if he believes one of them is you..." the man shrugged. "I owe him my life many times over."

Gabrick would never call anyone a crete again. "Take me to the alley. I can save him from the enforcers." He paused. Should he tell the man everything? If he knew the truth, he might change his mind about helping. "But if I kill the enforcers, they might take it out on your people."

The man laughed. "You've been seen. Everywhere you've been, the emperor is murdering anyone who might have known of your existence. Our entire community will be razed to the ground."

Gabrick's heart dropped. He hadn't known, hadn't realized the extent of the danger they'd placed these people in.

The man winked. "But whispers are faster than enforcers. The emperor cannot hide your existence, no matter how he tries. And when they raze our homes, all of us who defy him will already be gone. Only the traitors, his disciples, will burn."

With that, he took Gabrick's arm and dragged him through another door. A few more turns and shoves, and Gabrick found himself in an alley, two gray-clad guards having just rushed by, guns out, in hot pursuit of a middle-aged man with a limp—Chuluun. The man who'd helped him, handed him a knife and shut the door in his face.

Gabrick took in his surroundings, unable to figure out where in the maze of huts and hovels he stood. He'd have liked to skirt around, but he had a lousy sense of direction. At least Den had taught him stealth. He ran behind the enforcers on silent feet. They stopped right as Gabrick came close. A fifth-tier held Chuluun's stick-like arm in a tight grip. The ragged purple cloth tied round the man's bulging biceps marked him as a province enforcer.

"Where's the boy?"

When Chuluun didn't answer, the man backhanded him. The enforcer closest to Gabrick laughed, giving Gabrick the opportunity he needed. He plunged his knife between the man's ribs. As Den would say, the only silent man was a dead one.

Chuluun pointed at Gabrick as the enforcer turned in his direction. "He's right there."

The man's comrade slumped into the dirt. Chuluun's attacker spun his pistol toward Gabrick, but much too slow. Gabrick ducked under the man's arm, pushing it up as he lunged. As one, he and Chuluun plunged knives into the man's side. Gabrick wouldn't have been surprised to hear their metal tips clang together. The pistol slid from lifeless fingers, the man's eyes rolled up, and he slumped down not far from his partner. Gabrick flipped the safety on and tucked the long-barreled pistol into the back of his pants.

"Get out of here," Gabrick told him. "I'm going to find Mari."

Chuluun pushed Gabrick toward the hut he'd come from. "One of my boys is watching her. There are too many enforcers and seekers out there for you to reach her without being spotted."

"She risked her life for us. I'm not going to leave her."

"Getting yourself caught or killed won't help her." Chuluun continued to shove Gabrick forward. He was strong for such a small, skinny man. "She can call the plants if she needs help, but she can't do that if they use you as a hostage. When the time comes, my boy will bring her to meet us."

The door opened. Gabrick let Chuluun push him through. "Promise me you'll find her."

"I think she's every bit as important as you. I'll do everything in my power to keep her alive, but in an hour or less there'll be nothing left here but charred bodies and ash. We must leave. Now."

Gabrick entered another false wall, climbing down into a basement. Through a maze of corridors, up to another house, across an alley, down into another underground hideout, hallway, and up again. Gabrick and Chuluun avoided the enforcers, ending up at the edge of the slums outside the city, eventually reaching a hidden cove well south of the main docks.

Den and Aednat waited for him. Gabrick ignored Den's scowl as he accepted Aednat's embrace.

"Mari?" she asked.

Gabrick glanced at Chuluun and shook his head. "She can defend herself, but I hope she doesn't go into another trance."

61

Small homes and alleys surrounded Mariessa, making her feel like a slip of water running between hills and rocks with no control over direction. Positive that she'd turned around and started back to the center, she exited the mass of decrepit structures and found herself on a wider street leading to an open area dusted with fallen snow—the community center. Small footprints marked where a child had run home as the enforcers came close.

Not too far from Mariessa, a squat structure with ill-fitting boards faced the quiet square. Crudely carved images of Vasheri and their creations circled wooden pillars of irregular size on the front step. So similar to the humble church of her childhood, Mariessa felt drawn to the little building. The scuttle of feet, cries of mothers and children surprised by the enforcers' appearance, echoed behind her.

Skirting brown, sleeping foliage, their roots waiting for spring, she crossed the wide dirt road. As she made her way between the pillars, boards squeaked in protest, straining against the orange-crusted nails keeping them in place. She slipped through the front door, opening it as little as possible.

In the dim light of two poorly-charged lightstones, Mariessa surveyed the small chapel. Low benches, similar to those in Keran but of a different wood and backless, formed the few simple rows from the front altar to where Mariessa stood. Carved of the same light-hued wood as the benches, with the same crude lack of expertise as the pillars outside, the altar exhibited the Vasheri's creations. Depictions of vines and trees twisted up the four corners, twining together along the top edges. On the panel facing Mariessa, a jungle cat leapt from one side, a horse reared at the other, and a bird flew to the skies between them. She knew if she circled the altar one side would have waterfalls, rivers, and/or ocean shores; one side would depict mountains, cliffs, and unusual rock formations; and the other would show everything together, but under the influence of wind, storm, and lightning.

She took a few steps forward, her footprints making marks across the dusty floor. Though the top of the altar lacked the usual small plants kept at its corners, and no music, bird-song, or small fountains intruded on the deathly quiet, the traditional figurines had been placed to depict humanity—the Vasheri in mortal form. A woman knelt in the center, her hand held out to the congregation, a seed resting in her palm. It symbolized the giving of life to all creation. A man stood on each side of her, mouths open, singing praises to the Vasheri.

The entire room smelled of mold and stale sweat. The altar was dull, its crevices thick with dust. No plants lined the walls or even sat in the corners. Stained glass windows, so coated with grime she could only make out shapes but no color, refused to allow sunlight into the dreary unkempt room.

"A deserted church," she whispered to herself, feeling a deep sadness that these poor people, so like herself when impoverished in Keran, didn't even have the comfort of a functioning congregation.

She turned to leave. Before she reached the door, a man's gentle voice accosted her from the far shadows. "Can I help you, dear child?"

Mariessa started, releasing the tiniest scream. "I thought the place empty. I'm sorry to intrude."

"I just arrived." The man stepped into the pale light, almost as short as Mariessa but better fed, wearing a priest's sash across his shoulders that though expensive, had seen better days. Three-day stubble grew in patches across his jaw. He gestured with his head toward the shadow from which he'd emerged. "I came through the side door into my office when I heard footsteps within the chapel. You look frightened, child. How can I help you?"

Mariessa shook her head. "You can't. No one can. I should leave."

The man inclined his head in acceptance. "You might be surprised at what the church, or a meager priest, can accomplish."

She dared to hope. "Can you give me asylum? Can you hide me from the seekers?" Unbidden tears came to her eyes. "I don't want to kill anymore. I don't want to feel the plants strangle and mutilate people. I can't do it. I won't."

"Come, child." The man held out his arms. As if her feet acted on their own power, she found herself running to the priest, allowing him to enfold her in his arms. He nodded to a scrawny altar boy, who scurried away.

"Where is he—"

"Don't worry," said the priest. "I'll take care of you. All will be well."

Mariessa leaned her head against the priest's shoulder, closing her eyes and drifting peacefully amid his whispered words of comfort.

Movement near dilapidated curtains a few arms away caught their attention. The priest, still holding Mariessa in his arms, turned to one side, staring at the hole-ridden fabric, daring it to move again. The priest turned back, but Mariessa still had a view of the dirt-blackened edges. A narrow face peeked out from one side—Chuluun's son, Kushi.

"Go," the boy mouthed.

The priest stroked her hair. "You will be safe here, little sorceress. Stay with me and all your worries are eased."

The boy stuck his head out again, shaking it back and forth. He mimed putting both fingers in his ears, pointed to the door, and mouthed, "Run!"

Local enforcers, led by two seekers with green stones in their hands, burst into the room. The priest lifted Mariessa off the floor and slammed her onto a bench. Like a hunter trussing up a wild pig, his small fingers pulled cloth and rope from his pocket, gagged her, covered her hands with cloth then tied them together, and did the same to her feet.

The enforcers made it halfway down the aisle before the priest raised up a hand. "Keep your distance. I caught her, and I'll hand her to the emperor myself. Bring me to him."

A man pulled out a communication stone and had a mumbled conversation in the corner. Mariessa squirmed against her restraints, reached out with her mind for some scrap of a plant or a root. Though she sensed them outside, she had no contact with the earth to call for them. Forgotten was her oath not to kill. More than anything at that moment, she wanted to strangle the little man who'd beguiled her with lies.

The man with the communication stone smirked. "You've received your wish. The emperor is coming here."

The priest's eyes went wide. "I didn't tell you to summon him."

"But you refused to hand over the prize to his designated authorities. Like it or not, he's coming to you." Even lying down on the bench, Mariessa caught the man's evil grin. "I wonder how he'll kill you. Usually depends on his mood."

Twenty minutes later, the sight of the man who stepped through the door sent her into a panic. Peder, deeply tanned from his time chasing them in the wilderness, strode between the benches, suddenly making the room smaller.

"Ah," he smiled. "The elusive sorceress." He held up his seeking stone, casting a greenish light that illuminated the chapel more than its lightstones or deadened windows. "My stone, in particular, seems especially good at finding you. And now, I will get to kill you."

Peder pulled a knife from his boot. The blade reflected green. In two steps, he stood over Mariessa. He flipped the knife's position, plunging it deep into the priest's sternum. As he pulled it away, blood splattered across Mariessa's chin and chest. The priest slumped to the floor.

"A voice sorcerer may be hard to recognize," Peder said, "But the effect he had on the enforcers gave him away. No need for a stone." He came close, so his cold ice-blue eyes could stare into hers. "How does it feel to be betrayed by your own kind?"

That was why she'd been unable to resist. She'd never even heard of a voice sorcerer, but there was no question the man had entranced her against her common sense. And now she would die.

But Peder wiped the knife on a part of her sleeve that was still clean then sheathed it. "Bring in the cage," he ordered.

A handful of his black-clad soldiers struggled at the doors, bringing in the monstrosity. Mariessa's heart sank. A solid cube of hard iron, the thing would suffocate her spirit before Peder exacted any other revenge. Without bothering to remove her restraints, the soldiers gripped her by the backs of her arms, dragged her between the pews, and threw her in. Her head banged the side and she slammed her back into the corner. The door clanged shut, heavy bolts and locks grating into place as silent darkness enveloped her. The only light was a pale gray spot above her head where multiple holes had been drilled, large enough to let her breathe but not big enough for the smallest twig or leaf to make its way through. With the sudden quiet came an absolute certainty that this was the end. No matter her powers, they were useless to her now.

Mariessa's stomach leapt when the side of her cage rumbled, the whine of metal grating against metal making her wince and wish she could cover her ears. A sudden crack of pale light appeared along one side of her prison, widening as the metal plate overlaying the bars lifted half an arm. The light of the dingy church brightened her space like the morning sun when compared to the former smothering darkness.

The face that sneered back at her made the silent cell preferable. She might even hate this man more than Peder. The emperor's cold features, so like Gabrick's, but so different in expression, stared from the other side of thick metal bars. At first Mariessa thought it was only Gabrick's darkened hair that made him appear different from his father. But it was more than that. Not only were both Gabrick's eyes grey-green instead of one green and the other blue, but Gabrick's fierce gaze held a warmth and vulnerability that this man's didn't. Though they both exhibited intense passion, the emperor's eyes were cold, angry, and insane.

"How are you liking your accommodations, concubine? I think they're better than you deserve, but they'll have to suffice for now."

The gag in her mouth forced her to remain silent. She'd removed the fabric the priest had wrapped around her hands and she continued to work at the rope as she fixed Beht Han with a neutral, uncaring expression. The emperor's pride would never stand for it.

"Remove the gag!" he yelled at one of the provincial enforcers.

With trepidation, one of the men approached the bars, gesturing Mariessa forward. She almost refused, but doubted her obstinacy would be enough for the emperor to open the cage, not yet. She crawled on her buttocks to the small window, allowing the man's fingers—trembling with fear of her, the emperor, or both—to untie the gag. As he did, she caught the emperor rubbing at the white scar around his neck. It almost blended in with the natural folds of skin, but not quite. She smiled, snapping at the guard's hand as he finished with the gag.

"If you'll remember correctly, Your *Highness*," she said. "You never managed to make me a *real* concubine. Just a pretty girl you'll never be man enough to bed."

As she'd hoped, the man's temper flared. He rushed forward, gripping the metal bars. "I'm going to kill you, along with everything and everyone you've ever loved or known."

Mariessa laughed. "Den will never let you catch them."

The emperor puffed up with triumph. "I don't need them. I'll kill every man, woman, and child in that little village you came from. Leave nothing but charred flesh for the wild beasts."

Her laugh grew louder. The only one she might regret at all would be her childhood friend, Termien. "Yes, please. Most of them deserve worse. Do us all a favor and raze the entire country. They'll be happier below in Paradise." She remembered an old tale from her childhood. "You already have an entire nation and hundreds of Vasheri-blessed determined to bring about an end to your blasphemy. The more you kill, the more who will call for your death and your everlasting torment in limbo."

The emperor's face flushed with anger. "I am the mighty Lingdow, granted eternal life, and none dare attempt to touch me or my power."

"You're as crazy in the head as a pup-deprived tree lepur." She kicked her foot against the bars, hitting his hands and clanging the metal cage.

The emperor cursed, holding his injured fingers. "I'm going to kill you!" he screamed, pulling a sword from a sheath at his side.

Mariessa backed into the corner, hoping he couldn't angle the blade through the narrow slits between bars. As he was about to attempt it, Peder sidled up and whispered in the emperor's ear. A wicked grin replaced Beht Han's fury as fast as a water sleth going from left to right.

"Let's see if that boy you've become so fond of is as loyal to you as you are to him." He turned to the enforcers, seekers, and his few personal guard. "There's to be an execution in the community square an hour before sundown. Announce it to everyone in the region."

"After we raze the town?" one of them asked.

"No," said the emperor. "After her execution we'll eliminate the bystanders as Peder has suggested, and then we'll raze the community. Set up men in street-clothes around the square, to keep an eye out for the man and boy. Kill them on sight."

The men saluted. Four stayed to guard Mariessa inside the church, while the rest took up their places outside. The guard closest to her cage started scraping her little window closed as the emperor moved aside.

"They're gone by now!" yelled Mariessa. "You might as well kill me now because they'll never come."

The window paused for a moment, the emperor's wicked green eye showing through the remaining slit. "I know the boy, probably better than you. After all, he's me."

"No, he's not," said Mariessa, surprised by her own conviction. "He cares about people, tries to do what's right, and he would never do the horrible things you've done."

The emperor gave a dry chuckle, motioning the window shut. "I stand corrected. He's like I once was."

The metal clanged together and her world went dark.

62

Gabrick thrust his knuckles forward, aiming for Den's esophagus, the first time he'd ever seriously tried to injure his mentor. Den evaded, pushed down Gabrick's shoulder, grabbed one arm, and swept his feet out from under him. Gabrick lay gasping on the rocky shore, lucky he hadn't bashed his head against the rocks.

Den stood above him. "Calm down, boy. I'm not saying she doesn't deserve our help. I'm saying there's nothing we can do. That execution is a trap, and I know Peder. He'll have every avenue covered."

Sitting up with a groan, Gabrick put his head in his hands. Den was right and he knew it, but he couldn't simply leave her there. Gabrick's father would slice his sword across her neck, spill her blood into the streets like he'd done to Esterelle.

Gabrick raised his head, a dangerous excitement filling his mind. "Then we get her before the execution."

"We have no idea where—" Aednat began.

"No, but a seeker would, and they're still hanging around the district." He turned to Chuluun's son, Kushi, the one who'd come to tell them the news. "Would you recognize the men in the church, the ones who had stones?"

Kushi nodded. "I had to leave when the big man showed up. His eyes were too good at spotting shadows, but the others who'd waited for him, I could get you to one of them."

"I'm sure they've moved her," said Den. "By the time we find a seeker, steal his stone, and find Mariessa, it'll be time for the execution. It'll never work."

"How many times has she done things she shouldn't be able to do, nearly killed herself saving us?" Gabrick rose to his feet, brushing off the breeches. "We have to at least try."

He didn't add that he felt like he'd crumble if they failed. Gabrick didn't have many friends in his life. Aednat was the only one who'd ever counted. And Esterelle, who was dead now. He couldn't lose Mari. He wouldn't.

"This is a blistering fool's errand," muttered Den.

Aednat beamed at Gabrick. "Then let's be fools."

Gabrick had never loved her more than at that moment.

Finding the seeker turned out to be the easy part. Back to full strength, even missing a couple of fingers, Den was the formidable man Gabrick knew from watching his sparring matches with the emperor. In fact, Gabrick began to wonder if Den had held back with Beht Han. He took out a trained seeker in three seconds. Gabrick had counted.

Now they hunched in the shadows between two shacks, out of sight from the enforcer's soldiers, including men dressed in clothing too artificially shabby to really belong there. Vendors had set up shop in the square and along the wider thoroughfares. A number of people milled in the streets, purchasing cheap treats as they waited, curious about the upcoming execution.

Den held up the pulsing seeker stone. "I'm pretty sure she's in the church, but they could have moved her to the square already, beyond the building."

Slapping at his thigh, Kushi swore. "This is where they caught her. I shouldn't have wasted your time with the stupid seeker."

"None of us thought they'd keep her in the same place," said Gabrick.

Aednat glanced at the black-and-white pictures posted on the side of the church. "I'll go in and find out if she's really there. How do I signal you once I'm in?"

"You're not going in there alone." Den grasped her forearm, pulling her deeper into the shadows.

Pointing to the posters, she pulled her arm free. "They have three pictures up there. You, Gabrick, and Mariessa. I'm a slave. No one but you has ever taken a picture of me, and I'm of no interest to the emperor. Dressed like this," she gestured at Satsral's clothes, "they won't even see me."

"They'll see you when you enter that church."

Aednat smoothed her hair and pulled at her bodice, making it scoop low over her ample chest. Assuming an air of seductive innocence, she batted her eyelashes. "I'm just a wide-eyed, simple crete who stumbled into the church. They may attack me, but they won't shoot me."

Kushi stared at her chest as he spoke. "I can sneak in after her, the way I did for Mariessa. The emperor or that tall crazy man would notice me there, but not a few stupid soldiers."

"You're sure?" asked Den.

The boy nodded as Aednat sauntered into the street. She took her time, waiting until all the surveillance men had their backs turned, then stepped into the chapel's side door. Gabrick took the opportunity to slip behind a weed the size of a bush at the back of the building. From his vantage he saw Kushi step into the street and give a quick nod. When the men's backs were turned again, Kushi slipped into the building as did Gabrick.

The place stank of mildew, dirt, and fresh blood. Gabrick almost panicked at a dark stain beneath one of the benches. but when he scanned the room, he found the metal box. Where else to keep a plant sorceress but surrounded by metal, unable to touch dirt?

True to her prediction, Aednat flirted with the enforcers standing guard, her accent a near-perfect replica of the natives. She'd learned a lot on this trip.

Placing a slender hand on the nearest enforcer's arm, she caressed it as she gazed up at him, doe-eyed. "How do you get so strong? My brother works the fisheries, but his arm doesn't feel like this."

The soldier flexed. "You want a better look at these babies?"

Aednat lowered her eyes, but pressed against him. "Aren't you supposed to stay on guard duty? I don't want to get anyone in trouble."

"These guys will stay here and keep an eye out. We should be fine for a few minutes."

She eyed the other men hungrily, appearing as eager for them as the one with an arm around her waist. Gabrick would enjoy gutting the pompous demon.

"I think she might want more than one of us," his comrade laughed, half-joking, but with a definite hopeful tone.

She gave them an interested half-smile. "I've never been with more than one man at a time, and certainly not with men like you. I'm not sure I'd know what to do."

The men grinned. "We'll help you figure it out." The second soldier took her other side, wrapping his hand around her, opposite his comrade. Together, they ushered her into the room, their hands lowering as they walked. Yes, Gabrick would enjoy gutting them, but first things first.

So focused on her, they never detected Gabrick among the shadows near the priest's office door.

He was about to go after the two guards nearest Mari when he spotted Den behind them, a homemade garrote in one hand, his knife in the other.

Gabrick slipped into the room with Aednat, only to find one man unconscious on the floor, the other struggling against the sleeve of his uniform coat, twisted and wrapped around his neck. When did she learn to fight like this? No, Den had trained her almost as much as Gabrick. The question was when did she gain the moxie to fight like this?

Gabrick moved forward with his knife.

"No," said Aednat, grunting as she fought with the soldier. "We'll knock them out, but we don't have to kill them."

It was probably too late for Den's victims, but Gabrick didn't argue. "You'll have to tie them up, to give us time."

She nodded, wrenching harder with the fabric. "Get Mariessa."

Gabrick left her to tie the men, running back for Mari. Den was dumping the two soldiers' bodies behind the barren altar.

"They have keys?" Gabrick whispered.

Den checked, but shook his head. "Only Peder, or maybe the emperor."

Even a workman's hammer would have had trouble breaking the massive lock on Mari's cell and that would have made enough noise to alert every guard in the area. Gabrick searched the room, his eyes landing on the heartstone sconces. The crude, metal bases elongated into downward spikes. He jumped, ripping one from the wall, raining plaster onto himself and the floor, the lightstone clattering under a bench and turning the chapel to twilight. The sound echoed in the small chapel, but no one came bursting through the doors.

Cramming the spike between the lock's body and shank, he used all his strength and leverage. Muscles strained as he repositioned himself. The metal sconce started to bend. Sweat beaded on his forehead. "Limbo's imps!" he cursed. Just when he thought he'd lose hold on the bending spike, the lock finally snapped.

With a crash, the heavy lock fell to the floor. The sconce flew from Gabrick's hand, clattering across benches before landing. He stumbled backward, but managed to stay on his feet. The hinges on Mari's cell squeaked as the door angled open, but she didn't come out.

Afraid at what he might find, Gabrick opened the door further. The cage was dungeon black and silent. Like an angry mountain cat waiting for its moment, Mari screeched and sprung from the cell. She struck with such force Gabrick flew into the air before his back slid across the floor, pebbles and bits of mortar scraping into his skin. As his head hit ground, a makeshift garrote wrapped around his neck. Though not as professional as Den's, it was strong. He'd barely stopped sliding when he felt his air supply cut off.

"Gabrick?"

The rope instantly released and she sat up, her legs straddling his waist. She'd torn her long skirt to free up her movements and create her weapon. Sitting on top of him, the fabric pushed halfway up her thighs.

Gabrick coughed and sat up on one elbow. "You all right?" He pushed the hair from her face, then ran his hands up her arms, looking for wounds. "Did they hurt you?"

She scooted down, but then seemed to realize that wasn't any more appropriate than where she'd been before. Jumping to her feet, she extended a hand, helping him up. "You shouldn't have come. Peder has a trap set for you."

"During the execution," said Gabrick. "But he didn't expect us to find you beforehand."

"True," Peder stepped through an open front door. "But this will work." He moved aside and flicked his fingers in the air. Soldiers poured into the small space. "Kill them all."

Gabrick grabbed Mari round the waist and spun them behind the metal cage. Gunfire pinged against the metal surface. Bullets ricocheted and stripped wood from posts, benches, and the altar behind which Den crouched. Aednat was nowhere to be seen.

"I'm sorry," Gabrick told Mari. "I didn't mean for you to die this way."

"I'd rather it be like this than letting that demon cut off my head." Her slim, calloused hand touched his cheek. "Not that I'm not glad for the company, but I wish you'd run. You and Aednat could have made a life together."

But he didn't want a life with Aednat. He adored her, loved her, but she'd been right, it wasn't that kind of love.

The doors near the back of the church burst open and Gabrick knew it was over. They were surrounded on every side. But instead of soldiers, the church filled with peasants...peasants with guns. More peasants poured in behind the soldiers in the church, carrying nothing but clubs. The soldiers turned their attention to the new threat and the battle commenced.

As Gabrick and Mari were ushered to the back of the chapel, the men defending them began to fall, many of their old, manual-loading rifles backfiring. But as each man fell, another peasant rose to take his place. Gabrick would never call them cretes again. They were heroes.

Gunfire, men's screams, and the splatter of blood, mixed with the rising smoke filling the already dimly lit room. Gabrick had no idea of his direction, but he let the low-tiered heroes guide him until they'd made it out the door.

Mari immediately reached for the soil. "No time," said Chuluun, stepping from the same weed Gabrick had hidden behind earlier. "You're out, my men will retreat, and we must get you away from here. The emperor is coming with more men. A lot more."

Peder rounded the building, seeking stone in one hand, a protection stone in the other. He pocketed them both, pulling a pistol.

"Go!" yelled Chuluun, pointing to ten men, including his son, astride horses on the other side of the street. Hand in hand, they ran for the horses. Kishu held two for Gabrick and Mari while Den and Aednat already sat their own steeds.

Shots fired. Den and Aednat's horses bolted.

"Papi!" Kishu screamed.

Though he knew what had happened, Gabrick had to turn. Chuluun lay in the dirt, eyes staring up at the sky. Bullet holes riddled his chest.

Kishu dropped their horses' reins. Already skittish from the gunfire, they bolted. Gabrick caught the gray stallion by one rein, but the other barreled forward, unwittingly providing cover from Peder. It screamed in pain. Kishu moved to dismount and run to his father.

Gabrick pushed the boy back in the saddle. "He doesn't want you dead, too." The boy struggled, trying to get down. "For your mother, your sisters, you have to take care of them."

Kishu stilled. Peder dumped the pistols' spent cartridges, loading more. The dead horse collapsed, leaving them in the open. With an angry glare, Kishu kicked his horse and took off down the road. The others followed.

Mari had already mounted, waiting for Gabrick. He grabbed the pommel of the saddle, slapping the horse's rear. It bolted after the others, bullets swishing through its tail. As it ran, Gabrick held on, getting his foot into the stirrup and mounting behind Mari.

"Wish I had a gun," he said. "I'd put a bullet between that daffing terdo's eyes."

Mari gave a short laugh. "My slang and yours don't go together well." She reached into her dress, pulling out a gun. She handed it to him. "I picked it up on the way out, but didn't think to use it. I've never fired one."

In exchange, he handed her his knife. She slid it into her leg sheath, though it's larger size cut at the leather and left a good share of blade visible.

"We're going to change positions," he said into her ear. "So I can have better aim."

He swung around Mariessa, taking her place in the saddle but facing backward. Pulling her onto his lap, her legs tightened around his torso. Mari held the reins, gripping him with her elbows, eyes barely above his shoulder.

Mud from the horses ahead splattered at his calves and back as one of his arms wrapped around her waist while the other held the gun.

When Peder showed, Gabrick gripped the back of Mari's dress. "Run this horse for all it's worth. Run it 'till it's dead."

"Why?" She glanced back. "Holy Vasheri."

Peder wasn't chasing them on horseback. Why would he? Driving a military vehicle, the kind with wide all-terrain tires and a machine-gun mounted on the back, Gabrick could see Peder's wide-mouthed grin, out of gunshot range.

"Den!" Gabrick tried yelling ahead, but the man couldn't hear him.

Another twenty lengths and Gabrick could hear the truck's engine. Den looked back, the same panic suddenly showing on his face as Gabrick's. Taking hold of one of Aednat's reins, Den turned their horses, leaving the group and heading toward the seashore. Mari followed, but they hadn't gone far when their horse tripped.

The gun flew from Gabrick's grip but he didn't care. He was more concerned with cradling Mari's head as they hit the rocks jutting up from deep patches of moist soil. When they finally stopped, Mari slammed her fingers into the mud. "There's nothing here but moss and small weeds."

Gabrick saw her strain, jaw tight and trembling. The shore here wasn't like the harbor in Haigang. Swift tides and rough oceans meant the sea plants wouldn't grow as big or as long. There wasn't a tree along this stretch for miles. If she tried to bring her powers to bear she'd kill herself.

"No!" Gabrick hauled her to her feet. Mud splattered from her hand, across his chest.

"He'll kill us!" Mari protested. "I have to do this."

Gabrick scooped her into his arms, running between the rocks, after Den and Aednat. "You're too tired. You'll kill yourself."

She didn't deny it. "But if I don't, he'll kill us all."

"Like Aednat said, 'All in this together,' remember? If we go down, we're taking him with us."

Even Peder's war truck didn't have what it took to deal with the rocks scoring the ground. The sound of it gunning its engines finally stopped. Gabrick didn't need to look to know Peder would follow them on foot.

He and Mari caught up with Aednat and Den in time to see that none of it mattered. They'd reached the ocean's edge, but not as intended. The cliff drop was higher than expected, and there was a fifty-fifty chance of landing on a rock. They might merely break an arm or a leg, but more likely, they'd bust their skulls or snap their spines.

63

Surrounded by his personal guard, Han arrived at the church to find the community center and building deserted. The broken, bullet-ridden cage that had kept the sorceress contained leaned to one side, the door creaking on a broken hinge. Dead enforcers and civilians littered the floor, strung across overturned benches, and huddled in the corners, their blood and fluids mingling together in a growing stench that made Han's lip curl.

"Peder!" he yelled. A moment later his communication stone warmed his side. He pulled it from inside his yellow robe. "What happened?"

Peder's voice came out in gasps. "They escaped. We're—"

"That much is obvious! You swore to me this trap would work. Now I have all four of them loose again."

"Not for long." The roar of a military truck, bouncing over rough terrain, echoed in the background. "I am having them in sight, Your Highness. We will be shooting so many holes into them they won't be recognizable to their own mothers."

"None of those simpletons have mothers," Han said. "But what about the sorceress? You know she could call an entire forest down on you."

"Not in this place. It's empty, rocky coast-land. I see nothing big enough here to make more than a slap to the face."

Han motioned to his guards to follow, running out of the church to his car. "How far ahead are you?"

"Close," said Peder. "We have left the church less than five minutes."

"I'm going to join you. I want to see Den's face when he dies."

"If you're not here, do you still want me to kill them?"

Han took the driver's seat, relegating his men to passengers, and slammed his foot down on the gas pedal. Mud and gravel spun from the wheels as he shifted gears. He didn't drive often, but he knew how and he'd made sure he was good. He threw the communication stone to one of his men to hold.

"Yes," he said. "Take any chance to kill them that's offered. But I want their heads in one piece. I'm going to set them on spikes outside the palace."

Peder hesitated. "Yes...yes, sir."

Han knew it was barbaric. A symbol of supremacy from centuries past. But Den deserved it. And so did the worthless children he'd kept so close to his heart.

Han forgot about his guards, intent on the retreating fugitives. They'd gone on foot, running for the shore. Peder ran after them, only a few lengths ahead. Han caught up with him as the terrain sloped toward the ocean. By the way Den and the others skidded to a halt, Han knew their pat ended in a cliff; the kind Den and the others obviously didn't dare jump. He had them. At last, Den would pay for everything he'd done.

64

Rocks below, Peder and the emperor facing them, Gabrick wasn't sure which fate would be worse.

"Jump," said Den.

Wide-eyed, Gabrick took another look at the crashing ocean. He'd never survive the fall let alone those deceptively mild waves throwing him from one rock to the next.

The emperor aimed his gun.

"Jump!" yelled Den.

The gun fired. From Den's other side, Aednat leaped at Gabrick. As she passed Den, she jerked in mid-air. Den's gun discharged in the emperor's direction, but Aednat had thrown off his aim. It went wide.

Aednat rammed into Gabrick, gripping his shirt with clenched fists. He tried to catch her, but she held none of her own weight. One step back. Two. Only loose rock for traction. Aednat did for them what Gabrick couldn't. She gripped the cliff's edge with her feet, pushing them both into the air. It wouldn't be enough to evade the rocks, but they'd be well away from the cliff face as they plummeted to their deaths.

Gabrick held her tight in his arms, even as her fingers released his shirt. Her body went limp, angling them to one side instead of feet first. Gabrick tried to keep them vertical, tried to keep his body beneath hers, but couldn't. They hit, Aednat slapping the water first.

Saltwater shot up his nose, into his eyes. The pressure didn't take his breath away nearly as much as the cold. Liquid ice.

Aednat hit a rock. Her body jerked with the impact. It jerked again as a wave forced his body to batter her against it. They tumbled to one side. A wave picked them up, slamming him into a jutting spire. Like a monstrous hand, the wave ripped Aednat from his grasp. He clawed for her, but she swept past.

A rope landed in the retreating wave. He had no idea where it had come from. He didn't care. He grabbed hold. Something brushed his foot. On instinct, he dove. Catching hold of Aednat's rippling dress, Gabrick struggled under water with her, forcing the looped rope around her torso, giving it a double tug. He could only hope that whoever held the other side, friend or foe, would understand.

Aednat was pulled from Gabrick's grip, disappearing into the dark water as he came up for air. His mouth filled with foam, another wave pushing him down, tumbling him against rock after rock, scraping his legs, his feet, his side. He covered his head as it slammed against one of the more jagged outcroppings. Something snapped. Blood swirled around him. Gabrick cried out, but his lungs only filled with more water. The wave receded, giving him a single gasp of air. He tried to swim, but one of his arms refused to cooperate.

Another swell approached. The rope looped around his neck. He had just enough time to pull his working arm through before the wave threw him back. The rope went taut. Water forced its way down his throat, into his lungs. Then he was up, gliding over the surface like a shark after prey. His dangling legs still struck rocks hiding beneath the surface. They scratched and tore at his skin. The water fought to keep its victim, continuing to bang him from one impossibly hard surface to another.

∿∿∿

Mariessa almost grabbed for Gabrick before he and Aednat went over, but the emperor wasn't the only one with a gun. Horrified, she watched as Peder adjusted his aim, Gabrick in his sights.

The blade strapped to her thigh was bulky, a military blade, not a throwing knife. But she'd been doing this since a child, and this time, there was no hesitation. She slipped the knife from its sheath, took aim, and threw with all her might.

Like an arrow sprung from a bow, the blade flew straight and true. The weight changed its trajectory more than she'd expected, but it stabbed Peder as well as if she'd stood by his side. The gun dropped from his fingers and he gripped the blade protruding from his stomach. The heart would have been better, but the look in his eye suggested she may have done well enough.

The emperor and Den faced off, each with a pistol aimed at the other. His soldiers filled in behind them, pulling up their weapons but waiting for orders.

"Shall we die together?" Den asked. "You used to say that was how this would all end."

The emperor shook his head, the side of one lip curling in a sneer. "You ruined that when you chose the whore over me."

Den smiled. "Get over yourself already." He pulled the trigger. The gun clicked.

The emperor laughed. "You always did have trouble keeping track of your ammunition."

Mariessa didn't wait for the return shot. They might survive the rocks, but Den wouldn't survive a bullet to the head. Grabbing his arm, she pushed them both off the edge. A shot rang out. Den grunted, jerking sideways, but she kept hold of him. Together they tumbled down the cliff, not through the air like Gabrick and Aednat, but bouncing on the rough rocks toward their deaths below.

A third of the way down, Mariessa released Den and began scraping her fingers along the cliff face. It didn't matter how far they had left to go. Only touching the soil mattered. Scraggly bushes, roots, and grass, reached out to ease her descent, not large or strong enough to defend them, but enough to help.

Den's "oomph" sounded below, but she didn't let herself look. Too soon it was her turn. She hit the cliff's base and cried out.

Strands of slimy seaweed wrapped around her and Den, forming living ropes that used the rocks and each other to pull them through the oncoming waves, little by little, toward the boat Mariessa had seen come into view. They left the spires of rocks as a rope landed across Mariessa's back.

The smell of salt and sea permeated the boat's wooden planks. Men wrapped a number of thick blankets around the both of them. Den's shoulder had a bullet hole, but the bullet had gone clean through, not much more than a scratch. He would heal.

One of the men clasped the hand on his good arm. "Chid Den. At last we find you." The man held out his vowels and cut off the sounds Gabrick had called hard consonants. The result was strange, but pleasant.

"How?" Den asked.

"We have searched and hoped since the ship was lost in Haigang. But you may thank your friends who are gathering to their boats a few miles to the south. They told us where to find you."

Something splashed near the rocks, catching the man's eye, but neither Mariessa nor Den paid it any attention. Two still figures lay on the ship's deck. Mariessa ran to Gabrick's side, Den to Aednat's.

In the distance, rifles discharged, bullets descending like torrential rain.

65

The bullet had hit Den. Han was sure. Blood had spattered as Den disappeared over the cliff's edge. Even if he'd missed vital organs, Den couldn't have survived the fall. He'd gone down at a worse angle than the boy and his pathetic servant-girl.

Before Han could check over the edge, Peder's blood-stained hand pulled at his robes. "Please, oh Holiness. Heal me."

Han stared down at the man, gasping with pain, his entire front soaked in blood. Peder had been one of Han's strongest, most loyal servants. He could save him. He had a healing stone inside his robes.

"Why should I?" Han asked.

Peder seemed almost at a loss for words, or perhaps the blood in his lungs made speech difficult. "You are the mighty Lingdow. I have served you, will continue to serve you, for eternity." If he'd stopped there, such reverence and belief probably would have convinced Han. "I will stay by your side and you need never doubt my loyalty."

Han had sent Den plunging to his death. He had no one else at his side. Not Esterelle, not Bow Quing, and now, not Den.

He placed a hand on Peder's shoulder, leaned down, and yanked the blade from his gut, listening as it squelched from the flesh. With a grateful smile, Peder placed his hand over the gushing wound, waiting for the healing stone.

Han thrust the knife between Peder's ribs, into his heart. "There is no one I can trust. No one, ever again."

He shoved the man's lifeless body over the edge, watching it tumble to the bottom, hitting rock, bouncing out, hitting rock again, bouncing once more before splashing into the ocean, joining Den's. But there was no sign of Den's body, not even a spattering of blood or a scrap of clothing.

A search of the rocks below, the roiling waves, revealed nothing. He strained his gaze farther out. The pitch-coated boat almost blended with the darkening waters. Twilight's grays, deepening toward black, had tried to hide the vessel, but the outline of Den, running across the deck toward two corpses, was unmistakable.

Han spun to the enforcers behind him. "You let them live! You imbeciles!" Striding to the nearest of the guard, he yanked the man's gun away, turned it on him, and shot him in the heart. Many of the others took a step back and Han realized what could happen if they chose to defend themselves.

"Don't let them get away," he yelled, turning toward the cliff. "Fire!"

With the command, he started the first shots, his guard following his example along with the rest of the provincial enforcers. At first, the plunk of bullets on wood made him think they might reach their target, but they only damaged the empty prow, and then not even that.

"Stop." He waved the soldiers down. "Halt!" One more bullet discharged then all was quiet. Han shook his fist in the air. "I will find you, Den! You are dead to me and I'll not rest until I see your head adorning the palace gates!"

Han turned to his personal guard. "You will accompany me back to Han City. There will be no plane so we have a long drive. Acquire the necessary soldiers." To one of the provincial officers he said, "Find that boat. Swim to it if you have to, but if you and twenty men of your choice don't reach it and kill every person on it, with bodies as proof, you'll be executed."

He assigned a couple of seekers to enforce his commands and left the cliff, striding toward his car. Behind him, men screamed as they were thrown into the ocean. Others began making their way back to the car and the road, hoping to cut the boat off.

In the midst of it all, a voice Han hadn't heard in eighteen years filled the air. It was as if a demon yelled from the vastness of limbo, using the moonlight-tinged clouds as a loudspeaker.

Panic gripped Han's heart like he'd never experienced before, not even when he'd heard the old crone's threats from her own mouth.

66

A commotion near the ship's edge caught Gabrick's attention, pulling him from his plunge into darkness.

Mari's face came into view, her expression of fear turning to joy, then sorrow.

"Thank the Vasheri." Gabrick lifted a shivering hand to her cold cheek. "You survived."

Gunfire echoed from the cliff's edge again. The ocean spit and bounced as if the clouds had opened. Some of the bullets hit wood, making Gabrick flinch, but then the thuds stopped.

He returned his focus to Mari, her sorrowful gaze directed at someone beside him. Gabrick tried to lift himself onto one elbow, but fell back. Mari put a trembling hand under one shoulder, urging him up.

"In a minute," he said, breathing hard with the pain.

She prodded him up. "I don't think you have that long."

"Butterflower," Den sobbed from somewhere close. "My sweet Aednat."

Near to panic, Gabrick let Mari help him, getting to his good elbow then sitting up. Covered in blankets, he hadn't felt Aednat lying next to him. Her honey-brown skin had turned deathly pale. Fresh blood slipped from between her lips. Eyes blinking rapidly, she fought death with the same vigor that she'd loved life.

Gabrick tried to speak, but the words choked in his throat.

"You...," Aednat whispered between blood-filled gasps. "...the one. Prophecy." She fumbled at her waist, but couldn't control her shaking fingers. "Keep...my stone."

Gabrick took her fumbling hand in his and nodded, tears streaming down his cheeks. Mari did what Aednat couldn't manage, reaching inside Aednat's dress, pulling out the wrapped stone she'd kept with her throughout the entire journey, placing it in her hand.

"Save Eleven," Aednat cried, louder than anything she'd said to that point. "Don't...don't let the emperor..."

"I won't let the emperor have him, Aednat," Gabrick cried. "I won't"

She gave a minute shake to her head. "Too late. Don't let him keep..."

Den raised his head a fraction. "We'll kill him. We'll free the boy. I promise you that."

She relaxed against the deck, her message delivered, the fight won. "Love you...love all...all..."

She stilled, her eyes staring upward. Gabrick choked back a sob, but couldn't stop the unrelenting tears falling onto Aednat's sodden blankets.

Mari huddled in on herself, rocking back and forth as if she could somehow shut the pain away.

Gabrick wrapped his good arm around her. She buried her face against his bare chest, tears mixing with the blood still dripping from his many scrapes and wounds. After a moment, he pulled her onto his lap, letting his own tears and sobs release onto her neck and shoulder. They clung to one another like two newly-made orphans with no one else in the world.

Sudden movement near Aednat brought everyone to attention. Den snatched the cloth-covered stone from her limp hand, rolling it out of its tattered wrapping and into his palm. He held it up like a beacon in the dark night, the red a pulsing heartbeat, and the white striations shining brighter than the sliver of the moon reflecting off billowing clouds.

A deep voice resonated through the air, echoing off the cliff walls, and against the ocean waves. It was an old voice, a woman's voice, but filled with such power Gabrick felt the words shake him from the inside:

"From a lonely god, the boy will come.
The son of none, yet fathered by many, a replica of his enemy.
The legions below gather to his standard, though they despise his unholy
visage.
They will call him
Savior.

His enemy will destroy him, yet he will rise again.
His father will seek to possess him, yet he will take possession.
His forebears will lie to him, yet he will discover them.
They will call him
Truth.

From beneath the earth, Vasheri vie for him
Walking the land, animals give him teeth.
Water and sky, rock and stone, lift him above all others.
They will call him
Warrior.

He will face his past and lose.
He will face the world and conquer.
He will face himself and crumble.
They will call him
Destroyer.

In victory he finds defeat.
In love he finds power.
In destruction, the world finds an end.
In sacrifice, the boy made man finds redemption.
They will call him
Emperor.

Death will follow him,
It will accompany him,
It will precede him,
And it will be his legacy.
They will call him
Thirteen."

"I will find you, Han!" Den yelled into the night. "I will make this prophecy come true, no matter the cost. You will die and your poisoned empire will fall! I swear it on the soil, the waters, and the sky. By Paradise below, the land of our trials, and the never-ending skies of limbo. May the Vasheri cease my existence in all three realms if I do not keep to my task!"

Mari gasped.

"What does that mean?" Gabrick asked.

"It's an unholy vow," she said. "He's swearing by everything in creation, including his own existence."

Gabrick glanced down at Aednat. "Then I'll join him in his unholy vow. I—"

Mari placed a finger over his lips. "Shh. Now is the time for grief, not rash promises."

He wanted to argue with her, he wanted to yell at the heavens, threaten his father as Den had done, but something in Mari's eyes held him.

"She's been everything to me," he said. "The only person who ever mattered."

Mari nodded, her sad expression deepening. "I know."

As Den rewrapped the stone, Gabrick clenched Mari's small frame. He didn't think he could survive another breath without Aednat so he drew on Mari's strength, his grip the desperate plea of a lost soul.

The boat pulled anchor, dark sails rising, and they disappeared into the night.

67

Dipping her hand into the water, Mariessa encouraged the plant life around them to speed their progress. She'd done this a number of times, holding her hand in the cold ocean as long as she could stand. Making their way down the coast, the land coming in and out of sight, the greenery had increased little by little as they made their way southward. Neither she nor Gabrick had inquired of their destination. It was enough for now that they were relatively safe. It seemed a lifetime since they hadn't had someone chasing them, their lives in constant danger.

She glanced behind her, Gabrick sitting by Aednat's wrapped body with his arm in a sling. He'd only left her side to take care of bodily needs and to change into thick weather-coated wool clothing and leather shoes so he wouldn't freeze in the winter weather.

They'd tried to give Mariessa a dress, but she'd refused. Instead she'd cinched the tie of a loose pair of men's pants round her thin waist, rolled the cuffs of the stiffened fabric, and added a thick gray shirt and a darker long coat. She probably looked the part of a pirate more than any of the men running ship, but she didn't care.

When she had some time, she'd sew pockets into the pants with hidden slits, giving her access to her knives. For now, she carried one on each thigh, three strapped round her waist, one on each arm, and one at her left ankle. She never wanted to be caught without one again.

The ship's leader, Najee Zareb Kuhani—Najee seeming to be their title for captain—strode by. Mari tapped his black-skinned arm, the way the younger subordinates did, speaking Imperium as slowly and distinctly as she could manage.

"There." She pointed to a curving peninsula. "We can observe Shangsan for

Aednat."

The man spoke something in his own language. "We have not time. It better we give her to the ocean than risk being taken."

They'd had this argument before. "She'll have a proper ceremony." Part of Mariessa wanted to pull a knife and threaten to gut him. "Look. There's plenty of tree cover and the land bar is thin, which means the dirt will be soft. Shangsan in a place like that won't take more than two days. I've set us far ahead of where we would normally be, and we're well away from the imperial ships. We can spare two days."

"Hah," Zareb laughed like the short yip of a dog. "I never see death-wait less than five days. We not have five days."

"She's right." Den spoke from behind them. Mariessa hadn't seen him since he'd gone below decks after they'd lost sight of the cliff. "Your country has harder soil, and even when the rains come there aren't enough xicao in the ground to consume the body faster than five days. Here, where animals wash to shore and the soil is always moist, the ground will be swarming with them. I doubt the ceremony need last more than twenty-four hours."

"You be sure?" Zareb asked.

Den nodded. "She would have wanted this, and it's important to the young ones."

With that, he disappeared again.

A few hours later, Gabrick and Mariessa said their words over Aednat, though neither of them could say much through the clenching in their throats. Den shook his head, not saying anything at all.

Gabrick managed some last words as they lay her body in a depression they'd carved from the ground. "She made people warm inside, brought out the best in everyone. Even a spoiled, twisted yenk like me."

He lay a thick evergreen branch over her body as the first xicao became visible above the soil.

Mariessa followed Gabrick with the next branch. "May you find peace below with your Vasheri brothers and sisters."

Gabrick stood at her side and she wrapped her fingers in his. He squeezed, speaking to Aednat one last time. "We'll get him back to you," Gabrick promised. "Wherever you are, if there's some part of us that lives on and goes to Paradise, I promise, Eleven will return to you."

Mariessa touched fingers to her forehead, a Kerokan sign that Aednat would never be forgotten. "Yenna, my sister."

"Yenna?" asked Gabrick

"It's a very old religious term. Priest Yosel used to say it sometimes. It means agreement of soul. Something you don't think about with your head, but you feel it in your heart."

"Yenna," Den repeated, nodding.

Mariessa touched a hand to his arm like she had a dozen times. As before, he shrugged her off, wincing at the pain in his wrapped shoulder, returning to his place in the shadows. Crouching by a tree, he held his head in his hands, taking deep breaths.

Mariessa released Gabrick, but he put his uninjured arm around her shoulders. "Please stay." He gestured to a fallen log not too far from Aednat's disintegrating body. "I know I'm not much company, but—"

"It's okay." Mariessa put an arm around his waist and they made their way to the fallen tree, sending a pungent odor of evergreen and damp fungus into the air.

In silence, they leaned against one another, Mariessa's head against his chest, him resting his cheek against the top of her frizzy hair.

Once they'd conducted the Liwu-shijan, presenting Aednat's heartstone to Den, they would start their journey in earnest. Today she would hold her friend, comfort him, and they would mourn. Tomorrow, they could make plans for the future.

Thirteen: The Number Prophecy Book 2

Coming July 2016

Acknowledgements

The concept for The Number Prophecy came from my children's obsession with picking up rocks. Soon after I started working on a series, a fellow author made the comment, "I am so sick of fantasy books with a magic stone. Can't people come up with anything else?" I appreciated the challenge as I thought to myself, "Yep, multiple magic stones, and not from some elf or long past magi, but a creation derived from a vital inner organ, representative of a person's soul—their heart.

A special thank you to Steven Novak for taking my ideas and turning them into a marvelous cover that embodied all my thoughts and goals for the opening of such a dark YA series.

(http://www.novakillustration.com)

Jen Hendricks did such a great job editing Fourteen that I had to hire her for the latest book in my Mankind's Redemption series as well. She gives me her thoughts and fixes my grammar faux-pas without interfering with my work. It's always nice to work with people like that.

Hugs and more hugs to my fans/beta readers who gave me pre-publishing feedback: Kim Mlazgar, Quint Seymore, Rachel Hanley, John D. Payne, Jon Hodge, Marsheila Rockwell and Evan Braun. I appreciate your time and patience.

I have to mention Quint one more time. He made fan art of Gabrick and Aednat on the Deviant Art website. I can't think of a greater compliment. (http://qtroubadour.deviantart.com/art/Limping-Home-368271205)

Last, but not least, I want to thank my family. They put up with the time I spend writing and even had patience with my rock-fetish phase. They are the best!

About the Author

Colette Black keeps a messy house and a clean mind (most of the time) as she types the stories swirling through her brain. Fascinated with early sci-fi horrors like *The Blob*, *Tarantula*, and *Planet of the Apes* she also grew to love great fantasy literature, such as C.S. Lewis' *Narnia* series, Terry Brooks *Shannara*, and Lloyd Alexander's *Chronicles of Prydain*. As the years passed and the pestering stories demanded they be told, it's no wonder that there's a little bit of science, fantasy, and horror in everything she writes...and romance. You must have romance.

Find out more at www. coletteblack.net